The Wise and Foolish Virgins

Don Hannah was born and raised in Canada. His plays include *The Wedding Script*, winner of the Chalmers Award, *Rubber Dolly*, *Running Far Back* and *The Wooden Hill*, based on the journals of L. M. Montgomery. This is his first novel.

The Wise and Foolish Virgins

DON HANNAH

Granta Books
London

Granta Publications, 2/3 Hanover Yard, London N1 8BE

First published in Great Britain by Granta Books 1999.
This edition published by Granta Books 2000.

A CIP catalogue record for this book
is available from the British Library.

1 3 5 7 9 10 8 6 4 2

Printed and bound in Great Britain by
Mackays of Chatham plc

For Marion R. Hannah ✣
and ✣
John and Marion Hannah ✣

"Continent, city, country, society:
the choice is never wide and never free
And here, or there ... No. Should we have stayed at home,
wherever that may be?"

ELIZABETH BISHOP
"Questions of Travel"

SLEEPERS/AWAKE ✣✣✣

For as long as he could remember, Sandy had been humiliated in his sleep. If he were walking down Main Street in his dreams, his pants and underwear would suddenly disappear, his shirt-tails flap up like blinds. Miss Bradley, his primary-school teacher, would drag him half-naked to the front of the classroom, where he would realize in a panic that he did not know if there was one "p" or two in "apple." Young boys, long since men — many of them, like Miss Bradley, dead and gone — would point at him and snicker. Once his mother had crawled from her deathbed to tell him that he would have to live somewhere else from now on because she was going to adopt Liberace. In the corner of that dream, Sandy could see Reverend Lewis tuning a grand piano in his bedroom; there was laughter and the clinking of glasses from the kitchen: Mother and Liberace were drinking martinis.

On this July morning, at six-thirty, he found himself hiding from his father in the graveyard, under a Christmas tree. Joey Mullins was beside him — they were late for something important — and Margaret Saunders was standing on his family plot in a black brassiere. "Sandy Whyte," she cried, "I know where you are!" She spun around, pointing at him, and Sandy woke up in a sweat.

Where had he been? Who had been taunting him? Had he wet the bed?

Bed-wetting was a recent fear; or maybe an old one that the incontinence of his mother's last days had dragged up from his subconscious. She had woken up soaking wet almost every morning: "Please don't humiliate me in front of strangers, Sandy. I don't want anyone else to change me but you. I can wait until you have a minute. It's not uncomfortable until it gets cold, dear, and Lord knows I haven't been able to smell anything good or bad for years."

Well, his bed was dry, thank God; he had not crossed that horrible line yet. He turned on the little radio that kept him company when he woke up at the crack of dawn. It galled him that the rest of the world could sleep untroubled until noon if it wanted — even his mother had slept in occasionally — while each and every day of Sandy's life began with this lonely injustice.

A choir was singing: it was Sunday. He would have to drag himself over to the church and listen to another sermon from that dreary little woman. Then the horror of Coffee and Conversation in the vestry. And the minister had called yesterday — there was a meeting of the Cemetery Committee at 12:30. Reverend Motier lived her life for useless meetings.

The cemetery — had he been dreaming about the cemetery? He could not remember clearly. The birds were making a racket in the maple trees outside; songbirds were singing frantically, their clear notes punctuated by screeches from crows. He could hear rustles and cooing in the attic — pigeons had found another hole under the eaves. *Damn things*. He'd have to hire somebody to fix it. The old house was getting out of control. He sighed and lay quietly. What was worse? The indignities of sleep or the thousand quiet outrages that awaited him as soon as his feet touched the bedroom floor?

An orange bar of sunrise gleamed between the sill and the bottom of the blind in the east window of the bay. Well, at least it might be a nice Sunday, weatherwise. There was that.

He had woken up in this bed in this room for most of his life, and very little had been changed since he was moved here from the crib in his parents' bedroom almost sixty-five years ago. His only time away from home had been in 1948, when he was eighteen and had decided to study psychology. He had gone to university for one term, sharing a dormitory room with an engineering freshman from Montreal, a little ignoramus named Neil. When Neil was sober, he pointedly ignored Sandy, but every weekend he drank and teased him mercilessly. "I know a girl named Sandy, and about the same size as you, too. If you're nice to her, maybe she'll loan you something pretty for the Christmas dance." The other engineers would listen outside the door and cackle. It had been unbearable.

The sunlight caught a corner of the picture on the wall across from his bed and shone back in his eyes. It was a photo of Sandy's high-school graduation that his mother had hung there when he was packing for university. "This room will always belong to my little boy," she had said sadly, "no matter how far away he may be." She had taken down the chromo print of *Samuel in Prayer* and hung Sandy on its nail. It was the only picture of himself that Sandy could bear. The black robe made him look sturdier than he had ever felt himself to be; its dark folds hid his little paunch and the soft hands that had always seemed so embarrassingly awkward whenever he felt he was being watched.

When he told them that he had decided not to return to university, his mother had kissed him and his father said he was thankful that Sandy had finally smartened up. "Anything you need to know about running the store, you can learn from me," the old man had said. "Anything else you want to find out you can get in a book. Psychology is for fools."

Since then, the longest he had been away was a day or two every few years on overnight buying trips for the store.

The photograph had slipped from its mat and was crooked inside the frame. "I can take this apart and straighten it for you," Gloria Maurice had said. That was three years ago, the first and last time she had attacked his room during spring cleaning. Sandy had hovered about so nervously that she was relieved when he finally said, "You don't need to waste your time in here. I'll take care of the inner sanctum." She had giggled at his little joke and avoided this end of the upstairs ever since.

His bed was cast iron, painted white, with brass posts: once it had seemed immense, but for almost fifty years now his feet had stuck through the bars at the bottom. Grandfather may have been a giant in business, but he was short in life. Well, everybody was then. Sandy was only five foot eight, so the shortness of his grandparents' old bed was a comfort; it made him feel tall. He had almost bought a new mattress ten years ago but had laid a sheet of plywood under the old one instead. He had read about the practice in the hints column of a newspaper. It was thrifty and, besides, it made him feel up to date. It was supposed to make the world of difference to his constant backache, but it did not. Over the years he had stained the mattress so badly that he did not know how to get rid of it without having people talk. When Gloria came on Tuesdays to clean, she left fresh sheets on a chair in the hall; he insisted on making the bed himself. The task had become more difficult as the mattress grew thin and lumpy over time, but if he let Gloria do it, she would know what he'd been up to before he fell asleep.

Gloria. *Dammit.* After he got back from church he would have to begin tidying up the house so that it would be respectable enough for her to clean. It had always been hard for him to allow a stranger into the place, but his mother's condition had forced him to. (The days of live-in servants had ended when old Jeannette Petipas died in her sleep in the little attic room the week after her nephew was lost at Normandy.) The fact that Gloria was a Catholic had helped; he didn't need to have some nosy girl from the United Church running home with tales to tell. He had even come to admire Gloria because she cleaned quietly and thoroughly and, although she was overweight, she wasn't slovenly; she was as neat as her work. Occasionally they would have coffee together in the kitchen and she would timidly ask him questions about the history of the town. She looked up to him.

The orange light was softening. He did not want to get out of bed. He would like to live his life right here in this room, sheltered in the warm cocoon of familiarity. Here alone was comfort and safety from the prying eyes of the world. Mother had hung the striped curtains in 1960 and, as far as Sandy was concerned, they still made the room look modern. Grandmother Synton had made the quilts in her youth; the yellowing chenille bedspread was a wedding present to his parents from Aunt Sis in Boston. The oak armchair that had been rescued from the Synton farm stood a few feet away from the bed and, as Sandy no longer hung everything neatly in the closet, was draped with clothes. Only one of the dresser drawers was shut; clothes were spilling out of the others. Tucked into the closed drawer was a small cardboard box containing all that remained of his mother. He had put her ashes in the one place he knew Gloria could not stumble upon them, and the door to her bedroom was always closed because he couldn't bear to look inside it as he passed. When Gloria went in there once a month to dust, he kept himself busy in his own room down the hall. Every time he walked past that ominous closed door, he felt ashamed.

"Only people with filthy secrets shut their bedroom doors, Sandy."

Mother would never leave him, no matter how many pairs of underwear he left draped over chairs.

He tried not to resent Gloria's weekly intrusions, because he knew that if it weren't for her the entire house would be a mess. He wanted her to tell people that he was fastidious. Whatever else they might say about him, he wanted it known that he was clean.

The choir on the radio was singing Bach, a cantata. Was it *Sleepers, Awake*? He thought so. He'd know when they reached the chorale — "Zion Hears the Watchman Singing." Right now it sounded familiar but he couldn't place it for certain.

Sandy had always prided himself on his ability to identify composers. Mother had told her friends that he had perfect pitch. He didn't. He knew enough about good music to know that he knew nothing, but to the people around here he was an expert simply because he listened to it. Like everything else in his life, it seemed that his appreciation for classical music set him apart from everyone else.

Something about Christmas, he realized suddenly, remembering a piece of his dream. *Something about Christmas and Mother?* He lay quietly, trying to make sense of a Christmas tree hovering beside the big Whyte family gravestone, but the image dwindled and was gone before he could fathom it. Christmas was a bad sign. He hated Christmas. Even when his mother was alive it had been the saddest day on the calendar. Last year, halfway though

White Christmas, he had shut off the television and packed away her decorations, vowing never to bring them down from the attic again.

The clock in the front hall was striking the last quarter-hour. He leaned over and turned up the radio: Bach flooded the room. He thought of all the empty rooms below him, the sun coming through the kitchen windows, the pale light in the parlour at the front of the house. The day would be more bearable if the whole house could be filled with Bach. All he would have to do is buy a recording and, of course, something to play it on: the turntable on the old hi-fi in the parlour had seized up years ago. He could buy a new one if he wanted to; after all, the house was his now. Once he had even driven to a new music store in Moncton to do just that. He had wandered up and down the aisles, looking at all the sleek, black equipment, without a clue as to what any of it was used for. The deafening music blasting throughout the store had turned his confusion to anger when a stupid-looking French clerk eyed him smugly and told him that people didn't even listen to records any more. Sandy had turned abruptly and stormed out, hoping that someone in charge would see his reaction and give the impudent boy an earful. It was terrible the way clerks treated customers these days.

He knew that he was not a very illustrious conclusion to the Whyte legacy. Their house was named The Oaks, although no one under sixty called it that now. It had been one of the four grand houses that dominated all aspects of life in Membartouche. From his office at the Whyte Brothers Company Store, Sandy's great-grandfather Captain William Whyte had ruled the town. The Oaks had been his castle. In summers a long time ago, the women of the Whyte family had reigned over tea parties on the large veranda, and the circular driveway had been filled first with buggies, then with cars. The veranda had been magnificent back then, with a wonderful view of the Membartouche River and Bay. But Sandy's father had divided the land on the other side of Main Street into lots and sold them off: rooftops and trees obscured the bay now.

Sandy hated the changes in the town. Progress to these people meant nothing more than finding a cheap way to make things ugly. The Membartouche Mall, a three-storey eyesore sheathed in dark corrugated metal, had devoured half of the old downtown — except, of course, for Whyte's Store. Even though it was closed, it was a landmark, and Sandy refused to sell it. When the last of his employees died, he had let it dribble out of business. The blinds were not pulled down, nor the doors boarded up, until after his mother had died.

Last year there had been a scheme to spruce up the downtown. Sandy, who knew more about local history than any of those fools, had been an advisor, but no one had wanted to listen to him or spend any money, and he became upset when the results of months of meetings had been Christmas lights on the edges of all the buildings. "It looks like Disneyland," he complained. "*Oui*," the mayor replied, beaming. "Yes, it's so beautiful now. Finally it looks like *someplace*." When ten immense concrete planters were craned onto the sidewalks, Sandy had left the committee in disgust. The planters blocked pedestrians and were soon filled with dying pansies and litter. As far as Sandy was concerned, all of the town's promise lay in the past.

For centuries, Micmacs had come here in summers, setting up camp on the south shore of the shallow bay. When his father was young, they arrived on the point every June; sixty years ago, they came to town only at Easter time. Huge Micmac women, dozens of baskets looped about their arms, or strung across their backs like bright, fat wings, had walked from door to door, the air about them thick with the scent of sweetgrass. Little Sandy had watched them in awe. He shivered with pleasure at the thought that such mysterious visitors had once lived here. He felt that both he and the town were moving forward from a glorious beginning, but now he knew that he was the last of his line and the last of any promise the town had once possessed. "Never forget who you are," Mother had said. But who he was meant nothing these days. His mother's passing had made him even more of a relic. In the library downstairs was a cardboard box filled with notes for the history of Membartouche that he wanted to write, but the story made him so depressed that he could do nothing but rearrange his outlines over and over. He could not get past the opening sentence: "Membartouche is an Indian name derived from the name of the first Christian convert in New France." He could not figure out how to avoid using the word "name" twice in the same sentence.

The chorale had already begun; the slow, sweet opening melody was so familiar that he had not noticed it until the tenor started to sing. He was almost certain it was *Sleepers, Awake*. He might not understand the workings of modern hi-fi systems but he knew better than any rude French clerk the difference between good music and noise.

Soon he would have to get up and have breakfast. He thought that, after Mother died, he would be able to stay in bed as long as he wanted and not feel any guilt. He had been wrong.

When she was in the long, tedious process of dying, one of his first thoughts was that eventually he would no longer be forced to face down a bowl of oatmeal each and every morning of his life. "It sticks to your gizzard," she had said — one of the few up-country expressions that her marriage had not broken. When she was bedridden, she would let no one but Sandy do the cooking, and he was forced to make a pot of oatmeal at night "the good old-fashioned way" and feed it to her in the morning.

Mother insisted that he have his bowl sitting at her bedside. "No one likes to eat all by themselves, Sandy." At first it was pleasant enough. "This is just the way I like it," she'd say. "Will you pick up a few things for me? I'd like to finish that needlepoint and I'm all out of crimson for robin red breast." In the last months of her life she just lay there and did nothing but cry. Sandy would force the porridge down his throat, but she'd barely eat a spoonful of her own. "Please don't forget me. Don't make your poor old mother eat alone." And he never did. He came home from the store for lunch, and had his dinner on a TV tray while the television flickered on his father's dresser at the foot of the bed.

Now that she was gone, he found that nothing but oatmeal appealed to him first thing in the morning. He'd given up on eggs years ago; they made him nauseated. Besides, he could never figure them out: they were either too runny or too hard. Toast caught in his throat; he could stomach it only at lunch time smothered with Cheez Whiz. He hated jellies, despised jams. And the boxes of dry cereal in the supermarket confused him. They all seemed to be designed for children, and he was afraid of picking up the wrong one, because the clerks might snicker. So he continued with oatmeal. It was waiting for him downstairs in the top of the double boiler.

The Bach was finished and the news was about to start. Sandy's underwear was on the floor by the bed. He pulled it on and walked down the hall, turning his head the other way as he neared his mother's door.

In the bathroom he peed noisily with the door open, hosing a circle around and around the edges of the bowl, then washed and lathered his face with soap. With the first stroke of his razor, he nicked himself on the chin. He felt the cut and lifted his eyes to the mirror: a small red pearl was hanging below his lip.

"Dammit."

The face in the mirror looked too much like his father's. Sandy had wished he could grow a beard since his mother first pointed out the resemblance on his forty-fifth birthday, just months after cancer had finally taken the old man out of his life. "It's a comfort to me, dear, really and truly. A great comfort." It was the opposite for her son. But a beard was out of the question, thanks to that hippy minister.

Reverend Lewis had been young and athletic, and loathed by Sandy because he questioned Sandy's every move as head of the Session. When the minister had started to grow a trim little beard, Sandy had come home from a Wednesday-night meeting and said to Mother, "This takes the cake! That miserable long hair wasn't enough! Now he's trying to look like the Lord Jesus Christ himself!" Mother had nodded and repeated her son's remarks over tea at the next meeting of the Ladies' Aid. She'd had no use for Reverend Lewis since his guitar first made its appearance one Sunday morning halfway through the service. It was bad enough that Mrs. Lewis ran around in outfits that emphasized her pregnancy, but to have her standing next to the pulpit bold as brass screeching away while her husband looked at her adoringly and played on that thing like a cowboy, well, something had to be done.

"I say either that beard goes, or he does," Sandy ranted.

Together, mother and son had fanned the flames until Reverend Lewis, his beard intact, had been sent to another charge, one where there were young people.

"Let him poison their impressionable little minds," said Sandy. "At least he's out of our hair." Mother had nodded.

No, a beard was out of the question. His father's face scowled as Sandy rubbed an old styptic-pencil stub on the fresh cut. Then, when that didn't quite work, he held a wad of toilet paper against his chin.

A snatch of last night's dream suddenly came back to him. *Something about Margaret Saunders. Something about Christmas and the graveyard and Margaret.* Had she been spending the holiday with his family? He had a recollection of her turning to him, her face and neck creamy white, her shoulders bare, while his father shouted something in the background. *Had she said something?* He could not remember the context.

He gingerly peeled the paper away, but a fresh drop of blood appeared on his chin. "Dammit. Dammit all to hell." He put the paper back and pressed harder. *Why a dream about Margaret? And why Christmas, that most miserable of all days?* Fifty-five years ago he had played Joseph in the Sunday-school pageant and sang "Oh Holy Night." His mother had combed a bit of olive oil into his hair to make it shine in the candlelight. The Ladies' Aid ladies had fussed over him; the organist had slipped him a nickel; and, afterwards, Mother had wrapped her arms about him and called him "her little Caruso." His father had merely grunted. When Sandy went into the store a few days later, Father had said, "Well well well, if it isn't Little Gatuso." The men who worked for Father had all laughed. Sandy hated the store.

"Why in hell do I work so hard?" his father had said constantly. "What's the point in building all of this up just so you can inherit it and lose the whole enterprise in six months?" But the glory days were long gone even then, and when Sandy did inherit the store he was surprised to find that Father had not been an astute businessman at all. If he had not been selling off the Captain's lands, they would have had nothing. The books were in terrible shape, the building falling apart. There was fifty-year-old stock in the storeroom. Sandy hired people to set the place straight and then he ran it smoothly and with a distinct lack of ambition. After Mother's death, he had just walked away from it. "You have an obligation to this business, to the church and to the town." His father's tone of voice implied that Sandy was completely inadequate to the task. He grew up feeling that his inheritance was a life sentence, but all of his father's big talk about Grandfather starting the business with a keg of nails and a dream, and going on to be a pillar in the town and the church was nothing but hot air. Father had prided himself that he had convinced Sandy to stay put; he never found out about the true horrors of university, the taunts of that lame-brained engineering student and his cronies. It was years before Sandy suspected that Father was frightened by the idea of his education.

He had longed for his father's death, thinking that, once they were free of him, he and his mother would be happy together. He imagined them travelling in tropical locations, sightseeing in the land of Egypt. With her husband's death, Sandy's mother would finally be free to become fun and intelligent, like Katharine Hepburn. But the depth of his mother's love for her husband frightened him as he grew to realize it. Once the old man was gone, she became very quiet. She no longer said "Your father" as in "Your father likes his potatoes whipped with cream." Instead, she would stare at the baked potato Sandy had put on her plate, cut with a cross and smushed up with a dab of sour cream and garnished with some fresh parsley, just like a restaurant potato, and she would sigh and say, "Alex did so love his whipped potatoes." She barely ate, as if she could take no pleasure in anything without her husband's presence. His clothes still hung in her closet; his dresser remained stocked with his underwear and socks. She went on living as if his death were only an extended vacation. She retreated further into the house; suddenly it seemed there was no longer a reason to go into the living room, then the dining room.

Sandy tried preparing suppers from *The Joy of Cooking*, but she would see him heading for the dining room with the linen place mats and say, "Oh, let's not bother making a fuss" and take out the green plastic place mats with embossed tulips, bits of egg and fuzz permanently embedded in their petals, and put them on the kitchen table. Then even her arrival in the kitchen became an event.

For the last two years of her life, she left her bedroom only for trips to the toilet. She lay there watching things that appalled her son: country music programs, quiz shows, wrestling. "Remember when Alex bought this set?" she would say. "It was the first one in town. Remember how much we loved Liberace? He used to wink at me."

"I hated Liberace," he wanted to protest, but by then she would be crying quietly.

Sandy had continued to feel that his life might be filled with promise until Mother died. But then the inevitability of his days was as obvious as his thinning grey hair and his thickening gut. Misery became an easier alternative than change. It wasn't until the old girl was gone that he truly realized that he would never get any younger. A shining future was behind him now, had faded away years ago. He no longer thought of himself as an optimist. All those transformations that would come with the passing of Mother were not to be. There was nothing glorious in the fact that he could watch television in his underwear without constantly looking towards a door she would never walk through again.

The day of the funeral he had come home from the church and walked straight to her bedroom. He had lain down on her bed, pulled his pants to his knees, and masturbated, feeling younger than he'd felt for years. But ten minutes later, sticky and overcome with guilt, he'd had that vague, pathetic feeling that he sometimes remembered from sleep.

He had loved his mother so much when he was a child. They had sat on the back steps, surrounded by her flowers, and played "patty-cake, patty-cake, baker's man." He remembered her oatmeal cookies: thick and chewy and creamy white, they glowed in the faint light of the pantry when he snuck there to grab a handful. She gave him picture books that were really for grown-ups: paintings by Rembrandt and Van Eyck. She read to him: *A Child's Garden of Verses* and *Bible Bedtime Stories*. Whenever a rainbow appeared in the sky, she would ask, "What was God's promise to Noah?" and he would answer, "No more floods——"

Margaret had been wearing a black brassiere!

What in the name of God had he been dreaming about?

And then he moaned low and loud as he realized that Joey Mullins had been in his dream, too. Nothing humiliating was ever lost; it slyly filed itself away and went on haunting.

When he was ten, he had gone exploring in the woods up past the orchard with Joey. He was one of the older boys in Sandy's class, and all one summer they had played together. There was a special place near the river where there used to be a stand of silver birch, and one day when they were up there, Joey had rolled up his sleeves. Sandy couldn't believe that he had such big muscles. He could not stop staring at them. The two years separating him from Joey suddenly felt like decades. They used to pee in the woods, and once, when they were swimming in the river, Joey lay floating on his back and held his jimmy-john in one hand and peed into the air. Sandy laughed so hard that he almost drowned.

In dreams Joey's arms were like far-off hills that Sandy stumbled towards.

How did the mind work? He should have stayed in university: he would have been a psychologist, respected, but more importantly, he would know his own brain inside out. If only it could be stretched out on a desk like a topographical map. He could imagine himself small and wandering through it, exploring — the way he and Joey used to wander through the back-fields and woods, the curves of the river, and had come to understand their boyhood world, how it would look from the air. He wished that he knew first-hand about electrical charges being signalled by events, sparks shooting through cords in his head like lightning — storms and earthquakes, weather in his brain. But he supposed that an earthquake wasn't really weather. The brain was as vast and complex as a planet. It was magnificent. He had always believed that he possessed the peculiar brain of an artist.

But Father and those brutes in engineering had put the kibosh on university and medical school and he had given up on studying psychology. "You could always go back," Margaret had said to him, but both of them knew it was an impossibility.

Margaret in a brassiere!

Why must he still be troubled by that sad look on her face? When he thought about her, he got goose bumps and his stomach felt delicate. He had liked Margaret very much, if the truth be known. She had a dark blue suit that she bought in Saint John that made her look very smart and, before she and that crazy sister of hers moved to a Holy Roller congregation, she used to come to the United Church in a hat. For years he had sat in the Whyte pew with his parents, listening to her voice singing in the congregation behind them. It seemed to him that she felt the hymns in a way that no one else did. Why hadn't she understood his feelings for her? They were not like his feelings for Joey; they were proper, they were grown up. And hadn't he defied his mother by going out with her? "She's nice enough I suppose, dear, but that mother of hers was so *common*. And I do not want to have her foolish sister showing up here whenever she feels like it." He had been prepared to make sacrifices for the sake of companionship, but, in the end, his mother had been

right: Margaret was common. Yet, he felt little remorse about
the times they were seen together. Who else was there around
here for either of them to be seen with? No one smart enough,
that's for sure. Still, he must feel guilty if he were hauling her out
of his subconscious and sticking her in his dreams.

He studied his father's face in the mirror. How unfair every
little thing was: how infuriating that he should have grown into
the face he had hated all his life. "Dammit," he muttered.
"Thanks to you, everything I know about the brain I got from
the *Reader's Digest* — 'I Am Joe's Brain.'"

He stared into his own eyes, then turned away.

Other people's lives pushed onward, lines moving up and
down through the hills and valleys of time, but Sandy felt that
his was barely vibrating in the same place. It wasn't even like
running on the spot.

His cut was healing and, back in his room, he dressed in yesterday's undershirt and socks, a yellowing shirt, and his old grey
suit, then padded down the back stairs to the kitchen. The oatmeal was a little on the thin side today and the milk was starting to turn. He was running low on brown sugar. He sighed as
he placed his bowl of half-eaten breakfast in the sink and filled
it with water so that he wouldn't have to go at the porridge crust
with an S.O.S pad that evening. He would listen to the radio for
a bit, and then go to church and try to stay awake through
another sermon on the meaning of Jesus in a Changing World.
He would suffer through Coffee and Conversation and then the
Cemetery Committee. He would come back and start getting
the house ready for Gloria and her vacuum on Tuesday. He
might even go for a drive down shore and have a lobster roll at
a take-out — a little treat. (Although as soon as he thought this,
he knew that he would never do such a thing.) Tomorrow he
would have to find someone to fix the hole in the eaves. He

would try to force himself to sit at the desk and finish an entire paragraph.

"Membartouche is an Indian name derived from the name of the first Christian convert in New France . . ."

How could he have arrived in his sixties with so much promise and so little accomplished? Artists leave something for the world, but everything he had to leave was locked up in his brain, hoarded so long it was his alone. The century would be over in five years, and he would have added nothing to it, nothing at all. *And one day Gloria will find me dead in the bathroom and that will be that.*

But it was two minutes later, as Sandy turned off the faucet and looked out the kitchen window and into the backyard, that he first saw the tall boy dart from the corner to the fence. The boy stopped and, taking some food from his pocket, perched brazenly on the top of the fence and gobbled it down. He was looking up at the back of the house. *How dare he!* Sandy thought, grabbing the binoculars that his mother had used for birdwatching. *Who is that?*

Sandy had never seen him before. He was a stranger. The boy's hair had fallen over his face. He licked his fingers, then pushed it back. "Oh," Sandy suddenly whispered. "Oh." Then the boy swung around and, jumping off the far side of the fence, sauntered away through the old orchard.

The vibrating line of Sandy's life leapt with his heart and, for the first time in many years, lurched forward.

TWO

S aturday night at the Maurice house had been a misery for the whole family. Junior and Danny had both arrived in the afternoon and, by eleven o'clock, neither one had uttered a single nice word. Danny had hardly said anything at all, and Junior was so grumpy that every time he opened his mouth he made somebody angry. Their sister, Gloria, wanted to tell them both to smarten up. She'd let Mama go to Ste. Anne's by herself so that she could be at home with them, and they didn't seem to care if she was there or not. When Mama came back from Mass, she and Pop — who *never* quarrelled out loud — had a fight over a piece of bread. Pop said that he wanted toast for his bedtime snack and Mama handed him the slice. He said it felt stale, she said it was fine, and five minutes later things had gotten so far out of hand that Mama was saying, "Throw it out then, throw the old bread out!" while he said, "Oh, give me the damn thing and I'll eat it!" Gloria tried not to pick sides, but she ended up on Mama's because she felt guilty for having let her go to Mass alone. Junior left the TV blaring when their fight became louder than Wrestling and went into the kitchen to side in with Pop, who told him to get lost. Gloria told her brother to mind his own business, but she had ended up arguing with her mother. Then she went out to talk to Danny on the back steps; he had thrown back so much rye all evening that his words were slurred. "Jusch stay outuv it," he said gently, touching her on the knee with his bad arm. "Oh, to hell with everybody," she muttered, and went to bed.

Gloria had not put in such a sleepless night for years. Even as she turned out the light, she had known that sleep would not find her soon. But she didn't want to read, and she certainly didn't want to try keeping a conversation going with *that* bunch. The breeze from her window was warm and she could hear a bad local band playing golden oldies at the Dart Club down the street. The songs made her sad because she was no longer a little girl lying in bed listening to them with excitement, thrilled at the prospect of becoming a teenager. On any other night she would have closed the window, but tonight she was lying very still, sometimes moving her lips, whispering songs that she hadn't thought of for twenty years.

Mama and Pop had gone to bed without speaking, but within five minutes they were both snoring to beat the band, as if this had been a night like any other. Gloria figured that was probably a good thing: maybe they wouldn't get up on the wrong side of bed tomorrow morning. She knew that they would complain about how the noise from the Club had kept them up half the night; they always did. Danny said that they had been complaining about it every Saturday and Sunday morning since the Club opened in 1967, Centennial Year. The day she came home from cleaning Sandy Whyte's house and told them that in his opinion Centennial Year hadn't done Membartouche any favours, even Pop had admitted that "Lord High Muck-a-Muck" was right, "for once." When she told Sandy Whyte that her father said "Some Centennial project! That damn Club looks like an old potato barn," he had nodded in agreement. It was a bright blue concrete-block eyesore and everybody hated it. Everybody, that is, except her oldest brother. Junior went drinking there whenever he came home.

Junior was in his old room. His suitcase was open on the floor with all his clothes spilling out of it. On the other bed, Danny's little overnight bag was zipped shut. After half an hour she heard Danny come up the stairs and go to the bathroom, then stumble back downstairs again. She waited to hear the fridge door open and close, the rattle of the ice-cube tray, and she shook her head. In a couple of days Raymond would be here, and then her whole family would be home for the first time in years. But what good would that be if they weren't going to get along? Gloria wanted this week to be special, but it was going to pieces before it even got under way. She suspected that people were angry at her for organizing a family reunion, but hadn't that been the right thing to do? Wasn't getting your family together something that normal people did all the time?

Gloria lay very still for a long while. She knew that downstairs Danny had poured himself another rye and pretty soon would fall asleep on the couch with the glass still in his hand. It was so late. There would be a last dance at the Club, and then everybody there would get in their cars and roar their mufflers and screech their tires, until, finally, everything in Membartouche would be quiet. And still she wouldn't sleep.

She watched the new moon move across the sky. It was no longer the moon of her childhood, the one that shone magically down on her brothers and her on summer nights. That moon had always been full, the sky around it crazy with stars and the possibility of comets. In those days she and her brothers could turn the house into anything they wanted: a hospital, a restaurant, a ship sailing to China. Why did everything change when you grew up?

After Mama went to Mass, Gloria had gone into the living room to ask Junior and Pop what they were watching on TV.

"You make a better door than a window, Lard Arse," Junior cracked. She wanted to say something about his big old beer gut and the pot calling the kettle black, but she didn't because that would make things worse. She just moved out of his way. She hated it when people made fun of her weight, even if they were only teasing.

"What's on?" she asked.

"If you'd shut up and look, you could figure it out for yourself," Junior replied, not even glancing at her. Pop said nothing, just tossed the *TV Guide* on the floor and walked out.

If they were still little kids, the future might still be filled with promise. Junior might never get into trouble. Danny would still have his hand. And little Raymond could appear at the top of the stairs after supper, tripping over the hem of Grandmama's old dress, getting ready to make his entrance as the Queen of England. He would prance through the house, making fun of everybody that they knew in Membartouche. One summer he showed Gloria how to make grass skirts and they danced the hula around the supper table. He sang in a high, silly voice, and Junior called him "Koomba Cod Snot, the Hawaiian Pineapple Singer." Even Pop laughed when Raymond's Queen Elizabeth told them about having tea at Sandy Whyte's place. Nobody was supposed to think that Sandy Whyte was a fairy because his family had been so high and mighty, but everybody did. The whole town whispered about it. People could be so mean about things they knew nothing about — *meaner* even, Gloria thought. People in town had whispered things about Raymond, too, and she knew that was one of the reasons he had moved away and left her. "It's too small and narrow-minded," he told her when he came home after his first year at art college. "I'm not coming back next year." On Tuesdays, when she cleaned Sandy Whyte's, she sometimes wished that her family had a house that was big and important. Maybe then her brother would come home more often. He would have felt safer there.

Of all the places where she worked, Sandy Whyte's was her favourite, because it was filled with interesting things. "Here's more old junk," Mama kept whispering to her the one time Gloria had brought her in to help with the cleaning. Except for the silverware and the dishes, her mother had found fault with everything: the faded rugs; the formal-looking settees that looked like grim old ladies; the shelves of dark leather books that were so intimidating Gloria could not believe anyone had ever read them, not even Sandy Whyte. Old Mrs. Whyte had died and Gloria thought that they would be cleaning out her bedroom; instead, Sandy had wanted them to spend the whole day down on the first floor. Gloria kept telling her mother that the things she was finding fault with were antiques, but she gave up when Mama pointed triumphantly at a stuffed blue jay in the bell jar on the mantelpiece. "Gloria, smarten up. Just because some ratty old thing's loaded with bugs doesn't make it an *antique*."

Mrs. Whyte's bedroom door had always been closed to keep the vacuum from bothering her. The one time Gloria had seen Mrs. Whyte, Sandy was helping her to the bathroom; she was confused and frail, and Gloria thought that Sandy was very patient and tender with her. She had been dead nearly a year before Sandy asked Gloria to dust her room, and Gloria saw that he had loved the old lady so deeply he couldn't bear to throw out any of her things. She never told anyone about the housecoat on the hook inside the door or the slippers beside the bed, because people would use them in a cruel way and gossip. When other people she worked for said leading things like "If that old house could speak, the tales it could tell…," she would nod and talk about the books, or the oak panelling, or the antiques.

Of all the people she knew, Gloria felt, Raymond alone would appreciate the contents of Sandy Whyte's home. Strangely enough, this was where she missed him the most. She smiled at the thought of poking around the old rooms with Raymond, opening drawers, going through closets, exploring. She had never done anything snoopy on her own; she just imagined the fun she could have doing it with her youngest brother.

When he came home and they were all together, could things be wonderful again? She hated it when people went away, even for a short time. When Mama went to Great-Aunt Erna's in Boston the time that Grandmama died, Gloria had only been four. She still had a vague memory of blue suitcases, and the out-fit she wore as she ran up and down the platform of the Moncton train station: short overalls with a bunny's head appliquéd on the bib, the fat pink ears stretched over her chest and buttoned onto suspender straps. She found it at the bottom of the ragbag in the closet when she was fifteen and, instead of feeling that she had found something precious, was only filled with loss.

Raymond used to read Nancy Drew books out loud to her when they were little; the stories seemed far-off and glamorous to her because Nancy Drew lived in the States. When Mama had gone there, Gloria had imagined her visit all mixed up with stories of girl detectives and roadsters. When her friend Lavinia Gautier first showed her holy cards of Jesus all whipped and bloody and talked to her about the Office of the Virgin, Gloria had pictured a sacred detective agency down the street from the house she had imagined for Great-Aunt Erna: Nancy Drew and the Immaculate Conception answered the telephone and solved mysteries together. They found things, the way that she and Raymond could if they teamed up. Once you were grown up, you stopped teaming up with people — except to get married, but that was a whole different thing.

Gloria remembered her brothers taking turns holding her hands and spinning her around and around in the yard. She yearned for the sweet, long-ago sensation of her feet leaving the ground and flying out behind her. Now she was in her thirties and fat and no one would ever twirl her in the air again.

It was Gloria who had phoned Junior and Danny to tell them that Raymond was coming for a visit. Junior would be at home anyway; Ginette had left him, moving back to Halifax so she could be closer to her kids, and he said he was fed up with his own cooking. "He'll be living here again, if we're not careful," Pop said to Mama. Danny said he had some holidays coming and didn't feel like going anywhere this year. What a laugh — Danny had never gone anywhere in his life, except to Toronto once to visit Raymond, and that time he was supposed to stay for two weeks but came back more than a whole week early. Even Gloria had been further away than he had. Four years ago she'd won a week's trip to Jamaica at the mall and had taken Mama with her. It was pretty, but neither of them liked the heat much, and, although it was summer there, the sun went down at six o'clock. Both she and her mother were uncomfortable having black people wait on them. One of the maids had asked them questions about Canada. Gloria told her that she was a cleaning lady, too, in the hopes that they might be friends, but it didn't work out that way. The whole trip made her glad that she hadn't moved away; even if some people in Membartouche were mean to her, they still felt safer than strangers.

Her brothers did not sound too interested in seeing Raymond and she wondered if Raymond was interested in seeing them. When she phoned him in Toronto, he said that he'd been thinking a lot about coming down and that he might bring a friend. "I've been dreaming about the beach," he told her, "and thinking about how we always talked about sailing up the coast. Maybe we can rent a sailboat, or maybe you know somebody who can take us out? And I want to go up to the Bouctouche Dune. Oh, and can you phone somebody and find out when the sandpipers come to the Bay of Fundy? We always meant to go see them and we never did, and I have to see them for sure." He rambled on and on about how beautiful New Brunswick was and how he missed it. Gloria thought he was probably a little drunk and her heart sank. Danny drank enough for everybody, and Junior wasn't too far behind. She had always thought that she could count on Raymond, but he had not said one word about people he wanted to see, just places and things. Still, she knew that Raymond used to be everybody's favourite, and maybe he could make the rest of the family have a good time.

The older boys had been home last Christmas, and as far as Gloria was concerned it had been the worst on record, worse even than the one when Junior got arrested for stealing their presents at the Moncton Mall. At least that time she'd had a talk with Danny that she still thought about sometimes. It was a long, serious talk, a rare event for both of them. Mama and Pop were at the jail and, although a snowstorm raged outside, the house seemed very still, as if it were listening. But last Christmas nobody had said much; they all just sat around looking miserable. Nobody even paid much attention to the funny presents that Gloria had bought. Danny grinned once, when Junior opened his and it was a wind-up hula dancer with bouncing breasts, but Junior had just looked at her and said, "You never gonna grow up?" and dropped it back in the box. He was in a bad mood the whole time because Ginette was spending Christmas in Halifax with her ex-husband. Even Mama's turkey was bad; it was all dried out and she hadn't put enough summer savory in the dressing. None of them had any fun any more. It was as if fun were something everybody had grown too big for, like her old bunny overalls.

She and Danny hardly ever saw each other, even though they lived so close. Well, Danny hardly ever saw anybody except the people who lived in the apartment building he looked after, and he told her that mostly they talked to him about the weather or complained about the washers in the basement. He had once loved a woman who lived there, but it had ended badly. Gloria knew about it because he had told her that he was seeing a woman named Marsha. A few weeks later when she tried to tease him about her, he said to never mention Marsha again because she had made fun of his arm.

"Still waters run deep" was all that Mama ever said whenever Gloria asked her mother why Danny was so quiet. This was even before the accident. Danny didn't have friends like the others had, and he never went out with girls all through school.

"But he keeps locking himself up in the bedroom. He don't even read in there. Just lies on the bed playing 'Oh! Susanna' and 'Alouette' over and over again on the mouth organ."

"Still waters run deep," said Mama. "Maybe he wants to be a musician someday."

Gloria didn't think so. Danny never even played the chorus of "Oh! Susanna" and he made the same mistakes every time.

That Christmas when they had their long talk, Danny told her that his hand still bothered him. It ached a lot and he felt an itch on his little finger, like a mosquito bite. He held up the stump — his arm ended a couple of inches below his elbow —

and gestured with his chin to a place about a foot away from the end of it. The itch was right there, he said, out in the air where there was nothing. Then he told her that he remembered seeing his hand. He saw it lying there in the long grass, holding onto a rock. But they told him, no, he could not possibly remember it. He'd been asleep when the car left the road, and unconscious when he was dragged from the wreck and taken to the hospital. But he could see it: each blade of grass, the stone in his fingers, the piece of bone sticking out like something in the butcher's shop. The doctors and the police told him he was wrong — they had found his hand inside the upturned car after the ambulance had taken him away. Junior says he's crazy, and he was there. He was driving, he saw the whole thing. But Danny told her it was like a picture. An ant was even running along a blade of grass beside his thumb. It was as real to him as the itch he couldn't scratch. He described it so well that she could see it just like he said. It was in Gloria's memory now, too.

They'd even talked about the time she thought she saw the Virgin Mary up in the woods behind the nuns' pasture, and all the trouble that brought her. "If I'd only come home like I was supposed to," she said, "I wouldn't have had all that grief. Virgin Mary almost ruined my life." Danny had nodded and said he sure wished he'd never gotten in the car with Junior that night. Although the accident had not been Junior's fault — the station wagon full of couples screeching their way from one high-school graduation party to another had crossed over the white line and smashed into them head-on in their own lane — he had been drinking and had dragged Danny along with him. Junior should have graduated with that class, and he wanted to drive down to the cottages where the parties would be and let the air out of people's tires. So a part of Danny blamed his brother for being so stupid. Gloria was surprised when he told her that he hated losing his hand so much that for a long time he had thought about killing himself. She was so glad he hadn't died that night that she thought his hand was a small price to pay.

That Christmas was the first time she realized how much she missed being a little girl. "Maybe that's why people grow up and have kids," Danny had said. "They think it will make them happy again."

The moon slipped from sight behind the edge of the window. The night was so clear that the sky had a faint pearly glow. Gloria felt that she would never sleep again in her whole life.

Junior was waiting to fall asleep, too. He hadn't meant to be so cranky, but every time he opened his mouth and tried to say something funny, something sour-sounding came out instead. But who could be interested in all of Gloria's jabbering about lobster suppers and family reunions and "remember-that-time-when?" — all of the crap that happened when they were kids? All he wanted was to relax and eat Mama's food and think about what he would do with the rest of his life. He had promised Ginette that he would smarten up, but he had broken his promises to her all the way along.

He was still trying to figure out if he loved her. He thought he did, but when he said "I love you," she called him a liar. "Don't be stupid," he said, hoping she'd stay and argue with him.

"If you loved me," she answered as she zipped her suitcase shut, "you'd go out and get a decent job. If you loved me, I wouldn't keep finding those goddam titty magazines stashed away all over the place."

Maybe it was Gloria's constant yapping about when they were kids that was keeping him awake. He kept thinking about the stupid things he had done back then. Would he be in the mess he was in now if hadn't chased Raymond and Gloria around the backyard and up into a tree with one of Pop's hammers? If he hadn't tossed dogshit onto Sandy Whyte's steps that Hallowe'en? If he'd never broken into any of those cottages?

He had broken into the first one when he was ten years old. He pried open a shutter in the back, lifted the sash, and crawled in. He knew there was no danger of being caught: the Melanson family lived in the city and, at that time of year — it was early October — only came out on Sundays for a drive. It was a warm evening. Indian summer. There was no danger, but the excitement of being somewhere illicit gave him such a thrill that almost from the moment his feet touched the floor below the window he could feel a boner growing in his pants. The memory of that feeling could still excite him, even all these years later.

He had tiptoed around the bedroom, and then explored the tiny kitchen and the living room filled with old furniture. Clamshell ashtrays were on the end tables beside the sagging couch, a row of *Reader's Digest* Condensed Books was on a shelf between the shuttered windows. Even though he hadn't broken in to steal anything — he just wanted to go inside to see what was there — he was disappointed that there seemed to be nothing worth taking. He went through the kitchen cupboards, finding only a set of blue Melmac dishes and a box of safety matches. But then, back in the bedroom, hidden away under the newspaper lining of a bottom bureau drawer, he found the magazine with photographs of two girls with silvery stars on their nipples. They were wearing black panties and sitting on a sofa in a room with paintings of horses' heads on the wall.

He didn't want to get caught with the magazine — Mama would have a fit — so he put it back in the drawer. But he returned to the cottage all that winter, and then he started going into others. Mostly there was nothing interesting — everybody who owned a cottage seemed to love *Reader's Digest* — but sometimes there were *Playboy*s or an old *Hustler* beside the toilet. If there were no dirty magazines, he would get back at the owners by finding something to take: an old teapot for Gloria to use with her dolls or a transistor radio to give to one of the girls from school.

When he was thirteen he coaxed Donna Ambrose through the window of the Melanson cottage and onto the Melansons' bed. "Jeeze, Junior, I dunno," she said. "What if we get caught?"

He lifted up Donna's sweater and started kneading her breasts like bread dough. She slapped his hands away with a little flurry of cuffs.

"Hey, don't just grab them. Jeez! They're alive, you know! They ain't dead, they can feel!"

"You promised me I could play with them!"

"Here," she said, taking something from her purse. "I stole one of the old man's Sheiks. Let's get it over with. This place gives me the creeps."

That night Junior was reborn with a secret identity. For the next four years, when cottagers arrived in late May to open their places for the summer and survey the damage, the husbands would look in the bedrooms while their wives and children sat waiting in their cars. "Well?" the women would ask. The husbands would nod their heads in disgust. Someone had broken in and left a used condom in the centre of each bed. They were Junior's calling cards, like the Lone Ranger's silver bullets. The summer people started calling him "the Sheik" and complaining to the police about how nothing was safe any more and the world was going to hell in a handcart.

Danny had been the first person to figure out that his brother was the Sheik.

"I think that Sheik guy must be real cool," Junior said one night in the yard after supper. School was over; he had failed

Grade Twelve for the first time and had gotten a job at the fish plant. Danny was getting ready for summer school — he wanted to get his New Math out of the way before next year. It was the summer before Raymond started junior high, and he was acting like it would change his life. Gloria was starting to hang around with Lavinia Gautier, who was trying to convince her to be a nun when she grew up. It was the summer when all of them realized that they were growing too old to play the games that they loved: too old to play hide-and-go-seek, too grown up to have circuses in the backyard with the other kids on the street. Now they were old enough to be sick of one another.

Junior looked around at everybody, then off into the darkness of the yard. "A real cool guy," he said longingly.

"Mama says he's a pig," Gloria said. "And Lavinia says he's going to hell for sure."

"I bet he's a fruit," said Raymond nervously, looking from one brother to the next. Lately he'd been saying "fruit" whenever he got the chance. Sometimes Junior told him to quit it or people would start calling him one. But before Junior could say a word, Danny stood up.

"How can you guys be so stupid," said Danny. "It's just Junior acting like a big shot."

"Is not!" said Junior.

"Is too!" said Danny.

"Is not! Liar!" But after Gloria and Raymond went inside to watch *Cabaret* on the Saturday-night movie, Junior grabbed Danny's shirt and said, "Don't you dare say nuthin."

Danny turned away from him. "I'm gonna go watch the movie."

"You're turning into a fruit, like Raymond," Junior replied. But Danny was gone and he was alone.

Junior still felt terrible about taking Danny along with him that night after he failed Grade Twelve for the second time, but the people that he couldn't forgive were the sons of bitches who graduated. He cursed all those rich kids whose tires he'd wanted to flatten. If it hadn't taken Danny so long to make up his mind about whether he was going to go or not, they would never have been on the road when that other car came at them. And that car should never have been there to begin with: if Danny had only said "yes" when he first asked him, it would have been stranded in front of a cottage with four flats.

Damn them. Damn every last one of them. And their stupid girl-friends, too.

He knew that his brother was sitting up downstairs with a drink. Before the accident, Danny had planned to start technical school in the fall; he was going to learn a trade so he could work his way through university and never get in debt. It wasn't fair.

Most nights Junior would have gone and joined him, but tonight he couldn't somehow. If Danny were to come to bed right now, Junior would have to pretend to be asleep, so his brother wouldn't think he wasn't interested in drinking with him.

When Ginette left this time, he was heartsick. He realized that she was different from other girls. No one before her had ever made him feel half as excited as the pictures he found in magazines. Ginette made him feel that he might not want the magazines someday, that he would wake up some morning and not need them. Yet something inside still made him go to the little *dépanneur* that sold them. He promised himself that he would just look, then that he would just buy one, but he always left with a small bundle that he had to smuggle back into the apartment. Somehow sneaking them home and hiding them from Ginette was a part of their temptation.

Whenever he had dreams that were sexy, he was always sneaking through a window into a room filled with dirty magazines. There they would be: piles and piles of them stacked high to the rafters, the bare breasts on their covers immense and creamy. He would wander among them, beside himself with happiness. A warehouse of earthly delights.

Downstairs, Danny knew that he should go to bed. Mama would get upset and go all quiet if she found him on the couch in the morning, and Pop would be mad. But he was so tired all of a sudden, too tired to move. He thought that tomorrow he should take Gloria for a drive — to the beach, maybe — and try to talk with her. He was worried about all her plans for this reunion business; those sorts of things never worked out, and she should know that. Hadn't she grown up in a family, for chrissakes? She seemed to think that Raymond would be interested in the dumb things that people did around here, but Raymond was from Away now. He went to fancy restaurants and ordered food they had never even heard of. He had friends who painted modern art. He even listened to that opera junk on the radio. Everyone used to tease him about being a fruit until they all realized that he probably was one after all; then nobody mentioned it, because they were embarrassed. When Danny had come back from Toronto a week early, he knew that everybody at home thought that this was the reason, but it wasn't, really. Danny had changed his ticket because he didn't know what to say to Raymond's friends about their big, confusing paintings, and because he didn't understand what was written on the menus in the restaurants that Raymond took him to for supper. He had come home early because Raymond ate *dinner* — he didn't even call it *supper* any more. He belonged to a strange, new world, and Danny did not want to do something stupid and shame them both. Their brother would not be interested in Gloria's family reunion.

Poor Gloria, who never seemed to want or expect much from life, seemed to think that Raymond could bring her something. Danny couldn't conceive what it might be — he just knew that he did not want to see her disappointed.

It was very late. He wished he were in bed. If he moved right now, he could be there before he fell asleep. Then his glass slipped to the floor and the slim ice cube and a few drops of rye slid out onto the carpet. He was dead to the world.

Sometime in the middle of the night, Gloria imagined that the house was a big sleeping thing, like a giant, and that she was its heart, pumping away while everything else lay quietly. It was almost four when she finally drifted off to where her brothers and the Blessed Virgin were waiting for her. The moon had floated so far away that, even if she had stood at the window, she would not have been able to see it. It had vanished behind the trees.

THREE

M innie was banging the cupboard doors in the kitchen downstairs; she yanked open the pot drawer under the stove and slammed it shut. She whacked a frying pan against a burner. *She thinks that if she makes a big enough commotion I'll come running down and fix her breakfast*, Margaret thought. But Margaret was not ready to face her; it would take more than a lot of noise to drag her out of bed and down into the day just yet. Her mother's Bible was propped open on her lap, but even though she wasn't prepared for tonight's meeting, she was so upset that she couldn't concentrate on the Psalms. Minnie was a dim irritation in the background — she could just wait. She could make some toast and just bide her time. Margaret did not want to see anybody — especially, she thought, her sister. Last night she had dreamed about their father and she was furious.

He had been in trouble, and she, somehow, had been responsible. "Daddy, are you all right? Is everything going to be okay?"

And then he looked at her the way he had all those years ago when he lifted her up so that she stood in front of him on the dining-room table — smiling that pathetic smile that made her squirm. "Dance, Sweetheart," he would say.

She had wrestled and kicked her top sheet into a ball under the quilt at the foot of the bed. At least she had woken up before he had done anything to her — something had saved her from that disaster. After all, if you dreamed that you died, you would pass away right there in your sleep. She had been saved — like in a falling dream when you woke up just before you hit the ground, she had escaped. But she could not be grateful for any dream in which she was a child again, a foolish little girl who thought it was her fault. How could she be so stupid? Fear and guilt tracked her through her sleep and, when they caught up with her, they always wore her father's terrible face.

Other people would not look twice at that face. Round and bland, it had no distinguishing features beyond their own lack of distinction. It wasn't that he looked innocent, he just didn't look like much of anything. A potato, she thought. Except that potatoes were good for you.

Why was she such a fool in her sleep? His fat little hands — even the fingers were sweaty. She imagined that he was standing beside her bedroom door; she stuck out her tongue and made a face. "Daddy, are you all right?" she hissed, her voice thick with sarcasm. Then she tortured herself by dragging up the memory of the dining-room table.

"Stand still," he would whisper, pulling at her panties as she stood in front of him, looking down at him sitting there, her underwear becoming two swollen rings about her ankles. "Now dance, Sweetheart."

"But I'll trip."

"I'll catch you. I'd never let my little girl fall down." That rancid smile of his: so kind, so sweet. His needs were embarrassing. They were pathetic.

And where was her mother? "Mommy will catch us." Hoping it would make him stop. "But we're not doing anything wrong, Sweetheart." Whispering: "It's just a secret." Mommy was always away: at the store buying something for dinner, or upstairs cleaning out the closet.

She didn't know if she could smell his panic all those years ago, or if she sensed it now from the distance of time. His eyes darting about, the drops of perspiration on his forehead like sweat on a boiled egg.

When her mother went to Saint John to visit Aunt Thea, he took her into their bedroom and said, "You don't have to sleep all by yourself this week" — as if her mother had been mean to her by making her stay alone in her bed. Those fingers would push at her, they would pull her inside out. Now, sixty years later, whenever a large man stood close to her, Margaret would shudder and move away.

The back door slammed shut. Minnie was marching across the porch beneath Margaret's bedroom window and rattling the garbage can. She banged the lid. Margaret sighed and rolled her eyes. Then Minnie banged the garbage can again and clomped back into the house. The door slammed a second time. *I'm not going to budge*, Margaret thought. *Not an inch*.

Every wall in their house had ears. At night, she could hear her sister moan and complain to herself from the bathroom. Minnie enjoyed poor health, and Margaret had learned long ago never to ask the fatal question "How are you today?" because the answer was an inventory of woe. There was no privacy anywhere. It had been years since Margaret allowed herself to have a bowel movement when her sister was upstairs. "Aren't you the lucky one," Minnie would say with a sigh. "I haven't been regular since nineteen eighty-five."

How on earth had her mother been so deaf?

Her father kept their secret confined to the house until the day he put down his newspaper and said, "I think I'll take Margaret to the pictures this week." He winked at her behind Mother's back, and she had been foolish enough to think that it was a peace offering. If only her mother hadn't hated the movies.

"That Wayne Saunders dotes on his child," women said to their husbands. "Why can't you spend more time with your kids?" People told her she was lucky; Mrs. Bourque in the box office put down her knitting and smiled at her, called her "the lucky girl." Five-year-old Margaret believed it until the lights went down. Sitting together, the smell of popcorn and stale air telling her that they were somewhere important, he held her hand, he rubbed her knee. "Do you want to sit on my lap, Sweetheart?" She shook her head, hoping that he wouldn't press the point in public.

Most of *Little Miss Broadway* was a blur in her head, but memory keeps clear and intact the agonizing moment when she stared up at the screen in horror as Shirley Temple started to dance. She was terrified because she knew that soon someone would pick up little Shirley and place her on a dining-room table, where she would be forced to do what Margaret had to do for her father. She tried not to burst into tears. Shirley swayed back and forth, rolling her eyes upwards and wiggling her index fingers. Margaret wanted to pee. She shut her eyes and held her breath. The popcorn smell was thick — she could feel it brushing against her face. The music was loud and fuzzy and seemed to be coming from far away. And Daddy's voice was far, far away too. "Margaret? Are you all right? Margaret! Open your eyes." She did and the dance was over. As Shirley bowed and curtsied, Margaret knew that she was an ungrateful daughter. Daddy smiled wider than anyone else at the theatre, and when the movie ended he started the applause. If she were Shirley Temple, it wouldn't hurt. Poor Daddy.

In the lobby afterwards, when Mrs. Bourque asked her if she liked the movie, she didn't know what to say. Mrs. Bourque was bending over her, touching her forehead. "Too much excitement," she said to Daddy, and then she turned back to Margaret.

"Did you like Shirley Temple?"

Margaret nodded. "My favourite part was when they took down her pants," she said, not wanting to disappoint her father.

"She's half-asleep," Daddy said, and he thanked Mrs. Bourque and carried Margaret home. And that night, as her mother tucked her in, he stood nervously in the bedroom door. "Will you come to the pictures next time, Mommy?"

"They give me a headache."

"Me too!" Margaret cried.

On her next birthday her father and mother came into her bedroom with a big box. They sat on the bed as she unwrapped her very own Shirley Temple doll. "Oh, Wayne," her mother said. "She's so happy that she doesn't know what to say."

THEN SINGS MY SOUL,
MY SAVIOUR GOD TO THEE
HOW GREAT THOU ART,
HOW GREAT THOU ART

Minnie had turned the kitchen radio up full tilt, and a church choir blared up through the floor. Another pan slammed on the stove. Margaret put her fingers in her ears. The noise was so deafening that even Minnie could not stand it and, after a few moments, turned the radio down. Poor Minnie. She needed to be the centre of attention. Unlike her sister, she could not bear to be alone.

Minnie was born a few months after Daddy went Overseas and died; every November Mrs. Saunders dragged her daughters to the park to stick a wreath by the memorial. He hadn't even died in action, hadn't even gotten near the war itself. He had arrived in England and, a few nights later, was watching a drunken brawl when a bottle came sailing out of the fray and smashed against his head. He never regained consciousness. Her mother didn't tell her this until Margaret was sixteen — for ten years she had felt sinful for thanking the anonymous Nazi soldier whom she assumed had been responsible.

For the rest of her mother's life, Margaret longed to interrupt her tales of Wayne the War Hero with the ridiculous truth of that deadly bottle, but she couldn't. "Poor wee Minnie," their mother said, sighing. "She never even knew her own father. He died before he ever saw her sweet little face." Consequently, Margaret was expected to pamper her sister.

She had not known quite what to make of Minnie: she was certainly pretty and Margaret was very happy that her sister would never have to live through the nightmare of Daddy. Truly happy. But she resented Minnie for having such an easy time of it. It wasn't fair. And so, occasionally, Margaret would mildly torture her sister, just to even the score a bit. She might sneak up on her and prick her with a pin — just enough to give Minnie a start — or trip her, accidentally on purpose. Sometimes she hid Minnie's favourite toys. She gave her sister the Shirley Temple doll so that it would no longer watch her every night. "Oh Margaret, what an angel you are," her mother said. "I know how much that means to you!" A few weeks later, when she saw that Minnie had forgotten it in the yard after a tea party with her toys, she hid it. Margaret and Mother searched for hours with a hysterical Minnie, to no avail. Later, Margaret took the doll from its hiding place — she had stuffed it inside the dirt bag of the Electrolux — and smuggled it into the field, where she went at its head with a rock. Then she dragged Shirley into the woods by the feet, and swung the doll back and forth, bashing its head against the sticky trunks of spruce trees. Minnie still believes that a nasty French girl snuck into the yard and spirited Shirley away; that's what Margaret whispered to her at bedtime. (Minnie, as a result, grew up believing that all French girls were inherently dishonest.) When their mother told her friends that she was so lucky to have Margaret to help her out and that Margaret loved her sister "just like a little doll," Margaret felt horrible. She tortured herself with the picture of Minnie being bashed by rocks and dragged up into the woods. She really did love Minnie — Minnie was sweet, after all — but she just couldn't stop herself from tormenting her. The tortures were never direct, and Minnie continued to blame her misfortunes on a parade of invisible French girls, Indians, and gypsies. Minnie knew that her older sister worshipped the ground she walked on and would do anything for her — their mother had told her so.

Poor Minnie was so gullible that she believed her tormentors could sneak into the house and balance glass marbles on the top edge of her bedroom door. She would push the door open into the ambush and the big allies would bounce off her skull. Margaret would run and hold her terrified sister, kiss the bumps on her head to calm her down, and help her collect the marbles from where they ricocheted about the room. It never occurred to Minnie that her own sister would stand on a chair in the hallway, carefully sneaking her fingers up through the crack of the almost-closed door and placing the marbles there in a wobbly row. Margaret could not do such a thing; Margaret was her best friend. She believed this all through school. She was stunned when her sister finished business college and went looking for work, was sick with grief when Margaret started working at a bank in Moncton thirty miles away. She couldn't believe that Margaret would want to spend her days without her. She sulked when Margaret took the morning train at seven, and sulked when she finally came home at night. When John Morton, the new bank manager, first asked her sister out for dinner and a movie, Minnie was upset because she was not invited. One Sunday he came out to Membartouche and took Margaret for a long, dull drive after church. "Why can't you take your sister?" Mrs. Saunders asked as Margaret sat waiting for him.

"John's going to pick up some friends of his," she lied. "There won't be room in the car for Minnie."

Mrs. Saunders looked miserable and stared out the window. "She'll get her own boyfriend soon, too, I suppose, and I'll be all alone in the world. Mr. Churchill and that rotten old Hitler sure made a mess of my life."

Although she was happy to spend as much time as possible away from Minnie, Margaret continued to date John Morton primarily because he never touched her. She listened with a sense of relief to his unhappy stories of the beautiful fiancée who had run off with his shiftless brother.

Not long after she graduated from high school, Minnie married the Fool. Arthur Snow was a shy sort of fellow who might occasionally sidle up to you at a party with a rye and ginger in his hand and say, "I heard a cute little story at the office. An Irishman, a Frenchman, and a Chinaman were all out fishing one day, when along comes this Jew ..." Who but Minnie could laugh at those darn things? Her high-school yearbook had called her "good fun" and "high-spirited," but Margaret figured that was a nice way of saying that she had the attention span of a flea.

Margaret persuaded John to come to the wedding with her. Mother grabbed him at the reception and talked for half an hour about Minnie's fatal mistake. "That Arthur Snow is a Fool," she said. "If only Margaret had spent more time with her sister, poor Minnie wouldn't have married the first man to walk in the door." John smiled awkwardly and tried to get Mrs. Saunders to change the subject; Minnie's husband was standing right behind them with an empty glass and an emptier look on his face. Shortly afterwards, John was transferred to a branch in Nova Scotia. Although Margaret was not sorry to see him go, she enjoyed secretly blaming her mother and sister for destroying her one chance at happiness.

"That Arthur Snow is a Fool."

Mother had said it first when a giggling Minnie showed them her diamond, and Margaret had agreed with her, although her reasons were very different from her mother's. Minnie prattled day and night just to hear herself talk. She would sit for hours yakking about how she planned to redecorate their new house, but she did nothing. "What if we painted the kitchen robin's-egg blue?" she would say, flipping through magazines at the table while Margaret and her mother scrubbed her cupboards. "But maybe sunshine yellow would be better. Which do you think is the more sporty? I wish I had a breakfast nook. Arthur promised me a breakfast nook. He promised me that, you know. He's going to take out that wall by the shed and put in a lovely breakfast nook with a plate rack."

Minnie had been a very pretty girl and was good fun. She certainly knew how to laugh, and Margaret thought that was the main reason the Fool had married her. Her laugh was infectious mostly because it was so loud and outlandish that people had to laugh when she did — but no one was laughing with her. After a certain point, Minnie's braying started to drive people crazy.

No one in their right mind would go to the movies with her — she would drown out the actors at the most inappropriate moments — and, if she went to a party, first the wives, then the husbands, would start retreating into other rooms. There had been a kind of novelty in her being such a pretty girl with such a crazed laugh, but when she started to go to fat it was as if she were finally growing into the sound. The pounds started piling up just months into the marriage, and her shrieking lost its charm. Margaret felt terribly guilty and responsible. This was what happened when you tormented your sister. Minnie became a cross for her to bear, and Margaret blamed no one but herself.

The Fool was a quiet man who never offered an opinion. If someone were making a strong point, he would stand to one side bobbing his head up and down. "Yessir. Yessir," he'd say. He had no family except for an estranged sister somewhere in Alberta. He had come to town to be a clerk in the Fisheries office; he went to his Lodge meetings; he did a bit of gardening in the summer; and, for a few months, he doted on Minnie. No one but Margaret understood why he might not be happy to come home from work every day and find his wife sitting at the kitchen table while her mother cooked supper. Less than a month after the Snows came back from their Cavendish Beach honeymoon, Mrs. Saunders began going over in the afternoons "to help Minnie out." In the beginning, she came home and ate supper with Margaret, but soon she was staying "to help Minnie with the dishes." It was only a matter of months before she started spending the night. When the Snows' six-month anniversary came around, the closet in their spare bedroom was half-filled with her clothes.

"I think they'd like more time to themselves," Margaret ventured one Sunday evening as she and her mother were eating a pork roast. Arthur had taken Minnie to the Starlight Lounge in

Moncton for smorgasbord, and Mrs. Saunders was sour and slighted.

"But the Fool never says a word!" she barked. "Poor Minnie gets so lonely."

Arthur began to stay outside the house, where he developed a greater love for gardening. His mother-in-law would watch him through the kitchen window, shaking her head sadly and saying, "Not a damn thing the Fool plants will ever come up." But most of it did; the Fool would bring her beautiful fat vegetables that she stuck in Minnie's pressure cooker and blasted. "I boiled the life out of these carrots, but I had to do *something!* I never saw such miserable produce in my life."

Mother had her first stroke while pickling. She was furiously dicing the Fool's green tomatoes for chow-chow when the knife fell out of her hand. She followed it to the floor. Over the next few days her daughters sat nervously by her hospital bed. The doctor said Mother was making a remarkable recovery, but when she was able to talk again, she spoke only to her late husband and Winston Churchill. Moments after Minnie and Arthur walked into her semi-private room one afternoon with a bouquet from his garden, a second stroke killed her instantly.

A few months later — five weeks to the day after their first anniversary — the Fool set off for a Lodge meeting one night and didn't come back. Minnie phoned Margaret in a panic. The next day, they discovered that he no longer worked for Fisheries — he had given his notice the month before — and the joint bank account was half-gone. The two sisters went to Minnie's bank and checked the safety-deposit box. Their mother's few bits of jewellery were still there, as well as a Hallmark card with the note: "Minnie, very sorry, Arthur." Membartouche never heard from him again. Minnie moved back home and her weeping proved to be as resonant as her laughter.

"Every time I think of that breakfast nook, my heart just breaks," Minnie said when she sold the house.

Minnie tromped up the stairs and was starting to storm about in her bedroom across the hall. Her dresser drawers screeched open and banged shut, the hangers scraped across the pole in the closet as she shunted her dresses back and forth. She stamped her feet on the hardwood floor. Margaret knew that she would have to get out of bed soon. If she did not cook Minnie some breakfast, her sister would eat every sweet in the kitchen; if she did not take her to church, Minnie would slam around the house all day and pout.

She and Minnie no longer went to church in town: Minnie had discovered the Church of the Water of Life when a young couple arrived at the kitchen door three years ago. When Margaret came back from the supermarket, she was introduced to Bob and Cindy, who helped her lug the groceries in from the car. "You must be Margaret," Bob said. "We've heard so much about you." The next day they arrived at nine in the morning to take Minnie and Margaret to their church in the city. The service was long, and something about it disturbed Margaret, but Minnie had a whale of a time. She sang at the top of her lungs and gave a moving testimonial about how low she had been after the Fool had walked out on her. She beamed through her tears as the congregation surrounded her afterwards, holding her and patting her hand. A few months later, Margaret allowed herself to be baptised by immersion, mainly because she had come to dread seeing Sandy Whyte at the United Church every Sunday morning.

Because Membartouche was a small town, and because they had both been in their early thirties and unmarried, there were rumours before Sandy ever asked her out. When he finally did, they were alone in the church early on Easter morning and she was arranging Mrs. Whyte's daffodils and tulips in a large vase beside the altar. Margaret simply said "yes" and steeled herself for a dull evening, which she got — although she had to admit that it was a pleasant change from Minnie. They went out again. Mostly they talked about church business, about his store, and about her job at the bank, and although she didn't feel completely at ease with Sandy at first, she didn't feel threatened either. She knew that old Mrs. Whyte did not approve of her, and this, somehow, made her continue to see Sandy after she knew that their relationship would never lead to anything romantic. One Friday night they had dinner at the Hotel, and once he drove her to Moncton to see a Katharine Hepburn movie. It was more of a distraction than an affair; but then Sandy suggested that he could teach her how to drive.

From the moment she sat behind the wheel and drove up into the woods at the end of Dorchester Street, she felt the thrill of a true, deep passion. She came to love everything about driving: the wind blowing her hair through the open window, the satisfaction of coordinating the clutch and the gear shift from first to second to third to fourth, the pleasure of acceleration when she eased her foot down and the car zoomed forward. She loved the speed and she loved the fact that she controlled it. She even loved Sandy's growing nervousness beside her as he glanced over at the speedometer. "I'd watch that speed limit a bit more closely, if I were you," he'd say. It was a few weeks before she realized that he hated driving himself; he enjoyed having her take him places. They both discovered how much they loved getting out of town. She drove up the coast and travelled inland on dusty dirt roads to explore abandoned cemeteries beside rivers with ancient, unfathomable Micmac names. They went south and drank iced tea beside the old Acadian dykes on the Tantramar

Marshes. They sped along the far side of the Petitcodiac River into the gentle Appalachian woods and farms of Albert County.

She began to brighten up whenever Sandy came to take her for a lesson. She had never before been so happy. Was this what her father had robbed her of — the simple and extreme moments of bliss that filled other people's lives so easily? On those Sunday afternoons, she felt that she and Sandy were driving off for adventures into a new world, a world without the bank and Minnie, an adult world where adventure was possible. They talked about the town, they gossiped mildly about the church; they never mentioned their respective families except to politely inquire about their health.

"How is your mother doing?"

"The same, fine. And your sister?"

"The same. Fine."

What they enjoyed most was talking about the land, the Indians, the old French and Scottish settlers. During the week she read books on local history and studied large government maps. "Planning your next *excursion*?" Minnie would say sourly. Once, when they were returning from the Maine border, Sandy had said, "I wonder how long it would take to drive to Nantucket," and Margaret realized that both of them were wishing that they could travel further. But an overnight trip was out of the question. People would talk and, besides, they had responsibilities at home.

Often she sang hymns as they drove along. He was too timid to join in, but he would hum the melodies and encourage her. "That was lovely. Can you sing 'Tell Me the Old, Old Story'?" or "What next? How about 'Jesus Bids Us Shine'?" Margaret treasured the simple faith from the hymns of her childhood: this faith was a part of her, it had sustained her through those terrible years with her father, and she loved it still, as naturally as she loved the countryside. All that summer and fall, Sandy and his little grey Austin allowed her to escape from the cramped world with Minnie in her father's house and glimpse a wider, more glorious one.

In this world of darkness
so we must shine
You in your small corner
and I in mine.

It was on a fall drive to see the leaves in Albert County that Sandy surprised her by touching her. They were parked on a side road, looking across a valley at hillsides blazing with orange and red maples. Margaret had never felt happier in her life, and told him so. Sandy placed a nervous hand on her leg, and suddenly Margaret was confused because it seemed to her that in such a moment she was not on her guard. She shrank away and then stepped out of the car.

Before Daddy went Overseas, her parents had taken her to the town beach for a swim after supper. He cupped his hands, holding them out to her like a stirrup, and she lifted her foot, placing it in his wide palms. She stepped up, putting her hands on his forehead for balance, as he called out, "Ready, hold your breath!" and her mother shouted, "One Two Three!" Then he shot her up in the air like a rocket. She sailed up and up, flipping over backwards and sliding back into the water. The three of them were standing together and laughing, and at that moment she believed that they lived for her. She was their beach toy, a spinning top. She wanted to do tricks for them: each jump higher, each dive deeper, and each time they would move closer to her until their arms were around each other and, slippery as a little fish, Margaret would shoot up between them, laughing in delight, flying quick circles in the air around them like a bird.

"Higher, Dad! Higher!"

But her mother was suddenly moving towards the shore, and in that moment her father touched her, slid his big hand up the inside of her leg and shoved his finger under the edge of her bathing suit. She went as rigid as stone and fell into the sea.

She could not look at Sandy that Sunday afternoon when she returned to the car and said that she had to get back home. She was still a little girl frightened of a hand on her leg, but she felt like her mother, too, turning her back and walking away. "I promised Minnie I'd make some cookies," she said.

Their friendship ended that winter. Margaret and her sister were in Saint John visiting Aunt Thea when Sandy was in the city on business. She told Minnie that she was going to the Loyalist Burial Ground to look at the headstones, but she drifted into the lobby of the Admiral Beatty Hotel, where Sandy was staying. Although she sensed that he was dreading their secret meeting as much as she was, it seemed the inevitable destination of all their Sunday drives.

As she took off her dress and stood in his hotel room in her slip, Sandy stared at the dark stubble under her arms and turned quite pale. He mumbled something that she could not understand, took a step towards the bathroom door, and fainted. Margaret was horrified and relieved. She knelt beside him, holding his head in her lap, and talked very sweetly to him. He said that maybe he should lie down; she helped him to the bed, where he immediately started to snore. It made her think of the way that she had pretended to sleep when her father used to come into her room, and suddenly she felt protective of Sandy. She sat quietly on the other side of the bed.

"Sandy," she said, "it would have been nice if this had worked out, but we both knew it wouldn't." Although she had heard people whisper unkind things about him, she was not entirely sure what their cruel words meant. She suspected that he was frightened of sex, and she tried to talk to him about this. After all, her father had ensured that her own meagre sexual appetite consisted mostly of dread. She had sensed that this was their unspoken yet strongest bond of friendship. Here, in the strange intimacy of a hotel bedroom, she wanted to tell him about her father.

But as soon as she said "I know it's not me, it's all women, isn't it, Sandy?" he turned away from her, his body tight with rage. "*Get. Out.*" he said; the words were whispered but he was screaming. "*Get out of here!*"

Neither of them said a word when everyone started talking about how old Mrs. Whyte had come between them. They saw each other only on Sundays at church. For years Sandy and his mother sat together in the Whyte pew at the front, both of them snubbing Margaret and her sister. After the old lady became bedridden, there was something about Sandy's isolation from the congregation behind him that set Margaret's teeth on edge. For years she dreaded church because Sandy would be sitting up there in his regal, holier-than-thou family pew. The sight of his bowed head could send her into a fury as dark as the memories of her father. It was so unjust; this was the one place she had felt free from the burden of her life. And so, she had gone along with her sister and joined the Church of the Water of Life. In no time at all, she was in charge of the Flower Committee and typing up a weekly newsletter. After she retired from the bank, she agreed to help with the phones at the Save the Children Hotline. Her passion for the cause surprised her; she had never really thought about abortion before.

Which is why she was lying in bed this Sunday morning with the Bible propped open on her lap to the Psalms. There was a meeting of the volunteers tonight: an American preacher and his wife, both active in the pro-life movement, would be speaking, and Florence Jenson had called yesterday and asked if she would read "something inspirational." She had been looking through the later psalms — she was certain that there was a number 9 in the one she wanted — and in Psalm 109 her eye stuck on "Let his children be fatherless, and his wife a widow."

And she had remembered the dream about her father.

She read the beginning of the psalm again, softly whispering the verses that spoke to her.

"'For the mouth of the wicked and the mouth of the deceitful are opened against me: they have spoken against me with a lying tongue.

"'They compassed me about also with words of hatred: and fought against me without a cause.'"

Yes, she thought, *yes.*

"'Set thou a wicked man over him: and let Satan stand at his right hand.

"'When he shall be judged, let him be condemned: and let his prayer become sin.'"

Let him be condemned: and let his prayer become sin.

She wished she had written those words herself. She wished she could engrave them in granite on her father's grave in England.

Margaret had never thought about Satan a great deal — she'd had her father to contend with and he was evil enough — but, like David in his psalm, she had been unjustly treated. Her father had done her a great wrong and, as a result, she had been denied her place in the world. She had been forced to move through her own life like an outsider. She watched other people move with ease through their lives and was bitterly angry. She'd see them laughing over their carts at the grocery store or sitting on their porches while their children played in the yard. They were as much an affront to her as the stupid girls she saw necking in the park with their boyfriends. They flaunted the ease of their lives.

She started scanning through the Bible and found what she wanted in Psalm 139.

... thou hast covered me in my mother's womb. I will praise thee for I am fearfully and wonderfully made: marvellous are thy works; and that my soul knoweth right well.

"'Covered me in my mother's womb,'" she whispered.

My substance was not hid from thee, when I was made in secret, and curiously wrought in the lowest parts of the earth.

A few verses later was her lesson: *Do not I hate them, O Lord, that hate thee? and am not I grieved with those that rise up against thee? I hate them with a perfect hatred; I count them mine enemies.*

Yes, this was what she wanted. The abortionists were, like her father, destroyers of life: they were her enemies. She turned on her side and the Bible slipped off her lap and dropped to the floor.

Covered me in my mother's womb. She thought of God tenderly placing a tiny quilt over her.

Minnie's sharp little ears heard the Bible hit the floor and, no longer able to contain herself, she shoved open Margaret's door and stood looking at her sister from the hall.

"If you're feeling poorly," she said, "you better call the doctor. Otherwise, if you don't get up, we won't have time to eat before church."

"All right." Margaret got out of bed. She pushed back the quilt and reached down to straighten out the scrunched-up sheet. Suddenly something perverse in her decided to rein in a bit of Minnie's control over the day. "Let's go to the United Church instead this morning."

"Why on earth do you want to do that?"

"I think we should still show up once in a while. Besides, I have to go into Moncton for my meeting tonight. I'd rather just make one trip to town." Margaret found the top edge of her sheet and pulled it up. Minnie's jaw dropped into her double chins, and she jumped into the room, her chubby fingers pointing at the sheet hanging in her sister's hand.

"What in the name of God were you up to?"

An ugly tear gaped from the bottom of the sheet halfway up to Margaret's fist.

FOUR

On Sunday morning at seven o'clock, Chaleur was up and dressed and out the door. All week he'd looked forward to staying with Annette while she babysat her sister's kids, but she picked a fight with him last night halfway through *Thelma and Louise* and said she didn't want to see him. He hoped that she'd feel bad and try phoning him in a couple of hours; just to show her how much he didn't care, nobody at home would be able to tell her where he was. They wouldn't even know if he'd come home last night. She'd been so bitchy to him all week that he figured she wanted to break up with him, and so he'd said something about the movie that he knew would get her started. There was no way that he was going to let her think that it mattered to him. "Fucking bitch," he'd said all the way home from her sister's. "Fucking bitch." He'd thrown his beer bottle at a stop sign, but it had missed and thumped off a car window. If he stayed at the house today he knew he'd fight with everybody, so the best thing to do was take off.

From the first week after his family had moved to Membartouche, Chaleur headed off into the woods every chance he got. He was twelve then and didn't want to talk to anybody. His mother had married a jerk, his little brother had tricked everyone into thinking that he was some kind of holy saint, and there was no one in the woods to nag him. When he was home, he wanted to be alone in his room, his music obliterating Mom and Rory screeching over the TV or their constant praises for Ralphie, who never got into trouble. "Why can't you be more like your brother?" they said every day of the week, while Ralphie, who snuck into his room and stole his stuff, stood smirking behind them, making the "L" for Loser sign with his fingers and pointing at Chaleur. Ralphie even said that he couldn't remember their real father. "Rory's more my dad than yours," he bragged.

Rory was loud and stupid and always referred to Chaleur as "your little Frenchman," as in "Guess what your little Frenchman was up to today?" Everything he did rubbed Rory the wrong way. Chaleur's father was a Boudreau from outside Caraquet and his mother was Acadian on her mother's side, but it was like she didn't believe she had any French attachments at all. Except for Chaleur. She never stood up for the French, ever. Her life was a series of Rory-driven confrontations and she knew better than to get her back up when he started baiting her. Rory never hit her, even though he said he was going to slap her silly about once every hour, because he was too lazy to get up and fight; but he had such a mean tongue that it was easier to go along with him. "Your little Frenchman's been stealing my beer," Rory bellowed from the fridge. "Your little Frenchman left a mess in here," he hollered from the bathroom. "Where the hell is that little Frenchman? I'm gonna wring his stupid neck!" The only remark she made to her son when Rory ranted and raved was "Don't let him get your goat."

Practically the only thing that made him feel French at all was that his stepfather hated every Frenchman on the face of the earth. Chaleur couldn't speak a word of it any more, and the school he went to in the city was English. "Baa baa baa le petit mouton noir" was the only French that he remembered. It was from a long time ago, when he sat with his father and Grand-mère in her kitchen. It was warm by the stove, and her hands were scratchy when she touched his face. "Baa baa baa le petit mouton noir," she cooed, rocking him in her big chair. If only his father's heart had been stronger. It had been big, why wasn't it strong? That was one of the last things Grandmère had said to him: his dad's heart was too big. They were standing outside the church before the funeral. It had been a warm summer day, but Chaleur keeps mixing it up in his head with a memory of going to midnight Mass with her the next Christmas, he and Grand-mère shivering in the freezing rain.

He can hardly remember his father: just vague memories of being lifted into the air by a man who was the size of a moun-tain, who smelled like pine trees and had a big laugh. He recalled visiting his grandmother on the farm near Caraquet where his father had been a little boy. He used to try to picture the room exactly, pretending that he was sitting in her lap and looking around. He knew that his father was in the room with them, but when he tries to find him, all he can see are corners and edges of things, and all the chairs are empty. He can see the Aunt Jemima salt and pepper shakers that look like toys, and the kitchen cot where the cats slept. There is a door to the pantry where the shelves go way, way up and Grandmère keeps her cookies. The little rug that they sit him on has a house on it, and a sleigh: Grandmère made it all by herself. His father's toys are in an old cardboard box behind the door to the back stairs — an elephant, a police car, a broken Ferris wheel: the toys are the treasures that he never can find in his dreams. But his father is nowhere to be seen, as if he were locked so far away that Chaleur can remember only bits and pieces of him.

After his dad died he hardly ever saw Grandmère again. She had to sell the farm and move into one of those homes where they keep old people tied to the bed. He wanted to go see her, but after Rory moved in with them, his mother stopped their Sunday visits. He ran away once to see her, but old age had taken her mind away and she didn't know who he was. He hitch-hiked back home and no one had even missed him. Then they left the Miramichi and moved to Membartouche and Grandmère was far away.

"Tell your little Frenchman to turn that goddam racket off before I go in there and smash his friggin' stereo."

He had to steal headphones from Zellers so he could listen to Guns N' Roses in peace and quiet. The big sound filled up the emptiness he felt and made it possible for him to stay in his room without going crazy. The music sounded exactly the way he felt: *Don't trust anybody*, the songs screamed to him; *the world is mean and you are all alone.* Sometimes when he was kissing Annette he wanted to hold her tight and have the music roar around them like a video, his tongue in her mouth, searching for new meanings to the words Axl Rose poured into the air. He felt that they were alone in a beautiful place, like the top of a mountain, and even if the rest of the world hated them, it didn't matter, because everything outside their bodies was small and stupid. Now that she was mad at him for no reason, he was all alone again and it was worse than it had been before he ever touched her. He had thought that there was a space in the songs for her; suddenly those very same songs made him lonelier than he had ever been. He hoped that she felt worse than he did.

In the woods he never wanted to hear anything except the soft wind and the birds. He would steal a couple of his step-father's beers and head out into the secrecy that surrounded the town. There were crows and ravens that made the woods sound lonely and scary, and chickadees that made it sound safe; he'd seen a porcupine and followed a stream from the river up to a beaver dam. He waited and waited, but the beavers never showed. Once he'd seen a deer in a clearing. She was the most beautiful thing that he'd ever seen and it bugged him that she bolted and ran away in an instant. But you couldn't tell an animal that you wanted to be its friend; they all thought that you wanted to kill them. And maybe, if he had a rifle, he would have.

He was sixteen now and went to the woods only a couple of times a week. Annette never wanted to go, and he had been stupid enough to do whatever she wanted. He used to walk halfway across town and turn up Dorchester Street; after a mile or so he would cross the four-lane highway that bypassed Membartouche and follow what was left of the street until it dwindled into a wood road. Then it was almost a half an hour before he could take an old trail down to the river. But last year he had found a shorter way. He thought he would try to get back to town by following the river downstream — he only had to take off his sneakers and wade in two places — and then he found a path that was so overgrown he wouldn't have seen it unless he was looking really hard. Following it through a mile or so of spruce, he'd crossed over the old railway bed and through a small stand of poplars, then come out in an old field almost filled with alders about a half-mile from the river. There was an overgrown orchard at the far end. After that, all he had to do was jump over a fence and sneak across a backyard and he was almost home. It saved him about half an hour and, if he made it through the backyard without anybody in the big house seeing him, no one at all would know where he'd been.

It was going to be a nice day. The sun had filled the kitchen with yellow light when he took a couple of Rory's beers and a package of bologna from the fridge. He liked the house best when it was quiet and pretty like this, before anybody else was up. Outside, the sun glittered on the river, and the bay was a deep, rich blue. He walked along the road, taking out a piece of bologna, pulling off the rind, and rolling it up like a cigar before he ate it. When he was sure no one was looking, he ran across the lawn of the old Whyte place and snuck along the edge of the big house — the only person who lived in it was an old fart who was probably half-blind anyway. From the street, the house looked like a millionaire lived there, but it was shabby when you got close. He didn't even need his glasses to see that. The paint was peeling on the clapboards and some of them looked rotten. The grass in the yard needed to be cut. It was easy to jump over the back fence because it was broken in places. He sat on the fence and ate another piece of bologna, looking up at the back of the house. Someday, he wanted to have a house like that. It was so big that if you had a party and got tired of it, you could just go to another room somewhere and be by yourself. It was crazy that they were all crammed into the dump he lived in while one old guy had this whole place to himself — the Whyte place was so big that, if they lived in it, whole weeks could go by before he would even have to see Rory.

But then he saw something move in the kitchen window, so he hopped off the fence and started walking through the orchard. He took his glasses out of his pocket and put them on. Nobody could see him now and he didn't want to miss anything. What he liked best about the long hike to his favourite spot was that he didn't have to think when he was walking. He knew he should be thinking about Annette right now, but he didn't want to. The sun was getting higher — it would be nice up there today.

When he first started going to the woods, he'd found an old hunting shack and he hung out in it. It was as dark and musty as a cellar inside, and the few bits of furniture in it were all broken. All around it were bottles, many of them smashed. He figured that a long time ago it had been owned by men who stood in the doorway, tossing their empties into the bush. Maybe his dad had been a guy like that. The shack was so old that Chaleur decided everybody else in the world had forgotten about it, so it could belong to him. It was too bad it was falling apart, because he knew that it was a place where he could have been happy.

When he was twelve, he sat inside the crooked doorway and imagined going home and finding all of his family dead. Sometimes it was bloody — their throats slit and blood spattered on the walls like in a horror movie — and sometimes they were just propped up dead on the sofa. "Carbon monoxide," the cop would say, and Chaleur would be allowed to live by himself from now on. Sometimes he would just imagine going home and the cops would be waiting to tell him that they'd all been killed in a car accident. He knew that was the best one, because he wouldn't have to think about the bodies in the house, but most of the time he was so mad that he wanted the satisfaction and danger of finding them. He loved thinking about what it would be like to wake up all alone in the house and have girls over. Back then he thought that when he was old enough to have a girlfriend, he would run away with her and bring her to his shack. They would live like a love song turned up really loud. Even when he was twelve, he wanted that girl to be Annette MacNeil.

He knows now that he was a stupid kid back then, four years ago. He didn't know anything. Annette would never know how much he'd let her mean to him. He'd never let her know now, ever.

He stopped and looked back through the orchard towards the old house. He should wear his glasses when he sneaks across that yard; maybe the old guy had seen him. Yeah, well, he could just go fuck himself. "Go fuck yourself," he said aloud. He picked up a rock and fired it at a blue jay. Missed.

One day he'd heard men's voices coming from inside the shack and he realized that other people still knew about it. He'd ducked down in the bushes, his heart suddenly pounding so loud he thought the strangers might hear it. At first he was going to sneak up so that he could look through the window, but instead he turned around and walked away. He was afraid of getting caught and, besides, he didn't want to know who they were. They might be escaped convicts from the Penitentiary, which would be dangerous, or, even worse, they might be guys that he saw downtown or at school and then he would know that the woods didn't belong to him. He didn't want to share the woods at all.

He decided that it would be better if he built a secret place, a hidden place, and then he could go there and always be by himself. Just a little lean-to tucked into a hillside further upstream. He even made plans, sketches in the back of his scribblers at school, and a couple of weeks after he heard the voices in the shack he found just the right place for it, set high enough up on the rise above the river that no one could sneak up on him, and hidden away in an evergreen grove so that it wouldn't stick out. But the place he found was so smooth to lie on and so sheltered by a giant pine tree that in the end he decided to just go there and not build anything. He took some glass jars from the kitchen cupboard and stashed them away in the bushes — he could hide the things he wanted to keep up there in them.

The first year he went to the woods, he liked to explore, but after a while he just wanted the quiet. He'd sit on a rock in the river near his spot on the hill, his bare feet in the cool water, and spend a long time thinking about Annette. She was in his class at school and he liked her because she seemed older than the rest of them. She wasn't hard, but she had a tough way of talking that he admired. Her laugh was low and quick, and sometimes she seemed to look at him from a deep place. When he thought about being sized up, he imagined someone's eyes moving up and down him slowly; Annette took you in with a quick, powerful stare. He loved her legs in her little short skirts: they were solid and pretty — not like most of the girls, who wanted their legs to look like sticks. But she wasn't fat either. He thought about her lying back and opening those legs for him like a pair of soft scissors. He'd lie down on top of her and she'd bend her legs, bringing her knees up under his armpits, her ankles holding him at the small of his back.

When he was thirteen years old, this was his favourite thing in the whole world to think about up in the woods, sitting on his favourite rock, drinking some of Rory's beer.

Back then, he'd only talked to her a couple of times, but they'd made each other laugh. She went out with Rocky Arsenault then; he towered over everybody and played hockey so violently that people said he'd make the NHL someday. He'd heard Annette say things like "You know how much Gretzky makes? His wife can have everything she wants. They live like a couple of movie stars." Annette ran on the beach every morning with Rocky. In the winter, she stayed at the high school and ran around the track while Rocky was at hockey practice. One of the first times Chaleur talked to her, he asked her if she wanted to be a professional athlete, and she said one in the family was going to be enough, and besides they'd make her quit smoking. She smoked long menthol cigarettes, and Chaleur started smoking the same brand himself, secretly, in the woods. He always had a pack of them stashed away up there in an old mayonnaise jar. His mom and his stepfather both smoked like chimneys, but when he tried to smoke at home they called him stupid and told him it would stunt his growth.

Back then, when he wasn't imagining his whole family being dead, he thought about ways he and Annette could be together deep in the spruce grove near the river. He figured that something big would have to happen to bring them together. Maybe if the whole town burnt down, or maybe a big gas leak. An earthquake, or a hurricane forcing them to move inland. He wanted her so powerfully and she seemed so unobtainable that people would have to die before he could get her.

He would start by thinking about something like the gas leak: everybody would be running around, trying to get away from downtown because the whole place was going to blow up. He'd see Annette and rescue her, taking her up into the woods. She'd be amazed that he knew his way around them so well, and they'd be lying down beside each other when finally it would happen. But then, when he got to the part where her knees were moving up his sides, just when her ankles were about to cross themselves in the small of his back, some weird doubt would set in. *What kind of gas leak? Would there be other people in the woods too? Where was Rocky?* So he'd think back to downtown and have an earthquake split Main Street in two.

He'd see her standing there helpless as a store fell on Rocky, then he'd run and grab her hand and they'd escape into the woods. She'd be amazed that he knew his way around so well, and then he was at the part with her ankles crossing themselves, when he realized that if Rocky had just been killed that she'd be really upset, and either she wouldn't do it with him or it wouldn't mean anything to her if she did. So his mind would end up back on Main Street, and just as the earthquake was about to start and the building going to fall, Rocky would leave her and run away screaming like the big chickenshit he was and Chaleur would run in to save her. *Yes.* Then the woods and her ankles and — *but wouldn't they have helicopters flying over looking at stuff? Looking for survivors?*

He wanted to go out with Annette so badly, but he just couldn't think of a way to make it happen. He ran through every disaster he could think of, but there was a flaw each time and he'd end up without her. Back then he figured that disasters were big things — now, suddenly, he knew that a disaster could happen just because you said *Thelma and Louise* sucked.

"If you don't like it, why don't you just leave?" she'd said.

"All right then."

"And take your friggin' empties with you."

It hadn't taken a fire or an earthquake to bring them together either. Rocky had taken a swing at her one night after losing a game and she'd broken up with him — it turned out he was already going out with Gina Estabrooks anyway. A few weeks later Annette and Chaleur ran into each other at the video store. She wanted to see the latest *Nightmare on Elm Street* and he'd just rented it. "I'm babysitting for my sister," she said. "Why don't you bring it over after I get the kids to bed and let me watch it with you."

"What time?"

"Nine?"

He stole a few of his stepfather's beers and was at the door five minutes early. "All the girls think you're cute," she said. "Some of them think you're stuck-up, but I told them you were just shy. I like guys who are shy."

"Then why'd you go out with Rocky?"

"He had a shy part," she said.

"Yeah? Where?"

She smiled and rolled her eyes. "Wouldn't you like to know."
Then she took a drag on her cigarette. "Unfortunately," she said,
"Rocky is a moron."

That was last fall. She was probably calling him a moron
right now.

"Fucking bitch."

And after he'd been so nice to her. He brought her stuff all
the time — things she liked to eat — and he always paid for the
videos. And he'd been trying to figure out how to get that ring
for her that she liked so much. It was in a store window in the
Moncton Mall.

He was afraid to touch her at first because he was worried
that it wouldn't be as good as he dreamt it could be. But it was.
Every time she went babysitting, he would meet her and they
would neck while watching the movie. This was fine with him
— he pretended to like horror movies, but really they scared
him: he rented them only because he thought watching them
might make him braver. Annette loved them because they made
her laugh. "It's so phoney" she'd cackle as guts spilled out of
someone's stomach. "My little niece could've made those out of
plasticine." What bothered Chaleur was knowing that something terrible was always going to happen. The violence was
never as bad as the worry about it: he hated the dread. Luckily,
the dread was what Annette considered the boring parts, so he
could neck with her during those, stopping when the music signalled something violent was starting.

The first time they went all the way was when she was babysitting the weekend that her cousin went to Halifax for a wedding. They hadn't planned to do it really — they had never even
talked about doing it — but just before midnight she broke away

from him and went rummaging in her purse. "Here," she said, holding up a condom. "I don't want any excuses. You gotta wear the friggin' thing."

He grinned and took another one out of his jeans pocket. "I guess this means we can do it twice," he'd said.

Afterwards she told him that she'd never done it with Rocky, even though he'd begged her.

"Why not?"

"'Cause he's the kind of guy who'd blab it all over town," she said, looking at him very hard. Then she turned away, "You'd be nuts to screw a guy like that before he married you."

They had always used a safe. Every single time they had used a safe. He had never even argued, the way some guys did. So it wasn't fair that she wanted to break up with him.

He hid his bottle under the bank where the river was shallow to cool it off. He had never brought Annette to this place. "You think I'm nuts?" she said. "Woods are full of morons. They shoot at you and then they say, 'I thought you was a deer.'" What did she know? The river bed was full of smooth stones, every one of them was beautiful, even the way they fit in your hand was beautiful. If you could stop the water, build a dam upstream, then the river would be like a road of stones between the sandstone ledges of the banks. It would be awesome. There was a reddish-brown tinge to the water. A teacher in school had said something once about looking at the world through rose-coloured glasses, and Chaleur thought that's what it was like looking down into the river at the stones on the bottom. Sometimes, if he sat still and stared long enough, he might see a trout. Annette was crazy.

He walked up the little hill past his secret place, and took a cigarette out of the jar he had stashed there. This was it for him — no more menthol cigarettes after today. He would change brands. Nothing in his life would have anything to do with her.

He lit it and walked to the top of the spruce grove. The smoke was stale and a little damp. It went out a couple of times. Every time he lit it, he cursed Annette.

He looked at the river snaking along below. Just downstream it turned and widened and was very still. The view always made him think of his father, who loved to work in the woods. Clumps of water lilies with yellow flowers grew there — as exotic to him as giraffes — and right there is where he sometimes saw black ducks and mallards. He had heard his mother tell Rory about the time Dad had come home from work and told her they were cutting down some of the most beautiful timber he had ever seen. "Said he wanted to build me a house out of it," she said. Rory just snorted.

The breeze stopped and the trees were silent. In the near distance, he could hear crows. They always seemed to caw from somewhere deeper in the woods — their sound telling him how much of the woods he will never know. But this time it sounded like there were a lot of them. Then he saw first one, then another, flying towards the south. He imagined a clearing filled with them and decided to follow the sound upstream. Maybe they were mating, maybe all of them were over there mating and he would get to see how birds did it. If he stayed here, he would do nothing but think about Annette anyway. He ground out the cigarette with his heel.

Twenty minutes later he was edging his way through clumps of densely packed spruce along the steep bank. The crows were very loud — it sounded like there were dozens of them — and he could see one or two arching in the air around the next bend. The river was shallow here and walking on the bank was hard — branches scratched his face, knocking his glasses to the ground — so he took off his sneakers and socks. He didn't bother rolling up his jeans because the air was so warm they would take no time to dry, and anyway he liked the feel of wet pants on his legs. The stones were slippery and uneven under his feet.

Just past the bend in the river a huge pine tree hung out over the water. Spring freshets had torn away the bank: some of the pine's roots stuck out into the air. By next year it would crash into the trees on the other side of the river. The crows were whirling around it, cawing and screeching; he had never seen so many all at once, and more of them seemed to be arriving every minute. That many crows made him feel creepy. Was he in danger? What if he was trespassing on something secret, some secret crow thing that no one had ever seen before? He sloshed over to the opposite bank as quietly as he could and found a place where he could sit. He figured that there must be forty or fifty of them — the noise was deafening. But they weren't paying any attention to him at all. What was making them crazy? It was hard to see through the branches of the pine, so he wiped his feet dry with his socks, put on his sneakers, and climbed up the bank.

They were trying to get at something way up in the pine tree, something sitting close to the trunk on a branch. The screaming crows were wheeling around it in wild circles.

It was a dog! They were trying to kill a dog! How could a dog have climbed up so far?

He wished he could see better. There was another big pine on his side of the river, so he made for that and shimmied ten or so feet up the trunk. He hoisted himself up into a branch and climbed until he came to a wide crook and sat there, his arms and legs around the trunk.

It wasn't a dog at all, but an owl. A huge horned owl. It was sitting very still, moving its head slowly around, as calm as could be, while the crows seemed to be getting more frantic by the minute. More and more of them were arriving and their flapping seemed to get faster and crazier. The owl would jerk out its head when one swooped too close. Chaleur realized that if it made a false move, it was done for; if it tried to fly away, a black screaming cloud would drag it to the ground and peck it to bits. It would have to stay here for as long as the crows did and be on guard. He started screaming at them.

"Go 'way!" he hollered. "Get outta there!"

But the crows didn't even let on that they had heard him. He sat on the branch for a long time looking over at the owl. What terrible thing had it done for the crows to hate it so much? Killed one of them? Robbed their nests? Smashed and eaten their eggs? Or was it simply because it was an owl and crows hated owls?

Yes, maybe it was hated for being what it was, the same way people like Rory hated him because he was Chaleur.

BRIDE / GROOMS ✛
✛
✛

Most of the sunlight that shone on the stained glass of the Whyte Memorial Window was trapped and held there; it gleamed above the choir like barley candy. A patient-looking Jesus stood in the middle, wearing a bulky grey robe over a purple smock; pale and willowy, he held out his hands in what should not have looked so much like a shrug. The thin, long bars of yellow that radiated from the black circles in his palms dribbled to the ground, where purple and red roses shone about the scroll reading: "To the Glory of God and the Loving Memory of Captain William Whyte" — Sandy's great-grandfather. In the narrow window on the left, Mary stood with hands clasped in prayer, her blue gown edged in gold; John the Baptist was on the right, holding the gospels. Angels hovered in the air on either side of Jesus, the feathers in their wings gleaming dark purple and red in the sunshine. A lamb peeked out from behind his robe. All of them, even the lamb, had haloes of frosted white glass. All three windows were edged with little pillars and buttresses of grey and mauve, as if some fantastic gothic building had been designed simply for the figures to stand in. At the age of ten, Sandy had been racked by guilt because he had wondered if Jesus wore underwear beneath that robe. "What does a Scotsman wear under his kilt?" crept sinfully into his mind when he looked at the window.

Mary's feet were hidden by the scroll for his grandmother, Erminda Whyte; John the Baptist's, by his Uncle Jeremiah's. Each figure was outlined in black, like a picture in a colouring book, and the green glass surrounding them clearly showed that they stood at the entrance to a garden. *A Child's Garden of Verses*, Sandy used to think, because Mother was reading Stevenson to him when he spent his earliest Sunday mornings staring at his family's window. Back then he had wished it were possible to step inside that world of richness. The flowers would taste like sweets.

On a day as sunny as this, the light pushed through the brightest shades, and stray reds and yellows dappled the choir loft and the altar; the dusty air of the church was sprinkled with dots of colour. Reverend Motier had just stepped into a spot of sunlight; crimson specks bounced across her shoulders. She was a short, cheerful woman who smiled constantly and touched her parishioners' arms in a lingering way when she spoke in her careful, serene voice. Sandy loathed her. Every word that she uttered was cant. When he spoke of her out loud to himself at home, he always called her "that sanctimonious little dwarf."

Today's sermon, yet again, was about the challenges facing Christians in Contemporary Society. Her answer to the problem, as usual, was to send more money. At this very moment, the world's problems were centred on the purchase of a plough for a village in Africa. She had pictures.

The Whyte pew was in the front row, dead centre. Sandy was forced to sit alone and ramrod straight as an example to the congregation behind him. He was rarely absent because he knew that if he were away, everyone in the congregation would talk about it over their Sunday dinners. The position of his pew made him as much a fixture in the church as the window. His great-grandparents had sat here; sixty years ago he was expected to sit as rigid as stone beside his severe grandfather, that grand old pillar of Membartouche, A.D. Whyte, Captain William's son, the donor of the window. Sandy remembers the old man's dark mahogany coffin and the church packed for the funeral: the entire town had turned out. That, too, had been expected.

When Sandy died there would not be such a crowd — the entire church membership and all their lapsed offspring wouldn't total half that number these days. He was among the most doggedly faithful. How many hours of his life had he spent sitting right here in this very spot? One long hour a week, fifty-two weeks a year, for sixty-odd years. How much time was that exactly? Sixty times fifty-two. He couldn't figure it without moving his lips. If the dwarf noticed, let her think he was praying.

Six twos are twelve, carry the one, six fives are thirty and one — three thousand, one hundred and twenty hours. Now twenty-four hours a day, so divide that by twenty-four and — Dammit, more than a hundred days.

And how many memorable moments? A sermon by a substitute preacher about the leap of faith — that was back when he was dating Margaret Saunders and it had given him something to think about for weeks. "I don't know, Sandy," she had said. "Why try to intellectualize these things? We go to church for emotional reasons, not rational ones." He used to like talking to Margaret. That sermon was the only time he'd ever heard anything halfway intelligent come from this pulpit. Well, so much for memorable moments. Oh — family funerals. Well, best not to think about those.

That was it. Unless he counted his appearance at the Christmas pageant —

Christmas! Now there was another, what — fifty-odd hours to add on. More than two whole days spent listening to the choir drag its way through the same six carols. There were so few children now that they didn't even have a pageant any more, just some horrible party that he couldn't miss because he supplied the candies and had paid for a new Santa Claus suit ten years ago.

"You will join us, won't you, Mr. Whyte?"

"Oh, Sandy you have to come. It's a tradition."

Tradition nothing; it was money. They were always after him for money. Reverend Motier was smiling at him right now while she held up a picture of a baked-mud hut.

A plough! Some of his good money should be funnelled back into the church itself. Look at that floor — it badly needed painting and the old wine-coloured rugs in the aisles were faded and worn through in places. At a meeting of the Session last winter, he had complained about the old altar cloth — it was in shreds — and the minister had gone home and resourcefully stitched together the pink and blue felt horror that was now draped over the old one. "IHS," it said, in a border of yellow stars and daffodils that she'd cut out all by herself. The clever little thing — she was resourceful in every useless way imaginable. The organist didn't like her either; he could tell that by the way she bashed her way through the new hymns that Motier favoured: the ones with all that feminist He/She/God business. Alphie Johnson had been church organist for forty-seven years, and she used her choir selections to wage war on the contemporary church. The hymn sung during the offering was the only one that she alone could pick — and it never came from the new hymn book. Quite often she chose hymns that weren't from the old one either; she favoured the gospel hymns that women had played on their parlour pianos fifty years ago. Although Sandy thought, quite frankly, that her choices were scandalous — the United Church had its roots in Presbyterianism, after all — he delighted in knowing that Motier was sitting behind the pulpit fuming whenever the choir launched into something like "There Is a Fountain Filled with Blood."

Motier was moving around again; as she turned, the crimson light sparkled on the end of her nose. She never stood behind the pulpit. She couldn't; she was too short. She began her sermons off to one side and then wandered around with a microphone in her hand like a cheap singer. Sandy had fought against the sound system — ministers used to pride themselves on their ability as orators. People used to travel for miles to hear a man who knew how to speak. But the generations on either side of him had won out. The young ones wanted "to bring the church into the twentieth century" — as if Sandy had been born in the nineteenth — and the older ones wanted loudspeakers because they were all going deaf and they complained that no one knew how to talk without mumbling any more.

"A new plough would enable Akpomay's family to plant their crops in half the time."

Oh, spare us, she was holding up a chart. When had sermons become these sob-sister versions of the morning news? Bombings, widows and orphans in Central Europe, China. Sandy had nothing against Akpomay and her family, but he would like to hear a sermon about something like the leap of faith once in a while. Why couldn't the Motiers of this world acknowledge that it wasn't always easy to believe in God? Our own lives were not the lives of happy-go-lucky sheep. She went on and on about the horrors of the world without ever stopping to realize that the tragedies befalling the likes of her poor little Akpomay might possibly shake an intelligent parishioner's faith. Didn't they study these things at divinity school? Or was religious philosophy a thing of the past?

A cloud must have passed in front of the sun. The window had dimmed, but then it was bright again.

What does a Scotsman wear under his kilt?

He couldn't settle into the routine of the church service, couldn't be lulled into its boredom, although he knew that no one sitting behind him would suspect that anything was unusual. He had arrived in church early: he wanted to be one of the first ones there simply because he didn't want to have to see anybody until the miserable thing was over. Then he would have to deal with Coffee and Conversation and the Cemetery Committee. Both would be endless today.

His hands were clasped in his lap: he curled his little finger and rubbed it against his crotch.

When he saw the boy on his fence this morning, Sandy had gone out into his backyard. He didn't know what he was looking for, or why, or what he would say if he met the trespasser. The door in the back shed behind the kitchen was still swollen with spring damp and he had to shove against it with his shoulder to get it open. Then he'd almost put his foot through the back steps: they were so rotten in places that he knew they couldn't be repaired; the whole thing would have to be replaced. He hadn't been in the yard since last fall — he hardly ever went out there, and he had to admit it was a sorry disgrace. His mother's tulips and daffodils still came up every spring, but the rest of the yard was a mess, her gardens in ruin. He hired one of the Gallants who worked at the cemetery to look after the place, but other than pushing a lawnmower around as slowly as possible, the man obviously did nothing. The grass was deep and growing over the edges of the old beds. Until the death of his father, his mother had kept the borders as crisp as paper. Now, the lilacs were full of dead wood, and his great-grandmother's ornamental shrubs were gone. The last remaining one, the snowball tree, had been crushed in an ice storm last winter. The whole thing would have to go. When he called someone to get the pigeons out of the attic, he'd better tell them to clear up all this culch while they were at it.

The sunlight had been glittering through the maples at the back of the yard. They had not been there when he was a boy, and their size astounded him; he had lived so long that huge trees had grown up where only bushes once had been. Back then there had been one maple; now it stood miserably in the corner, looking old and battered, most of its branches empty of leaves, the dead limbs stretched through it like veins. Most of the old oaks that the house was named for were shattered or gone. The new maples were tall and sturdy; in places, they had shoved the old wooden fence out of the way.

Sandy walked through the grass towards the fence. He had walked along the top of it when he was young; no one could manage that feat with what remained. In one place, it sagged so far forward that it almost touched the grass. The old stile had fallen away long ago; only the barest traces of its steps remained. At the beginning of summer his mother had always placed her pots of kitchen geraniums on the right-hand sides of those steps. "Don't go any further than the stile, Sandy," she would call from the back door. He had especially loved to climb it and look out at the orchard when the apple trees were in bloom.

When had he last been in the orchard? Ages ago. He knew that people went there to steal his apples, or used to — the fruit probably wasn't worth eating any more. Good for cooking maybe. But the sort of people who stole apples were not the sort who baked pies. There was no trace of the boy. Up past the trees was the field where his great-grandfather's barns had once stood. Beyond that lay the woods. His father used to rent out the field to a Frenchman from the bridge who had a half-dozen cows. Deer sometimes had come out of the woods at night; they would come across the train tracks and down into the pasture to lick at the big blue cake of salt.

Very early one morning, when he was five, a buck had strayed from up there and wandered down through the orchard. Sandy was sitting with Mother on the back steps — she had her coffee outside in fine weather so she could admire her flowers. Sandy always had a coffee cup filled with warm milk and sugar, with just enough coffee in it to give it a little colour. The deer had looked over the fence into the yard. "Shhh," whispered Mother. "Don't move, Sweetheart." She was smiling. The deer took no notice of them. It looked about and then calmly walked over the stile into the yard and started eating the flowers. "We should really do something," Mother whispered, but her smile only deepened. The deer wandered through the garden, trampling snapdragons and peonies. It was nibbling away at her perennial bed; they could hear it munching the tender leaves. His mother giggled. Sandy could not contain his joy any longer; he put his cup gently on the steps and started to walk towards the animal. He didn't want to scare it, but he had only taken a few steps when it bolted. It leapt in the air and the ground actually shook as it landed in the middle of the lawn before it vanished around the corner. Sandy ran along the side of the house after it. "Sandy!" his mother called, but he ignored her. He watched the deer cross the front lawn and dart up Main Street. He expected a sound as glorious as trumpets, but heard only the short bursts of a horn.

He wanted to go and follow it, but his mother took him into the house. When Father came home for lunch, he told them it had been hit by a fish truck, and had limped over to the train station, where a policeman had to shoot it.

For his twelfth birthday, Mother had given him a book called *The Great Masters of Europe* that contained a fold-out colour picture of Van Eyck's *Adoration of the Lamb* from the Ghent altarpiece: green, green grass and lovely fruit trees with little crowds of people strolling under them. It was the most perfect lawn he could imagine, and that is how he still imagines his backyard when he thinks of that morning when the deer walked into it. A complete, perfect world, totally beautiful, endlessly explorable. Outside its boundaries, nothing was safe.

Standing by the relics of the stile — a rotten board still fastened to the fence, a line of rusty nail heads — he could see only the barest traces of that beauty around him.

He looked into the overgrown orchard. The grass was long, the trees grown wild and wormy. Alders were moving in from the edges.

When the boy had looked up at the house to see if anyone was watching him, his hair had fallen down over his face. And that movement, and the gesture of the boy's hand as he brushed it back, was what brought Sandy into the yard. Until that moment he had been furious that someone was trespassing. Then, suddenly, a wisp of last night's dream flickered in his imagination and he thought of Joey Mullins. He wished he could stare at the boy and not be seen, to have the boy in his yard and watch him through the window.

The boy had been eating something. Sandy wanted to find some trace, knowing that if he did he would be disappointed because the boy had littered — people had no respect for property nowadays — but at the same time, he needed some tangible proof of this boy to come into his hands. A long string of bologna rind was on the ground at the foot of the fence, so fresh that the ants had not yet found it. He picked it up and ran it through his fingers like a string of sweaty beads.

It wasn't easy to get over the fence, but he managed it. He had almost sold the orchard a few years ago, until it came to him that it would be possible to run a street through from the River Road and behind his house. He could not bear the idea of having the old orchard and field subdivided into bungalows, of having that many more people living so close. Now he was even happier that he hadn't. His heart was beating wildly and he wanted to sing. He walked a few steps, then looked all about him. He could hear the LeBlancs from the house next door, but they lived in another world. He could not see them, no one could see him. No one had ever seen him really; he had been living secretly all his life. He walked towards a clump of alders and moved into a little space between them. All he could smell was green. He could hear insects buzzing about, a blue jay calling. The orchard was alive. Very tenderly he opened the zipper on his pants and reached inside. He took out his penis and started to pee into the alder bushes, just like when he was a boy and the bathroom was miles away. He thought of Joey Mullins floating on his back in the river and peeing into the air. He laughed aloud. Then he shook the last drops and stood for a moment. The air was so good!

Gently he tucked the bologna rind into his underwear with his penis and zipped up his fly. He wiped his hand on some alder leaves, backed out of the bushes, and looked about. Then he turned and walked back towards the house. At the fence he stopped and ran his hand against the front of his pants. Money jingled in his pocket.

Sandy reached in and took out the small handful of change. He left a dollar on the fence where the boy had been sitting and, walking back to the house, dropped the rest, dollars, quarters, and dimes, in a little trail towards the back door.

Softly and tenderly Jesus is calling
Calling for you and for me

The choir had already started singing.

The sermon had dribbled away to such nothingness that he hadn't even realized she was finished. Lionel Motier and Bob Jones were moving slowly up the aisle with the collection plates while the choir sang. Sandy looked up at his family's window and wished he were at home, watching the backyard for a glimpse. When he reached into his pants for the collection envelope, he moved his fingers, pushing the warm rind against his genitals.

Come home! Come ho-o-ome
Ye who are weary, Come ho-o-ome

When he dropped his contribution onto the plate, he was smiling and humming along softly with the choir. He looked up into Lionel's startled face and blushed.

At the end of the service, he sat in the pew, knowing the congregation would think that he was praying, but he was trying to will away the stiffness in his crotch. The church was almost empty when he finally got up. His erection dwindled and shrank the moment he saw Margaret Saunders and her sister talking to Lionel and the minister.

"Sandy Whyte," Minnie cooed. "Well well well. Long time no see." She giggled.

"Good morning, Sandy." Margaret was cool but friendly. A little embarrassed, he thought.

"Good morning, ladies. Interesting sermon, Mrs. Motier. As usual."

"Thank you, Mr. Whyte. Isn't it wonderful to have our two lost lambs back in the fold this morning?"

Minnie giggled, but Margaret's face sank. *Stupid dwarf,* Sandy thought, then he rescued Margaret by saying, "Are you coming into the vestry for coffee?"

"Thanks, Sandy," said Margaret, adding, "but we can't stay long."

"I'll join you as soon as I get rid of my ecclesiastical garb," the dwarf tittered. Minnie whooped and Sandy led Margaret into the vestry. "I'm sorry," he muttered.

"Oh," Margaret replied. "But she means well, I suppose."

"I suppose."

A couple of dozen people were already there. Hilda Jones and Ernestine Taylor from the choir were pouring at a table near the kitchen door. Women from the congregation were sitting in chairs along the opposite wall; the men were standing in a group near the open door to the parking lot. Outside, some of them were smoking. Both Sandy and Margaret knew that the moment they walked into the vestry together they would become the subject of conversations for the rest of the day. Old Mrs. Motier, the minister's mother-in-law, turned away the moment she saw them.

"Hello, you two." Hilda smiled. "Well well well. Coffee or tea?"

"Isn't Minnie coming?" asked Ernestine, but at that moment she walked in with the minister and her husband. "Oh, there she is! Hello, Minnie!" She waved, and Minnie grinned and nodded her head.

Minnie and the Motiers were talking at the vestry door. Sandy suddenly remembered that last night he had dreamed of Margaret in a brassiere and, for the second time that morning, he blushed.

"Black coffee, please," Margaret said.

"The same," said Sandy. "With cream."

Margaret looked down at the table. "Oh, you're all out of china. That's too bad."

Hilda handed her a styrofoam cup. "No dear, we don't bother with it any more. It's not worth it — someone just has to stay and wash up."

"A big bone of contention," said Ernestine, pouring cream for Sandy. "Many lectures from On High about the environment. But You Know Who wasn't about to give up her Sunday afternoons for a sink full of dirty dishes."

"Ernestine!" hissed Hilda.

"Thank you, ladies." Sandy smiled, ushering Margaret away from the table.

"The natives are restless," she said a moment later as they stood with their styrofoam cups in the middle of the room. The women were watching them from their chairs; the men, from the door.

"You've been going to another church, I take it."

"Sometimes. How have you been?"

"The same as ever. And you?"

"Yes. The same."

There was nothing else that either of them could think of to say. Thirty years ago, people were certain that they would be married. There had been things to talk about then; now there was an awkward silence. Sandy realized that if they had married, by now they might have a boy who was even older than the one in his yard. After a long silence he cleared his throat. He fought the terrible urge to put his hand in his pocket and manipulate the bologna rind. Minnie was about to join them with that damned prattle of hers.

"Oh, Lionel," she was saying as the two of them came over with their coffee. "People don't understand, they don't! Some mornings my head just throbs. People who don't have migraines simply have no idea."

Sandy recalled that Lionel had been in the hospital this spring. "You've been fine since the surgery, haven't you, Lionel?"

"Surgery!" Minnie exclaimed, her eyes widening. "You poor thing! When was this?"

"April. Yes, thank you, Sandy. Everything's tip-top."

Minnie looked at Lionel greedily. "You poor man. Was it your heart?"

"No," said Lionel looking at the floor.

"What then, if I may be so bold?"

"Minnie," Margaret warned.

Minnie ignored her sister. "I take it then that it was something of a personal nature," she said sadly.

"Just a little prostate trouble."

"Oh, that's awful!" Minnie said, "I had that after Mother died and the pain was something terrible!"

Lionel raised his head and looked at her, not knowing what to say next.

"Oh, Minnie." Margaret sighed.

"What?"

At that moment the minister arrived and coyly hooked her arm through Sandy's.

"Are we all ready for the Cemetery Committee?" She beamed.

SIX

R aymond was feverish throughout the night on the train, but he knew that it was nothing to worry about, he was just excited to be going home. When they changed trains and boarded the Ocean Limited in Montreal earlier in the day, he had gone straight to the last car and sat upstairs at the front of the dome. Hal could go to his berth whenever he wanted, Raymond said, but he was going to ride all the way in the observation car. In order to save twenty-five dollars apiece, Hal had insisted on upper berths.

"Liked being shipped home in a coffin" was Raymond's comment last week as they walked away from the wicket at Union Station.

"Fifty bucks means that we can eat and drink beer on the way down," Hal replied.

"Little Miss Practical," said Raymond.

He loved the observation car because he felt above everything else, in a place of privilege. Because he had been born on the East Coast, and because his father had worked for the CNR, he felt entitled to it: he was connected to the Ocean Limited by birthright. The train snaked out below and ahead of them, moving steadily east through the countryside that led homeward.

"Where are we now, do you think?" Hal asked.

Raymond shrugged.

"I'm going to go get my Walkman. You want anything?"

Raymond shook his head. "No, I'm happy listening to the train."

"Back in a few minutes." And Hal was gone.

The noisy click-clack and hum was interrupted only when the engine sounded its whistle, a lonely wail that came from so far ahead of them that the rest of the train seemed to be straining to reach it. A wigwag's bell clanged beside them. They were passing a level crossing, and the houses and barns down the long road looked like toys. A little boy and his mother were waving from the front seat of their truck. Raymond waved back, smiling. In a seat behind him an old lady's laughing voice called out "Hello, hello!" and he knew that she was waving too. Raymond suddenly felt light-headed.

"What are you grinning about?" Hal asked when he came back.

Raymond shrugged. "Beats me."

The evening star appeared in the dark blue behind them, and they watched the new moon come up over a long field that gleamed bright yellow-green in the early twilight. Every hour or so, Hal went to the smoking lounge below for a cigarette and came back with a beer for Raymond. For a time, the moon held its course with the train, as if Raymond and the moon were two

constant points; between them, the surging countryside and the
great distance of sky. Hal bought chicken-salad sandwiches from
the bartender and they ate them as the moon arched up over the
glass roof and stars arrived as sharp and clear as the lights of a
nearby town. The other passengers around them came and went,
talking in quiet voices, and the Ocean roared over rivers and
plunged into the deepness of forests. If he were outside in the
fields and woods, Raymond knew that his train would be only a
few moments of sound hurtling past, but inside, he was safe at
the heart of something. He thought of the little boy in the truck,
of how his mother would be tucking him into bed, of how trains
might soar through his dreams tonight. He thought of the engineers up at the front, the cooks and waiters, and the conductors
and porters moving through each car, yet it seemed to him that
the Ocean was independent of them all. It was sailing eastward
with a mind of its own, and everything else in the world was
asleep and waiting.

He was taking Hal to meet his family and to show him New
Brunswick. Hal had never been east of Montreal, and Raymond
knew that until he walked down Main Street past Whyte's Store
or went swimming in the strait beside the Bouctouche Dune,
that Hal would never truly know him. He worried about what
Hal might discover — he wasn't afraid of anything in particular,
but he had a nagging anxiety that Hal might come back to
Toronto and leave him. The land of your childhood was a land
of secrets. How Hal would get along with Raymond's family was
anybody's guess. Gloria would be fine, and Mama and Pop too,
probably. Danny might be uncomfortable, but you never knew
with Danny, he was always so damn quiet. But Junior; God only
knows what Junior would say or do. "But I love Junior," Hal
had told him. "No, you don't. You don't even know him. You
just love my stories *about* Junior."

Hal had become envious of Raymond's stories about the people and places that fell under the heading of home. It seemed to encompass everything that he had never known. His own father was a banker, and he had grown up in split-level houses in suburbs with secondary names like White Rock, Dorval, Mississauga. His father's offices had been in Vancouver, Montreal, and Toronto, but Hal, along with his mother and sisters, lived on the edges of his job and the cities he left for each morning at seven. His sisters were older: each one was married and living in the suburb where she had graduated from high school. He knew his other relatives only from the family photos they sent at Christmas. He did not even have a clear picture of the back lots and parks that he had played in; they all blurred together. He could never pin down his past. Did he start smoking with Jason Furlong in Dorval behind the *dépanneur* or was it with Donny Morrison at the Mississauga Town Centre? He could not say for sure. Clarity was restricted to only the worst moments. When he was fifteen in Mississauga, he had been expelled from school when the vice-principal caught him giving Tony Giovinazzo a blow job in the staff washroom. Mrs. Dewey had opened the door with a key, screeched, and started whacking Hal about the shoulders and back with her purse. "Get up off your knees!" she demanded; "Young man, get up off your knees this instant!" His parents had responded by returning to church after a ten-year hiatus, where they followed the advice of the minister, who recommended a Christian psychiatrist. Dr. Glower gave him a prescription for Valium, told him to pray whenever he felt wicked and to stop wearing pastel shirts.

Secretly Hal wanted to adopt Raymond's world, but feared that it would not have him. He never told Raymond as much. Instead he said things like "I'll guess I'll just have to go to my grave without ever having seen the Tidal Bore."

"And die all the better for it," Raymond replied.

Going East was an idea they had batted back and forth for two years, and Raymond had always decided that the trip was impossible.

Hal, you'd hate it there.

But Hal, there's nothing to do.

Oh Hal, it's the asshole at the centre of the earth.

Then Raymond had talked to his sister on the phone and changed his mind. "Gloria wants to organize a family reunion," Raymond said when Hal came back from his walk. "I told her we'd go."

"God, what threats did the poor woman have to use?"

"None. Well, I figure that no one will want to have much to do with us anyway so we'll be able to do what we want. Besides, we'll get out of this fucking heat."

Hal didn't argue with his reasoning. It was too hot.

But then, after weeks of punishing humidity, it had been beautiful yesterday when they left Toronto. Thunderstorms had cleared the air the night before and, when they looked out the window Monday morning, they could see the city clearly above the trees on the far side of the Don Valley; the CN Tower and bank buildings weren't lost in a sickening haze. "Wouldn't you know it," Hal had said; "it's finally decent the day we're leaving." But Raymond had taken the change in weather as a sign, a good omen. "Do you know what everyone back home will say to us tomorrow? 'You brought the good weather with you.' I bet you anything everyone will say that." For the last month they had been forced to sleep with the roar of a huge square fan at the foot of the bed; without it, they had lain awake with the heat pressing down on them, thick and heavy. Both of them were so skinny now that they hated sleeping without covers. "Look at us," Hal had said one night as they lay naked together. "We look like a couple of goddam Christs from the Middle Ages."

Last night, Raymond had woken up barely an hour after he'd fallen asleep and mistaken the deafening fan for the noise of the train. "I'm already halfway there," he thought joyfully, until he sat up in bed and saw lightning fill the bedroom window. And then, still half-asleep, he'd started to cry. He knew it was nothing but guilt. He wished that Gloria and her reunion were drawing him home, but he knew it was the disease moving in his blood that was sending him back to Membartouche.

They were in northern New Brunswick now: there was more spruce. It was deep in the night and Hal was sleeping, his head slumped on Raymond's shoulder. Raymond thought that he really should go to the sleeping car; it was unfair to make Hal sit up with him. But he knew that he would lie awake up there, feeling trapped under the curved ceiling of the upper berth. He would not be able to see where they were; he would miss everything. Besides, Hal was a big boy, he could go to bed any time he wanted.

The train had slowed down and stopped; they were off on a siding in the bush waiting for a freight train to pass. It was impossible to tell how far these tracks were from any other human life. Outside the windows, all was still. There could be villages nearby, ahead of them and beyond the tracks. Or perhaps there was only a fisherman sleeping in a tent by a river in the woods. Or someone in a truck parked on an old wood road. Or no one and nothing for miles. New Brunswick was small on the map, but the woods were endless; there were trees that no human eyes would ever see. The moon had disappeared and the stars were brighter. In the city, he could see the Big Dipper on a clear night. Out here the names of every constellation that Miss Rodd had drawn on the blackboard came back to him. The Milky Way

was as immediate and mysterious as the forest. His head was
warm. *Damn air-conditioning*, he thought. *We'll all catch summer
colds.*

Then the train shivered, and suddenly they were gliding
slowly backwards, giving him the chance to see details in the
woods that he might have missed only moments before. Raymond watched carefully, knowing he would be given the opportunity to look on these very trees on this one night only.
Everywhere there were spruce, many of them fallen and held up
at sharp angles by the tangle of their upper branches. There was
a stand of thin silver birch that gleamed in the darkness, and
poplars were growing around what remained of an old shed. Hal
shifted slightly in his sleep. His Walkman was playing a Philip
Glass tape over and over, a low droning that Raymond could
just hear. There was an empty beer can between Hal's legs, and
Raymond reached down and put it in the garbage bag under the
window. Then he leaned over and found the Walkman tucked
in beside the arm of Hal's seat. He shut it off. Outside the train
there was not a breath of wind; the poplar leaves were as still as
could be. He felt an itch in his throat; he tried to swallow it, but
instead he coughed. His chest hurt. Whenever he felt that ache,
he imagined that his bones were wearing down, becoming as
thin and fine as twigs. When he coughed they could snap and
his whole body might collapse. He lay his left hand on top of
Hal's right one and pressed his forehead against the window.

Hal could sleep through anything. The thunder last night
had cracked the air, the windows had rattled, but he hadn't
stirred. Sometimes when Raymond couldn't sleep, he would get
out of bed and sit at his drafting table in the other end of the
apartment, trying to work and listening to music: Billie Holiday
and Montserrat Caballé — all he demanded of music nowadays
was that it make him cry. Hal never noticed. He fell into sleep as

soon as he said goodnight, and rarely moved until morning. Sometimes he murmured, whispering words so low and fast that Raymond could never make sense of them. He would lean over, his ear hovering above Hal's mouth. The next morning he would say, "You were talking in your sleep again."

"Really? What did I say?"

"Beats me, it sounded like mana-mana-mana. Or bwana-bwana-bwana. Maybe you were talking in tongues."

"Maybe I'm Pentecostal in my sleep."

"No, you don't thrash around enough."

Hal was the first person he had ever slept with who never complained about his snoring. Sometimes it was so loud that he woke himself up. When he was a kid, his brothers had teased him that he snored as loudly as their parents. "Like havin a friggin' truck in the room" was how Junior had put it. Whenever he made love to someone for the first time, he had always turned to him when he said goodnight and said, "I'm sorry, but I have a terrible confession to make. I snore."

His parents no doubt were snoring away now, a powerful commotion of honks and sputters that would be filling all the upstairs rooms. Mostly they snorted in unison, as regular as feet marching slowly in step, but sometimes, when their breathing was not together, they sounded like two gruff voices calling and responding, a strange duet in the night language of animals. Asleep, they were never independent from each other: snoring fused them into one noisy being that never stopped communicating with itself. It was as if they had been together for so long that they could not be separate in anything. Perhaps, thought Raymond, they even dreamed the same dreams.

Raymond has dreams in which he curls up like a ball, his head pressed into his knees, his arms tightly locked around his legs, and floats about the house. His ability to float is all about balance; he steers his way around corners by shifting his head and leaning into the turn. He is never more than five feet in the air, and if he loosens the grip of his arms about his legs, he will fall. He glides down the hallway outside his parents' bedroom and pauses, hovering at the top of the stairs. Then, leaning his head forward, he dips downward and slides through the air over the steps. Halfway down, he lifts his head to straighten up, then, turning it to the right, he drifts up over the banister railing and drops slowly into the hall. He moves about the downstairs, squeezing himself tighter to make himself go higher, just grazing the backs of chairs and the buffet, and lowering his head to duck under ceiling lights and slide through the tops of doorways.

Mama and Pop, Junior, Danny, and Gloria are all sitting around the table when he floats into the kitchen, where, wiggling his bum, he slaloms little zigzags in the air just above their heads. Little Gloria claps her hands and calls out, "Look, everybody, look! It's Raymond! And he's a balloon!"

He loved Gloria and hoped that, of all his family, she would take to Hal. He knew that it had been a mistake to have gone so long without seeing her. They sent each other postcards, and a couple of times a year they talked on the phone. She was the Queen of Remember When.

Remember when we had the circus in the backyard?

Remember when Alphonse gave Pop all those lobsters?

Remember when Glenda used to pay you a nickel to let her comb your hair?

She had the most infectious laugh he knew — it invited you back to the times that she longed to talk about. What he loved most about her was that she could make him remember that he had been happy. He wanted the three of them to drive up the coast and spend a day walking along the dune at Bouctouche.

They would take bottles of wine and sandwiches with them in the old picnic basket from the attic, and throw their scraps to the gulls. There would be no one else for miles around. Gloria would make them laugh as he and Hal walked along the edge of the strait for hours, the sun turning them as brown as berries.

He was holding Hal's hand, aware that his own was damp and hot. He looked down at the sleeping face. It was amazing how much adults could look like children when they slept. It was so late that there was no one else in the car behind them, so he kissed the top of Hal's head.

Who would go first? Hal said this question was one of the things that kept them together. Which one? They talked about it a lot — who would be the widow.

"Well, of the two of us, I *would* look better in black," Hal said.

"Yes, you'd give Rose Kennedy herself a run for her money."

"That I would."

"But don't forget — if *I* win the Widows' Tournament, there'll be someone to keep the Christians at bay."

"The Christians" were Hal's parents.

"You're right," said Hal. "If I die without you, they'll swoop down out of the hills of Mississauga and carry my ashes away. Some minister I've never laid eyes on will read Generic Eulogy Number Four: 'He is better off in the Hands of God.' Then they'll sing all the hymns I never liked."

The night that Gloria had phoned, they had walked down the street to Riverdale Park. "There's one thing I have to do when I go home," Raymond said. "I have to figure out where I want you to fling my ashes."

"Oh, doesn't that sound like fun!"

"Well, I have to let you know on the *off* chance that *you* win the Tournament of Widows."

"And what happens if I don't? Where do you plan on scattering me?"

"Wherever you want me to. Just tell me."

"I don't know," he said flatly.

They had reached the park and sat down on the steep hill in the dark. For a few minutes neither of them said anything.

"Did I ever tell you about the time I had sex once, right here in this very park?"

"A thousand times, Raymond. At least."

"Really?"

"He was such a big brute of a guy that you thought he might beat you up, but he didn't — he took you down beside the bridge and then the earth moved and a thousand stars exploded in the sky."

"And afterwards——"

"Afterwards there was a parking ticket on his pick-up truck and he told you it was worth every penny and drove you home like a respectable Christian woman. I've heard it a million times."

"Oh." Raymond had gotten to his feet and was looking down the hillside. He could feel the heat rolling up from the Parkway. "Well, I'm sorry I'm so boring."

After a moment Hal said, "I'm sorry I was snappy," and reached over to touch Raymond's leg.

Raymond was still looking down towards the little footbridge. "I can't remember telling you that before."

When they were back in the lobby waiting for the elevator, Hal said, "The problem is that there's nowhere that matters enough to me. If I'd had great sex in the park, I'd say 'Scatter me there with my happy memories of youth.' But I didn't. You always win in the memories department."

Raymond wanted to change the subject. From the very first time they had talked, when they were walking down Church

Street after their friend Clive's funeral, he had courted Hal with stories about his past. He had broken the misery of that afternoon by making Hal laugh. Sometimes in bed Hal would say, "Tell me a story," and Raymond would talk about Membartouche, about hiding firecrackers inside votive candles and sneaking them into Ste. Anne's, or about his brothers convincing Gloria that "Titsy" was Miss Rodd's real first name. Although Hal still asked for stories, lately he seemed to resent them; he was acting as if his own life had not been worth living.

Later, lying in bed, Hal said, "The sad truth is that all I know about my ashes is what I don't want."

"The Christians."

"Yep."

A few minutes later Raymond whispered, "I don't have to be scattered in New Brunswick, you know. We could find a nice little plot together right here in our very own home town." He hoped that Hal couldn't hear the resignation in his voice. Why was it so hard for him to think of himself and Hal as a couple?

The train stretched out ahead of them in the stillness and dark, its cars full of sleeping people going home or going off on holiday; it was a long silver elegy for something he could not quite name. In a few hours Gloria would meet them at the station. She would be surprised by his thinness — all of them would — and he didn't know what he would say about it, if anything. "I came home for your chicken, Mama, so you could fatten me up."

A summer tan would make him feel better. Once he gets over the difficulty of appearing on the beach in a bathing suit — the lesions on his side were dark and frightening. Yesterday, after he delivered the new menu layouts to a restaurant in Yorkville, he had gone into Lichtman's to check the tide schedules in the

New Brunswick newspapers. He wanted to go swimming with Hal on the day they arrived.

The freight train finally arrived, flowing past them with the steady rhythm of its cars. Hal opened his eyes and looked about.

"Where are we?"

"Stuck on one of the more isolated sidings of the National Dream."

"Oh."

"Do you want to go to the sleeping car?"

Hal nodded and snuggled his head nearer to Raymond's. "Did she cancel?" His voice sounded thick and stupid.

"Who?"

"Monsterfat Caballé."

"You're dreaming. Hal? . . . Hal?"

But Hal was asleep again.

Just after the freight had passed, in the moment before the train started up again, a nighthawk scooped down low, flew lazily above the cars, and disappeared over the woods. Raymond knew that somewhere out there was another smaller bird, or a rabbit, or maybe a sleeping mouse that would not know it had been seen from the air until it was too late. It was just waiting to be caught. Waiting and not even knowing it was waiting.

SEVEN ✢

"I gotta talk to you," Annette said when she phoned him Monday afternoon.

"So talk." If she wanted to break up with him they might as well get it over with.

"Not on the phone."

"Where then?"

"Meet me on the beach after supper."

Chaleur had decided that he wouldn't beg her. He would tell her that he loved her — he was pretty sure he did — and if that didn't mean anything, he would let her go. Maybe he would tell her that it was the best six months of his life, but that was it. He would never beg.

He drove down to the beach on his brother's bicycle; it was an easy ride, but it still made him all sweaty. The weatherman had said that a heatwave was coming.

Annette was waiting for him in the parking lot near the light-house, leaning against her sister's car and smoking. As he was gliding up, she dropped the cigarette and ground it out under her foot. She did not look at him; she kept grinding until the paper split and the tobacco was smeared over the asphalt.

"Hi," he said. He locked the bike against a fence.

"Hi." She kicked off her sandals and threw them in the car. "Let's go for a walk."

"Sure."

"Want to put your shoes in the car?" She was holding the driver's door open for him.

He sat on the fence and took off his sneakers and threw them into the front seat. Annette slammed the door and moved towards the beach, striding quickly ahead of him like she was mad. He wanted to call out for her to wait up, but he was afraid that she might blow up and say something mean. A couple came towards them on the boardwalk drinking Cokes; two little girls were turning cartwheels beside them in the grass.

"Look, Mommy, look! I'm way better than Holly!"

"She is not!"

"Is too!"

Kids made him crazy; he didn't know how Annette could stand to babysit so much. She was standing on the top of the dune, looking out across the bay towards the strait. As soon as he caught up with her, she moved on ahead without turning to look at him. At the edge of the sand she stopped and they walked together. She kept kicking at the water. He wanted to hold her hand, but there was a wall around her. He was starting to get as angry as she seemed to be. "What's the matter?"

"Not yet." Although most of the tourists had left for the day, there were a few cottage families walking along the beach, children and dogs were running up and down the sand.

"Why not?" She was screwed up so tight and her voice was so hard that he was ready to leave right now. It was like the dread part in a horror movie, like up ahead something terrible was going to happen to both of them, and nothing he could do would save them from it.

"'Cause I don't wanna cry in front of these jerks, okay?"

"Oh." He followed along behind her for a few minutes until they reached the far end, where the beach started to get marshy. Then she slowed down and stood looking out at the bay. When she turned back towards him, the last thing he expected her to say was "Well, I'm pregnant."

"What?"

"You heard me." She started walking again, and then stopped a few feet ahead of him.

"But how?" he said.

She turned around and, for the first time, she looked squarely at him. "Oh maybe because we were fucking," she said bitterly.

"I know but——"

"I dunno how it happened."

"But we always used a safe."

"I know."

"Fuck."

She twisted her toes into the wet sand. "Aren't you gonna ask me if I'm sure it's yours?"

"Ain't it?"

"Yeah."

"Then why'd you want me to ask?"

"Guys always do."

"Yeah?" He was standing beside her now.

"Yeah."

"Who else knows?"

"Nobody. Mom and Dad find out, they'd kill me. And you."

"Shit. You sure? I mean, about being pregnant?"

"Yeah, I'm sure. I bought a test from the drugstore. I went to one in Moncton. If I'd gone here everybody in town would know by now."

They faced the bay. There was a cloud bank on the horizon — the sun was going down behind it and it was becoming more and more golden. A woman was swimming out past the third sandbar, a tiny dark figure moving steadily towards the shore. He could tell it was a woman because the sun bounced off her white bathing cap like a little buoy. He felt like he was somebody else, some stranger.

"What're you gonna do?" he said. The look on her face let him know that he had said something wrong. "I mean, what're *we* gonna do?" he said, touching her hand.

"We're gonna have an abortion, that's what we're gonna do," she said, pulling her hand away.

"No fucking way!" he said, surprised at how hard the words came out.

"What?"

"We're not gonna kill a baby." Things were happening too fast — he was getting mad at her for even thinking about it.

"Don't go all Christian on me."

"Fuck this." He thought about running away, about taking Annette up into the woods and fixing up the hunting shack, about living up in the woods with her and their baby.

"Oh, right. So instead we quit school, get married, and then what? Get jobs at McDonald's? Go on welfare?"

"Fuck." He thought about how much Annette's mother and father would hate him. He imagined them coming to see his mother and Rory, then all the terrible things that Rory would say. "Couldn't we give it away? Like to somebody who wants a baby?"

"If you think I'm gonna stay pregnant, and have everybody in town talk about me like I'm a tramp, then you're nuts."

"Couldn't you sell it?"

"You are nuts. No. You go to an abortion clinic, you have an abortion, and nobody knows a thing."

"Can't we sue the people who make the safes?"

"Like we've got proof you had one on."

"But we did."

"You got a witness?"

"Oh." This was the most grown-up thing that had ever happened to him — why did he suddenly feel like a little kid? He started kicking at the little waves lapping the shore. "Fuck fuck fuck fuck fuck."

"I gotta sit down," Annette said, and they walked across the beach to where she could sit at the foot of a little dune. The sun was shining through a gap in the clouds and everything in sight was rich and clear. Annette hugged her legs, put her forehead on her knees.

"When my period was late, at first I thought I was sick, but really I knew."

"How?"

"I just knew. Fuck, I hate biology," she said taking a cigarette from her package and lighting it.

He knew that pregnant women were supposed to quit smoking, but he decided that he had better not say so.

"It's not much bigger than a cornflake," she said. "Yet."

He sat down beside her and, because he didn't know what to say, he put his arm around her shoulder. He was watching the woman in the bathing cap: she was closer now, lying on her back and lazily kicking her feet. He felt that Annette's body was even more strange and amazing than he did before: there was a whole other person inside it now. He thought of the tiny cornflake baby swimming inside her, like the woman moving steadily to shore, only the baby was inside a huge place, like a cave in *Journey to the Center of the Earth*. He wondered if it looked like him already. Right now it was small enough to sit on the end of his finger, like a bee.

"A baby," he said.

"Oh fuck," she said and blew a stream of smoke out her mouth and nose.

She was not moving closer to him, snuggling in the way she always did when he put his arm around her. He wanted to pull her closer, but he was afraid to, afraid that she might shove him away. She just sat next to him smoking, as rigid as a stone, so he fell back against the dune and started to pound at the sand with his fists. He was angry that she was pregnant and angrier that she wanted to kill his baby.

"Look," he said, "I think you should think some more———"

"Think some more! Jesus fuck, I wish to God I could stop thinking! It's all I've done for a friggin' week! I haven't had any sleep since this started." She could not look at him. Neither one of them knew what to say. They both were looking out at the water, wishing that there was no one else on the beach. Chaleur hated all those people with their kids and dogs running around. He wanted to stand up and tell them all to fuck off.

And then Annette started to talk. "I used to think about having babies," she said. "I thought about finishing school and getting my nursing and getting married and having kids. My sister has a hard time with her two, but she gets along with George okay, and they have enough money to pay the bills and stuff."

This is what happens to grown-up people, he thought. *They think about money.*

"I put her kids to bed when I look after them, and pretend sometimes that they're mine. I think about what it must be like to have something that needs you that much."

I need you that much, he thought, but he was afraid that she would laugh, so he said nothing.

"Jackie says that she needs her kids as much as they need her, but I don't understand that part; she says that I won't until I have one of my own. She told me that as soon as the first one was born she knew she would kill anybody who tried to hurt it. I think I understand that, but I don't feel it."

"You'd be a good mother," he said.

"Yeah, right." The sound of her own voice scared her so she said, "Someday. But not now."

"Did you tell your sister?"

"Not yet. I think I will though. She won't tell Mom and Dad."

He had been looking at her face, thinking of how it changed when they were making out on her sister's couch. How sweaty she got and how he would lick the sweat off her forehead. He turned away. "Shit," he said softly.

"I'm scared about the abortion."

"That's what I mean."

"What?"

"We should think about something else."

"Chaleur, for fucksake."

"I mean, I don't think we should kill the baby."

"What's with you? You sound like Father Caissie at the Right To Life."

"But it's killing."

"You think I don't know that!"

"Then why do it?"

"Give me an alternative that doesn't screw me up for the rest of my life."

But all he could think of was living in the woods and he knew that was a stupid idea. "There's gotta be an answer. Something we haven't thought of yet."

"Right." She shoved the cigarette into the sand.

She was fed up with him, he could feel that. He wanted to be able to say something that would bring her back, but nothing was big enough to say. He was picking up fistfuls of sand and squeezing them, letting the sand trickle out in little mounds on either side of him.

"I wish I could sing," he said.

She looked at him and started to laugh. "What?"

"I just said I wished I could sing. I didn't think it was that funny."

"Why'd you say it?"

"I dunno. Maybe I feel like singing. I dunno."

"What would you sing?"

He looked out at the swimmer who was walking in the shallow water towards the shore. He shrugged. "'Don't Cry,'" he said.

"Then sing it."

"You know I can't sing."

"Right. And Axl Rose can."

"He's a great singer."

She looked at him. "Jesus, are you fulla shit," she said kindly.

He shrugged and looked at the sand falling from his hand.

She reached inside her jeans and pulled out a piece of newspaper and handed it to him. On it was a tiny ad that started off "Pregnant? Confused?"

"It's the abortion number," she said. "I'm scared to call it by myself. Will you come with me to the pay phone?"

"But Jesus, killing a baby."

"Chaleur, for shit sakes! It's not a baby yet — it's a cornflake!"

"But——"

"Look. I take care of kids all the time, I know what this means. If I have a baby right now it means everything changes and it's all bad."

"Everything's already changed," he said. He wanted to kiss her, but he couldn't; she might not want him to touch her ever again. "Which time was it?" he said. "When it happened?"

"The night we watched *Ghoulies*, I figure."

"Fuck," he said. "Wasn't even a good movie."

Annette laughed. "I love you," she said.

That made him feel better, but he had to figure out a way to make her keep the baby.

They walked over to the beach house and he stood beside her at the pay phone when she made the call. "It don't make any sense," she said to the lady on the phone. "We always used protection." Then she rolled her eyes at Chaleur and said, "A, you know, a safe."

Chaleur was thinking that if she was going to go through with this, she was going to do it on her own. But then he thought that maybe if he went with her he could show her how terrible the abortion people really were. He wanted to run away.

"He's my boyfriend," Annette was saying, and she smiled at him before turning away and talking in a quiet voice he couldn't understand. She had wanted him to be with her when she made the call, but at that instant he knew that she had already begun to form an alliance with the abortion people.

"What? I beg your pardon?" She was listening again. "You want us both to talk to a counsellor? When?" Then she was waving at him.

"Lemme check." She put her hand over the receiver. "Day after tomorrow," she said to him. "Wednesday, two o'clock. That okay?"

He shrugged. "Yeah."

The sun was going down now. There was a space between the bottom of the clouds and the sea where it suddenly appeared — a fat, orange ball. Everyone at the beach except for Annette was watching it. The swimming lady walked past him with a towel around her shoulders. She had just taken off her bathing cap and was shaking her hair. She was older than Chaleur had thought; her hair was grey and her skin all loose and flabby.

"Lovely evening." She smiled as she walked past him. He didn't answer. Everyone was happy except for Chaleur and Annette, everyone else in the whole world.

Annette was still quietly talking, and he was frightened at what she might be saying. He walked a little further away from her. A part of him was relieved that she didn't want to break up with him after all, but his worries about that seemed stupid now, and far away. A gull screeched in the air a few feet over his head.

"She seemed nice," Annette said, after she had hung up the phone. "She sounded like a nice lady."

I bet, Chaleur thought; *she's a fucking baby killer*. But he knew better than to say this out loud.

He wanted to drive the bicycle home, but because it did not have a light and because it was starting to get dark, Annette had a fit and so he put it in the trunk of the car. "I'm worried enough without worrying about you getting run over by a drunk," she said. They hardly spoke when she drove him into town and parked in front of her sister's house.

"What're you gonna do tomorrow?" she said after he took the bike out of the trunk.

"I dunno. Go up to the woods maybe."

"Be careful up there."

"Why?"

"'Cause there's creeps that hang out up there."

He sighed. She kissed him.

"The day after tomorrow," she said. "Call me tomorrow night and we'll figure everything out."

"Yeah." He wanted to kiss her again, but he was starting to get mad at her for being bossy, so he wheeled the bicycle away and swung up onto it. He hoped that she was standing beside the car, watching him drive away, like a girl in a movie.

When he got back home, Rory hollered at him because he had run out of beer during *WWF* and had to go out and buy some. Chaleur reached into his pocket and pulled out a balled-up five-dollar bill that he had found in the backyard of the old Whyte place. In the last couple of days, there had been money lying all over the yard; that old guy was so rich that he probably did not even know it was falling out of his pockets. "Here," he said, tossing it in Rory's lap.

"I don't want your fucking money, just keep your hands off my beer," Rory said, putting the bill in his shirt pocket.

Chaleur went into the kitchen and snuck a beer from the fridge. He hid it inside the top of his jeans and pulled out his tee shirt to cover it. Outside his bedroom, his mother told him that he was selfish for taking his kid brother's bike without asking, because Ralphie had wanted to play with his friends and had not been able to because they were all on their bikes. He told her he would never do it again and she said, "Right, that's what you always say," and went in to watch TV with Rory. Chaleur shut his door, and then took the beer out of his pants. Ralphie had written "FREAK" across Axl Rose's chest on the poster by his bed. He sat up in bed drinking the beer, hoping it might calm him down. He wanted to play his music really loud, but that would just bring Rory into his room; he couldn't use his head-phones because then they might sneak up on him and catch him drinking. His mind was angry and racing, and he thought that he probably would not be able to get to sleep for a long while.

Tomorrow he would go to the woods and think the whole thing through, and then he would know what to do.

He thought about the little baby inside Annette. He thought about how his dad had loved his mother and how once he, too, had been no bigger than a cornflake. He had read in a magazine that Axl Rose could remember all the bad stuff that had happened in his family when he was a little baby; he could even remember being born. Chaleur tried to remember back that far, but all he could think of was the way his dad looked in the picture in his dresser drawer, standing in front of their old house on the Miramichi in a plaid coat, holding Chaleur up on his shoulder. It was winter and Chaleur was wearing a snowsuit. His dad was smiling so big that the cigarette in his mouth was pointing almost straight up. But Chaleur could not even remember the day that the picture had been taken. If only Dad's heart had not been so big, he would still be alive and his mom would never have met Rory. They would never have moved to this place. But then he would never have met Annette. But then Annette would not be pregnant. Not by him at least. One thing that he was sure of was that when his baby was born he would love it the way that his dad had loved him. He would crawl around on the floor with it and give it presents. When it grew up and brought home pictures from school, he would put them right up on their fridge and he would never say "What's this supposed to be?" and laugh.

How could someone remember what happened when they were being born? The whole idea of being inside his mother and coming out between her legs made him sick. She had never quit smoking when she was pregnant, he was sure of that.

He lay quietly for a long time. Rory and his mother had a fight and went to bed; later he could hear her laughing and screeching the way she did when Rory tickled her.

Is that what would happen to him if he convinced Annette to have the baby? Would they get married and have all those fights?

When he did sleep, he did not dream about Annette at all. He was in his grandmother's kitchen trying to find his dad, who was hiding, and everywhere he looked he found money in the grass.

The next morning he filled his knapsack with beer from the fridge before anyone was up. On his way out the door, he saw a bottle of rye on the counter and took that too.

EIGHT ✛

Margaret was surprised by the uneasiness she felt sitting in her old church on Sunday morning, a sense very much like dread. She had always felt safe in the stiff old pews and, if truth be told, she preferred it to the excitement of the Water of Life. Despite the fact that her father had been a part of this church — she remembered him passing the collection plate — she had always been able to be here with him and know that there was no danger. Even though she had not always been certain that what he did to her was wrong in the eyes of the world, little Margaret had always known that it would be wrong to do it in church. This was the one place where she had always been safe from his fingers, and for that reason she felt guilty that she had so easily gone along with Minnie and moved her membership to the Church of the Water of Life.

She sat through the service, ignoring Minnie, who shifted constantly and sighed beside her. She was aware of the minister — but of hardly a word the woman said — and of Sandy Whyte sitting a dozen rows ahead of them. If Minnie made her think of a huge, hyperactive child, then Sandy sat like a quiet, little boy with his head slightly bowed. He was so lonely-looking up there that her old anger for him moved towards pity.

She tried to concentrate on the sunlight playing on the window above the choir loft; it was so pretty that she hoped it might relax her. Her purse was wedged next to Minnie and her hands were folded neatly on her lap; she tried not to grip her own fingers too tightly. She stood awkwardly during the hymns, shoving the spine of the open hymn book hard against the pew in front of her. The familiar words looked strange on the page, as if they were written in a language she no longer knew. She barely whispered them. As the service moved through the sermon, the offering, and on to the benediction, she felt that she was slowly being wound as tightly as a clock spring; if she snapped, what terrible thing might happen? Her body was as tense as the stillness before a summer storm, but outwardly she seemed very hushed and calm. She might even have been smiling.

Margaret realized that she missed the old God she had known all her life, the God of the United Church, so simple and benign, the hero of so many Sunday-school stories. He felt safer than the God at the Water of Life. All through the Sunday service she felt queasy, as if her new God had followed her there and was upset.

Afterwards, talking to Sandy Whyte added more weight to the way she was feeling. She was confused by the absurd tenderness she felt towards him, a tenderness that made her want to run away from him as quickly as possible. He was so polite and sad, and although they had nothing to say to each other, the silence between them was a kind of bond. "Neither of us suffers fools gladly," it said, "and here we are in a room full of them." She left the United Church deeply troubled.

"Well, that wasn't so bad," Minnie said as they walked home after Coffee and Conversation. She started to giggle. "Except for my slacks."

Minnie had split the seam on her rear end while she was talking to the minister's husband.

Later, while she sat at the table watching Margaret peel the potatoes for Sunday dinner, she broke a long silence with "Well, I must say that you and Sandy Whyte were pretty chummy."

Margaret ignored the remark. While she had been working on the potatoes, a peculiar sensation had overwhelmed her; it was as if she were somehow somewhere else, far away. She felt as if she were looking down on the potatoes from a great height. Her hands worked the peeler automatically, the muscles in her fingers moving as involuntarily as her heart. Her own hands looked foreign to her — they could have been two strange beasts performing a ritual on the counter top far below her. They would be fine on their own and she could allow herself to be led somewhere else. But just as she was about to open something — a door? a curtain? — and see where exactly, Minnie's voice dragged her back to the kitchen.

"Well, I must say that you and Sandy Whyte were pretty chummy."

It took all of Margaret's energy to finish making dinner, and Minnie's only comment had been "These potatoes are a little on the raw side."

"Well, I'm sorry. You cook them next time."

"I wasn't complaining. Don't bite my head off."

But that was precisely what Margaret had wanted to do: on top of everything else she had been mad at Minnie for days.

"What's wrong with you?"

"I'm running late." She picked up her plate and walked into the kitchen. "Don't bother with the dishes," she called out. "I'll do them when I get home." She waited in vain for Minnie to protest, to say "No, I'll do them for a change," but Minnie was silent. Margaret quietly found her purse, picked up her sweater and her Bible, and took the car keys off the hook by the back door. "I'm off."

Minnie did not reply.

"I'm off."

After a pause to indicate that it did not matter to her one way or the other, Minnie sighed. "Well, have a good time."

A good time. She had wanted to phone in sick, but she would rather go to the Hotline meeting than spend another five minutes with her sister. She had not asked her to come along and she knew that this was why Minnie was being so sullen. But from the beginning her sister had always said, "I'd be no good on that hotline, I'm too sensitive," so why should she feel left out? Although Margaret had to admit that had never stopped her from coming to all the meetings and holding forth with opinions on everything.

As she drove along the highway, she banged the palms of her hands against the steering wheel and said, "I just want her to get off my back! That's all! Off my back!"

Why was it necessary to say those words aloud? To whom could she ever possibly speak them? She continued to talk, complaining loudly about her sister, all the while imagining that she was telling these things to Sandy Whyte. "What am I going to do with her?" she declared. "What could anyone do with her?" She knew that Sandy would have no answers to these questions either, and when she left the highway and drove into the city, she wondered if she should have been trying to talk to God.

There were not as many people at the meeting as she had expected and, to Margaret's surprise, no one asked her about

Minnie. She had waited outside in her car until 7:29 so that she could go straight to her seat without having to talk to anyone. Bob and Cindy were welcoming people at the door, and even they did not mention her sister. Bob simply touched her arm and smiled and Cindy gave her a hug. "We're so happy to see you," she said. Margaret wondered if she had ever heard Cindy use the word "I," and if her "we's" referred to herself and Bob or to the church as a whole.

Florence Jenson welcomed their guest speakers and asked Margaret to read from the Scriptures. Margaret opened the meeting with Psalm 139. Her voice was timid at first, but she gathered strength as she moved through the verses, each one more affirming than the last. At the end, she hit every word like a little bell.

Search me, O God, and know my heart: try me, and know my thoughts: And see if there be any wicked way in me, and lead me in the way everlasting.

The Reverend and Mrs. Dooney were both tall and blond, their accents inviting. They thanked Margaret for her reading, calling her "sister" in a way that drew her to them.

"Let's begin with singing," Mrs. Dooney said brightly.

"Yes," said her husband. "Let's start with that grand old hymn 'When Mothers of Salem.'" Margaret had just gotten back to her seat when the assembly rose to its feet and Mrs. Dooney sat down at the piano.

Margaret had always loved to sing. She knew that her voice was unexceptional, but it was clear and true, and during all those years at the United Church she had steered it cleanly over Alphie Johnson's slow tempos, unconcerned that the congregation and the choir dragged just slightly behind her like a little weight. Her voice guided her through the familiar landscape of comforting words that she treasured and loved and sang for herself. At first she had been both troubled and excited by the singing at the

Church of Water of Life: it was so loud and powerful that she was afraid of becoming lost in it. When she and Minnie had started attending their services she moved her lips timidly, never committing herself. Lately, however, she had started to surrender. There was a peculiar sensation when she was singing here, as if the boundaries between herself and all the others in the congregation were dissolving, as if she were no longer singing for herself alone.

In the spring, on the Sunday after Easter, Minnie had stood beside her and started to speak in tongues. "Ee ya," Minnie had said, "Ee ya yaddar mecca!" But before she could go any further, Margaret's hand reached out and pinched a roll of fat on her sister's waist and Minnie's mouth clamped shut. Margaret knew that she was an old faker.

"You never let me have any fun," Minnie said later.

"I just didn't want you to embarrass yourself, that's all."

"Humph." Minnie knew that, whenever the congregation began to shout their praises to God and to speak in tongues, it was Margaret who was embarrassed.

In late April, Minnie claimed to have a cold and had stayed in bed the day the church travelled by bus to march in front of the abortion clinic in the capital, and there Margaret had felt that she was truly a part of something bigger than herself. Her heart had ached as she stood outside the fine old home that had been turned into an abortion mill; she thought of the little deaths inside it. What monsters could do such a thing? And suddenly she felt that she could see through the cream-coloured clapboard to a room where a man in a white coat was bending over something. When he turned and glared at her, she realized to her horror that he looked like her father.

But Jesus saw them ere they fled,
and sweetly smiled, and kindly said,

'Suffer little children
To come unto Me.'

When the hymn was over, the Americans began to preach.
The Reverend Dooney referred to Margaret's reading and quoted
her psalm. "Thank you, Sister," he said — and, indeed, at that
moment she felt that she was more his sister than she was Minnie's.

Mrs. Dooney spoke of King Herod, how he had slain all
those babies, but could not destroy Jesus Christ. Good had tri-
umphed away back then and Christ's blood would triumph over
the evil of abortion today. When Reverend Dooney talked about
the Great River of Zion, Margaret felt it was so close that she
could jump in her car and drive there on the highway. The unobtainable seemed so close that the world around her began to fade
— the words of the preacher and his wife became a pure air that
swirled about her. It was sweet, and when she moved her tongue
between her lips she could taste it, like milk and honey.

Then, as she realized that this air was the air she had longed to
breathe all her life, everything about her became sharp and intense,
as if the room were glowing, and the assembly began to converge.
All about her, individual bodies and faces were shifting, they were
flowing into one being. As the Reverend Dooney talked about
their mission, about closing the abortion mills all across America
and Canada, Margaret thought of herself at Christ's side as he
overturned tables and drove the moneylenders out of the temple.
They, too, had her father's face. The skin on her arms tingled.

How unlike the sermon she had sat through that very morning! The air in this room was not empty and dry, the odd stray
word floating over to her like a wisp of smoke. It was filled with
words so passionate that they brushed against her skin. Her new
God was saying to her, "There, Margaret, there; there is the place,
just ahead."

She opened her mouth to catch the words in her throat, and they began to fill her. "There is a fountain filled with blood," the words said as they lifted her up, "There is a fountain filled with blood, drawn from Immanuel's veins." The words bounced her in the air, pushing and sliding over and under her. And then they were swirling about her so fast that she could no longer catch them all — they began to spill out of her. She was a fountain of words that could not be contained. They began to pour out of her in a song. She was singing about her life and her Jesus, singing in the sweet secret language of God. She was David singing in the lost language of the Psalms, loud and clear. The room swirled about her. Were her own words mingling with the voices calling towards her? Or were they searching for her, following her like a voice in the wilderness? The words came faster and faster, and she was dimly aware that people were suddenly pressing closer to her. She was nearing the summit and they were coming behind her. When she sensed how near they were to her, she stopped. Everyone had surrounded her, and the Americans were saying "Hallelujah!"

"Yes, Sister, speak!" Reverend Dooney called out. "Speak out the Lord's truth!" She turned and looked down at their open faces.

What had she been saying? What truths could have poured from her throat? She felt suspended a few inches above the floor; it seemed that everyone was looking up to her, amazed that she could float above them. She thought of Minnie, how envious she would be, and then of Sandy's sad face that morning. She had reached a moment of time where she had the opportunity to understand something; it seemed as if she could hang in the air and see everything in a new, clear way. But then she suddenly saw Sandy that afternoon in the little room of the Admiral Beatty Hotel when he started to faint. She reached out her hand as he was sliding to the carpet.

And then God flew out of her body and she fell to the floor.

When she awoke, she seemed to be in a strange and unfamiliar place and she was very frightened. Everyone around her was whispering — sharp, soft sounds like the hissing of angels' wings. "Give her air," someone was saying, and, when she sat up, the Dooneys started to clap and soon the room was filled with applause. It embarrassed her, but the sound was loud and soothing, like a heavy rain.

"God has a purpose for you, Sister," Mrs. Dooney said as she helped Margaret back to her chair. Bob and Cindy moved close to her, and Cindy held her hand. As soon as the meeting was over, she slipped away.

She did not even remember driving home. She was opening the back door when Minnie's voice made her aware that she had lost all track of time, as if she had been a passenger in her own car, or as if she had missed the ride home altogether and God had simply deposited her Volvo in the driveway.

"Well?" Minnie asked.

"It was a good meeting, and I'm exhausted," she replied as she walked though the kitchen.

"Better than the United Church?"

Margaret was moving up the back stairs.

"I'll bet it wasn't as much fun as Coffee and Conversation with your old boyfriend!"

Margaret pretended not to hear her sister and went straight to bed. Minnie had not done the dishes and, for the first time in her life, Margaret decided that they could wait until the morning. She knew that if she spent another five minutes downstairs that her sister would find a way to mention both Sandy Whyte and the raw potatoes again.

She was so tired that she fell into a deep sleep and, if she dreamed at all, could not remember a single detail when she awoke on Monday morning. "The sleep of the dead," she thought, thankfully.

She had the dishes washed first thing and put breakfast on the table before Minnie was up. As soon as she heard her sister start to come down the back stairs, she took her coffee out into the yard. She was bewildered when she thought of last night. *"God has a purpose for you, Sister."* Had the holy spirit flowed through her veins like blood? That seemed the only way she could describe it to herself. But how could that be possible? She yearned to talk to someone, but who? There was no one in the world who could be her confidant. Other people might be able to talk to their families, but she knew that the last person on the face of the earth who could help her was Minnie. She wondered if perhaps she could talk to Sandy Whyte. Was there anything left of their old friendship? She thought of their Sunday drives in his little Austin, but then she thought of the room in the Admiral Beatty Hotel and all those Sundays afterwards when he and his mother had turned their backs to her.

She spent the entire day trying to avoid her sister, but, no matter where she went, Minnie was always beside her. At six o'clock she would have to drive into the city and work her shift on the Hotline; she wanted to phone someone and say that she couldn't make it. But she was afraid that if she didn't show up that people might talk about what had happened last night even more, and she did not want them to talk about it at all. She certainly did not want her sister to find out, but keeping it secret would be impossible. Minnie would find out and hound her to death.

At lunch time Minnie said, "I slept something terrible last night. I think it must have been those potatoes."

In the afternoon, just before it was time for her story on the television, she came into the kitchen and said, "Well, at least those potatoes cleaned me right out, but now I've got the trots — did you use all the Kaopectate?"

At supper time she picked at her vegetables. "I'm still feeling a little tender after those potatoes." But she ate two pieces of cake.

Margaret took her can of ginger ale from the fridge, gathered up the rest of her things, and headed for the door. "Do you mind doing the dishes tonight?" she said. "I don't want to be late." She did not wait for an answer.

When she arrived at the Hotline office, she put the ginger ale on the desk and hung her sweater over the back of a chair; she sat down, holding her purse on her lap, and stared at the phone. She did not want it to ring. Ever. Florence Jenson had left a note saying that she had to leave her shift early because her daughter was visiting from Halifax; it was propped up against a little framed snapshot of her grandson. Margaret picked it up.

What did people see in their own flesh and blood that was so special? Was it the recognition of something so simple as the family nose? Something familiar about the eyes? Margaret felt that her ties to her own sister were woven as much of guilt and fury as they were of blood.

When she first became involved with the Hotline, there had been training sessions where many people cried — women who'd had abortions in the past and had come to see the error of their ways, ministers who talked about the sanctity of life, women like Florence who seemed terrified that their own children would have abortions — and Margaret had cried too. But she had been standing next to her sister, and Minnie's sobbing had eclipsed her own and embarrassed her. When Margaret was driving them home afterwards, Minnie had turned to her and said, "Well, that was more fun than I thought it would be." And then later, "I couldn't talk to those girls on the phones. I'm too delicate."

While all the other volunteers on the Hotline seemed to have spent most of their lives thinking about the tragedy of abortion, Margaret herself had never spent a great deal of time thinking about it at all. She had always known that it was wrong, of course, but abortion was one of those things, like welfare, or the Vietnam War, or drug addiction, that was an issue for other people; it had never touched her life directly until she had imagined the doctor in the white coat with her father's face. She wondered now if that vision was connected to her performance last night. She knew that her father was the reason that she had committed herself to the Hotline.

She put the snapshot face down on a far corner of the desk and stared at the wall.

The little foetuses on the poster in front of her were all lined up in their various stages of growth. Margaret knew that they were not accurately drawn — their faces were more like babies' than foetuses' — but, even so, they still looked inhuman to her. She knew that they were supposed to be cute, but cute was a concept she had never understood. Shirley Temple had been cute, Minnie adored television shows that were cute — but, to Margaret, cuteness had always been a mask painted on top of something frightening. The little faces seemed to be a part of the same lie as her old Shirley Temple doll beaming happily from the chair beside her bed while her father's hands wounded her under the covers. The truth was convincing enough — why twist it with cuddly pictures?

Sandy Whyte had shown her a picture of a painting once, an angel telling Mary that she was carrying the Son of God. "The Annunciation," the Catholics called it. There was a ray of sunlight streaming through the window towards Mary, and a wee little Jesus was sailing down it with a tiny cross over his shoulder. Every pregnancy was tragic.

How could God have entered into her? She had seen God all her life: in flowers, in the wind sweeping across the Tantramar Marshes, in the sun setting on Membartouche Bay, but she had never encountered God in people and she had never felt God within herself. How could she be certain that last night was anything other than a *performance*? When Minnie pulled stunts like that, Margaret had always assumed that her sister knew what she was doing. Had she spoken in tongues in the same way that Minnie cried her big, salty crocodile tears?

With the exception of a wrong number — a man who tried to sell her a vacuum cleaner — the phone did not ring for an hour and a half. It was nearly time for Margaret to leave when it did, and the sound made her heart sink. She almost let it ring through to the answering machine, but she knew that whoever came in for the next shift would want to know why.

"Hello," she said.

"Hi, I need to talk to somebody because I'm like, pregnant?" It was a young voice, a teenager. She was trying to talk calmly, but Margaret could see through that. They always tried to sound bored at first, these girls, but if they stayed on the line for more than ten minutes they were in tears. This one claimed that she had used protection, but then most of them said that.

"What kind of protection was it?"

"A, you know, a safe."

"A condom."

"Whatever."

A bunch of little liars, these teenagers, and Margaret always had to keep telling herself that she should not believe that they deserved everything they got. They were dirty girls who came from that dirty world where her father had lived, the world that he had tried to drag her into. Margaret saw them necking in the park when she went to the post office. They crawled over their boyfriends with one eye to the sidewalk and, if you looked at them for more than a second, they hollered out, "What're you looking at?" and stuck their middle fingers in the air. After Margaret walked past them they would laugh like screech owls. Why was the world so full of these stupid girls?

"And how far along are you?"

"I just did the test last week, so a couple a, three weeks. What do I do?"

"Well, you should come in for counselling before you do anything. What is your relationship with the father?"

"He's my boyfriend."

Margaret waited for the girl to volunteer more information. She could hear a steady noise in the background, like a bad connection, and people's voices in the distance. When the pause started to lengthen uncomfortably she said, "So you're in a strong relationship."

"I guess."

Margaret waited again. As she was about to break the silence the girl said, "He's right here with me. He doesn't want the abortion."

"Oh." So she thought that she was calling the abortion clinic. She made a note to that effect on the form she had started for the girl. Someone would meet with the two and talk to them about problem solving and the options that were open to them. Someone would deal with the sanctity of life and show them how they could organize a support network. If they were religious — which was highly doubtful these days — the counsellor would try to confirm their belief. Whatever it took to help the innocent child.

The noise in the background seemed louder, as if there were more activity around the girl. "What's that sound?" Margaret asked, but as soon as she spoke she could see the beach where she used to swim with her parents.

"Huh? What sound?"

"It's waves. It's the sea."

"Yeah, we're at the beach."

"Yes." Margaret turned and looked towards the little west window at the back of the office. The clouds were golden; that same sun was setting on this girl at the beach. There was another pause. "How old are you?"

"Why do I have to tell you that?"

"I don't need your name, but I need your age for my records. Just for the sheet I have to fill in at the end of my shift."

"Oh. Sixteen."

"And how old is the father?"

"Same as me."

That could mean fifteen, Margaret figured. Sixteen-year-olds usually said they were eighteen. "I think you should come in as soon as possible" — Margaret looked at the chart. "Wednesday at two?"

"Lemme check."

Margaret's throat was parched, but her can of ginger ale was empty; it was amazing how a short conversation could dry her out. Because it had been a slow night, she had already packed up to leave; her lozenges were stowed away in her purse. She glanced towards the window and, just then, the sun broke through and filled the room with orange.

"*Oh.*"

The room was suddenly larger, magical somehow. She held up her hand: in the glowing, her skin looked younger. The girl came back and said that Wednesday was fine and that she would have to borrow a car to come to the meeting. For some reason, Margaret was thinking that the girl had short, dark hair.

"Would you like to use your own name or a code name?"

"Oh, um, a code."

"Well then, what shall we call you?"

"Um, I don't know."

"Just pick anything, dear." Some others at the Hotline were not keen on Margaret's penchant for anonymity, but Margaret felt that it was more effective with the teenagers. She knew the cloak-and-dagger aspect would get her in their good graces. "A name from a picture or television."

"Carrie."

"Carrie it is. What a pretty name."

"I guess."

"Well, we look forward to seeing you, dear."

"Oh," the girl said.

"Well, goodbye."

"Oh." She seemed surprised that the call was over. "I ..."

"Yes?"

"Well, I'm ... It's just that ..."

"What is it? Just tell me what's on your mind."

"I'm frightened."

"I understand."

"No, I mean, why is the whole world so scary all of a sudden?"

"Well, you have a lot of thinking to do." Margaret had the unexpected feeling that her words were as useless as Reverend Motier's had been on Sunday morning.

"I know that, but ... I just feel, I dunno, like I don't understand how I feel, and I dunno what I think even. Look, my boyfriend, like right now he's over there looking out at the bay and, I mean, I love him, you know, but ..."

"Yes?"

"Like, if this were five years from now and we were still together I think I'd be really happy. But I don't know. I mean, we were getting along okay, like things were fine, but now this ...

I mean, something is *inside* me now. I didn't plan it, didn't want it, but here it is, and I don't trust ... I mean, the way I feel about *him* even."

"Who?" asked Margaret. "God?"

"No, my boyfriend. Why would you think I mean God?"

"Just the way you said 'him.'"

"Oh."

"Do you believe in God?"

"I guess so, but so what?"

"Well, there's strength there for some people." Margaret felt a warm breeze on her skin; she glanced at the window again but it was closed.

"Maybe if this was like Bible times and God still talked to people, but ... I guess, what I mean is, I don't think I know who I am any more."

"Oh," said Margaret, wishing an answer could spring to mind. But she knew that whatever she might say would be a lie. And then she knew as well that this was why she could not think of anyone to talk to about her episode last night: she did not want the useless comfort of a pat answer. "Go on," she said. "Please."

"But that's all. I'm not me any more."

Margaret said nothing. The skin on her arms was starting to tingle, and the air about her seemed more bracing. *Salty*, she thought.

"Do you know what he said after I told him? He said that he wished he could sing."

"Oh." For suddenly Margaret knew that it was the wind from the beach on her skin and it seemed that the girl was standing near her. She saw the black receiver of the pay phone against the girl's cheek. A gull flew above them — she saw it before she heard the screech through the telephone. Both of them looked up at the same moment. Then the girl turned to look at someone.

"Well," the girl said. "Thanks. See you Wednesday."

But Margaret was trying to see the boy standing a few feet away.

"Goodbye."

"Wait!" Margaret called, but the line went dead, the girl disappeared, and the sun vanished, leaving the room looking cold and barren.

Margaret sat very still. She had seen the girl, but as she tried to remember every detail, the particulars began sliding away.

Dark hair, she thought, *short. The boy* —

But she had seen nothing of the boy. The vision was fading as surely as a dream. That dream about her father — what did she remember? That she had dreamed about him, that it had been unpleasant and frightening, but the details were lost in waking.

The phone did not ring again. Before she left, she picked up the schedule for the week and wrote that she could not do her next shift and, instead, she would come in on Wednesday and counsel.

When Bob dropped Cindy off to replace her, she was out the door before they could to do more than exchange pleasantries.

She needed to get away and think things through, but she was so muddled that she could not imagine where she could go to do that. Just some quiet place where she could be by herself. "A crisis of faith," Margaret said aloud as she drove back home. "That's what this is all about. A crisis of faith."

She knew that her sister would be waiting up for her, dying to hear the details of the evening.

"But it's confidential!"

"But I'm your sister," Minnie would say in her are-you-out-of-your-mind tone of voice. She would have spent the entire evening stuffing her face and watching television.

A crisis of faith.

The phrase both thrilled and frightened her. She was driving home along the four-lane highway, her heart beating too rapidly and her foot too heavy on the accelerator. She looked at the speedometer and was shocked to see that she was twenty kilometres over the limit. She lifted her foot and coasted down. She did not want to go home, and here she was racing to get there. There was hardly any traffic in her lanes, and there were so many cars on the other side of the barrier going towards the city, as if there were an exodus from her home town. They were families coming back from the shore, of course. They had spent their day playing in the sand, watching their children paddle in the water. The shore. She decided to drive there. She would go for a walk along the beach. Maybe she would see the girl.

"I would know her in a second," she told herself as she drove through town and turned off at Gould's Corner to go down to the beach.

Margaret parked her car and walked across the lot. She gave wide berth to a parked van where some teenagers were drinking; the music from inside it was pounding so loudly that it seemed impossible for the van not to be bouncing up and down. For a moment she was worried that the girl on the phone might be there, but she dismissed the thought.

The beach was dark and lonely, and the sand was damp when she sat down. Still, the air was warm and there was a breeze off the water that ruffled her hair. She thought of how long it had been since she had really talked to someone. She thought of Sandy Whyte sitting all alone in his pew at the front of the church. And then she heard the girl's voice as clearly as if she were sitting next to her.

"I don't think I know who I am any more."

Margaret did not have to look; she knew there was no one there. And yet she felt that there was, in the same way that she had felt herself standing beside the girl when they talked on the phone. It was frightening, as her own voice had been frightening when it pulled her into the air at the meeting last night. How could these things be happening to her?

At the United Church good manners and good taste prevented intimate talk about God. She could go to Easter services and listen to the choir sing "Christ the Lord Is Risen Today" without being confronted with the brute facts of the resurrection. He had been dead. He had been buried. The beginnings of putrefaction. Worms. His hair and fingernails had gone on growing. Then the lifeless limbs had started to move again. The heart had begun slowly to beat. There were holes in his hands and feet, in his side. At the Church of the Water of Life they knew this was a fact and knew that people who did not believe in it as fact were not true Christians. But these facts scared her and she did not want to believe them. They were not a part of the God who had comforted her throughout childhood. She worried that she had been lying to herself and to God when she had been rebaptised.

So then, why would God enter into her?

"God has a purpose for you, Sister," Mrs. Dooney had said.

But what on earth could it possibly be?

Because of the way that Margaret and Sandy Whyte had looked at each other after church, Minnie was worried that her sister might decide to start seeing him again, and so she had spent the evening on the phone catching up on all the local gossip. Mrs. LeBlanc, who lived next door to The Oaks, had seen Sandy out behind his house the day before, relieving himself in the bushes. "Disgusting!" she said.

Minnie was tickled pink.

NINE

The dough was all wrong under Mama's fingers — she would never get it to roll out properly. It would be too thick and turn out tough instead of flaky. Even though she had only made one bad batch of piecrust in her life — and that was before she was married — she had this same fear every time she formed the dough into balls and lined them up on the wax paper beside her bread board. Her own mother (now there was a woman who could make a piecrust, and without a recipe) had told her, "You're hopeless around the house," and Mama had gone on believing her long after the old lady had gone away to Aunt Erna's and died. After she and Pop were married and he moved into the house, her mother had started criticizing her even more. Whenever she made supper, her mother would sit at the table, rolling her eyes. "Rose, I swear to God, you couldn't parboil shit for a tramp." It was supposed to be a joke, but Mama had never found it very funny.

Her fingers had felt fat and stupid all morning: first thing, while contemplating the Second Sorrowful Mystery in the wicker rocker out on the veranda, she had fumbled her rosary — it had plunged from her hand and snagged on a loose piece of wicker on the leg of the chair. When she tried to tug it free, she pulled too hard and it felt like it might break. It was terrible how a few seconds of panic could upset the rest of your day.

She whispered a prayer to help her hands with the dough.

Hail, holy Queen, Mother of Mercy, our life, our sweetness, and our hope! To you do we cry, poor banished children of Eve. To you do we send our sighs, mourning and weeping in this valley of tears —

The dough felt a little better. Oh, well, maybe this batch would be all right yet.

Mama knew that she would never enjoy making pies even though she loved the warm, sweet smell that would soon fill the kitchen, even though they would look so pretty when she took them out of the oven. Her family could finish off a pie in seconds. Putting one on the table was like dropping a chicken in front of a den of foxes — no cries of admiration, no thank-yous, they just gorged themselves and took off. It was a lot of bother for nothing. She wished that she could just go and buy a gallon of ice cream at the Co-op. But she had a hard time with store-bought food. In her heart she believed that if she did not bake pies and cakes from scratch, or knead bread dough and let it rise, or stuff chickens with her mother's summer-savory dressing, or spend two weeks every September putting up jars of the mustard pickles and chow-chows, the jams and jellies that she had eaten when she was a girl — if she did not do these things, then she would not qualify as a good mother. This was why she got up every morning and started cleaning the house as soon as she had the coffee on. It was why there was always a washing in by 9:00 a.m. It would be so nice if she were able to make pies or do the housework without the fear that she was doing it badly. Some people loved to do these things — why not her? Gloria could clean house in her sleep; it came as naturally to her as breathing. But with Mama it was always this terrible battle with dirt and dough.

Strawberry-rhubarb was Raymond's favourite pie, and she was making them as a peace offering for all her unkind thoughts about the way he lived up in Toronto. When he was growing up, they had all doted on him. He was quiet, but not so quiet as Danny, and he got in trouble, but not so badly as Junior — most days he made them laugh. "That kid's more comical than the TV," Pop used to say. Although neither of them had ever mentioned it out loud, Raymond had been special to them both because he had been born after her mother left the house and moved to Boston: he was the first child who was really and truly all theirs.

When she realized that he did sinful things with other men — and she had known it herself long before Junior had opened his big trap and said it out loud to her and Pop — she had been cut to the quick; but she understood later that she would have been just as deeply hurt if he had married a nice girl and moved next door. He could only have made her happy if he had been able to stay a little boy for the rest of his days. That's why it was easier to love him if he stayed away and lived his own life in Ontario, leaving the memory of little Raymond safe inside her. There were lots of his kind of people on television these days; many of them were supposed to be funny, but a lot of them were angry and sick, and all of them made her upset.

Hail, holy Queen, Mother of Mercy, our life, our sweetness, and our hope —

Raymond was the late baby she had not planned and, without her own mother around to find fault with every move she made, she had hoped he could be the perfect one; but instead she had raised someone who lived his life far away from her.

To you do we cry, poor banished children of Eve —

She wished she could recover that clean feeling she used to have after confession when she was a girl, coming out of the church into a bright world of promise, but these days it all seemed to go by rote; after Father Pelletier absolved her, things felt just the same. Lately, when she watched the news on the TV, she felt like a fool — here she was confessing to unkind thoughts while other people ran through elementary schools with guns, while governments turned poor people out into the streets. Maybe Pop was right to stay away from church. But no. She could never do that because it had mattered to her so much. God and the Virgin had been told all of her worst sins and she had been forgiven.

Turn, then, O most gracious Advocate, your eyes of mercy toward us, and after this our exile show unto us the blessed fruit of your womb, Jesus.

The crust had rolled out not too badly after all, and she had mixed an egg in with the sugar and fruit so that the filling would be thick and rich. Would Raymond tell her that they were still his favourite pies and give her a kiss? "I spent the whole train ride thinking of your pies, Mama."

O clement, O loving, O sweet Virgin Mary.

Mama eased a top crust off the rolling pin onto the pie and fluted the edges. She wished that she could be like other mothers, the ones she talked to after Mass or at Bingo who could say things like "My son's home from Calgary this week" or "We were over at my daughter's for dinner on Sunday" — mothers who were comfortable with their children's lives. When she thought about seeing Raymond again, Mama felt sick and was overcome with a flatulence that was pure misery. Her insides bubbled like oatmeal on a slow boil, the pockets of gas rolling through her so violently that it seemed impossible that such turbulence couldn't be noticed through her clothing.

The disruptions in her bowels confounded her. If the mere thought of one of her children could have this terrible power over her body, shouldn't that child be Junior? After all, he was the troublemaker, that one, a constant source of grief and disappointment. When he was a teenager, every time the phone rang late at night, Pop would say "What's that damn kid done now?" And Junior had done it all — break and enter, drunk and disorderly, theft — an endlessly sad list that continued on even past that horrible June night on the beach road when Junior and Danny were pulled from what was left of the old Ford Falcon. Why should Raymond throw her body into chaos while Junior just made her shake her head with resignation?

Her mother had wanted her to give Junior up for adoption, but Mama refused and Pop had married her. When the old lady eventually went to live with her sister in Boston, Mama thought for a while that she had actually won the lifelong battle with her mother.

"I can't sit here and watch you and that husband of yours ruin those kids. Erna's got her own place in Boston now and wants me to go and live with her."

She had tried to love all her children equally, but was that even possible? Had Raymond been special to her just because she had been able to change his diapers without having her mother glaring behind her, telling her that she was going about it all wrong? Had Junior gotten into so much trouble because she had been pregnant with him before Pop gave her the little diamond engagement ring? Had Danny lost his hand because, years before, she had not listened to the old lady when she said, "You're spoiling that child, Rose, you're spoiling that child rotten"?

When other mothers talked about their families getting together, why did it all seem so effortless for them? "You're hopeless, Rose," her mother had said, and maybe she had been right. One thing she knew for certain: family life was easiest when nothing important was happening. The miseries arose at Christmas, on anniversaries, at family reunions.

Damn that Gloria for turning this into a big deal.

While Gloria was standing on the platform, looking down the tracks for Raymond's train, she was annoyed at herself for even thinking about whether or not Sandy Whyte would be upset if she skipped cleaning this week. She had already changed it from today until tomorrow — what would he do if she called tonight to change it again? And why was she worried about what he thought anyway? She had no problem telling the other people she worked for that she was taking the week off, why was she different around him? There was just so much to be done at home and her brothers were useless at all of it. Mama was getting grumpy and needed her help. Gloria had convinced her that they should have a big feed of lobster on Thursday night — with the good china, and French wine that came with a cork, and candles in the silver holders that Gloria had given her parents the first year she had a job — but she knew that the day-to-day meals would be the real chore. And she wanted them to have time to *do* things — to go to the beach or play cards, or maybe they could pile into a couple of cars and go to the Neptune Drive-In in Shediac. She had wanted everybody to come to the station and give Raymond a big welcome, to have all of them standing on the platform when the train came in, like the happy family that she remembered, but no one seemed interested. Only Danny had driven into Moncton with her; he was waiting in the parking lot. Mama was back home making Raymond's favourite pies, and Junior and Pop were downshore looking at a car. So much for the welcoming committee — here she was all by herself.

She guessed that she found it hard to tell Sandy Whyte about the reunion because he was the only person left in his whole family; it might make him feel lonely. Well, if he knew how hard it was to have a family, he might not feel that way at all. He might just count his blessings.

As soon as she heard the train whistle from across the city, she started to bounce on her feet with excitement. She turned back to Danny and nodded her head, but he wasn't even looking her way. She thought about going to get him, but then she could see the Ocean Limited coming from far down the tracks. People were coming out of the station with their suitcases, and the platform around her was filling up. She looked back towards the parking lot; Danny had finally gotten out of the car and was standing beside it. She knew that he would not come out on the platform with her because he would not want people to think he was corny. As the train eased in and the diesel pulled past her and slowed down to a stop, she looked in every window and at all the doors. Suddenly people were walking past her in both directions: the people from the coach cars were coming towards her with weary smiles and their families were moving into their arms. Everybody seemed tired and happy. Old ladies and families were moving from the far end of the train where the sleeping cars were. She jumped up and down, looking for Raymond over their heads.

A skinny old man smiled at her and waved. At first she thought he looked an awful lot like Raymond. His hair was very short and thin, and his skin was stretched tight, as if all the flesh had left his face. He looked like someone who had seen a terrible thing and never recovered from the shock. Then her own face flushed hot with panic — it *was* Raymond.

He walked over to her, grinning, and dropped his bag on the platform. As soon as she hugged him — he was all bone — she knew the reason why he looked so bad and, wiping her eyes she said, "Look at me. I'm so happy to see you that I'm crying like a baby."

A tall man with the same short haircut was standing beside him. "Gloria, this is Hal," he said. "Hal, this vision of loveliness is my favourite sister."

"Your only sister," she said giving him a gentle cuff on the arm. "Hello, Hal."

She was about to shake his hand when Hal surprised her by giving her a hug — he was as thin as her brother — and she understood that he was not someone that Raymond had met on the train but that he was coming to stay with them. Had he said something on the phone about a friend? Yes, but she thought that he would phone back and tell her for sure. When he had called to tell her which train to meet had he said "I" or "we"? What would Mama and Pop think? Worse, what would Junior *say*?

"You two are going to have to sleep in the same bed," she said suddenly, and then she laughed when they did.

Danny watched the three of them from beside the car thinking how strange it was that although he had never seen a person with AIDS before, he recognized it as soon as he saw his brother get off the train. He had been worried about Raymond for the last few years, but had never talked about it. He knew that Mama was worried too, because the other night when they were alone in the garden she had tried to bring it up. He told her not to be crazy. Now he was mad at Raymond for being so stupid and getting sick. And what was he doing bringing some boyfriend home without telling them? Could he have told Gloria and she was so ditsy that she forgot to tell anyone else? He opened the trunk of the car and then went around to the front as the others approached him. He held out his left hand so that Raymond's friend would not be embarrassed and try to shake the wrong one.

But Hal stuck out his own left hand right away and, smiling, said he was glad to meet him.

"You got more bags?" Danny asked Raymond.

"Yeah, Hal and I'll go wait in line at the baggage counter."

"I'll go with you," said Gloria.

"Then I'll wait here," Hal said. He did not want to go inside where he would not be allowed to smoke. He sniffed the air and leaned up against the car. "What a great day."

"You must've brought the good weather with you," Gloria said, and Raymond turned to wink at Hal as he followed her to the baggage counter.

Hal had thought the station would be stone, and old, with covered platforms and historical plaques. Instead he was standing next to a cement-block shoebox surrounded by parking lots — there was a mall behind them. He liked the look of Raymond's brother but didn't know what to say to him.

Danny cleared his throat and watched the train; the way Hal kept gawking over at him made him nervous.

"You haven't had good weather?" Hal asked after a minute.

"Hasn't been bad."

"Oh. Well, I hope it stays like this." Hal was surprised at how much Danny and Raymond looked alike — he had seen pictures, but none of them recent — there were also traces of Raymond in Gloria: something vague and familiar even in the plumpness about her mouth and chin. Raymond had always called her a "big gal," but he hadn't expected her to be so fat. "Has it been warm?"

Danny shook his head. "Nah."

He offered Danny a cigarette. Danny had not really looked at him yet, not even when they shook hands.

"Thanks, but I got me own right here." Danny had his own cigarette out and lit before Hal could fish his lighter out of his knapsack.

They smoked in silence until Hal began to feel awkward. "Did you know I was coming?" he asked.

Danny shrugged. "Everything'll be fine," he said and moved his cigarette in the air to indicate that there was nothing to worry about. Hal found little comfort in this, and the strange familiarities in Danny's face didn't help. "I'm going to go see what the delay is," he said.

"Always takes forever," Danny said. And then he added, "Bad system. They gotta bad system. Those fools couldn't organize a dresser drawer."

It seemed to take for ever to get out of the city, too, even though Raymond chattered happily away beside Hal in the back seat.

"The high school where we all went is up that street. Has it changed any?"

"New gym," Danny grunted.

"I hear it's lovely," Gloria said. She was approaching a green light and had started slowing down in case the light turned yellow before she got to the intersection.

"Ha."

"Oh, Danny, don't be so negative." She gave his arm a swat with the back of her hand.

The light still shone green and Raymond said, "I had a girlfriend who lived over there."

"Where?"

"In an old apartment building down there. Is she still around?"

"Therese Moore? I think so," Gloria said. "Oh shut up!" she called out to the driver behind her who had started to honk his horn.

"You never told me you went out with girls," Hal said.

"I didn't know any better then. Is she married?"

"I don't know, Raymond. You were the only person who ever liked her. Now be quiet, I have to concentrate." The light had not turned red and she had stopped in the middle of the intersection to make a left turn. She hit the signal and waited patiently for an approaching car.

"Gloria, by the time that guy gets here the light will be red and he'll have to stop."

"Shut up, Danny."

"It's yellow," Danny said. "Go."

"Shut up."

"*Go go go!*" Danny shouted, startling her so much that she hit the gas, squealing the tires as she shot through the turn.

"Don't do that to me!"

"Friggin' women," Danny moaned.

A moment later, Gloria looked at Raymond in the rear-view mirror. "I heard she got a divorce."

"Who?"

"Therese."

"Oh. I thought you said I was the only one who ever liked her."

"She got a divorce from some guy she met at the Vet College. Isn't that right, Danny?"

"How the frig should I know?"

"Oh look." Raymond pointed. "Glenda painted her house."

"Who's Glenda?" Hal asked.

"Our cousin. The one who paid me money to let her comb my hair."

"Right."

"A nickel," Gloria said. "She moved. Hasn't lived there for ages."

"Where'd she move to?"

"In with some guy in Gunningsville. A real creep, eh, Danny?"

"I guess."

"Well, his family's probably saying the same thing about her," Raymond said.

"He has no family."

"How come?" Raymond was leaning forward with his chin on the back of the front seat in between his brother and sister. He looked at Danny when he spoke, wanting him to say more than two words.

"When he got outta jail, they'd all took off on him. Moved up to Ontario. Didn't they, Danny?"

"Why was he in jail?"

"Arson, I think. Burnt a covered bridge down, wasn't it?" A moment later she said casually, "They say he got his sister in trouble."

"What?" Hal said softly.

"I went to high school with her," Gloria continued. "What a big dumb thing she was. Leena or Lana I think her name was. Something like that. Big dumb thing."

"Glenda can pick 'em, that's for sure." Raymond patted Hal's knee and winked at him. "So how are Mama and Pop?"

"Pretty good. Pop's downshore with Junior today looking at cars."

"How is the Sheik?"

"For godsakes don't call him that or we'll all suffer!"

"Why?"

"Ginette moved to Halifax for good, so he's real cranky."

"That's too bad. Has he said much about it?"

"Not to me. He and Danny went over to the Club the other night — he say anything then?"

Danny shook his head.

"Just stay out of his hair for a couple of days." There was another green light ahead and she was slowing down again. When Danny moaned, she said, "Holy Mother of God, will you stop being such a back-seat driver!" The light turned amber and then red and she stopped the car. "There, see, Smarty Pants?" After a moment she said, "Leena, I'm sure it was Leena. Doesn't matter anyway."

"No, it doesn't." Raymond settled back next to Hal.

"Big dumb thing."

Although Raymond's hand was resting on his knee, Hal felt very far away from him; he couldn't believe that Raymond hadn't told his family that he was coming. He almost wished that Danny or Gloria would ask him something but he knew that they wouldn't — he could sense that he made them nervous. And he couldn't think of anything to ask them. He wished that he hadn't hugged Gloria.

When they were finally on the four-lane — Gloria chugging along at a safe ten kilometres below the speed limit — the land was so familiar to Raymond: the woods and fields outside the car reminding him of all the times he had driven this road in childhood and adolescence. There was no history here for Hal, Raymond thought. He knew that it must look much the same to him as the views from the train. There was no way that he could share Raymond's understanding of home.

He was suddenly very tired. He was rubbing Hal's knee gently back and forth, and the movement seemed like a lullaby. "We're almost there," he said quietly. He thought he could see the bay ahead of them, a deeper blue low in the sky where the woods seemed to meet the highway on the horizon ahead. He leaned his chin on the back of the front seat. "So how's the swimming this year, Sis?"

"I don't know anyone who's been in. Do you, Danny?"

Danny barely shook his head.

"Pop and I drove past the beach one day last week and there seemed to be lots of cars there. Cottage people have been back for ages."

"Don't you guys go to the beach ever?"

"Ha," said Danny.

Raymond leaned back and slumped his head on Hal's shoulder. "A nice quick dip is what I need right now. How about you?"

"Whatever," Hal said. It sounded good, but he was tired and he knew that Raymond would be asleep before too long. He wasn't comfortable having Raymond touch him with the others so close — Gloria kept stealing glances at them in the rear-view mirror.

"Look there," Raymond said, pointing to a dozen or so brown cows on a hillside bordered by the woods. How could he explain to Hal that they were special to him because he had seen cows on that same spot for as far back as he could remember?

Moments later, as Gloria turned onto the ramp from the highway to the road into town, a shiver of sadness passed through him. When he was seventeen he had driven past the handsomest hitch-hiker imaginable at this very intersection and, ever since, for the moment it took to take the turn off into Membartouche he thought of lost opportunities, of a life he might have had if only he'd dared to stop the car that one time.

After they drove over the bridge and onto Main Street, Raymond pointed out a big old house set back from the road. "Sandy Whyte's place," he said. "The local fruit."

"I've gotta phone him," Gloria moaned. "I just can't do his place this week."

"Hal and I'll help you."

"Are you nuts?"

"No, I'm just nosy. I haven't been inside since I was a kid."

"What were you doing in there?"

"Christmas party. I went with a girl from their church. Sherri Dobbins."

"With the bad, bad acne. I remember her."

The town was unlike the one Hal had imagined: he'd wanted tree-lined streets and little old clapboard buildings, white steeples with weathervanes, but most of the buildings were new and anonymous and there were no trees downtown. This Main Street could be anywhere. It was so crowded with crosswalks that it took for ever to drive through.

Raymond moaned, "Place looks as crappy as ever."

"We've got a McDonald's now, Raymond," Gloria said.

"Where?"

"Other side of town. A McDonald's, a Tim Horton's, a Wendy's, a Kentucky Fried. The whole nine yards."

"Is the Grill still open?"

Danny turned slowly around. "You nuts?" he said.

"It's gone?"

"Raymond," Gloria said, "it closed before you left. You were still in high school."

"God, I can't remember."

"You took me there the week it closed and bought me a banana split," she said.

"Oh yeah." This sounded familiar, but he was not sure he remembered.

They were passing Whyte's Store; the paint on the sign was faded and peeling, the blinds in the window bleached out by the sun. "Boy that place has gone to hell. It's falling apart."

They drove past the new concrete Drug Mart. "There was a nice old building there once."

"Sandy Whyte tried to save it but he didn't get far. You can all say what you like about him, but he's the only person around who ever tried to save anything."

Raymond was trying to remember where the old Grill had been. It had been on a corner — was it near the new drugstore? The town has changed too much, he thought. When you leave something behind it goes on without you.

"I don't live here any more," he said, as if he had just realized it. He reached for Hal's hand.

"Hal," said Danny without turning his head. "Tell that friend of yours he isn't too swift." Gloria gave him a poke with her hand.

Mama was taking the pies out of the oven when the back door opened and Gloria called out.

"Mama, guess who I found hanging around at the train station?"

"Just a second!" She put the pies on top of the stove and shut the oven door. She came out of the old pantry with a pot holder in each hand. She looked tired, Raymond thought, and she hugged him so tightly that he resented it.

"Mama, this is my friend Hal."

Her son's friend was standing just inside the back door behind Danny and smiling at her. "Hello," he said, "I'm very happy to meet you."

"Why didn't you tell us you were bringing someone?" She swatted Raymond gently with the pot holders and then dropped them both on the table.

"I told Gloria."

"You said *maybe*," Gloria replied sheepishly. She had hoped that nobody would say anything in front of Raymond's friend. Hal would think they were not polite.

"I did not."

"Gloria," Mama said, "you always were hopeless. Hal, don't mind them. Good to have you."

Hal wished that he believed her; he felt very self-conscious.

"Are you hungry?" she asked, poking Raymond in the ribs with her finger. "You look like you haven't had a decent meal in weeks." She turned to Hal, "Does my son eat up there?"

"Like a horse, Mrs. Maurice."

"Please call me Mama——"

"Mrs. Maurice was my mother-in-law's name," Raymond and Gloria finished at the same time.

"Don't pay any attention to these brats," she said.

"I smell rhubarb pies."

"Strawberry-rhubarb, and they're not for you."

"Who are they for then?"

"They're for Hal." Mama thought she should make the poor man welcome even if it was the last thing on earth she felt like doing. "You'll have to ask him if you can have any. Come on in and shut the door before the place fills up with flies. I'm sorry that I didn't know you were coming, because now you'll have to sleep with Raymond up in the attic. I bet he didn't tell you how bad he snores. Bad boy." And she poked him again. He was terrifyingly thin.

"That's okay," Hal said. "I know he snores."

"He'd sleep through a war." Raymond grinned and Hal thought this visit would be so much simpler if he and Raymond pretended to be friends instead of lovers. He moved aside when Raymond touched his shoulder.

"Gloria, make yourself useful and show the boys where they'll be staying, will you? And get those suitcases out of here to avoid the confusion."

"Grab your bags," Gloria said, leading the way, and Raymond and Hal followed her up the stairs. Mama turned to Danny and shook her head. As soon as she heard the attic door open and knew they were out of earshot, she said, "He doesn't look too good."

"Yeah, I know."

"Well, I'm glad he's home, and I hope Gloria's happy." She started to go back to her pies. "That fella with him …"

"His boyfriend."

"What'll Pop say?"

"Nothing, as usual. Junior's the one with the big mouth."

Mama picked up the pot holders and shook her head. "Pop and I were so worried that he would get that little Moore girl pregnant back in high school." She went back to the pantry.

"So?"

"Maybe it would have been better if he had."

Danny followed her. "Mama, you couldn't stand Therese Moore. You said she was crazy."

"Yeah, but she was normal."

Danny wanted a drink, but Mama was near the fridge so he went out into the yard. He thought that he should try to head off Junior and Pop before they saw Raymond and his friend, but wasn't sure what he would say to them.

"I don't know, he doesn't look too good," Mama said, but Danny was gone.

TEN ✛

With the house in darkness, Sandy hoped that he could not be seen watching from his mother's bedroom window. He had dragged her vanity chair to the big upstairs bay at the back of the house and was sitting with his knees pressed against the sill. Leaning forwards, elbows on knees, he pressed the binoculars against his eyes, and roamed through the maples to peer at the apple trees and into the dark greens of the alders. It was early dusk and the orchard was a mysterious place; it was the time of day when rabbits appeared — if there were still rabbits this close to town — and birds flew to their nests for the night. The orchard was quiet and still.

Sandy bitterly regretted that he had somehow missed the spring, had not even been interested in it. When the apple trees had been in bloom this year, he had barely noticed; now he wished that he had walked through them, pulling their branches down to his face the way Mother had done when he was young. "Oh, Sandy, don't they smell good enough to eat?" she had said, and then laughed for a long time after he sang out "Apple blossom pie." (It became one of those anecdotes that he grew to hate; at the end of her life, she was always saying things like "Remember when you asked me to make you some apple-blossom pie?" He came to feel that everything she loved about him came from the nursery.) But this evening the memory of those mornings in the orchard was so strong that he could smell the blossoms in the stale air of her room. They overpowered the faint antiseptic odours and mingled with faint traces of her Yardley's powder, making the air potent and sweet. He remembered her dress with the strawberries on it, and the memory was so keen, it was as if she had been here and wearing it only moments before.

When he was able to get away from church on Sunday afternoon, he had looked all over the attic for his childhood books and finally found them buried in a box under the eaves. Tucked away beneath his mother's old Books of the Month was a little stack: *Tom Swift and the Floating Island*, Ernest Thompson Seton's *Two Little Savages*, James Fenimore Cooper's *The Deerslayer*, *Bible Bedtime Stories*, and, the object of his search, *The Great Masters of Europe*. It had a musty smell, but the colours on the fold-out plates were still vibrant. The central panel of the Ghent altarpiece filled him with an ache that he couldn't define or describe. It was yearning and loss and expectation all together in one enormous mystery. At the age of twelve, when he first opened up the glossy page and saw it all spread out before him, *Adoration of the Lamb* had the familiarity of a dream, as if he had always been longing for the beauties of that landscape and the painting had only confirmed his desires. The little white flowers on the grass were the ones he had seen in the woods in the spring, the roses and lilies were Mother's garden. On hills and valleys in the distance, the thickets and groves of miniature trees were wait-ing for him.

Four groups dressed in brilliant colours were converging on a clearing where the Lamb of God stood on an altar surrounded by fourteen angels. At the very top of the panel, in the centre, hovered a dove surrounded by glory. Fistfuls of golden rays, the most delicate and precise light imaginable, beckoned the four groups forward. No one was singing, but there was singing in the air. Some of the angels held the instruments of the passion — the cross, the spear, the vinegar sponge — and two of them were swinging censers: those censers were the only movement in the painting. The rest of the angels were praying. The colours were so bright — all those varieties of green in the grass and the trees, and the red and blue robes stood out like folded jewels in the sunshine. The painting was about a moment of arrival. Sandy felt that everyone had been singing just moments ago, and now that they were converging and could see the Lamb, some had fallen to their knees and the others simply stopped in their tracks, their songs still hanging in the air. The apostles and prophets in simple dun-coloured robes were the ones kneeling. The patriarchs were very serious-looking in their splendid hats. The saints and martyrs had an air of calm about them, and their golden crowns and the rich crimson of their robes gave them an enormous authority. Coming down from the right, a troop of ladies with their heads bowed carried palm branches, the virgin saints. This was the group he had always felt closest to — it was their sweetness — and, anyway, most of the men looked terribly stern and serious.

The virgins all looked pregnant, but Sandy knew this was convention in late Gothic art. He would tell the boy this when they studied the painting together. They would sit beside each other at the dining-room table with the book open in front of them. He would point out the figures that he knew. The patriarch in white was probably Virgil. (He would have to explain who Virgil was, exactly. The education system, like everything else today, had gone to hell.) The martyr on the far right was the patron saint of Ghent. He remembered his mother pointing to that figure, her voice heavy with scorn and warning. She had been concerned that her son cared so much about what was clearly a Roman Catholic painting and felt it necessary to point out every unsavoury aspect. "Look at this fellow over here, Sandy! What's he holding? It looks like a pair of tongs with a tongue in it! Catholics are a morbid bunch. Don't ever let the minister see this picture!" But the horrors of martyrdom only thrilled him when he was little. This clearing was such a beautiful place that the past difficulties of its inhabitants only made it more interesting. "Where is this place?" he had asked as soon as he saw it. "Well, I guess it's supposed to be heaven, Sandy, but really it's the world that the painters knew."

When he had shown it to his father, he had been told that it should be called *Wishful Thinking* because Catholics "didn't have a hope in hell of getting into heaven." That was Father's idea of a joke.

It seemed to him now with his binoculars scanning the trees and bushes, looking up towards the woods, that he was getting closer and closer to the moment in the painting. The moment when the goal is almost reached and the pilgrims pause. This was the ultimate moment of the *Adoration* — the whole purpose of the panels beside it — because when the crowds got to the Lamb, what could there be to do next? It wasn't like earth, where you achieved your goal and died; after all, they were already dead. Would they drink the blood that poured from the Lamb's breast into a golden cup? Would they simply worship for a while and then go home? But where was home? In those splendid cathe-drals just over the hills? The painting was a constant richness to him because the mysteries kept expanding; if his eyes explored it for ever, there would always be something new and fresh.

The window was open a little; he could hear the last of the birds, and bats were beginning to skitter about the air in the yard. Of course the Van Eycks had made the world their heaven — it was so beautiful. There was every reason to be filled with such trembling, such anticipation. It seemed that all of his life of unhappiness and, yes, martyrdom had been leading up to this great moment. Like the four groups in the painting, he felt that his life was about to converge.

Because of this he was able to disregard the troubles on Sunday. There had been disaster and tension at the Cemetery Committee: Joan Leeman had discovered (to her immense delight, thought Sandy) that someone was already buried in her sister's plot. Sarah had died in Toronto and wanted her ashes buried at home, but the gravedigger had hit old wood. Sandy must have made a mistake on the ground plans when he was assigning plots. "Not all of us have the protection of concrete," Joan had said smugly, trying to humiliate Sandy. She was an old snake to bring that up; it was a clear indication that the woman had no decency whatsoever and that, like the rest of her clan, she was as common as mud. Everyone knew the story and Sandy had hoped that he had heard the end of it long ago, but the Leemans were the last people to let someone rest in peace.

Sandy's father had insisted that he be buried in concrete and that his wife be beside him in a block of it herself. Mother had tried to argue with him, but he had been determined. "Promise me you'll have concrete, too," he said to her near the end. "Promise me, Grace." He believed that concrete would make him fresher on Judgment Day. When the last trumpet sounded, he and his wife would be raised more incorruptible than anyone else in the whole cemetery and would be the purest couple for miles around. At the time of his father's death, as Sandy stood with his mother in the cemetery while the concrete was being poured into the grave, he could sense that everyone at the graveside was dying to go home and gossip. He and his mother both knew that the church was divided on the issue and both sides were mean. One half said that she was burying her husband in concrete because she thought the Whytes were so good they could even be spared the indignity of worms, while the other half shook their heads and said that Sandy wanted him in concrete to make sure he would never get up again. Sandy had made it clear that concrete was his father's wish and not his mother's or his own, but what did these people care for the truth? When she was near her own end, she had made him promise that he would spare her from concrete. "I couldn't bear to have your father see me like this," she cried. "He won't recognize an eighty-five-year-old woman! No concrete, Sandy, *please* promise me, *please*. Just get them to cremate me and you can put me out in my poor old garden."

Sandy and the boy would scatter her ashes in the yard at this very time of day.

He had apologized to Joan Leeman and made a show of going through all the plots and ground plans to discover how the error had occurred. He knew that it had been a simple mistake, a matter of a few feet, nothing more. It galled him to think that he was apologizing to the old witch, but it was the most expedient way of getting the meeting over with so that he could get back home. He was furious with the dwarf for not telling him why the committee was meeting. She had wanted to talk to him afterwards, but he had pleaded a headache and left. Maybe they all wanted him off the committee, which was just fine as far as he was concerned. He had more important things to do with his time.

He had spent the last two days at watch in the window.

The boy had come through his yard every day, which made Sandy think that he had probably been trespassing for a while. On Sunday evening when he returned through the orchard, the boy had seen the money right away. Glancing up at the house when he stopped to pick it up, he had given Sandy a few clear seconds view of his face. But his glance had been so sudden, and Sandy was so afraid he had might be seen, that the binoculars had jiggled. The boy had straight, dark hair, as long as a girl's, and features that seemed, to Sandy, of astounding purity and strength. His eyes were dark; his nose slender, but not thin, and wide at the base. His lips were thick enough to be sensuous. But it was his cheekbones that made Sandy's binoculars wobble. They were high, gently pointed, and gave the boy the look of an aristocrat. He had pocketed the change and gone around the corner and out of sight. Sandy had run through the upstairs, but by the time he got to the big hall window, the boy was already on Main Street. Sandy's heart was racing and he went to the kitchen to make some tea and calm down.

He wondered about the boy's life, but he wasn't sure what he wanted that life to be. It was doubtful that he lived by himself, but Sandy was sure that he was an outsider to his family, much as Sandy himself had been. Perhaps he was lonely and restless — that would explain the daily trips into the woods. Or maybe he was completely happy and at one with nature, like Ernest Thompson Seton's "Little Savages." Or perhaps something illegal was happening up in the woods — but what could that possibly be? Could the boy have a camp up there? He thought of how superior the boy was to Joey Mullins, how more refined he was, and intelligent. He might even be a hunter or a trapper. He thought of the Van Eyck angels with their splendid bird wings and wished that he could fly after the boy and watch him from the treetops. Then he would be able to see him cross over the old pasture and follow the river up past the sawmill. But no, the sawmill had been gone for thirty years at least. He imagined bits and pieces of the boy's walk southwards, deeper into the woods, and there, at the end, was the pool of water where the river turned and deepened and the boy was taking off his clothes and swimming. Sandy had not been to that pool in well over fifty years, but he assumed that it was still there. He had never gone back, not since Joey had punched him and called him a fruit. He had asked Joey to prove that his penis could shoot ten feet because Joey had bragged that he could hit the ceiling if he were lying down in bed playing with himself.

The boy would go to the pool and take off his clothes and go swimming. Sandy imagined the dark wetness that his body left on the large flat rock where he would dry himself in the sun. It was so exciting to Sandy that he could imagine the clearing from *Adoration of the Lamb* just around a bend in the river.

On Monday, the boy had walked through his yard around seven in the morning. He was wearing glasses — which made Sandy happy, perhaps the boy was a scholar — and he was looking about for money in the grass. He did not find the five-dollar bill that Sandy had wadded into a little ball and dropped near the fence long before sunrise. It had been a warm day, and Sandy saw a glimpse of bare skin: the boy's arms when he leaned down to pick up some silver in the grass, the small of his back when his shirt rode up a bit. After the boy disappeared into the apple trees, Sandy sat very still, thinking of those arms, the smooth skin under the boy's tee shirt, and he began imagining his knees, his armpits, his nipples, a small mole on his back. He thought of his feet, how each toe might look. With his magnifying glass he examined the bare feet of two praying apostles in the altarpiece. Both were kneeling, the bottoms of their feet sticking out from their robes behind them. He thought of the boy's strong and gentle arches, the thick big toes and the four smaller ones like descending notes on a scale. With each successive glimpse of the boy's face, he memorized every detail of perfection.

He had scanned the Van Eyck painting, hoping that, as a sign, the boy would be there; but the painting was filled with old men. In the rear of the crowd of bishops and confessors, there was a glimpse of a younger-looking figure, but all Sandy could see was a strong forehead with a thick crown of hair.

Around noon on Monday, Sandy went out into the yard to move the five-dollar bill, but it was gone. He cursed himself for not watching all day. The boy must have come back late in the morning and found it then. He left another one on the back steps and, although he waited patiently all of yesterday, his vigil was not rewarded. The bill was still there when he went to bed at midnight. He slept badly and dreamed that Margaret and Minnie were living in his kitchen. When he woke up, there was a crick in his neck and he could barely move his head.

The five dollars was gone when he checked first thing this morning, but maybe it had been windy in the night — the bill could easily have blown away. He kept watching and was delighted when the boy arrived early, at 8:00 a.m. He was carrying a knapsack and he walked through the yard more boldly than ever. He wore his glasses and marched brazenly across the grass and jumped the fallen fence without once looking up at the house. His boldness thrilled Sandy. That was the way to stride through life — as if a brass band were always playing to announce your arrivals, the trumpets' notes hanging in the clear air after you had passed.

Sandy was fighting the inclination to think of the boy in a sexual way. He had, of course, but the idea of the two of them together depressed him because it was the corruption of near perfection. He could not allow himself those kinds of thoughts. He was here to do the boy a service, to do for him all those things that no one had done for Sandy.

In the darkening room his legs had fallen asleep and he stood up to get his blood moving when something in the orchard caught his eye. He plopped back down and lifted the binoculars so quickly that he banged them against his forehead. There, walking with awkward grace among the trees, was his beloved. Before he reached the fence, he stopped and raised a bottle to his lips. He lost his footing for a second, but quickly regained it. He lifted the bottle over his head and swung his other arm about. Then he leaned against the fence and continued to drink. With some consternation, Sandy saw that the boy was upset. When he lowered the bottle he slapped it against his thigh while shaking his other hand up and down as if he were making a point to someone nearby. He raised the bottle again and drained it, then tossed it into the bushes. Sandy noted where the bottle landed: he would search for it in the morning. The boy remained leaning against the fence for what seemed like a long time, possibly a minute. His head was downcast and he shook it sadly. Was he ill? And then Sandy realized that he was quite drunk, which both excited and depressed him. For a moment he wished that he were old enough to get drunk too, and then he remembered that he was too old, and that "old" and "young" became confused and meaningless terms when one was in love. But none of this seemed important, because right there, so close, so near, was his beloved with a broken heart. Why was the object of his affections in such distress?

The boy jerked forward, shoving himself away from the fence, and took a few awkward steps, staggering a bit. Then he stumbled over what was left of the stile and stopped. He slumped down in Sandy's yard and leaned back against the old wood. He looked about and then took something from the grass — a quarter maybe — and examined it. Then he was looking up at the house. He looked from window to window — the back shed, the kitchen, the pantry, and upstairs to the bathroom — and then his eyes gazed right into Sandy's. For a horrifying moment Sandy believed he had been caught, but the boy's eyes registered nothing. After a moment, he fumbled in his knapsack and took out another bottle of beer.

For fifteen minutes, Sandy tried not to move, not to breathe. He tried to watch closely as the unhappy boy sullenly drank and stared into space. Night had fallen and the boy was barely visible, another shadow deepening in the yard below him. He was sitting with his legs outstretched on the grass, the bottle between his legs. After a while, it seemed that he might be asleep. For Sandy, at first there was excitement, and then anxiety, and then, as the minutes went by, he began to worry. What would he do if the boy stayed in the yard for hours? The grass would become wet in the night, the wind had already started to pick up, there was usually a cool night breeze off the bay. What would happen? Would he be forced to go downstairs and send the boy away for his own good? But if he did that, would he ever come back again? What if he went down and asked the boy to come inside — could he possibly do that? What would he say? He could think of nothing that was simple and sure enough. He might startle the boy and he would run away and never come back. Sandy's legs and arms were asleep and tingling, and yet he was afraid to move for fear that he would miss a second of this, the most important moment of his life.

But then the boy moved. He crawled up onto his knees and stood. From the way he weaved about, Sandy knew that the yard was reeling around him. He leaned against the fence, trying to steady himself, then he picked up his knapsack and looked about. Sandy was ready to go downstairs to try to help the poor thing find his way home, when he saw that the boy was walking towards the house, dragging his knapsack behind him. He stood up and looked down in the yard. The boy had made it to the back steps but, as he stepped up, the rotten wood gave way beneath him, and he fell. He was so close to the house that Sandy could no longer see him, even though he was pressing his face against the glass. He waited a moment, listening, not knowing what to do. Then, through the window, he heard the backshed door creak open.

Clutching the binoculars, Sandy gently pushed back the chair and started to walk around it and out the door, his ears alert to every sound. The floorboards in the hall had never creaked so loudly as they did as he moved across them to the back stairs. At the top he paused and heard nothing. The stairs squeaked as he tiptoed down.

In the dark kitchen, he banged against a chair, but at that very moment there was a crash in the back shed. He froze, staring at the kitchen door. He stood for five minutes not knowing what to do next. Then he placed the binoculars on the table very quietly, tiptoed to the door, unlocked it as gently as possible, and very slowly opened it.

The shed door was open and there was a bad sick smell. The boy was curled up on the floor beside the washing machine, his face lying beside a pool of vomit. Sandy watched him for what seemed like a very long time, and then went over and, crouching down, touched his shoulder very tentatively. The boy was out cold.

Sandy stayed beside him for a few minutes. Never, ever in his life had he been so close to anything so beautiful. He touched the boy's arm — the softness and strength of the skin as he cupped the bicep. The boy's glasses were crooked; he removed them and put them in his pocket, then he brushed back the boy's hair, and touched his face, the cheekbones, the nostrils, the lips.

Fifteen minutes later he stood up. He went into the kitchen and filled a dish pan with warm water and found a couple of towels. Back in the shed, he threw an old towel over the vomit, then dipped a clean dishrag into the soapy water and washed the boy's face. Very tenderly he wiped the boy's mouth and neck. He dipped the cloth in the water and rinsed it out. He wiped a bit of vomit from his hair — the softest, silkiest hair that Sandy could ever imagine. He was saving the boy's life. This was love, he thought, as he wiped the precious cheek clean. He rinsed the cloth again and cleaned a bit of vomit from the boy's jacket. Then he dropped the cloth into the dish pan and moved it to one side. He gathered up the towel and scrubbed the patch of floor. He tossed the towel out onto the steps, then carried the dish pan back into the kitchen. He washed his hands in the sink.

Tenderly, oh so tenderly, he put his hands under the boy's armpits and carefully hoisted him up. The back of the boy's head brushed against his legs, his stomach. Slowly and tenderly, he dragged the boy from the shed into the kitchen and laid him on the braided rug beside the table. Sandy went back to the shed and shut the outside door, then he picked up the knapsack and locked the kitchen door.

The boy had not moved. Sandy crouched down beside him and slid his arm under the boy's neck and then down to his shoulder blades. He slid his other one under his knees, and then he slowly stood up, carrying the limp body as gently as he could. The back stairs were too narrow, so he went down the hall to the front ones and started up. He was at the landing before he even thought about what he was doing and then had a sudden moment of panic because he realized that the boy was much too heavy for him. He would throw out his back, he would drop him, he would trip and kill them both, he was crazy!

But then he caught his breath and very calmly counted to three and climbed the rest of the way up and walked down the dark hallway to his mother's bedroom.

Then very tenderly he lay the boy down on the mattress. His heart was pounding so loudly he was sure it would wake him. When he stood up, his back cracked and, for the first time in many weeks, it stopped hurting. He turned on the soft little night light beside the door. He remembered a poem that his mother sometimes recited at bedtime after he had said his prayers. He sat on the edge of the bed and looked at the unconscious boy. "Little lamb, who made thee?" he whispered. "Dost thou know who made thee?" All was still and perfect for a very long time.

What would the boy do when he woke up? Would he leave? Would he ever know that Sandy was his saviour? Would he care? It would be much simpler if he could just stay like this, a sleeping beauty. Sandy would not defile him; he would care for him. He touched the boy's hand, raised it to his lips and kissed it. Must this end? It seemed unfair somehow; he had been waiting for so very long. He stood up and walked about the room. Hanging on a rack inside the closet door were his father's old ties. Sandy grabbed a handful of them and put them on the bed. And then tenderly, oh so tenderly, one after another, he tied the boy's arms and legs to the bedposts of his mother's bed. He opened his mother's cedar chest and took out her wedding-ring quilt and gently laid it over the boy so that he would not get cold.

He sat down calmly in a chair by the bedside. He wanted to turn on the radio and have Bach fill the room.

PURE LOVE ✛
✛
✛

ELEVEN

A crisis in the Middle East pre-empted Minnie's three-o'clock story just seconds after Georgette's evil twin turned up in town to seduce her brother-in-law and ruin his family name. When she first read about the episode in the *Soap Opera Guide* listings, Minnie had tried to convince Margaret to stay home and watch it with her — this, she felt, could be the episode that might finally convince her sister of the merits of her story — but Margaret had just looked at her in that horrible way of hers and gone back to doing the dishes. "It's your loss, dear," Minnie had said, as sweetly as possible. She wanted her story to be something that she and her sister could do together, something they could share, but Margaret was an old party-pooper, as usual.

After waiting patiently the whole day for it to come on the air, a bunch of thoughtless people had taken it all away. She was trying to console herself with a pan of Margaret's brownies; as she popped them into her mouth, she figured that her sister was at the root of this unhappy situation. After all, it was Margaret's fault that they did not have a satellite dish. A dish would not pre-empt her story for a bunch of foreigners running around with guns in their hands and dishtowels wrapped around their heads.

Life was so very unfair. She had hoped that when her sister retired from the bank things would change. She did not know how, exactly, but she thought that the house might become brighter. She had imagined Margaret's retirement in terms of large flat shapes — pinks and yellows and robin's-egg blues, the colours of old Sunday-school pictures that often came into her dreams. But now that Margaret was around so much, everything seemed to be duller and they never played together.

She brushed some crumbs from the magazine that was lying on her lap and turned to her favourite page, a full-sized photograph of the collector's plate that she wanted to own. A little girl in a big bonnet was sitting dreamily in a field of pretty pink flowers; a lamb lay at her feet, taking a nap. The sun was just coming up, and in the sky, which was a lovely bright, deep blue, the morning star glistened like a twinkling cross. The grass was the sweetest shade of green — "lime green" they called it in decorating magazines, but the limes she had seen in the supermarket were darker. "Lime green" was nicer than the real thing — it was a milky green, as soft as spun sugar.

Minnie popped another tiny brownie into her mouth and sucked it for a moment before biting into it. She had been having more problems with her dentures lately and Margaret had let this batch get a little too crusty.

The girl in the bonnet looked so happy sitting on her soft grey stone, and the flowers around her were so bright — Why was Margaret so opposed to beautiful things? They were simply make-up for their home, a little something to make it prettier. Minnie had adored make-up since she was fifteen. Rouge was her favourite thing. Everytime she rubbed it in she thought of coming indoors on a cold day for cookies and hot chocolate and having her mother say, "Old Jack Frost has put the roses in your cheeks." To get that pretty world back, she wanted to fill the house with pretty things. On the table beside her chair were china bunnies with pale pink ears asleep like darlings under quilts sprinkled with stars. On top of the television set, a skunk in a tall silk hat was sniffing a bunch of flowers. Minnie had named him Mr. Precious.

The plate that she fancied so much was called "Little Miss Morningstar." There was a whole set to collect with names like "Baby Moonbeam" and "Sunset Serenade." How lovely they would look on a plate rack in the dining room. But Margaret said that collector's plates were not practical and would not buy them for her.

There was a French lady down the street who had a wonderful ornament in her front yard. At first Minnie had thought it was a giant red mushroom, but then she realized that it was a cutout of a woman in a red dress bending over; all you could see of her was her legs and the big round shape of her bum. Every time she passed by that yard, Minnie had to chuckle. "Laugh at life," that was her motto. On Sunday, when she was telling the minister's husband about the ornament, she had split her slacks up the seam when she bent over. Did she blush and go all silly? Of course not. She laughed and made other people laugh by showing them her rear end. Prudish people upset her.

Which is one of reasons that Sandy Whyte offended her sensibilities. He never looked her in the eye, which meant he could not be trusted, and the man simply had no sense of humour. When she had turned to show him her backside in the church vestry, he had looked at her with scorn. Why did people call him an old woman? Women giggled at jokes, women were fun. He was an old prude. Now that was something no one could ever say about her.

What would she do if her sister were crazy enough to start going out with him again? She had not *yet* said anything about what she had heard from Mrs. LeBlanc. She knew her sister well enough to understand that if she said something at the wrong moment the whole thing could backfire and Margaret would start defending him. Going out and having a pee in his backyard! It was clear to anyone with a brain that the man was dirty-minded or going gaga; whatever he was, it was disgusting. Minnie wanted to talk to Mrs. LeBlanc right now, but she felt that she could not call again quite so soon — her pretext the other day had been a rummage sale at church with the proceeds for the Hotline. It was only a little white lie — because the LeBlancs were R.C., she knew they would be opposed to abortion.

"We give to our own Right To Life right here in town," Mrs. LeBlanc had said.

"Well, we all have to fight the good fight from whatever side we pray on," Minnie replied good-naturedly. It had not been hard after that to get Mrs. LeBlanc talking about her neighbour Sandy Whyte.

"I don't know how that Gloria Maurice can stand to go in there and clean up after him," the old lady said.

"Well, she's a bit simple, isn't she?" Minnie asked, as discreetly as possible.

"She's a troublemaker, that one. She tried to get us all in bad trouble with the bishop back when she was a little girl and lied about seeing the Virgin up in the old nuns' pasture."

But as interesting as dim-witted Gloria might be, Minnie had deftly steered the conversation back to Sandy Whyte.

"What does he do all day in that house?"

"They say he's working on a history of the town, but they been saying that for years."

"Who'd ever want to read the likes of that?"

"Do you know what I think? I think that whole history business is a front for him being so nosy. It's just an excuse for him to ask people all these questions about their relatives."

"I bet you're right," said Minnie. "You're as right as rain."

And that was when Minnie heard about Sandy in the bushes. The world was certainly a shocking place. Margaret said that she was not interested in Minnie's afternoon story because it was sordid and full of sex, but really, it was just like life, only with taste.

She had heard that Mrs. LeBlanc was famous for her rhubarb nut loaf; tomorrow she would call the old lady again and ask for the recipe. Minnie was prepared to go the full distance to spare her sister any future sorrow.

Minnie wished that she could be the little girl in the big bonnet sitting in the light of the rising sun. The lamb was making her think that maybe a nap would not be such a bad idea — after all, the news bulletin showed no signs of letting up, and the change in the weather had made the air muggy. She was feeling a bit drowsy. She had hit the mute button on her remote and occasionally glanced up to see big crowds of Jews and Arabs — she could not tell which was which and didn't care — they were all milling about and waving their arms.

There was precious little chance now of finding out what that scheming twin was really up to. If they did not rebroadcast the whole thing tomorrow, someone was going to hear from her. Maybe now Margaret would finally see reason and buy them the satellite dish. She thought of her story floating around way up in outer space, hovering above the world, unable to get into her television set. It was a waste and so terribly unfair. She was dimly aware that the magazine was sliding off her lap and onto the rug.

In her dream, Minnie went into a flying saucer that turned into a new branch of her bank, where she found Arthur hiding in a corner of the bright pink safety-deposit box. She began to cry because he was only two inches high. "I'll take you back, Sweetheart!" she said. "It doesn't matter to me how teeny you are!" But Arthur was pretending that he could not hear her. She could not bring herself to let him see that she knew he was trying to trick her. "Oh, Artie," she said. "Not deaf too!"

When she picked him up, as gently as she would a fluffy kitten, and held him close to her face, he stuck out his tongue at her and she cried again because she knew that she would love him for ever. Then she saw a big smear of lipstick on his back like a big kiss, and she knew that her sister had been kissing him.

"Oh no!" she said, and Arthur scurried away like a giggly mouse.

Just then, Sandy Whyte and Margaret walked right past her, arm in arm, without so much as saying a word. Minnie was so frightened that she woke up.

She sat quietly for a minute, her brain cloudy from sleep. Then she reached for a brownie. What would she do if her sister were crazy enough to start going out with that fool again?

An hour before they were supposed to be at the meeting with the abortion lady, Annette finally called Chaleur's house to find out what was keeping him. He was supposed to phone her last night and she had not called him then because she hated phoning his place; his mother was crazy and his stepfather was a creep. The phone rang over and over, each ring seeming to send Chaleur further away from her, before Rory finally answered.

"Yeah?" he said.

When she asked for Chaleur, he just said, "He ain't here," and hung up before she could ask him anything else.

She was at her sister's house — Jackie was out in the back-yard trying to cool off while Joanne and Evan played in the wading pool — and as soon as she hung up the phone it rang.

"Hello!"

But it was only her mother. "Annette, if Jackie doesn't need you this afternoon, I'm washing the curtains and could use a hand putting them back when they're dry."

"Okay, Mom."

"My eyes are shot. I can't stick those damn little hooks back in the right place."

"I'll check with Jackie. Look, if Chaleur phones me, be sure and tell him I'm here."

"Where else would I say you'd be?"

A half-hour later when there was still no sign of him, she borrowed her sister's car and drove down to his house. Chaleur's brother was sitting out on the back steps with one of the Smith kids, the fat one who was always hanging around the taxi store trying to bum cigarettes.

"Hey, Ralphie," Annette said. "Chaleur around?"

"Who wants to know?" he replied, and then he and his friend giggled.

"Very funny. Look, have you seen him since lunch?"

"Ask her for a smoke," the fat boy whispered.

"Give us a couple of weeds and I'll tell you."

"C'mon, Ralphie, you're too young to smoke. Have you seen your brother?"

"Don't get bitchy with us," Ralphie said, and he and his friend started laughing again because they were feeling big and important.

"Ralphie!" a voice screeched from the kitchen. "Who's out there?"

"Chaleurrrr's girrrrl," Ralphie answered, drawing both words out like it was the funniest thing in the whole world. "Say, I'm a poet and don't know it!" he said.

"Got a boat and can't row it," his friend finished, and they laughed so hard they almost fell over. Annette started to walk past them when Ralphie grabbed her leg, very near her crotch.

"Who said you could walk up my steps?" he said.

"Lay off!" Grabbing his hands, she shoved him away. She walked up the four steps to the creaky little back porch and knocked on the screen door. "Hello?" she called.

Chaleur's mother was standing in the middle of the kitchen with a bottle of beer in each hand. She turned her head towards the door. "What is it?"

"I was supposed to meet Chaleur. Do you know where he is?"

"Can't say." She set the beer down on the table and twisted off the caps.

"Did he say where he was going this morning?"

"Haven't seen him today at all." Her voice sounded as if she were long past the time when she could even make an effort to sound nice, but when she picked up the beer she took a step towards the door.

Then Rory's voice boomed from somewhere in the house. "Where's that friggin' beer?"

"Hold your horses, there's someone at the door!"

"Did he say anything yesterday, about where he was going?"

"Haven't seen him since night before last, when he finally come back after stealing poor little Ralphie's bike."

"Who the hell is it?" Rory called.

"It's just Annette! Hold your horses, I said!"

Annette looked away from the door — both boys were looking at her bum and whispering. What should she do next? She turned back to Chaleur's mother. "He wasn't home yesterday?"

"He was outta here at crow piss. Look, I dunno where he is and I don't care. When he's home all he does is sneak around the place and get on everybody's nerves."

"Is she deaf?" Rory called out. "I told her on the phone he wasn't here! Get her to tell that little Frenchman that he owes me a bottle of rye!"

"And he never came home?" What if he had taken off yesterday? He could be anywhere by now. She imagined him walking along the highway with his thumb out, the knapsack with "Guns N' Roses" written on it slung over his back.

"I'd be the last one to know. He never tells me a damn thing, just like his old man used to be."

"Could you please get him to call me as soon as he gets back?"

"Do I have to get that friggin' beer myself?" Rory hollered. "I'm dying of thirst in here!"

Without looking at Annette, Chaleur's mother nodded and turned away. Annette went to step off the porch, but both boys had stretched themselves out across the middle steps and were deliberately blocking her way. They were trying to look very bored and cool, but the Smith's kid's belly was shaking with the laughter he could not quite suppress.

"Excuse me," she said.

"We'll move if you let us touch your titties." The fat boy giggled.

"Move."

"You can't make us," said Ralphie. "This is my house and you're a trespasser."

She glared at them — enough of this stupid nonsense. "You move," Annette commanded, "and damn quick, or I'll kick your useless little nuts right out your backsides!"

"Ooh," said Ralphie. "She's a tough tittie."

But when Annette jumped down to the step directly above him and raised her foot above his crotch, both he and his friend scrambled to their feet.

"That's better," she said as she walked down the steps.

"Bitch," one of them muttered as she walked past.

Annette whirled around and grabbed them both by the ears. "I swear to Christ," she said, "you two are the most ignorant little shits I ever met! You ever speak to me like that again, I'll go straight to the cops and get them to call the Children's Aid and you'll be in such deep shit that no one'll even be able to see the tops of your stupid heads. You got me?"

When they glared at her, she yanked on their ears. "I said, You got me?"

"Yeah," the fat boy grunted.

She pushed them away and moved to the car. She drove away without looking back at them because she knew they would be sticking out their tongues and giving her the finger. Why, after living with that bunch, would Chaleur want to bring a baby into the world? They were enough to make you want to end the human race. Could she even blame him for taking off?

But if he had gone and left her all alone with this mess, she was going to kill him.

She knew that he went up to the woods to get away from his family, so she drove up Dorchester Street; five miles after the pavement ended, she pulled over and parked near the trail that led down to the river. She had hated this place ever since the spring that she and Jackie had come for a walk up here and someone had fired a BB gun at them. That was a long time ago: Jackie had just found out she was pregnant with Evan and he was five last month.

The trail had once been an old logging road; now it was almost overgrown. It was way too quiet — every ten feet a bird or some little animal would make a noise in the underbrush and scare her.

Of course there was no sign of him anywhere.

"Chaleur!" she called, standing beside the river where it turned and started moving faster. "Chaleur!"

But there was not even an echo: just the wind in the pine trees above her, the water in the river, and a lonely-sounding chickadee. She called out his name a few more times, and then just stood, shaking her head and shrugging her shoulders over and over. A few feet away, in a quiet part of the river, yellow water lilies were blooming. She heard a fish jump and watched the ripples spread out in soft circles.

"Chaa-leuur!" She waited for another minute, and then she left, looking around her nervously as she walked back to Jackie's car. As she was driving into town, she looked at her watch and knew that she was too late to make their appointment. When she got back to her sister's place, she took the telephone and locked herself in the bathroom.

"What's going on?" her sister asked through the door.

"I'll tell you later, s'nuthin'."

The woman who answered was not the same one she had talked to before; she was too perky-sounding, like one of those brain-dead supply teachers. Annette said, "I'd like to speak to the lady I was talking to before, on Monday night? I was supposed to meet her today."

"Just a minute."

Annette waited, sitting on the edge of the tub, and thinking that this was the worst day of her whole life.

"Hello?"

She knew right away that this was the same lady. "Hi. You're the person I was talking to before?"

"This is Carrie?"

"What? Oh yeah."

"Yes, it's me. They tried to tell me to go home, but I just knew that you'd be in touch. I had a feeling."

"Thanks. I just ... I phoned to say I'm sorry I missed the meeting."

"Something's wrong, isn't it? I can tell by your voice."

"Yes. I'll say."

"Can you tell me?"

"Um, well." Annette took a deep breath and then stated the horrible fact: "My boyfriend's disappeared. No one knows where he is."

The lady did not sound very surprised when she said "I'm sure he'll be back soon."

"He's never broken a promise to me before."

"Well, I hate to say it, dear, but you've never been pregnant before. Where are you now?"

"At my sister's. I can't talk very long." And then she whispered, "I'm worried and I'm so mad and ... And if he's taken off on me, I don't know what I'll do."

"Do you know where the benches are at the beach?"

"What?"

"The park benches, at the beach. On the far end, just past the First Aid station?"

"Yeah. Why?"

"I can meet you there in an hour."

This was the last thing that Annette expected and she was not sure what to say. Just then, her niece started screaming outside the bathroom door. "Just a sec," she said, covering the mouthpiece with her hand. "I'll be right out, Joanna, pipe down!"

"I gotta pee!"

"Use the toilet in the basement. I'm busy."

"Selfish!" the little girl said, stomping back down the hall towards the basement door.

"Hello? Sorry about that."

"You should talk to someone," the lady said. "Just to help you sort things out."

"I suppose."

"I can be there in an hour."

"An hour. Okay. Thanks, lady."

"I look forward to meeting you, Carrie."

Annette felt silly using a pretend name. "Lady?"

"Yes?"

"My name's really Annette."

"Oh. And my name's not really Lady, it's Margaret."

"Right. Thank you, Margaret."

"Yes, dear. Goodbye."

The phone rang as soon as she hung up, but it was only her mother again, so she had to tear over there first and help with the curtains. It seemed to take for ever, but it was really only about twenty minutes. Then she jumped in her sister's car without saying where she was going and drove straight to the beach.

She felt weird being there in her jeans and sweatshirt while everybody else was walking around in bathing suits, but she had not wanted to even wear shorts since she had taken the test from the drugstore. It was not only as if her clothes would hide the baby inside her, but, if she wore enough of them, she might be able to make it go away.

Just two days ago she had been right here with Chaleur — so where the hell was he now? Anger alternated with worry as she parked the car and lit a cigarette. If he had taken off on her, she was going to track him down and wring his neck. But then she thought about growing up with Rory and what it would be like having a horrible brother like Ralphie and she wanted to cry. She had always known he had a bad family, but now even they seemed worse.

Had he left her all alone because she wanted to have the abortion? If she had told him that she was having the baby, would he still be here? And did she love him so much that she would have the baby just to keep him close to her?

For some reason she seemed certain that the abortion lady, Margaret, could help answer all her questions.

TWELVE

Chaleur was trying to walk down a long hallway, but the walls and ceiling were getting so close that he could feel them pressing against his shoulders and the top of his head. He had found the secret passage behind his grandmother's stove, the place that would take him to his father, but he was running out of time: the walls had already started shrinking in on him and soon he would be stuck inside a house no bigger than a doll's. He would smother. He could hear voices from other rooms: somewhere a man and a woman were arguing in a language that he did not understand. In the distance a baby was crying. There was a smell like turned milk, and as it grew stronger he could feel the walls curdling as he brushed past them. Bits of them were flaking off and sticking to his arms like greasy snow.

"Dad?" he said. "Dad?"

There was a light ahead of him, like the ones in the high-school corridor; even though it was on, it was not very bright and did not help him to see the way clearly. He thought that he could hear his grandmother singing, but when he stopped to listen, the man and woman were shouting again; he knew that they were not his mother and Rory but that it was the same argument he had heard almost nightly through their bedroom walls. It was coming from below him, from a room beneath the cellar inside the earth.

His kid brother tore past him on a bicycle, sticking out his tongue and swerving so that one of the pedals scraped against Chaleur's leg. He was almost knocked over, and his leg felt like it was fastened to something heavy; he had to drag it behind him and the walking was slower.

"Dad?"

It was not fair that Ralphie would get to his father first; Ralphie bragged that he barely remembered him. Suddenly Chaleur could not remember if he and Ralphie even had the same father.

There was more bad milk; it was thick underfoot and it might be slippery, like slime-covered rocks in the river. It was hard walking on one foot. Ralphie knew how to fly — how come he had never learned? The milk smell was making him sick, his head was pounding. Someone was crying. It was the baby again, but older now; it was growing up too fast.

"Dad?"

And then he understood that before he could find his father he needed to reach the baby that was calling for him. Patches of stale milk were drying on the back of his hands, pinching his skin, so he tried to shake them off. He lifted his hands above his head to give them a good shake, but they became caught on something. When he tried to lower them, they were fastened together above his head. He yanked and pulled, but could not get them free, and that was when he knew he had been tricked: he had not found the secret passage after all. It was night in the woods and he was hanging from a high branch. In the distance, he could hear crows flying towards him.

"Dad!"

If only he were wearing his glasses they would not be able to peck out his eyes. He jerked his hands and then he was falling.

"Dad!"

He called out so loud that the noise startled him and he hit the soft ground. He tried to sit up, but he could not. He was no longer in the woods. It was dark but there was a window. He was in a bedroom, on a bed, unable to move. His hands and feet seemed to be tied, and when he struggled, the knots just became tighter. Maybe Rory had finally hated him so much that he had tied him up, but this was not his bedroom or any other one in his house. He had never dreamed about this place before; it was new. His head was killing him.

He tried looking around. It might be day outside, because there was a point of light at the edge of the window, but without his glasses he was not sure. It could be a street light. The room was very dark. He could hear birds, but they were pigeons, not forest birds. He twisted his head and saw a dark old dresser with a television sitting on it. The bed was the old-fashioned kind with brass posts, and it was to these that his arms and legs were tied. Maybe this was a whole different kind of dream, a horrible kind of nightmare.

As he became more aware of this new place, he knew that he was no longer searching for his father in a dream, that he was no longer even dreaming. He was awake and he was tied to a strange bed in a strange room. What could have happened? How could he have gotten to this place?

He had been in the woods — he remembered that — and was trying to figure out what to do about Annette. She was pregnant. No, that had been part of the terrible dream. They had walked along the beach and she had told him that she was pregnant —

But that did not feel like a dream, somehow, that felt real. Yes, because he was supposed to go talk to the abortion lady with her. That was right. On Wednesday. What day was this? His mind became less groggy with sleep, but his headache was growing into a heavy pounding. He began to struggle to free his arms and legs. Somehow, someone had tied him to a bed. Maybe they had found him in the woods. But this was not like the camp he had found up there. No one in the woods had a room like this. And besides, it did not sound like the woods. The birds were pigeons. Should he call for help? Or would that just bring the people who had captured him? Maybe they would kill him. He was so tired and sick-feeling. Maybe if he went back to sleep he might wake up again somewhere else. He was frightened and worried that he might cry. There was an old quilt on top of him that made him think of his grandmother.

He thought of Grandmère and how she had cried when he saw her tied to the bed in the Home. Could this be a place like that?

The pigeons were noisy, and they made him think that the rest of the world was going on without him. He had been hidden away. He tried to listen for other sounds that might help him, but the loudest sound in the room was the pounding of his heart, as if his ear were pressed right against it. It went back and forth like a rocking chair.

He had been in the woods and he'd been drinking. He remembered putting the empty bottles in the river, watching them bob in the stream before they finally sank. And he had drank more than beer — he'd stolen Rory's bottle of rye and had finished it off. That was why his head hurt so badly; he had a hangover. Then he'd come back, not wanting to go home, and not knowing where he could go. He remembered looking at the old Whyte house and maybe even going into the shed to sleep. Had that happened?

One night when Rory and his mother had taken Ralphie to the Moncton Mall, he drank so much that he couldn't remember what he did — a blackout, people called it. When he came to, he was in the cellar and had no idea how he got there. A blackout. That must have been what had happened. Maybe he had been caught inside the Whyte house and was in real bad trouble. He knew that sometimes people did terrible things in blackouts; they beat people up, killed them even. He and Annette had seen a movie where a woman woke up in bed next to a man she could not remember, with a knife sticking out of his heart.

What if he had done something terrible that he couldn't remember and they caught him and tied him up? Would the police be coming soon? He would have to go to court and maybe to jail and —

And Annette would get rid of their baby.

But right now Annette was very far away and he felt terrible that he had argued with her. If he could only be with her, he would hold her and kiss her and tell her how much he loved her. He tested each one of his bonds, starting with his left leg and moving around clockwise. There was more give on the ones binding his hands — he could move his elbows a little, but he could not get his hands near each other. The ropes were soft, and when he twisted his head to look up at his hands, he saw that they were ties, which for some reason frightened him even more. He started pulling his arms and legs, but all that this accomplished was to make the bed rock noisily, so he stopped. He had shaken off the quilt and it slid to the floor. He was terrified of what would happen when someone came into the room.

And just then, the bedroom door opened and someone did come in behind him, walking slowly to stand at the head of the bed, where Chaleur could not see. The room was very still — even the pigeons outside seemed to be listening.

Finally, Chaleur asked, "Who's there?"

At first his only answer was a sharp intake of breath.

"You were very sick," a man's voice said. "I saved you. I helped you." Although he sounded old, his voice made Chaleur think of an actor in some stupid school play who was saying words that someone else had written down. "I think you should stay quiet for a while."

"What're …"

"Yes?" The man moved closer to the bed and Chaleur could feel the warmth of his hand on the pillow near his head.

"What're you gonna do with me?"

The hand moved away. Chaleur caught a glimpse of it — it was old, like the man's voice when he said "I'll be back." And then Chaleur was all alone again.

He listened to footsteps walking away on a creaky wood floor and, hating himself for it, he started to cry.

Sandy had finally fallen asleep in the chair beside the bed and, when he woke up dreamless an hour or so later, he felt very refreshed. The boy was still asleep, stretched out like a starfish — if only this perfect time could go on and on so that Sandy could stay in it for as long as possible. But it would be dawn soon, and the boy would wake up. Sandy stood up and went to the window — there was quiet in the air and the sky was starting to lighten. He pulled down the blind and closed the curtains; the outside world did not have to interfere. As he tiptoed out of the room, he stopped beside the bed and touched the tender cheek. His whole body was singing — not since he was a little boy had he been so excited by the warmth of another human being.

He smiled as he left the room, shutting the door gently behind him, then he showered and changed into his good suit. Before he went downstairs to put on the coffee, he could not help himself: he peeked inside the bedroom and saw that nothing had changed. He almost went in to touch the boy again. *No*, he thought, *I'll just let him sleep*.

While the coffee was perking, he went out into the back shed to make sure that he had cleaned up all the traces of last night. He scrubbed the patch of floor again and opened the back door. Out in the yard, the air was very still and there were birds calling everywhere. He could faintly hear traffic humming in the air, and even this made him smile — he imagined the rest of the world driving away and leaving him alone in this new day.

The towel that he had used last night was still in the yard. When he went to pick it up, he saw that it was chewed and torn. Some animal had been at it — a dog, probably. He saw a beer bottle in the dewy grass under a bush and walked over to pick it up. He was taking it back into the house when he saw that old Mrs. LeBlanc from next door had come out into her yard and was smoking a cigarette and staring at him. Normally he would have nodded his head almost imperceptibly and she might have done the same, but this morning he smiled and, without thinking, waved at her. But he had raised the hand holding the bottle and she did not wave back. He shrugged and went into the house, where he shoved the towel into the garbage. He put the bottle in the sink.

He would have to be careful or someone might come and spoil everything. He would lock the house up, take the telephone off the hook, and erase the rest of the world. If Gloria came to clean, he would not answer the door. He should phone her, to tell her not to bother coming in for a while. But then again, why should he have to even talk to her? And what would he say?

He wanted to run upstairs — it all seemed like a wonderful dream — but decided that for good luck he would stand by the stove until the coffee was ready. The warm perked smell reminded him of his mother and he thought of how all of this would look to her. There was a boy upstairs in her bed, *tied* to her bed. In the eyes of Mother and the world, this was a bad thing, but he was moving beyond that tired, unhappy world now. What kind of influence could it ever have again?

Back in Sunday school he had been drilled in the Beatitudes, and the only one that had seized his attention was "Blessed are the meek: for they shall inherit the earth." He had thought that meeks were small, furry animals, like mink or weasels, and he had imagined them running across the lawn, covering it with a soft brown pelt. They would eat out of his hand. This idea had made him happy. But then, he discovered that the meek were not animals at all, but people who went around with their heads bowed down, doing as they were told, and that he was supposed to be one of them — submissive, obedient, and dull. Although he had inwardly rebelled, feeling that his version was far lovelier, he had said nothing. He listened attentively, memorized Scripture, and was patted on the head for being a good little boy. He had become one of the meek, growing up to inherit nothing but a life filled with loneliness, a business he hated, and a mother whose demands for his devotion had ruined his love for her.

Matthew 5:5 was a lie: the meek inherited nothing. You were told you would inherit the earth, then, when you had figured that one out, you were told that your reward was in heaven.

Throughout his life, the anger of the meek had been growing. Why should he care for a world that did not care for him?

All his life he had played by the rules, and none of them had made him happy. As the warm smell of coffee filled the room with comfort, he looked on all his kowtowing as a thing of the past. Even his kitchen could become a part of his new world; he had always hated the dark wainscotting — he and the boy would paint it white. Or even yellow. And there would be music.

He felt the old anger dissolving as his life gained purpose. The days of the future were not going to be like the days of the past. Each one would be thrilling and new and would provide reasons to go on living that had nothing to do with dull routine and the fear of others. Every waking moment would be filled with a bold gesture.

He opened a cupboard and took out the Rosenthal cup and saucer. It had always been the most elegant in the house: cream-coloured with a discreet design embossed in the china and a thin band of gold below the outside rim. He had loved it since he was a child, but Mother had always told him that it was too good to use, too good even for company. It had sat in the cupboard collecting dust for decades.

Very carefully, he washed it in the sink and then he poured his coffee into it. "And why shouldn't I?" he said aloud. He slammed the pot back on the stove to emphasize the point that his new-found joy was not a reward for the dutiful way he had lived his life, but was his because he had stepped outside of that world of committee meetings and impotent meekness to breathe a new, strong air. It was the air that Bach had breathed when his hand flew across empty staves, dropping notes from his pen like dark, brilliant stars. It was the air of the Van Eycks as they mixed oil with pigment and discovered the sweet green grass of heaven. Artists knew this joy and now he, Sandy Whyte, who had always been an outsider, a listener, a spectator, had joined the ranks of the mighty. He was no longer a member of any congregation: that world was so far, far behind him that it hardly even seemed to exist. The hands had fallen off the clock. Time of day, day of the week — none of this would matter any more. Here, in this house, in that magic room upstairs, he would keep the curtains drawn in a lovely and perpetual twilight. Because he had stopped playing by the rules, and had become courageous and true to what was possible, everything that he had yearned for was within his reach.

In the world outside, the sun was coming up.

How wonderful it would be if the boy simply agreed to Sandy's wishes; but he knew that the chances of that happening immediately were probably very slim. It was unfortunate that for a while he would have to remain here as a captive, but when he came to understand the new world that Sandy had to offer, they would be linked together. Captivated, both of them.

After his first coffee, he poured another cup and started to go upstairs. A shaft of sunlight shone through the branches of the maple trees beside the orchard and pierced the kitchen window, travelling across the room, through the door on the far wall and all the way down the long hallway. It gleamed in the dusty motes in the air and sparkled against the diamond panes of the front door at the other end of the house. As he walked along the hallway, Sandy lifted his hand and ran it flickering through the beam. To his knowledge, this had never happened before: the old house had been such a labyrinth that there was no way that a beam of pure light could pass directly through it. If he were to open the front door, the light would continue out into world. He walked under the sunbeam, and then turned and started up the stairs. Halfway up, he leaned over the banister and scooped his hand down into it, scattering the golden, floating dust like planets before the hand of God. Then a breeze rippled in the orchard and the leaves swayed, making the sunbeam flicker and then taking it away.

He had just reached the upstairs hall when he heard noises from Mother's room. The sounds startled him, and he spilled a bit of coffee on the floor. Bending down, he quietly set the cup beside the spill and mopped it up with a handkerchief from his pocket. He crept as silently as possible towards the bedroom door. He knew exactly what he would say.

As soon as he opened the door, he could tell that the boy had been struggling with his bonds. The quilt had fallen to the floor in a heap beside the bed. The boy's breathing was not the comfort it had been earlier — it was ragged and frightened-sounding, and for a terrible moment it echoed the last days of Mother in this same bed. The words he had planned to say flew out of his head and a ghastly feeling came over him. But then he concentrated on the tanned forearm beside the pillow: it was pointing towards him. He smiled and stepped into the room. He stood inside the door, not wanting the boy to see him just yet, and said nothing.

"Who's there?"

The voice startled him. It was not so sweet as he had imagined it would be. He thought of giving a made-up name, but that seemed absurd so he continued to say nothing. As the moment went on, he knew that he was in danger of losing all confidence. Then he realized that he could speak without answering the question.

"You were very sick," Sandy said quietly. "I saved you. I helped you." The boy was straining at his bonds and trying to look behind him. "I think you should stay quiet for a while."

The boy seemed to be thinking about this. He was so lovely. Could he possibly remember anything that had happened after he stumbled into the back shed? Did he know how tenderly Sandy had washed him? Did his body remember Sandy's hands gently wiping him clean? Sandy looked at the boy's arms, his hair spilling over the pillow. Although they had not changed since he kept his vigil by the bed, they were different somehow now that the boy was awake.

"Water?" the boy said. Of course he was parched, and Sandy thought of the centurion raising the sponge to Christ's lips. He knelt down so that he could not be seen and inched towards the head of the bed on his knees, reaching out his hand through the brass bars. That silky hair, that soft cheek had been his to touch less than an hour ago — he lay his hand on the pillow, realizing that he could not touch them so easily now.

"Yes?"

"What're you gonna do with me?"

No, not "water" but "what're" — Sandy pulled back his hand. It was much too early to answer this question. The boy would not yet understand that his intentions were honourable.

"I'll be back," he said and left the room. He walked down the hallway towards his own bedroom, picking up his coffee on the way. He placed it beside his bed. Without taking off his suit, he lay down and stared at the ceiling. He was not sure what to do next. If he made the wrong move, this perfect, delicate situation could turn sour. What would he do then? The boy needed to have confidence in him. *He'll have to be trained. Like a pet.*

As soon as he thought this, Sandy began to shiver.

No. No, it's not like that at all.

By mid-morning, Chaleur was as bored as he was frightened, and he had to go to the bathroom so badly that he was losing his mind.

"Hey!" he called out. "Buddy! Hey, buddy!"

Sandy ignored him for a few minutes, but realized that the neighbours might hear the shouting, so he got up and went to the bedroom door.

"Yes?" he said, not entering the room.

"I gotta go to the bathroom real bad."

"Oh." This was something that Sandy had not thought about and he cursed himself for being so stupid. His heart sank at the thought of what he would have to do; it was demeaning to them both.

Chaleur was twisting his head, trying to look towards the door.

Sandy took a step backwards into the dark of the hallway.

"C'mon. You gonna do something or just fucking stand there?"

"Don't swear."

"You'd swear too if you were tied up and gonna shit the bed."

The crassness of the boy made Sandy's stomach tighten.

"I'll be back."

"Jesus fuck, that's what you said five fucking hours ago. C'mon and let me go to the fucking toilet."

But Sandy was hurrying to the bathroom. He opened the linen closet and took out his mother's bedpan and, as he turned to leave, he saw himself in the old mirror above the sink. There he stood, pot-bellied and balding, his shoulders stooped, the bedpan clutched to his chest. The boy would make fun of the way he looked, he would be laughed at. He knew that he could not show the boy his face. He put the bedpan down and rummaged in the closet until he found one of his mother's formal hand towels. They were linen and for guests only, and all his life he had been told never to use them.

"Hey, you! Hey!" Chaleur knew that he was moments away from losing control and making this whole nightmare situation even worse. "Where the fuck are you?" He was clenching every muscle in his body and feeling that his bowels were about to erupt. "Jesus Christ," he groaned. "Jesus fucking Christ."

"Just a minute," Sandy called out as chipper as possible and he walked into the room with the bedpan trembling slightly in his hand. He had decided that a disguise might not be a bad idea for the time being and had tied the hand towel over the lower part of his face like a stage-coach robber from a Roy Rogers movie. On top of his head, he wore his mother's old shower cap.

Chaleur stared at him. He knew for sure now that he was in old man Whyte's house, and the old guy was crazier than anyone had ever said.

"Jesus Christ, took you long enough."

"Don't swear or I'll just walk out that door and never come back!"

Sandy's disguise had so startled Chaleur that he did not notice the bedpan for a few seconds.

"No fucking way," he said, "No fucking way I'm using that thing."

Sandy did not know what to do. But then, he acted as if it were still Mother lying in the bed.

"Calm down," he said, setting the bedpan on the mattress. "Just calm down."

He was starting to unfasten the boy's jeans when Chaleur started tossing about violently. "Get your hands off me, you fucking fruit. Get your fucking hands offa me!"

Sandy jumped back. A torrent of abuse was pouring out of the boy's mouth and there was real danger that he could be overheard from the street. Sandy reached inside his suit-jacket pocket and took out the coffee-stained handkerchief. He flapped it open, wadded it up, and stuck it in the boy's mouth, almost getting bitten in the process. Then he stood back.

"I did not want to do that," he said, "but you left me no choice. Now *lie still* or you'll mess yourself!" He was surprised by the power in his voice.

Chaleur had to stop struggling — if he did not concentrate on his breathing, the handkerchief would choke him. He lay quietly.

Sandy opened the boy's pants and pulled down the zipper.

"Lift your bum," he said, and pulled the pants down the boy's legs. How differently he had imagined his first glimpse of those legs and how differently he had imagined they would look. Not so skinny and pale, but sturdier and the walnut colour of the boy's arms. "Almost there," he said, and he tugged down the underwear. He was afraid to look at the boy's penis.

"Will you promise to be quiet?" he said.

Chaleur nodded.

Sandy took the gag from his mouth and opened it up. Daintily he spread it out over the boy's thighs. Then he put his arm under the boy's back, lifting him from the mattress as he slid the bedpan beneath him. From the lump under the handkerchief, he realized that the penis was pointing towards the boy's belly. He moved one finger towards it.

"Touch my dick and I'll kill you."

"Don't panic," he said. "We just don't want you to get wet." And with his finger he prodded the penis through the cotton handkerchief so that it was hanging down between the boy's legs. "There, all comfy?"

Chaleur glared at him. "I'll call you when I'm done," he said. Sandy stood quietly for a moment and then left the room. He did not want to listen, but he was barely out the door when Chaleur's bowels exploded into the bedpan.

A few minutes later, when the doorbell started to ring, he was gripped with fear.

Lying in agony on top of the bedpan, Chaleur heard it too, and prayed that his ordeal might be coming to an end.

THIRTEEN

It was almost eleven before they piled into the car: Junior and Danny up front and Raymond wedged in the back between Hal and his sister. Gloria had made sandwiches for them all and she had to go downtown twice because she forgot to buy pop. "I'm all buggered up this morning," she told Mama. "I just can't think straight."

Last night she had tried to keep things lively during supper, but Raymond had been the only other person who wanted to talk. In hopes that she could make them laugh, she had started to tell the story about the time they had dressed up the neighbourhood dogs for a circus in the backyard. No one but Hal seemed very interested, and she had not been sure if he was just trying to be polite. Did she like him? She wasn't sure. She knew that she should, of course, because Raymond must like him a lot, but he was so quiet and nervous that it hardly surprised her when

she overheard Junior calling him a "little fairy snob" to Danny.
Junior and Danny had hardly ever lifted their eyes from their
plates; they wolfed down their food and left the table as quickly
as they could.

Her little brother had not made things easier for any of them.
Without really telling anyone that he and Hal were sick, Raymond had talked as if they had known about it all along. He had
gone on about blood work and T-cell counts in the way that
Ruthie Crossman had blabbed about her first pregnancy. Everyone had been uncomfortable and not known what to say. Gloria
had wanted to ask what some things meant, but she was afraid
that Raymond and his boyfriend would think that she was stupid.
What were T-cells anyway? It was as if her brother was living in
a new place where they spoke a whole new language. All she was
sure of was that nothing Raymond talked about was good news.
If only someone else at the table would have tried to help her get
a conversation going.

So when Raymond said that he wanted to go up the coast
to the Bouctouche Dune, she had seized on the idea and committed her brothers to going. "We'd love to go with you!" she
said, clapping her hands. "What a great idea!" A nice drive and
a picnic might be just the thing to get things moving. She knew
that Raymond was the only one who really wanted to go.

Just after they finished Mama's pies, which Hal said were the
best he had ever eaten, Danny had asked, "So, Hal, what do you
do?" but when he answered that he worked in a bookstore,
Raymond had opened his big mouth and said "A *gay* bookstore"
in such a way that Gloria knew he wanted to make them all
squirm. Junior mumbled something and left the room. Gloria
couldn't help herself — she felt sorry for Hal.

This morning Raymond was up early, and he was down in
the kitchen driving Mama crazy because he wanted to make

pancakes for everybody. "Raymond," she said, "your brothers are still in bed, Pop only ever has toast, and Gloria and me had our bran flakes an hour ago."

"You've never had my pancakes. They melt in your mouth."

"Later in the week, okay?" She almost said "Why don't you go out and play" because he was nagging her like a little boy. He sat down in a chair by the kitchen counter, where he always seemed to be in her way. "Radio says it's gonna be a hot one today," she told him, "so I don't want to be in this kitchen after noon." She was peeling potatoes for a salad at suppertime. "Why don't you go down to the store with your sister?"

But Gloria had snuck out of the house without him. She was not sure what he might say to people in the grocery store and she wanted to get used to being around him more before they went out in public together. She felt so guilty about it that she bragged to everybody she saw that her whole family was home and even told the clerk at the check-out how much Raymond had made them all laugh at supper last night. "He's as funny as a fit," she said and tried to laugh as if she were remembering one of his jokes.

Raymond took yesterday's paper out on the back steps to read the obituaries, but the air seemed so clean to him that he could hardly concentrate. Whenever Mama looked out the window, she could see that his eyes were closed and his head was tilted back; he was sniffing the air like a little dog.

Hal had woken up early, but he stayed in bed, pretending to be asleep. He was worried about spending time with any of Raymond's family, even Gloria, who had, after all, tried to be nice to him. Mama had tried too, but she never looked at him when she spoke. Raymond's father had ignored him completely. The only thing he'd said so far was "I'd shake your hand but mine's all dirty." The people in this household made him nervous. He had not expected to be welcomed with open arms, but he could not tell if the Maurice family was acting out of shyness or resentment. And every time Raymond had opened his mouth he made things worse.

Raymond had been right about Junior though: it had been one thing to hear stories about Junior, but it was quite another thing to sit in a room with him. He looked big and flabby, but one look at his forearms told Hal that he was powerfully built, and the scratchy tattoo on one of them — "Ginette" it said — had convinced him that Junior was the kind of guy who would not think twice before he bashed the hell out of you. It did not take a genius to figure out that he was not pleased to see his kid brother, and even less thrilled to meet his brother's boyfriend. Last night Raymond had wanted to make love even though it was obvious that he was too tired to even start. "No, babe," Hal had said.

"I want everybody to hear us," Raymond said impishly.

"Well, I don't. Why are you acting so weird?" But Raymond had already started to snore. Hal watched him sleep, and then the exhaustion of the train ride finally caught up with him and he was dreaming about his own family.

Junior and Danny slept in till almost nine. When everyone else had gone to bed last night, they had headed down the street to the Club for a few beers. Neither one of them wanted to spend a day with Raymond and Hal on the Dune, but Mama had taken Pop aside after supper, and Pop had taken them aside after that and told them to do it as a favour to her.

"Those two don't look so hot," he said. "And if anything happened up there, Gloria would have too much on her hands."

"What the hell does Raymond want to go there for anyway?" Junior muttered.

Pop shrugged and shook his head. "It's a fine mess."

"We'll go tomorrow," Danny said. "But I don't think we should spend all week running the roads with Raymond. I don't think the kid's strong enough."

"Oh, Jesus," Junior moaned. "We're not gonna catch this, are we?"

"Oh c'mon, Junior. Even you know that's stupid."

"I do?" He was not happy about any of this. "Doctors don't know shit. We could all get this damn thing from the toilet after one of them has a crap."

Pop stood for a moment shaking his head. "A fine mess," he said again, and he turned and went back to Mama.

At the Club they had both been very quiet: Danny hardly said a word and Junior kept staring at his beer, saying "Jesus Christ" over and over like a sigh.

"You gonna call Ginette?" Danny had asked after last call.

"Aw, bite me," Junior answered. "You gonna call *Marsha*?" As soon as he said it, he felt terrible. Gloria had told him that Marsha had made fun of Danny's arm when she left him. They walked home in silence.

This morning they had both come down into the kitchen slightly hung over.

"Eat something quick," Mama said. And then, bending towards them, she whispered, "Your brother's been bugging me about wanting to make pancakes, so if you're already eating maybe he'll forget about it and stay out of my hair."

The three of them were looking out the window at Raymond, who was down on his hands and knees smelling the forget-me-nots by the lilac hedge. He was crawling back and forth between a blue patch and a pink one.

Danny sighed. "Poor little bugger."

"Jesus Christ."

Mama gave Junior a poke with the back of her hand. "Watch your tongue."

The Dune was almost an hour's drive up the coast. Raymond wanted them to take the old shore road that wound along the coast through village after village. "All aboard," he called out, "for Shediac, Grande-Digue, Cocagne, St. Thomas de Kent, Bouctouche, and the Great Bouctouche Dune!" But Junior, who was driving, said the shore drive was a waste of time — it would take them twice as long to get there.

"But Hal should see the coast."

"There's lots of time," Hal said.

"You have to drive through beautiful downtown Cocagne just once before you die."

"Oh Christ," Junior muttered, backing the car out of the driveway.

"I can see it another day, Raymond."

"Stop off at Sandy Whyte's place first," Gloria called out, relieved that she could change the subject. "I have to tell him that I can't clean this week and the phone's been busy all morning."

"Who's he got to talk to?" Junior asked.

"Every old woman in town," said Danny.

"You should drop in and see him, Raymond," Junior said. "He probably hasn't laid eyes on a real fruit in years."

"Kiss me arse."

"Dream on."

This exchange made Gloria relax just the tiniest bit. It was the first sign of their old banter and she welcomed it. Maybe they could find a way to tease each other and get along after all. Then, as they were waiting for the light at Main Street, Raymond pointed to an old lady walking through the tiny park.

"Look! It's old Vyia Rodd! Bitch!"

"Be quiet!" Gloria said, backhanding him sharply. "Vyia Rodd's been dead more than five years."

"Well who's that old bitch?"

"Her name's Mrs. Motier and her daughter-in-law's the minister at the United Church. You've never seen her before."

"Why didn't anybody tell me the old bitch was dead?" He turned to Hal. "She was our teacher in primary school."

"I know," said Hal. "You told me." Raymond had also told him that she had died, but Hal decided not to mention it.

Junior had to inch his way through town because Main Street was packed with tourists; it was fifteen minutes before he pulled into Sandy Whyte's, easing the car around the deep potholes in the big circular drive and stopping at the foot of the walk.

"I won't be a minute." Gloria ran up to the front door and rang the bell.

"This place looks like hell," Raymond said.

Junior shook his head. "The old fairy's not home."

"Car's there though," Danny said.

Gloria rang the bell again. She tried peering through the diamond windows of the big front door but could see nothing. The inside doors were closed too, the house shut up as tight as a drum. She leaned into the bell.

Junior honked the horn. "Leave him a note, for chrissakes," he called out, but there was no paper in the car and no one had a pen. Gloria rang the bell one last time.

"I'll try again on the way back," she said when she got back in the car. "I don't know where he could be."

"He musta heard Ahh was in town," Raymond crooned in a Southern accent, "an' he is out buyin' hisself a suitable outfit."

As they were pulling away, Hal turned around and looked back at the house. He could see a rotten board hanging under the eaves and pigeons walking along the edge of the roof. The paint was peeling and all the curtains were drawn — it was a house in mourning for itself. Then he could swear that the curtain in one of the upstairs windows was pushed back ever so slightly and a vague, grey figure brushed against it. He squinted, but the curtain was back in place as if it had not been touched for many years, and the old house seemed emptier than ever. Hal turned back and said nothing.

They drove up on the new highway, Raymond moaning all the way because there was no view, which, Hal had to admit, was certainly the truth. The road was a straight line through the woods a couple of miles inland; along its sides, flowerless overgrown grasses covered the embankment up to the bushes and trees. All of nature here seemed scruffy and poor. Even the signs along the road were shabby and tired-looking, like advertisements for places that had gone out of business long ago. Twice the car burst through the woods to cross wide, dull bridges, as ordinary as any concrete overpass, and Raymond pointed to their right, where the rivers widened downstream towards the villages along the coast.

"There's Shediac Bridge!" he said, or "There's Cocagne!"

"Some thrill," Junior muttered.

Raymond and Gloria yakked a bit in the back seat, and Hal, sitting beside them, hardly said a word. With all the windows wide open and the hot air roaring past, it was almost impossible to talk anyway.

Danny was in the front seat, looking straight ahead. He never turned around; he was thinking of the beer he had put in the trunk of the car, wondering how long he could wait before having one without his sister giving him a hard time. Junior was driving with his right hand; his left arm was out the open window and he was drumming a rhythm on the side of his car with two fingers. Ginette's favourite Randy Travis song had come into his head and he was rapping out the refrain to "Forever and Ever, Amen" over and over again. He was thinking about the time that her kids had come to stay with her and they had gone to the beach and played Frisbee with a stray dog.

He turned off at Bouctouche and they drove along the tiny main street, past the huge Catholic church, and then, on the other side of town, the convent and the graveyard.

"Slow down!" Raymond called and pointed past the graveyard out into the bay. "That's it, way out there."

Across the still, blue water Hal could see a long finger of land a mile or so away; near the water, it looked as green as a pasture, and, above that, the gently arching dunes were a soft silhouette along the horizon.

"There's buildings at the end, see? And a lighthouse."

Hal squinted, looking for them and, seconds after he found them, the small white dots that were these buildings wavered in the hot air. At that same moment, Raymond grabbed his hand, and Hal felt the connection between his lover's excitement and the Dune itself. Quiet and remote-looking across the bay, it seemed as strange and mysterious to Hal as he thought it must once have been to Raymond.

A few miles later, in the middle of a big bend in the road, Junior turned off and parked next to a handful of cars by a little beach. They could see a few women sitting together talking and watching their kids play in the water.

"God, I haven't been here for years," Gloria said.

"Me either," said Junior. "And I wish I could've kept it that way."

They were standing outside the car and Junior was unlocking the trunk. Danny and Hal said nothing.

"Don't be so full of shit," Raymond said.

"Just a crummy sandbar," Junior growled. "Beach in town is way better."

Raymond took off his shorts and threw them in the trunk. When he took off his shirt, Gloria and her brothers stared at him and then turned away. His pale chest was thin and hollow-looking and there were lesions along his side. Junior and Danny looked at her and she shook her head slightly as if to say "Not a word." Hal knew that Raymond had not noticed this exchange. He could feel that Junior was looking at him and knew there was nothing but anger in his face.

"I've got the pop," said Gloria. "Who wants to carry the picnic basket?"

"I'll take it." But when Hal reached for the basket, Danny took it out of his hand. "It's okay. I'll take it the first stretch," he said. "You guys start out, Junior and I'll be right behind you."

Raymond and Gloria were moving down the beach to the water's edge and Hal followed them. Danny kicked off his shoes and threw them in the trunk.

"This is fucking dandy," Junior whispered, and he slammed down the lid.

The dune stretched out from the coast at a forty-five-degree angle and moved out into the strait, a long thin peninsula of sand and grass. With Raymond leading the way, the five of them walked in single file on the wet sand at the edge of the water.

"Isn't it beautiful?" Raymond asked Hal. "I told you."

Hal nodded. It was beautiful. Long, lonely, and beautiful. They were walking along a fairly wide beach that sloped upwards from the shoreline to the crest of the dune, where grasses bent gently in the breeze. The light brown sand stretched as far ahead of them as he could see. "How long is it?"

"Six, seven miles."

"We're not going to the end, are we?"

"Not with me, you're not," Gloria said. "Let's just go till we get away from everybody and have some privacy."

"Skinny-dipping!" Raymond hollered and ran ahead through the water. The huge still gulls that were standing quietly on the tiny sandbars offshore flew away when he got close to them.

"That's the way seagulls should be," Hal said to Gloria. "The goddam ones in Toronto are real beggars. It's disgusting." She smiled and walked a bit ahead of him. Even though he had said "goddam" he knew that he sounded too formal. Why was it so hard to say anything that sounded natural? Gloria's big rump swayed ahead of him in her frilly pink bathing suit. Her yellow tee shirt said "No Problem" in faded red and green letters.

Raymond stopped to catch his breath. His body was already tired, but he was filled with exhilaration. Although the sun was hot, there was a wonderful breeze from the water. They were passing the remains of what looked like an old wharf, a couple of dozen pilings sunk in the sand. He pointed to one that stuck up only a foot or so; the sea had worn it down to a fine, soft point. "Wouldn't you like to sit on that!" he called out to Hal. "That there's a toy for a big girl!"

Danny wondered why Raymond was trying to make Hal feel uncomfortable. Hal said nothing, just picked up a piece of driftwood and flung it into the water.

"Nice pitch, Carter."

"Oh, Raymond, even I know that Joe Carter isn't a pitcher."

A strong current carried the driftwood along beside them like a faithful little boat.

As Raymond walked, he became silent. The dune was more than a place to go swimming or have a picnic, it was a kind of state that he knew he could never fully grasp. From the time he had first seen it, this place had echoed an isolation within him and brought him comfort: it made him ache.

Last year, when he had taught a design workshop on a reserve on Manitoulin Island, he had been driven around and shown the sacred Ojibway places. Raymond had felt the same stillness inside him that he felt here and, for the first time in years, had yearned for home. Toronto is where he would always live and, in all probability, where he would die, but when he called it "home" it did not make his bones shiver.

Although he knew that the dune shifted each year with the tides and storms, it would always be the same abiding place that he had discovered when he was in high school and used to borrow Pop's car to drive here and be alone. Back then he would come up by himself and walk all day. He would take off his clothes and walk naked along the edge of the strait, his clothes in a knapsack that he balanced on his head like an African. He would talk out loud, saying things like "I am a homosexual," things that he dared not say anywhere else. A part of him had wanted to find someone like himself walking along the shore, but another, equal portion had hoped to be perfectly alone and not see anybody, and, usually, he never did.

He had never walked all the way to the end of the dune.

A few sunbathers were scattered along the beach, so far apart that they were like little Crusoes living in their own lost worlds; everybody on the dune gave each other a wide berth. After an hour's walking, there was no one else. In all that time only one fishing boat passed by out in the strait.

It was so quiet that Hal felt they could have stepped outside of time. "I want to go up there and take a look around," he said to Raymond.

"Me too."

They crossed the beach and climbed up the side of the dune. At the crest, the air was a degree cooler, the sun more gentle on their skin. The sharp cord grass cut into Hal's feet, so he stood very still as he surveyed the other side. In a thousand varieties of green the grass stretched down a wider expanse than the beach towards the bay. Breezes swept across it in gentle surges: patches as dark as emerald were ruffled into olive or a soft milky green and then dark again. The leeward side of the dune was in constant motion. There were wild flowers everywhere, all of them tiny and bright, and grasshoppers and butterflies flickered in the air. Songbirds were calling and skimming over the surface of the grass — why could he not hear them from the beach side? An old thin road, more like a sandy path, curled through the grass. Across the bay they could see tiny cars travelling along the road that had brought them here. The cars seemed very far away, as if they were separated not only by water and distance, but by time as well. Raymond put his arm about Hal's waist and they stood together, looking down and around them.

"Look." Raymond was pointing at the dune lying ahead of them as far as they could see; it looked like it might go on forever. "Isn't it like the train?"

"What?"

"Like when we were on the train looking out at it ahead of us. Except that had woods on either side and this has water. It's the same kind of travelling."

"You idiot. This isn't moving."

"*Au contraire, mon chéri*, this is the most moving place on earth."

A few yards away from them a small, sand-coloured bird started hopping about frantically and whistling.

"Poor thing," Hal said. "She's got a broken wing."

"No. Her nest's nearby and she's trying to distract us. Piping plover." The little bird had started running; if her yellow-orange legs could make a noise, Raymond thought it would be click-

click-click-click. "They're almost extinct," he said. "Feathers for hats. Death by millinery. And dune buggy."

Gloria had waded in the water up to the bottom of her bathing suit. The drop off was fairly steep and she did not want to get her tee shirt wet. Her feet hurt from walking and she was getting hungry. She turned and watched Raymond and Hal standing together on the bluff. Her little brother was so skinny, so frail, that she wanted to hold him, but his skin and his body frightened her. She wished he would put on a shirt. She thought that Hal should make him do it — didn't he care about her brother? Junior and Danny had caught up with her and they were waiting as she waded back to the shore. Raymond jumped and slid down the sandy slope, yelping "Yi-yi-yi!" He started running further up the beach.

"Stop right there!" Junior hollered. "That's far enough."

"Oh come on," Raymond whined.

"It all looks the friggin' same no matter how far we go," Junior said, tossing his towel on the sand and sitting down on top of it.

"No, it doesn't," said Raymond. "And besides, the further we go …"

"Yeah?"

"Then the further out we are," he finished.

"Let's eat something," Hal said, walking over to the others.

Danny said, "Gimme a beer there, Sis."

Gloria had opened the cooler. As she started rooting around for the drinks, Raymond pulled down his bathing suit. "I'm going in," he said. There were more lesions on his thighs. His penis dangled between his skinny legs like a little snail. Tossing his trunks in the air, he shouted, "C'mon all you nudists!"

Nobody moved for a few seconds. Gloria caught her breath

and handed a can of beer to Danny. "Here you go," she said calmly.

Raymond looked from one to the other. "I can't believe that I'm the only nudist in the crowd!" he shouted.

"I hate swimming, you know that," Junior grunted.

"I'll have my beer first," said Danny, "then maybe I'll take a dip." But he did not want to take off his shirt and let Hal and Raymond see his arm.

"Gloria?"

"Well, I'm not going in bare naked, that's for sure." For a moment she did not know what to do. She could not stand here and let her brother run around without his clothes on. She looked at the strait and suddenly hauled off her tee shirt.

"Last one in's a rotten egg!" she called and ran past Raymond and into the water. He followed her, his penis bouncing up and down. "C'mon, Hal!"

Hal was so hungry that he did not want to go into the water. He took off his shirt, aware that Raymond's brothers were scrutinizing his back and legs.

"Well," he said, "I guess I better go in." But he just stood there.

"Hal?" Danny asked.

"Yeah?"

"Those marks, the ones on Raymond's side? What are they?"

"Kaposi's," he said. "Kaposi's sarcoma."

"Oh."

"It was a lot worse in April. He was hoping they'd be all gone before, you know, he came home."

"Sure."

"Hal! Hurry up, you big sissy!" Raymond was calling him. He shrugged and slowly turned and walked away from the brothers into the water, which was colder than he wanted it to be, but it did feel good after their long walk in the sun. He realized that Danny probably did not know anything about Kaposi's and that he should probably talk to him about it. It was not a task to look forward to. Ahead of him, Raymond was slapping the water, splashing and laughing.

On the shore, Danny took a long drink and looked away from the swimmers.

"Get me a beer, will you?" Junior demanded.

"I'm the friggin' cripple. Get it yourself."

"You're closer," Junior said, but he crawled over to the cooler and fished around inside it. "It's a friggin' freak show," he said sadly.

After a moment Danny said, "Raymond doesn't seem right somehow."

"Aren't you brilliant."

"No, don't you think he seems kind of, I dunno, like he's acting funny?"

"He always acted funny — he's a fruit!" After a minute he added, "I feel like kicking the shit out of his little fairy friend for getting him sick."

"They were both sick already when they met. Raymond told me last night. They met at a funeral for some guy they both knew."

"Dandy, that's just friggin' dandy."

Out in the water, Raymond lay floating on his back. The current was strong and he gave in to it, let it carry him along like Hal's faithful driftwood. If he just paddled a little with his feet, how long would it take him to reach the end of the dune? Way out there, miles from anything else, what could he find? He knew there was a lighthouse because he could see it from the shore, and there were other little specks of white. When he was young, he had imagined a little cove where he would meet a man who would take him into a cottage and hold him — he used to think about this on summer nights before he went to sleep. But he did not need that dream any more. There had been men since then; there was Hal, right now, right here with him. If he and Hal could go to the very end of the dune, would they find the place that would stop the yearning he felt? The water felt so clean, so good, that he kept drifting; he giggled — for the first time in months he felt happy.

Gloria and Hal had been swimming on their own for a few minutes when they realized that Raymond was not beside them. "Raymond?" she said. Hal lifted his head out of the water, looking around.

"He's over there,"

"This current's pretty strong," she said, and Hal nodded, following her as she swam towards her brother. In a minute she was beside him. He had spread his thin legs open in a vee, his penis had shrivelled up in the cool water and was stuck between his legs like a button.

"C'mon," said Hal swimming up to them, "I'm starving."

"Party-poopers."

"Raymond, c'mon!"

He rolled over onto his stomach and began to swim to shore. For a moment he panicked. The water started pulling him backwards and down, and his arms seemed so flimsy that he thought the current might snap them, but he struggled along with the others and soon his feet could touch the bottom. When the three of them came ashore they were all surprised that the strait had carried them fifty feet away from where Junior and Danny were sitting.

Gloria handed out egg-salad sandwiches and pop, and opened a big bag of potato chips. Raymond paced back and forth, singing "There's a Place for Us."

"Raymond," Junior said, "will you put your bathing suit on? Your sister's here, for chrissakes."

Raymond wiggled his hips. "Is my penis embarrassing you?" He made it bob up and down. The others looked away.

Gloria turned to Hal. "What's the height of conceit?" she said.

"Huh? I don't know."

"A fly, floating down the river with a hard-on, screaming 'Raise the drawbridge! Raise the drawbridge!'"

Raymond groaned when Hal laughed at her dumb joke, but he pulled on his bathing suit and sat down to eat with the others.

"Good sandwich, Sis," said Danny.

"Oh, they're all right, I suppose," she replied. "Thanks."

After lunch they moved closer to a curve in the dune and lay down in the shade. Raymond was beside Hal, staring out at the water. "Home," he said. "Home sweet home." He was face down on his towel, his shoulder brushing against Hal's. A few soft clouds were drifting by high above them and there was the occasional screech of a gull. Hal thought that, if it were night, they would be able to see every star in the universe. Everyone was very quiet. Everything had come to a lull. Whenever they opened their eyes, the world around them was white and blinding.

Gloria's cheek rested on her folded arms; she couldn't help herself — she kept sneaking looks at Raymond's spots. They made her think about watching *Ben Hur* on TV with him one Easter, about the part where Ben Hur found his mother and sister in the lepers' colony. They were ashamed, but Ben Hur had taken them to Jesus and they had been cured. She dozed, dreaming that she was trying to find Raymond, who was lost in the desert. "He's right around here," she kept saying, all the while looking at her watch because the movie was almost over. She went on walking, calling Raymond's name over and over.

A few feet away, his big hands folded on his beer belly, Junior was dreaming about sneaking Ginette through a window. When he started taking off her clothes, her breasts were brown-coloured and strange. At first he thought that her nipples had grown so big that they had spread out over her whole chest, but then he saw that this was not so. He pretended to touch them because he wanted her to think that he had not even noticed, but suddenly they jumped into his hands, startling him, and he woke up hearing her cry. A gull was screaming overhead. He muttered to himself and sat up. He went for a walk, taking off his sneakers and sticking his feet in the cool, salty water. Junior had always complained to Ginette when she made him wear a condom. "Why bother?" he had said. "Condoms are for kids." He had stopped wearing them when he slept with a girl from Moncton who was on the pill. Condoms were kid stuff from the days when the Sheik had tormented cottagers. He knew that it was impossible for him or Ginette to get sick the way that Raymond and his boyfriend were, so what was the point?

Danny and Hal could not sleep. Hal had brought along a book of poetry, and he read through Elizabeth Bishop's "Questions of Travel" over and over again, unable to concentrate because he was worried about the way Raymond was acting. Before their friend Clive jumped out that hospital window, he had been arrested for walking to the corner store half-naked. His body had been covered with lesions. Hal knew that he could not stand it if Raymond went crazy that way, and he realized that he wanted to be the first one to go. But if Raymond won the Widows' Tournament, who would there be to look after him? Raymond would be hopeless on his own.

Danny had stared at Raymond's back for a long time, wishing that he was the sort of person who could say something that would matter. He felt that he understood why Raymond was acting big and bratty, but he also understood why Junior was angry and upset. He wanted to sleep, even for a few minutes, but his hand was starting to bother him. As hard as he tried to ignore it, he could not stop imagining that it was itching. He cursed himself for being stupid enough to waste time wishing he could scratch the back of a hand that no longer existed. He drank another beer.

At three o'clock, Gloria sat up and said, "If we don't head back now, we'll be late for supper." She looked around. "Where's Junior?"

"Right here." He was walking up behind her; the bottoms of his jeans were wet.

"Raymond," Hal said, touching his lover's back. "Wake up, babe. Time to go."

Raymond lifted his head. "What?"

"Time to go."

"Oh." He rolled over onto his back and sat up. He looked down the beach to where the dune curved out into the strait a bit. Then, seeing something, he leaned forwards. "Oh, look," he said, pointing at the far-off crest. Silhouetted against the clouds, the grasses were gently moving in the breeze.

"What?" asked Gloria.

"I've dreamed about that little house and there it is."

"Where?"

"Right down there on the top of the dune."

Junior looked at Danny and shook his head.

"I can't see it, Raymond." Gloria stood up and squinted.

"Tell us about it," Hal said and he sat up on the sand beside Raymond.

"We must have walked to the end of the dune, because that's where I always thought that little house would be." He was smiling. "See the veranda?"

"I love verandas."

"And the porch swing?"

"The perfect place for mint juleps."

Raymond giggled. Gloria was still squinting with a puzzled look on her face. Danny touched her leg and when she looked at him he shook his head. She looked back at Raymond and then slowly sat down.

"Don't you love those shingles?" Raymond continued.

"What colour are they?"

"Junior would say grey, because they haven't been painted, but when the sun hits them the right way, they turn silver. They just shine."

Junior started to mutter something, but Danny shot him a look that said "Keep your big mouth shut."

"What else?" said Hal.

"Those great big windows with deep sills — you can sit on them when they're wide open. I bet they're covered with shells and little stones. Sand dollars. Don't you love walking on these soft wood floors in your bare feet? Sand between the planks. And when you go to bed at night the curtains blow halfway across the room and the air is so fresh you can sleep like a baby."

Gloria was getting upset: Raymond was talking about a cottage that wasn't there and Hal was leading him on. She didn't understand what was happening but she knew that she had to be a part of it. "Who lives there?" she asked.

Raymond moved to his feet. "Let's go see," he said.

"Jesus Christ."

"Junior!" Danny was standing.

Raymond looked over at the dune. He could see the little house flicker, an object wobbling in the heat. *It's winking at me*, he thought. Then he looked down at the others. They were all watching him. "What's wrong?" He looked back towards the house again. Where was it? "Am I the only one who can see it?" he asked.

Hal stood up next to him. "Apparently so."

Raymond suddenly looked confused. "Where am I?" he asked.

"You're with us, babe. On the big dune."

"That's what I thought. And you couldn't see the house?" He looked up at the dune. The little house with its veranda and silver shingles was gone.

"Must've been a mirage," Danny said.

And Gloria nodded her head. "Remember that time we was all out in Alphonse's boat and it was real hot that day and when we looked back at the point we could see the wharf double?"

Raymond nodded. "I think so," he said in a little voice.

"It must've been a cottage somewhere else," Danny said. "The sun is so hot it just looked like it was there."

"Yes. That must be it." Raymond sounded frightened.

"We've had too much sun," Hal said, tousling Raymond's hair. "We should be getting back."

Gloria started packing the basket, tossing everything in so quickly that she had to jam down the lid. She resented the way that Hal had touched Raymond's hair.

"Can't we swim back?" Raymond said, brightening.

"The current's too strong, we'd have to swim against it."

It was five o'clock before they got back to the car, which was hot as a furnace. Raymond crawled into the back seat and fell asleep. No one spoke. No one thought to remind Gloria that she had wanted to stop off at Sandy Whyte's place.

FOURTEEN

T he town beach was so jammed with tourists that the only parking spot Margaret could find was in the lot furthest from the water. When she got out of her car, she had to thread her way through a hot maze of asphalt and automobiles, resenting all the while the swarms of people from Away. How would she ever find that girl in this crowd? What on earth had she been thinking when she suggested that they meet? When the other women in the Hotline office overheard Margaret talking to the girl on the phone, they had looked at her as if she were crazy. The people here were looking at her the same way. Then she realized that in her dress and pantyhose, with her little white sling-back pumps, she was as out of place as she would have been in an evening gown at the post office. Everyone else was half-naked. She finally reached the path that circled past the canteen and walked along up a little hill to the benches.

A hedge separated her from all the people on the sand below. The beach looked common and ordinary through the thick, muggy heat. On Monday night, the dunes and the sea had been shrouded in the warm dark, and she had felt that she was on the edge of something boundless, unknowable; today there were so many people that the place looked a little banal: any beach, anywhere. The recent changes made the place unfamiliar to her. She had seen them before, of course — she had driven Minnie down to see the new landscaping, the paths and boardwalks, the canteen and beach houses — but whenever she thought about the beach, she thought about the place she had known as a little girl. She had come here with her parents and, early every July, the annual church picnic was held at the far end, past the lighthouse. The changes were practical and attractive and, she supposed, good for the environment, but they were not designed for local people. This was no longer the town beach; it existed for tourists.

She had pictured the girl so clearly the other night. Had she seen her on this beach or on the lost beach of her childhood? She could not be sure.

The asphalt was so hot that she could feel it burning through the soles of her shoes; when she reached the boardwalk, there was a little relief, but there was no breeze off the water. The air was thick and still. All the benches were occupied and no one in sight looked remotely like the girl on the telephone. Carrie. No, her name was Annette. She imagined her as small and dark with lovely plump arms.

On the closest bench, a big, sloppy woman with peroxided hair sat in cut-off jeans and an old tee shirt. A mess of half-naked children ran screaming around her, and she was smoking, not even trying to read the magazine that sat open on one great, sunburnt thigh. As Margaret walked past her, the woman barked at the boy who was lying across the bench beside her; he was ramming a small plastic car against the mountain of her body.

The next bench was no better: a grim-looking couple sat on it, glaring out at the water; it did not seem possible that they had spoken pleasantly to each other or anyone else for years. Their sunhats announced that they had both enjoyed themselves in Florida. Perhaps their children had sent them the hats: Bob and Cindy had given Minnie a tee shirt that claimed she had been to Disney World. The couple's tough, dark skin made Margaret think of reptiles, but their faces were neither so frightening nor so wise. They looked more like fleshy vegetables, with scowls.

There was flesh everywhere, and not much of it was attractive as far as she was concerned. One lovely-looking couple walked past her; tall and slender, with honey-coloured skin. The woman's blonde hair reminded her of the Dooneys. By now the Dooneys would be getting ready to preach to another group in another town. What a strange sort of existence that must be. What would they think of Margaret now? Was she doing something terribly wrong?

When the couple had walked a few steps ahead of her, she could see that they had their hands on each other's bums in a casual way that struck Margaret as bold enough to be indecent. And then, suddenly, the woman nuzzled the man's neck and, blocking the path, they stopped to kiss. Margaret had to step onto the grass to walk around them. Her left heel slipped on a pebble and she half-stumbled. The man said something in French to his wife and she giggled. Then Margaret knew that they were mean and showy; they were kissing each other just to make a spectacle of themselves.

On the third bench a large middle-aged man in a tiny bathing suit was sitting by himself, reading a thick book. The opposite end of his bench was her only choice. "Do you mind if I sit here?"

she asked. Without looking up, he grunted and shifted his body sightly away from her, and she sat, annoyed that he could not even pretend to be civil. He had the kind of abundant, wiry body hair that made her think of dirt. Her father had been quite hairless and doughy, yet she had always associated body hair with the weight of his crushing, dimpled flesh. She decided to ignore the man as completely as he was ignoring her.

She looked out over the hedge and down onto the beach; it was so crowded that she could scarcely see any sand at all. Under scads of beach umbrellas and lying on thousands of towels, what seemed like hundreds of thousands of people were all squeezed together along the strip between the dunes and the sea. Dogs barked, children shrieked and hollered, people laughed, and dozens of radios were in competition. Margaret looked up and down the beach — to her left, the people stretched as far as she could see and, to her right, they seemed to peter out a few hundred yards away, but the edge of a sandhill blocked her view. There was a time when so many people so involved in the enjoyment of their own lives would have caused her to feel alone and left out, but today she thought that she was the only person present who was not completely insane. How could anyone be fool enough to lie around half-naked in the sun, especially after the radio and television had been talking about skin cancer for years now? At the same time she knew that her pantyhose were ridiculous and her dress was too heavy for the weather. She was starting to sweat, and her legs felt like they were wrapped in rubber.

There was a sweet, rich smell in the air and, for a moment, she thought that the sullen man beside her was wearing perfume. But then she saw the roses. A bush of wild roses on the other side of the pathway was in bloom, and its old-fashioned smell was just for her. She shut her eyes and allowed their sweetness to take over her other senses. They were the roses that grew wild along the dusty roadsides where she and Sandy had taken their Sunday drives so many years ago. She had always associated them with old ladies and now she realized that she was becoming an old lady herself — to the girl she should be meeting soon, she would appear ancient.

Minnie's Fool had brought her roses from his garden one afternoon. At the time, she knew that his bouquet was only an excuse to get away from his mother-in-law for an hour — the old lady was practically living with him and Minnie by then. The roses had been as fat and full as peonies, and a deep, beet red. Margaret had hidden them in her room after he left because she knew that, if her mother saw them, she would start complaining. "You get the roses, while the Fool only brings us his miserable vegetables." They had been among the loveliest flowers she had ever seen. In all her life no one had brought her any others.

She sat very still with her eyes closed as the roses drifted across the pathway and filled her. She had not had real flowers in the house for years. Minnie had plastic flowers in her bedroom and, on the dining-room table, a vase of silk flowers that had once been electric blue and now had faded with dust and time. A little pink bunny stuck on the end of a stick was sitting in the middle of them. Margaret hated the look of the whole thing but had never dared to get rid of it. Lord, she was sick and tired of Minnie's culch — it was everywhere she looked. Minnie was always looking for something new to buy and, once it was in the house, she forgot about it and wanted something else.

The next time Margaret went into the city she would go to a florist and buy herself a great big bouquet.

"Margaret?"

A hand was touching her shoulder. "Excuse me?"

Margaret opened her eyes. A dark-haired girl was standing in front of her, bending towards her.

"Are you Margaret?"

"Yes." The girl had short, dark hair and thick, soft features. "Annette." This was exactly the young face she had seen when they had talked on the phone. Margaret's pulse quickened.

"I know I'm late. I got stuck at my mother's."

Margaret reached out and held the girl's hands. "Well, I'm awfully glad to meet you," she said. "I was just sitting here smelling the roses." Did the girl look tougher than she had imagined? She was not hard-looking though, but steady and solid.

The sullen man on the other side of the bench shifted his body again in a way that indicated that he was not about to move anywhere, and if they wanted to talk they had better do it somewhere else.

"Let's go for a little walk," Margaret said, getting up, and she and Annette began walking awkwardly down the path. The heat was pressing down on them with such force that it made Margaret feel light-headed.

"This is hardly the place for a serious conversation," she said. "I hadn't realized it would be so crowded."

"It's always like this on a hot day."

"I can't remember the last time I was here during the day."

Annette had seen Margaret before. She knew her as the old maid who lived with her sister in a big white house on Pleasant Street; she had gone there on Hallowe'en when she was little and been given chocolate bars. Because they were such a rich treat, so much better than Hallowe'en Kisses or an apple, she had grown up looking on that house with respectful awe. Recognizing Margaret had surprised her so that she had hung back, watching her. Once, when she and Chaleur were walking down Pleasant Street, she had told him that, when she got married, she wanted to live in a big, old-fashioned house. He had said that he liked old houses too because they reminded him of his grandmother.

And thinking of that had stopped her from holding back, of standing uncertainly staring at Margaret on the bench.

If his grandmother wasn't crazy and locked away in a Home, she thought, Chaleur might have run away to be with her. She knew how much he loved her because he talked about it sometimes, and once, when they spent the whole night together, he had called out to his grandmother in his sleep. He had sounded like a little boy and she had tucked her hand around his belly and pulled him close to her. She thought of the soft flesh there, the only softness on him, and she wanted to cry.

"I should have worn a hat," Margaret said. "The heat."

"I can't find him anywhere," Annette blurted out.

"Who? Oh, your fellow." For a moment Margaret had forgotten all about the boy. "Men," she said as wisely as possible, "are not always to be relied upon."

"He just disappeared. His family haven't seen him since Monday night."

"Have they called the police?"

"That bunch? They could care less."

"Oh. Well, maybe he just needs a little time to himself."

"It don't feel right though."

Doesn't, Margaret felt she should say, but instead she smiled, realizing that grammar counted for nothing.

A few yards away, just off the boardwalk, was the old clapboard lighthouse. The steps leading up to its locked door were in the shade. "Let's sit there." She pointed, moving a bit faster.

Annette nodded. She had no trouble walking down the soft slope, but Margaret's feet wobbled in the grass leading to the steps. The wooden stairs were worn smooth, almost soft, and the lighthouse blocked the noise from the beach behind them. It was set down in a slight gully between the dunes, so that they looked out at the hill that hid the parking lots. The people walking by on the boardwalk seemed to be miles and miles away. The shade was a relief and they both welcomed it. Margaret had sat on the lighthouse steps with Minnie when they were children at a church picnic, a corn boil, and Minnie had eaten a dozen ears and made herself sick. She sat down and Annette sat beside her.

"That's better. Now, Annette, tell me again. When did you find out?"

"Last week. I took one of those tests from the drugstore. Look, I know you think he's just taken off on me, but he isn't like that." Annette's voice had a little catch in it, as if she believed in Chaleur so strongly that her heart might break.

"I see." Margaret assumed that the boy was useless and had the poor girl hoodwinked. "What's his name, by the way?"

"Chaleur. His name's really Charles, but no one's ever called him that."

"Chaleur? That's different."

"It was his father's nickname for him."

"Is his father from the north of the province?"

"Yeah. He's dead now, ever since Chaleur was little, but he was from up near Caraquet, I think."

"That explains it, then, doesn't it?" Margaret thought of the place names that surrounded her town, old French and Indian names, and how they would sound if attached to people. Scoudouc, Bouctouche, Memramcook ...

But Annette was waiting for her to say something practical.

"Well, we need a strategy, don't we? We need to figure out what you are going to do for yourself and the baby, and we need to figure out where this Chaleur fellow of yours could be at."

Annette's heart sank when Margaret said the word "baby." Wasn't there another word she could use? But no one would ever say "your foetus"; that was too weird. The words were so important. There was a big difference to her between "I'm going to have a baby" and "I'm pregnant" — the second way sounded like she could do something about it.

"Why does he want you to keep the baby?" Margaret asked.

"I don't know. I was real surprised when he was dead set against the abortion."

"You argued."

"Yeah, I guess. He got all quiet. I keep hoping that he's given me time to myself to make up my own mind. But something inside tells me that he's in real trouble."

"If you don't mind, could you tell me more about him?" Despite the heat, a shiver raced through her.

Annette was looking up at the path that she and Margaret had just walked on, the same path that she and Chaleur had taken the night before last.

"I don't know where to start."

"Well, tell me a bit about his family."

"All right," she said and she talked about his stepfather, who was mean and stupid; about his horrible little brother, who was everybody's pet; about his mother, who had looked so worn out and tired at the kitchen door. She told bits of Chaleur's stories of his grandmother and father. Margaret listened, shaking her head or nodding, and, much to her surprise, she found herself drawn closer to this unhappy young woman. She closed her eyes, trying to imagine what this runaway boyfriend might look like; but every image she conjured up formed itself into her father.

While she talked, Annette couldn't help thinking about Chaleur's belly and how, after his lips, it was her favourite place to kiss him. His body was so skinny and tight, she loved that spot where there was some softness to him. Just above the line of pubic hair, which was as silky as the hair on his head, was the place that she would nuzzle against, moving her tongue in and out, kissing and licking him, and he would lie quietly, so happy, as she gathered up a small fold of white skin gently between her teeth and her lips and ran her tongue back and forth across it. When she did that, his whole body would shake and he would cry out, "Oh!" like it was a new surprise every time.

She had never gone all the way before Chaleur; he was the first guy who let her take the lead, slowly, so that their sex could be something that would shelter them, something that could build to the point where the rest of the world would be forgotten. When Rocky had put his fingers inside her, he could have been poking at her with a stick. But Chaleur had caressed her, stroking his fingers up and down there, pushing inside so gently it wasn't even like pushing, it was more like moving carefully into a shadowy room and exploring it in the dark. As if he were trying to memorize her with the ends of his fingers.

She was trying to concentrate, wanting to be as honest as she could. How could she explain the bad things about him to Margaret? He drank too much, he liked heavy metal — "It's like loud, shitty music," she said when Margaret looked baffled; "guys love it." He hated school for stupid reasons, he didn't know what he wanted to do besides get away from his family. But those were all things that she knew could change.

She could never tell anyone about the way his fingers touched her, and how that was something that never needed changing. The smart boys at school, the ones who had put "engineering" or "medical school" beside their pictures in the yearbook, they were the ones who could buy her a house and nice clothes, but she knew from the way that they looked at her that they would never in a million years be able to get as close to her as Chaleur could. Didn't it make more sense to start with someone who could touch her? Because in touching her, couldn't he find himself? The other boys thought they knew themselves already; they would never, ever, be able to find her.

Although she said nothing about sex to Margaret, the older woman knew that underlying all of Annette's words was the secret world that she had never found, a world that would allow someone else inside it. She knew that she would never be able to do this; it was too late and, besides, her father had barred the door.

Although they were out of the sun, the humidity was bothering her a great deal. The hill in front of her was unfocused and Annette's words were beginning to run together in her head.

"How do I get the abortion?" Annette said suddenly. "I know about it from books and a friend of my sister's had one, but you work there."

Margaret knew that she had to speak very carefully. She could not lie, but it was not yet time for the truth. She fell back on the facts she had memorized from the handbook at the Hotline office.

"Well, you know there are two procedures. In one, a little tube is put in the uterus, a little vacuum. The suction tears the baby apart and the placenta is torn from the uterus wall."

"I know, but there's nothing to tear apart — it's just like a little cornflake. That's not a D and C though, is it? What's a D and C?" She felt stupid asking. If she wanted to go to nursing school, shouldn't she should know things like this already?

"Dilation and curettage. The curettage is a knife, and it cuts up both the baby and the placenta and scrapes them out."

"Gross. How do you know which one to use? Do I have anything to say about that?"

"Do you realize how traumatic an abortion can be?"

Annette looked over at her, scrutinizing her. "Margaret, I'm not stupid," she said. "I know that an abortion will kill this foetus before it turns into a real baby. I know that some people think it's murder, and I'm all screwed up about that. But what I really know is that this isn't the way to have a baby, and I'm not going to do it."

Something inside of Margaret was strangling as surely as the dense air was catching in her throat. Her pantyhose seemed as thick and scratchy as wool. She was starting to feel faint and was suddenly panicked — remembering how she'd felt on Sunday night before her episode. She took a deep breath, unsure of what she would say next.

"The most important thing to think about right now," she found herself saying carefully as she reached down and unfastened first one shoe strap, then the other, "is that you make a decision that you can live with for the rest of your life, and one that you and your fellow will be happy with."

"That's this abortion," said Annette. "If he had to be a father right now, he'd have to get some crummy job. He'd never get anywhere."

Margaret took off her shoes and placed them carefully on the step beside her. "Wouldn't he be a good father?" she asked.

"I sure hope so. But how can you be a good father when you've got to work at McDonald's or something to pay the rent?"

"But he wants you to have the baby."

"I know. It's all a big mess, and the more I think about it the more messy it gets."

"Annette, it's a moral dilemma. And without them we'd just be animals."

"So what do I do?"

"You're a smart girl. You know that having an abortion isn't like having a tooth pulled at the dentist."

"I know I can't have this baby. I can't have a baby that would start off in such a hard way and would have a terrible life. I mean, what do I do about Chaleur?"

Suddenly Margaret saw her father and mother standing in their bedroom. What discussion would her parents have had when Wayne found out that he was about to be a father? Would there have been any discussion at all? Had the idea of her arrival made her parents happy? Had Wayne knelt down at her mother's feet and pressed his ear against her belly? As he listened, was he already starting to plan the ways that he would assault his young daughter? Did her father feel he could do whatever he wanted with her because he owned her?

"Margaret?"

Oh God, she thought, *please help me. All my words are useless.*

Her own father seemed so close to her that she could smell him in the thick heat.

"Are you all right?"

Annette seemed far away, at the end of a tunnel. How long had she been sitting here silently? She would collapse in this heat. She swallowed, and took another breath.

"Would you stand up?" Her voice was faint, remote, as if it had travelled a great distance.

"What?"

"Stand in front of me for a moment?"

The girl looked confused.

"Just stand up in front of me." She tried to smile. "If I don't get out of these darn pantyhose right now, I know I'll die right here on these lighthouse steps."

Annette looked at her and then she moved to the bottom of the steps. Behind her, Margaret lifted her seat in the air and reached up under her dress, tugging at the hose on her thighs, pulling them down until the crotch wadded up between her knees. The rush of air she felt against her legs was hot, but there was release. A swimmer whose lungs had finally reached the surface. Yes, this was helping. Yes, the world was clearer. She was so relieved that she relaxed and lost her balance. She fell backwards.

"Ow!"

Annette spun around. "Are you okay?"

"I busted my tail bone, but I think I'll live."

And suddenly both of them were young girls, laughing.

Annette helped to pull the pantyhose down over her ankles. They were torn from Margaret's nails, and Annette balled them up and carried them over to a garbage can sitting up beside the path.

Watching her come back, seeing the way that she was grinning at her, Margaret knew that when she got home, she would phone the abortion clinic and find out what she could. She knew it was wrong, that she was going too far, but God had not shown her any other way.

FIFTEEN

S andy watched Gloria give up on the doorbell and drive
away with her family; he would have to phone her after all
— last Christmas he had given her a key. He sighed, then
slowly walked to the bathroom, where he carefully put on his
disguise. He could smell the boy's bowel movement in the hall,
arrogant and rank. It would stay in his nose for the rest of the
day. He soaked a wash cloth in warm water and wrung it out,
he picked up a roll of toilet paper, and then he headed slowly
towards the back bedroom. It was all as if his mother were still
lying in her bed, making demands on him.

"Let's get you cleaned up," he said, as flatly as possible.

Chaleur turned away when Sandy came into the room. He
didn't know which was worse: lying on top of the bedpan filled
with shit or having the old creep clean him up. He shut his eyes

as Sandy leaned over him, lifting his bottom as high as the ties would permit and wiping and washing it. When Sandy sighed, Chaleur opened his eyes and glared at him. "You fucker," he said. "Lemme go, you rotten old fucker."

But Sandy said nothing. He did not even look into the boy's face because he knew that it would be ugly now. When he was pulling up his underwear and jeans, the sorry spectacle of the boy's pale legs and shrivelled penis distressed him. There was nothing secret now, just the banality of ordinary flesh. He picked up the bedpan from the floor and started towards the bathroom.

"Lemme go, you old fucker."

Sandy stopped at the door and turned around.

"I can gag you, you know." The bitchiness in his voice pleased him. He felt as if the boy had been giving him trouble for weeks now and he was fed up.

"Just fucking try!"

Sandy wanted to march back to the bed and slap the impudent little tough across the face. But instead he sighed.

"Watch yourself, young man, or there'll be serious trouble."

"When you gonna fucking lemme go?"

There was no answer. Sandy had left and was emptying the bedpan into the toilet. "Deaf old asshole," Chaleur said softly. But Sandy heard him as he began washing out the bedpan in the bathtub. With a sinking feeling, he realized that cleaning up after Mother had been more pleasant. She, at least, had thanked him.

"Hey, fucker! Hey, you old fucker!"

Sandy ignored him, but the shouting grew louder.

"Hey, you fucker! Lemme go! Lemme go!"

Sandy stopped scrubbing and listened. He began to worry about the neighbours.

"I'll kill you, you old fruit, swear to fuck I'll kill you!"

Then Chaleur was screaming and banging on the bed with

such a fury that he was started to shake the house. Sandy dropped the bedpan, chipping a piece of enamel off the tub.

"Dammit!"

He quickly checked his disguise in the mirror and hurried into the bedroom. The boy was yanking at the ties, pulling and screaming, like something wild caught in a trap. He was screeching and swearing, and the bedposts were pounding the floor as he banged up and down on the old mattress.

"Be quiet!"

But Chaleur thought that if he slammed around hard enough, the old fart would not be able to hold him down and someone would hear him. He was going to scream until the entire town heard him. He was going to holler and thrash and spit until the neighbours or the police broke down the door. "Help!" he screamed, "Fucking help me! Somebody fucking help me!"

With a swiftness that surprised them both, Sandy grabbed a cushion from the chair and jumped onto the bed. He squashed it into the boy's face and fell on top of it, shoving down with his elbows and upper body.

"Stop this! *Stop stop stop!*"

He had straddled the boy's chest and could feel it twisting and bucking between his thighs, Chaleur's muffled voice roared into the cushion. Sandy leaned his whole weight into it.

Chaleur was pinned, but he wriggled and fought until he could no longer breathe. The cushion was old and stale — his mouth and nose were filled with its stink. There was no way that he would give up, he would fight this old bugger until —

But then there was nothing to breathe but dust, and he collapsed, defeated.

Both men lay very still. The boy was as warm as blood. Sandy could feel the heart inside the sweaty chest pounding against his thighs. He squeezed tighter, and beneath him the body jerked faintly, awkwardly, the death throe of a small animal. Keeping his hands on the pillow, he pushed with his arms until he was sitting on Chaleur's stomach.

"I'm going to get up now," Sandy said calmly, "and I want you to be quiet. Understand?"

There was a muffled noise of assent.

Sandy slowly lifted the cushion, as if he were afraid that the boy might jump at him. Chaleur coughed. His face was red and sweaty, and there were tears in the corners of his eyes.

"This is the new rule," Sandy said. "The next time you pull a stunt like that, I put a gag on you. Understand?"

Chaleur glared at him.

"Understand?" Sandy thrust his body downwards against the boy and winded him.

Chaleur bit his lip and nodded. Anything to get this old creep off him.

"A gag. And I don't care if you choke on it. No more outbursts!"

Chaleur glared at him.

"You had better behave, young man."

"Fuck off," Chaleur said quietly.

Sandy slapped the boy's face. "That's for swearing," he said.

Chaleur rolled his eyes. "Jesus fuck."

Sandy stared down at the sullen, angry face. His worst fear was being confirmed: here was no little god, but a common hoodlum. He had wasted his love.

He climbed off the bed and started to leave the room.

"I don't want things to get out of hand," he said, not looking back.

"Just lemme go and I'm outta here," Chaleur said quietly.

Sandy stopped for a moment at the door. "We can work this out." But uncertainty had crept into his voice.

"Please, lemme go."

But Sandy was out the door. He went into the bathroom and tore off the shower cap. He pulled the towel from his face and threw it onto the floor. Then he got down on his knees beside the tub and violently finished scrubbing out the bedpan.

He was furious at the boy for making him hard inside his good suit pants.

Chaleur lay still, waiting for his heart to stop pounding. The ties were cutting into his wrists and ankles — his hands and feet were falling asleep and starting to tingle. He hoped that when his body calmed down it might shrink a little and the ties wouldn't hurt him so. He had always thought that his body was too small, his arms and legs puny and laughable, but now they seemed much too big. If he starved, just a little, could he slip free? But his aching head, his whole body was throbbing in pain and would never shrink.

Maybe the old guy would let him go soon. Or was he planning to keep him like this for ever? What had he done?

He tried not to think about food or cigarettes. He tried to concentrate on something else, anything. He stared at a crack in the ceiling plaster.

Why was he here? If the old guy was a fruit, why hadn't he tried anything? If he was psycho, like Freddy in *A Nightmare on Elm Street*, why wasn't he laughing crazy or sticking a knife at his throat? What did he mean when he said "We can work this out"? The old fart sounded the way that Chaleur sometimes felt when he had to deal with Ralphie, like he was fed up and had had enough. What would Ralphie do if someone tied him to a bed? What would his father have done?

The old fucker was finished in the bathroom and Chaleur heard him in the hall. He could sense him standing in the bedroom door.

"I'm going to get you something to eat," Sandy said. "I don't have to remind you to be quiet."

Then don't, you stupid old fucker, Chaleur thought as his eyes followed the crack across the ceiling to the wall above the window. Outside, so close, was the yard and the broken fence and the path through the orchard to the woods, but they might as well have been in China for all the good they were to him.

When Chaleur didn't respond, Sandy turned around and walked down the hall.

"Asshole," Chaleur whispered.

The crack on the ceiling was bugging him. If his dad had ever had a house like this, he would have kept it fixed up. He would have gotten a ladder and ripped off the peeling paint and torn down the ceiling around him. He would —

But he was wasting time. He had to try to figure out how to get out of this place, but could not think of anything that was practical. In the movies, he might have had a knife hidden somewhere, or maybe he could work one of his hands free. But nothing like that was possible. Quietly, he tugged at the ties.

He wondered if anyone had reported him missing. Not Rory, for sure. But his mother? Maybe Annette. But maybe she thought he had taken off on her because she was pregnant and wanted the abortion. Was he being punished because he thought she wanted to break up with him when really she was just upset because of the baby? He thought of the little baby and then thought of the old creep wiping his bum like he was still in diapers. Was he being punished because he got mad at her when she said that she wanted an abortion? Would she call the police and tell them that he was missing? Or was she just glad that he was out of her hair and she could get rid of the baby and go on with her life? Was there anyone anywhere who would miss him? He wanted to scream and jump, but he knew it wouldn't do any good. The old fucker had almost smothered him and had slapped him — he was crazy for sure and Chaleur was afraid of what else he might do. He was in the dread part of a horror movie and he was scared.

"Dad?" he whispered. "Dad? Can you help me?"

Downstairs, Sandy put bread in the toaster and poured the boy a glass of milk. But tied down like that — how could he drink out of a glass? He wondered if his old baby bottles were still somewhere in the house. Every little thing was suddenly a chore. He phoned Gloria's number.

"She's at the beach with her brothers," Mrs. Maurice said.

"Oh. It's Alexander Whyte. Could you tell her that I won't be needing her this week? Something's come up."

"I'll do that, Mr. Whyte. Are you going away?"

Nosy old witch. "Yes, that's it. I'm going out of town. Yes."

The moment he hung up the phone, the toast popped. He gave a startled little cry, then buttered it and, placing it on a tray beside the milk, walked up the back stairs. He was so preoccupied with figuring out how to manage the feeding that he forgot his disguise. At first he didn't realize what the boy meant when he looked at him and said, "That's even more scary."

He let the remark pass.

"Here," he said, "I'll prop you up a bit and feed you."

"I ain't hungry."

"You have to eat something."

"Make me."

Chaleur could not stand to look at the guy, and went back to staring at the crack on the ceiling. Sandy stood awkwardly for a moment with the toast and milk.

"Very well then." He set the tray on the dresser and left the room. Slowly he went down the hall to his bedroom, where he sat on the edge of his bed and began to talk quietly to himself.

He would have to gag the boy before he went to sleep and he needed to figure out how to do it.

It was a long, hot afternoon for both men. Sandy sat on his bed, looking at an assortment of possible muzzles: a wash cloth, a towel, a torn piece of bed sheet that he had found in Gloria's ragbag. He needed something that would keep the boy quiet but wouldn't hamper his breathing or make him choke. On television he had once seen someone gagged with very wide tape: he had tried piecing a large sticky gag together out of strips of Scotch tape from his desk but it hadn't worked. He held up a thick towel.

Last night had been the happiest of Sandy's life and now the memory of that joy was so tainted that he could vomit in disgust. All his hopes were gone: the boy was worth nothing. There was no poetry in his soul. He would never be able to appreciate a painting, or the music of Bach: he was the sort of young thug who would never have an original idea in his life.

Chaleur started banging the bed and screaming again in the late afternoon. Sandy walked quickly down the hall, covered his face with the pillow again, and gagged him with the strip of bed sheet. And then, without uttering a word, he walked slowly back to his room.

Chaleur bit into the gag; he twisted his head back and forth, trying to loosen it, and then, when he started to choke, he gave up.

The Oaks was sealed shut against the weather; the screen doors and windows had been leaning beside the washer and dryer in the back shed for years now. Sandy's mother used to hire a man to put the storm windows on every fall and take them off in late May, but when he told her that he could no longer climb the extension ladder — he was sixty — she never found anyone else to do it. "The night air bothers me anyway," she told Sandy. As a boy, he had hated the idea of strangers on ladders looking in from the outside — he was convinced that they might discover secrets and talk — and so he had not protested; the storm windows remained on the house winter and summer.

In the heat of a long day like this, the old house afforded no comfort. The air was thick and stale, the heat pushing down from the ceilings. The water pipes dripped with sweat. In the bathroom, a thin pool had formed beneath the old toilet tank and was inching towards a stain on the wainscotting in the corner. The bedrooms were ovens.

To keep from going crazy, Chaleur played Guns N' Roses songs over and over in his head, trying to work his way through a whole album. He was doing his best to think not just of the lyrics — he tried to remember every guitar chord, every drum beat, and put them in place. Sometimes he was so frustrated that nothing came, but then big chunks of sound popped up as clear as if he were wearing headphones and listening to it right then. The room was unbearable by mid-afternoon and he was starving, but after the humiliation of having the old bastard wipe and clean up his ass, there was no way he was going to be fed toast and milk like he was a helpless cripple or something. Every once in a while he struggled with the ties, but that was getting him nowhere. The heat made him dizzy; his hangover was killing him.

He decided not to use the bedpan again. He would mess the bed and then the old fucker would have to untie him to clean it up. It was the closest he could come to an escape plan.

Before he went downstairs and forced himself to eat a sandwich, Sandy went over to his dresser and took Mother's ashes out of the bottom drawer, and carried them back to the bed. He lay down and hugged them to his chest. Once this whole terrible ordeal was over, he would bury her in the garden.

Should Sandy simply let him go? The humiliation would be unbearable. People would avoid him at church. The world would laugh at him. He might even be arrested.

But the boy had broken into his house! He had thrown up all over his shed!

He looked down at the box containing his mother. "I should never have saved him," he whispered.

Chaleur could not tell if he was falling asleep or passing out from hunger and the oppressive heat. The pain of his hangover had spread throughout his dehydrated body. At one point, when he heard the toilet flushing, the sound of water so close by was such an agony that he began to beat his head against the pillow. If his skull broke open, maybe the pain would escape.

He dreamed that he was hiding from Rory, that he was in the woods, that he was tied to a bed. At times, in a groggy haze, he could not say for certain where he was. His body was numb and sweaty, he stuck to his clothes and his clothes stuck to the sheets. The pillow was pasted to his head.

At nine o'clock, Sandy came into the room to offer the boy some more food and found him sleeping. Outside in the garden, songbirds were singing as the sun went down. The sunlight pouring down the hallway was golden, and he could clearly see the boy lying in the soft yellow light, his skin as beautiful as a painting. Mother had died at noon, and there was something unnatural about her cold grey flesh in the bright light of day.

He moved quietly over to the bed. Chaleur's hair was damp and stuck to his face, and Sandy pushed it back from his forehead. How could anything so beautiful be so foul? In sleep, there was none of anger or crudeness that had twisted and maligned these features, and, to Sandy's confusion, the lovely body seemed filled with possibilities all over again.

Perhaps he had been too hasty; the fault was as much his own as the boy's. Perhaps here, still, might be the perfect vessel for his love. He knelt behind the head of the bed and very gently untied the strip of cloth. The boy did not wake up. He moved to the bedside and lifted the gag tenderly.

That perfect mouth could be taught to laugh, rather than hurl obscenities. He held the gag to his face and sniffed it, then pushed it against his mouth and nose.

Chaleur's body need not be a weapon against his own. Asleep, he was perfect again and Sandy knew that he could not harm him. He marvelled again at the cheekbones, the soft beard on the boy's cheek. Asleep, the boy was his again. Sandy knelt down beside the bed, placing the strip of cloth beside the pillow. He touched the boy's arm; the muscles were soft and relaxed in sleep.

He began to whisper.

"At evening when the lamp is lit,

Around the fire my parents sit ..."

He reached out and ran his finger along the thick fold of denim near the boy's zipper, as gently as an ant might walk over a thin leaf, or a feather might fall against his cheek.

"They sit at home and talk and sing,

And do not play at anything ..."

He moved his finger back and forth until the boy's flesh reached up from inside his clothing towards Sandy's touch. Then the sleeper gave a little moan that seemed, to Sandy, to be filled with joy. He opened his hand and lay the palm comfortingly across the warmth and, gently pressing it down, he watched the boy sleep.

So close to him, and yet so far away as to be unreachable, Chaleur in his dreams was moving at a great pace. Annette was ahead of him, and he was running towards her. She scooped him up into her arms like a little boy and held him to her breast as she ran to safety through a deep, spruce wood.

SIXTEEN

While she was running the vacuum cleaner over the rugs in the afternoon, Mama decided that Junior and Danny should move to the attic so that Raymond could sleep in the back bedroom. She knew how much he loved the attic — and she was more comfortable having him there, out of the way with his friend — but it was too hot. She was ready to argue with him if he put up a fight. When they all came back from their day at the Dune, one glance at Raymond convinced her that she was right; he looked much worse than he had in the morning before they left. She watched from the hall window as Junior drove the car into the yard. Raymond, looking exhausted and frail, leaned on his friend's shoulder as they walked towards the house. He lay down on the cot on the veranda and went right to sleep.

Gloria changed from her bathing suit and went to the kitchen to help Mama with supper, while Junior and Danny sat out on the back steps, drinking beer.

"Sandy Whyte called," Mama said. "He's going out of town and won't need you this week."

"Where could he be going?"

Mama shrugged.

Hal was on the front steps reading. He had decided to wait until after supper to wash off; the salt on his skin made it feel thicker, tougher. He liked the way it tingled. When Gloria came to get them for supper, he said, "I'll bring his plate out here, and make sure he eats."

"Oh, I'll eat here, too. Kitchen's way too hot."

So Gloria joined them, chattering about the past while she ate her cold chicken and potato salad on the front steps. Back in the kitchen Mama told her older sons why she wanted them to go upstairs and switch things around. "He's gonna have to lie down during the day," she said, "and that darn attic's a blast furnace until after midnight." Neither Junior or Danny talked about the way he had acted while they were at the Dune because they knew it would worry her more, but she figured that something must have happened because neither of them moaned or groaned, they just said they would go upstairs after supper and pack up their things.

"Gloria and I'll switch the bedding around in a little while, so don't you worry about that."

When Gloria came inside with the plates, Mama said, "How did he do?"

"Hal got him to eat most of it. They're working on their desserts right now."

"Good. Help your father with the dishes. I'm gonna take my shortcake out there. Can one of you be so kind as to make the tea?"

It felt nice and peaceful out on the veranda: the evening was starting to cool off. Raymond was propped up on a couple of pillows, and his friend was sitting on the floor, leaning back on the cot. They were both finishing up their strawberry shortcake.

"So how are you boys doing?" She did not look at either of them as she sat down in the wicker rocker.

"This is fabulous," Hal told her. "*Almost* as good as that pie you made for me yesterday."

"And the chicken," added Raymond. "Mama, you're going to make us fat." He did not look at her; he was gazing off at the sunset.

"Tea'll be ready soon."

"Just look at that sky," Raymond sighed.

"Yep." Mama nodded. "You'd have to go a long ways before you'd find a sky as pretty as the one we got right here." Holding her plate in her left hand, she cut down through the tender biscuit and took her first bite. "This old shortcake's not too bad after all."

"It's fabulous," Hal repeated.

All three of them were silent for a moment, and then Hal said, "It was beautiful on the Dune. It's so long, like you could walk for ever and never reach the end."

"Haven't been there for years. Never was a place we went to much, not with our own beach right here. You always liked it up there though, didn't you, Raymond?"

He nodded. Then he pointed with his right hand. "It's amazing. Just look at how that pink goes up and turns into green. Pale, pale green."

The house across the street was set on the upper edge of a wide lot, so that they were facing a deep yard of well-kept grass that ran back to a lilac hedge and a line of spruce trees. The sun had gone down behind the trees; above them the sky was a fiery pink that stretched up and faded into pastels. Floating high over the pointed spruce, one lone cloud still caught the sun, and for a few moments its bottom edge was golden.

"I have to say that your sister and I saw a couple a nice sunsets that time we was in Jamaica." She shook her head. "People there sure was different."

"You mean black," said Raymond.

"No, I don't; I mean different. Old Mrs. Vincent who comes to Mass is black and she's the same as the rest of us. People there were different."

"How so?" Hal asked.

"I don't mean the way they talked or anything — I mean, that was different, but — it was just the way — well, I felt like an outsider, that nobody really wanted me around. People kept hounding us for money."

"Boys oh boys, were they barking up the wrong tree," Raymond said.

"You can say that again." She had some more dessert and shrugged her shoulders. "I suppose they feel the same way about us that we feel about the crazy Americans coming here in the summer. Pretty place though, all the same. I'm glad I saw it once."

The cloud was drifting slowly towards the east; it was grey now, and flat-looking. The evening star was balanced on the top of a spruce tree, flickering as the branches moved in the breeze.

"I forgot the sky was so beautiful here," Raymond said.

"Oh, it's a beautiful place." Mama nodded. "There was a time you said you'd never leave it."

"Yes, and there was a time when I was eight years old." He paused. "Remember when Gloria and I decided to live under the veranda? You got so mad at us."

"Because I had to crawl under there and drag out your bed-

ding. I had to wash those darn sheets twice they were so filthy."
She almost smiled, and added affectionately, "You kids were bad."

"I'd forgotten about it till Gloria mentioned it at dinner."

"That sister of yours must be part elephant — she never forgets a damn thing."

"She's got an elephant's butt, that's for sure."

"Sssh! She lost ten pounds this winter at Weight Watchers
and it came off everywhere but there. Don't you dare say anything to her about her bum. She's real sensitive about it." She
had finished her shortcake and sat quietly rocking, still holding
the empty plate in her hand.

Hal looked over at her. "Have you lived here all your life?"

"Right here," she said. "Right here in this house." She sat
quietly for a moment. "Look, I've got the boys upstairs switching things around. They're going to sleep in the attic and you
two can have their beds from now on."

"What?" moaned Raymond. "Why?"

"I know you love that old attic, but if you want to lie down
during the day and have a nap, then that attic's too darn hot."

Hal looked at her and nodded. "I think that's a good idea,"
he said. "Thanks."

"I think it's a crappy idea."

"Raymond."

"She just wants us in those dinky twin beds."

"Oh, Raymond, come on."

"You can push the beds together for all I care," said Mama.
"I was just thinking of your comfort, that's all."

"Bullshit, you were——"

"Quiet!" Hal turned around and held Raymond's arm. "It'll
be much more comfortable and we're not going to argue about
it. All right?"

Raymond rolled his eyes. "Fuck."

The atmosphere had become uncomfortable and tense. Hal stood up and moved to the front steps, where he stretched and lit a cigarette. Mama scraped her plate violently and Raymond let out a sigh of exasperation. Hal knew that it was up to him to stop the silence growing between them. "It seems wonderful to me, you know, the idea of always living in the same place. My family moved all the time."

Mama said nothing, just nodded grimly as she rocked.

"It's fabulous that Raymond can come back to the house where he grew up. I've never even seen the house where my parents live now."

"Why not?" Mama asked. She set her fork down on her empty plate.

Hal shrugged, "Well——"

"They're Baptists," Raymond cut in sarcastically, "not open-minded Catholics like *we* are."

"The last time a man in this family went to Mass was so long ago even I've forgotten it." There was a childish edge to Mama's voice. "When Father Pelletier first came here, he thought I was a widow."

"Mass is a waste of time."

"Then why did you used to get up early and shine everyone's shoes before we went off to Ste. Anne's?"

"Oh please——"

"If it's a waste of time why were you always dragging your sister into the front closet and making her play confession behind the winter coats?"

"Mama, for godsakes."

She was looking in Hal's direction, but she didn't raise her eyes high enough to meet his; she spoke to his chest. "When he'd just started high school, he came to me one day and told me he was going to be a priest."

"Oh, God," Raymond moaned.

"Father Raymond," Hal said. "You never told me."

"What other option was there if you were a fag in this fucking place!"

Mama stopped rocking and wiggled in her chair. She exhaled sharply.

"I want to sleep in the attic."

"Well, you can't. And it's for your own good."

"Raymond," Hal said, "knock it off."

The awkward silence that followed was suddenly punctuated with a deep rippling sound, a series of gurgles, then a soft little pop. When Hal looked over at Mama, her face was clenched and she was staring painfully at her plate. She cleared her throat and started rocking again. The air on the veranda turned foul.

"What do I smell?" Raymond asked.

Hal glared at him.

"Don't you smell something?"

"*Raymond*."

There was a phoney innocence in Raymond's voice. "Like sulphur or——"

"Cut it out."

"But it's so *vile*. Stinky-stinky P.U."

Mama abruptly stood up and walked towards the door; she paused for a moment before opening it. She wished she could take him over her knee and give him a licking with the wooden spoon, but knew that if she even turned to look at him her body could explode again. "You're sleeping in the back bedroom!" she spat out angrily. "And that's that!" The screen door slammed behind her.

Hal looked at Raymond incredulously. "That's one of the meanest things I've ever seen anybody do."

Raymond shrugged. "You're the one who's always wanted to come here." He looked back at the evening star.

Hal stared at him, not knowing what to say next. Then he picked up their empty dessert plates and took them into the house.

Upstairs, Danny and Junior had packed their suitcases and carried them up to the attic.

Junior shook his head. "It's a fucking oven."

"It'll cool off." Danny collected some of Raymond and Hal's things. "Open that bag of theirs for me, will you?"

"This *fruity* one?" Junior said, pointing to a sleek-looking green case.

"Just open it."

Junior lifted the lid. "Jesus fucking Christ," he said, "take a look at this."

The suitcase was filled with pill bottles and ointments, jars full of vitamins. Danny shook his head and whistled.

"What the hell is all this stuff?"

"Pretty impressive, isn't it?" Hal had just come up the stairs and startled them.

"We was just packing your stuff up," Junior said defensively, as if he had been caught red-handed.

"It's okay, I know," Hal replied. The three of them were staring at the contents of the suitcase. "It's worse than my mother's purse."

"It's for Raymond's spots, isn't it?" said Danny.

Hal shook his head. "No, there's nothing we can do for them but radiation, and what's the point? Kaposi's are tumours. They'll just grow inwards eventually. Spread to the organs, the brain …"

He stopped. Despite the fact that he sensed they both wanted to know this, he knew that neither brother wanted to hear it. It was uncomfortable talking to them, but he felt that he should. "So all this stuff is just to try to build up our strength, mostly. I think a lot of it we just take to make ourselves feel like we're doing something. Some of it works." He felt like an adult talking to little boys. "Thanks for moving up here. Raymond's pissed off, but sometimes he doesn't know what's best for him."

"No problem," Danny said.

Junior was still staring at the suitcase. One whole side of it was filled with boxes of condoms. "Look at all the Sheiks," he said, dumbfounded.

"Raymond packed those. Wishful thinking."

Without offering to help carry anything down to the bedroom, Junior left them both and went downstairs to have a beer on the back porch.

When Pop realized that it was Raymond's friend taking a shower, he wandered out onto the veranda, thinking the coast was clear. He felt awkward talking to that man; he could not prevent the anger from boiling up in him, and he was afraid that he might say something bad. Mama was out there, sitting very still in the rocker, and Gloria was standing beside her. They looked like they were posing for a picture. "How's it going?" he asked.

"Sssh," Mama said, pointing to Raymond, who was sleeping on the cot. "He just drifted off," she whispered.

"Too much sun today," Gloria said softly. Both women did not move for a minute; they were quietly watching Raymond. It made Pop nervous and he was ready to turn back inside the house.

"Well, let's go change the beds," Mama said to Gloria, and the two of them left him alone with his son.

Night was falling. Pop stood on the veranda close to the door, rocking back and forth on his heels and toes, and softly whistled a few notes that sounded more like a bird call than the beginnings of a song. It was still too early for there to be much noise from the Club, although people were starting to arrive down there. A car door slammed and a woman laughed loudly. Without looking at Raymond, he went to the rocker and sat down.

The world was a funny place. Take this boy — not a boy now, of course, but a man. How did it happen that your own son could become such a stranger? Pop took a good look at him for the first time since he had come home. He had not wanted to look before because it seemed rude to stare, as if looking at Raymond were like gawking at something in a carnival sideshow.

His face had a strange colour, like he was always flushed, and his arms seemed as brittle as old kindling: he was as thin and sick as some foreigner on a TV ad for famine relief. Yet looking at him, Pop could still see the fat-faced little monkey who climbed over everything in the house, who shimmied up trees and the posts on the veranda, slid down the banister, swung from the clothesline. How could that little face be reconciled with this one? He felt tenderness for his boy, and revulsion as well.

Raymond had taken longer than the others to grow up. He wanted to play skin the cat longer: he bounced up and down on Pop's foot, crying "Giddyup, horsie" when he was really too big and heavy to do it any more. Pop remembered the weight of baby Raymond in his arms, and the feel of the Raymond's chubby little arms around his neck. He could see as clear as if it were yesterday the look on Raymond's face when he got caught doing something he wasn't supposed to, the way he couldn't stop himself from grinning. He had been a going concern.

All of that was still there, like history, in Raymond's sleeping face. Pop knew that his wife could see it, and the others, too, maybe. Gloria could, for sure. But that boyfriend fellow, he could see none of that. He knew nothing about who Raymond had been. Pop couldn't see how Hal had any right to be with Raymond at all. Had he felt the same way when Junior came home with Ginette? But Junior had not been as dear to him when he was little; besides, Junior and Ginette were normal. Both Mama and Pop had hoped that she would straighten Junior out. All that this boyfriend fellow had done was make Raymond sick. At least, that was how Pop saw things.

Maybe if one of his kids, just one, could give Mama and him a grandchild, maybe then things like this would not be so hard. He had not realized until Raymond came home how much he longed for one. Someone he and Mama could spoil: a little fellow who would look up at them and think that they knew all the answers. When kids grew up past a certain point, they wanted nothing from their parents any more, unless the old folks were rich and could give them a hand-out.

Raymond snorted and then started to snore. He sounded just like his mother. Pop looked out into the dark. He knew that he would outlive his own son. There was nothing that he could do for the boy, and he was thinking that all that was left between them were sad moments like this one.

He decided to go for a walk down to the wharf, so he got up and left his son sleeping alone on the cot in the night air.

Around eleven-thirty, about a half-hour after Mama and Pop went to bed, Raymond was still lying out on the veranda. He was awake now and feeling better. Hal was watching him from the rocker, creaking slowly back and forth. Gloria had covered her brother with an old quilt and was sitting at the foot of the cot with his feet resting on her lap. They were drinking rum and Cokes.

The night was soft and cool, and the nearest street light had burnt out, so they could see the stars. A rectangle of light came through the screen door, stretching across the veranda floor and down the steps into the yard. They could hear the jukebox playing from the Club. Danny and Junior were down there drinking.

"I'm glad there's no band tonight." Gloria sighed. "They're way more noisy."

The song on the jukebox was Patsy Cline singing "Sweet Dreams."

"Sis?"

"Yeah."

"What happened that time when you and Lavinia Gautier saw the Virgin?"

"Oh, Raymond, for cripes sakes."

"The virgin?" Hal asked. "Who's that?"

"The Virgin Mary," Raymond said. "You know, as in Holy-Mary-Mother-of-God-pray-for-us-sinners-now-and-at-the-hour-of-our-death-amen?"

"Oh." Hal nodded. He glanced at Gloria and then looked away.

"Aw, jeez, Raymond, now Hal's gonna think I'm nuts."

"Oh, no," said Hal. "No." He found it hard to believe that of the dozens of stories that Raymond had told him about the Maurice family he had failed to mention that his sister had seen the Virgin Mary.

Raymond laughed a little.

"What's so funny?" Gloria demanded.

"Nothing. She became a nun though, didn't she?"

"Lavinia? I guess so. She went to some convent up in Quebec. I don't know where she is now."

"Her family still around?"

"Raymond, her mom had cancer and her dad was killed in that car crash the year after you finished high school."

"Oh right, oh right. Down in Florida, or something."

Gloria nodded. "They've both been dead for years."

"And what happened to her brother?"

"He moved to Montreal, I think. He was a lot older than we were. Remember how old her parents were? They were like somebody's grandparents." She shook her head.

"Can you remember how mad Pop was when the priest came round? What was his name?"

"Father Flo."

"Whatever happened to him?"

"Had a nervous breakdown after all those kids who went to the Brothers' school claimed he felt them up when they was little."

"Did he go to court?"

"Naw, the Church packed him off somewheres else. Lavinia used to tell me that we were going to hell cause Pop sent us to the Protestant school, but I figure we're the lucky ones. Vyia Rodd was an old bitch, but she'd've dropped dead before she'd even think of doing sex things with us."

"She dropped dead before she even thought about sex, period," Raymond said. "Where did you see the Virgin, anyway? Was it over by the convent?"

Hal was watching Gloria, who had lowered her head and was staring at her feet. He wanted Raymond to talk about something else. The moon was shining through the trees. Hal stepped down off the veranda to look at it.

"Or was it up in the field past the nuns' garden?"

Gloria sighed and shook her head, and there was a long awkward moment.

"*O Fortuna*," Hal said grandly. "*Velut luna.*"

"*Casta Diva*," Raymond replied, grinning.

"*Konigin Der Nacht*," countered Hal.

Raymond shook his head. "The queen of the night wasn't the moon."

"Hmm," Hal said. "Then, *Mesicku na nebi hlubokem*." He curtsied. "Dvořák," he added. "*Rusalka*. 'The Song of the Moon.'"

Raymond sighed. "You always win."

"And what the frig was that?" Gloria asked.

"A medley," Raymond answered. "*Carmina Burana*, then the greatest role Joan Sutherland ever sang——"

"Arguably," said Hal.

"Arguably."

"Well, that's closer to English, but I still don't know."

"Just some songs about the moon."

"Oh. That opera crap."

"Right." Raymond was watching his sister. For some reason he did not want to let her off the hook. "So what happened with Lavinia anyway? I was away somewhere, I think."

"You were with Glenda at Aunt Mabel's — their cat was having kittens so you spent the week there. I don't wanna talk about it, Raymond, not now." She stood up. "Well, I'm going to bed."

"Goodnight, Gloria," Hal said, still standing out in the front yard.

"'Night, boys." And she went inside and up the stairs.

After a minute, Hal slowly came back onto the veranda. "What's with all this about the Virgin Mary?"

Raymond shrugged. "Gloria was in grade, I don't know, seven maybe. She and her friend were up behind the convent in the nuns' garden and came back home and said they'd seen her. They got in deep shit."

"What happened?"

"Not a soul believed them. Lavinia was a little religious fanatic and she led Gloria around by the nose. Mama told them to just forget about it, but Lavinia went to the priests. Father Flo came over here and called Gloria a liar. Pop threw him out and never went back to church. People started making fun of Gloria and called her crazy."

"So why did you bring it up?"

"I don't know. To see if it was real."

Hal sat down beside Raymond on the cot. "It was mean," he said. "Why are you being so mean?"

Gloria was not even sure herself any more if it had been real, and she was angry at Raymond for bringing it up in front of a stranger. Standing in the moonlight in the front bedroom, she buttoned up her nightgown and felt sad. She padded down to the bathroom and brushed her teeth extra hard, taking her anger out on her gums, which bled a little. She still thought about the Virgin a little bit each day, even though she tried not to; the memory made her upset. Lavinia Gautier had been her best friend, and they had stopped playing together after that summer. Everyone in town looked at her suspiciously from then on.

Lavinia took piano lessons from the nuns, and Gloria used to meet her afterwards: she would stand outside, under the convent window, listening to her play. There was a little piece that Gloria liked because it sounded just like a song that was on an old record they used to have, a pretty love song about gentle rain and meadows and birds serenading flowers. Lavinia had told her never to sing the words because the Hit Parade was bad and anything that the nuns taught you was holy. When Lavinia's lesson was finished, they would walk home together, up through the graveyard past the priests' graves, and across the nuns' vegetable garden and the fields. Sometimes Lavinia made her late for supper because she had to pray. They would sit beneath the big crucifix in the graveyard and talk about Lourdes; Lavinia talked about Lourdes the way that the other girls in school talked about boys. She had been so tiny and so strange, like a serious little doll. Gloria wondered if she was happy up in Quebec, married to Jesus.

When Gloria crawled into bed, she could not stop thinking about Lavinia. She thought of the ceiling in the convent chapel: the blueness of it, like the blue of the first robin's egg she had ever seen.

It was the last thing she thought of as she fell asleep.

"You want another beer?" Danny asked. "Give that attic more time to cool off."

"Yeah," said Junior, "I'll get her to send a couple over. I gotta take a piss." He left the table and headed for the washrooms. On the way he caught their waitress's attention, held up two fingers, and pointed back towards the table where Danny was sitting. She nodded.

While he was peeing, Junior tried to think of the waitress's name. He knew that she and Ginette had worked together somewhere once. He had been friendly with her all evening, but could not for the life of him remember her name.

There was no one at the pay phone beside the bathroom door. He stood and looked at it, then glanced back into the Club. The waitress was talking to Danny. Junior went to the phone and dialled. An operator told him that three minutes would cost four dollars, so he fed the coins into the phone.

He thought about the first thing that he would say. "I'm sorry I woke you up, but I have to talk to you." He said it a couple of times to himself while the phone started to ring. He pictured a black phone beside Ginette's bed in a little apartment in Halifax. He thought about her waking up and answering it. "I'm sorry I woke you up, but I have to talk to you." The phone went on ringing.

He let it ring twenty times.

SEVENTEEN

Her sister had snuck the phone into her bedroom to make a call so secret that Minnie was convinced she must be setting up an appointment with that stuck-up Sandy Whyte. Who else could it possibly be? Margaret's behaviour confirmed Minnie's deepest fear: something had passed between the two of them after church on Sunday while Minnie had been talking to the minister's husband. Her sister was about to make a fool of herself. This morning, she and Margaret had been sitting around after breakfast, talking about her frustrations with those clowns in the Middle East, and Minnie could not help but notice that Margaret was constantly stealing glances at the clock. Then, at nine on the dot, she had excused herself and gone upstairs.

Margaret had seemed a little odd these last few days, to say the least, and so Minnie was not altogether surprised when she heard her talking quietly in her room. She had tiptoed up the stairs and almost tripped over the phone cord that stretched across the floor from the telephone table in the upstairs hallway and under her sister's door. She tried to listen, but all she could make out was that Margaret's voice was low and serious, the inflections at the end of her sentences implying that she was asking a lot of questions. Then Minnie had shifted her weight, making a floorboard creak loudly, and Margaret's voice had dropped to a low whisper.

Minnie went into the bathroom and, after counting to fifty as quickly as she could, flushed the toilet — she did not want her sister to suspect that she had come upstairs to eavesdrop — and then she walked slowly past the closed bedroom door and down the stairs. She returned to the kitchen, where she sat idly dipping her fingers into the marmalade jar. She hated secrets that were not her own.

Maybe it was time to phone Mrs. LeBlanc and get herself invited over; she needed to have a long chat about Sandy Whyte.

But when she picked up the receiver and heard Margaret say "Friday afternoon, tomorrow," she realized that her sister was still on the line. Since she had unwittingly broken in on the conversation, she decided to listen just for a bit, but Margaret must have heard her because she said "I'll be off in a minute" in a very stern voice.

Minnie hung up and went back to the marmalade, licking off the bits of orange rind that stuck to her fingertips.

When her sister finally came downstairs, she did not even look at Minnie; she just marched through the kitchen and out the back door. Minnie went outside a few minutes later, but her sister was nowhere in sight. She could not have gone very far, because the car was still in the yard. Had she walked to Sandy Whyte's place? Minnie decided that there was no time to call Mrs. LeBlanc. She would have to drive there straight away and, if she saw Margaret en route, she might offer her a lift. That would shake her up. This whole thing had to be nipped in the bud.

She hadn't driven in a while, so she went very slowly. There was neither hide nor hair of Margaret on their street, or in the park, or anywhere on Main Street all the way to the Whyte house. Where on earth could she be? If she were already at The Oaks, she must have walked awfully darn fast.

When Minnie pulled into the driveway, Mrs. LeBlanc was sitting in a chair on her front porch, smoking a cigarette.

"Hello there," Minnie sang out, hefting herself out of the car. "I was going to call ahead but my sister's been yakking on the phone all the live-long day. I just dropped by to get your recipe for rhubarb nut loaf."

"That's a good recipe now too," the old lady said. "I miss it. My daughter, she won't let me bake now that they got that damn bakery at the supermarket."

Minnie was moving slowly along the walk from the driveway. "They make good doughnuts there, though, I have to say," she said.

Mrs. LeBlanc shrugged. "She tells me I don't have to bother cooking 'cause I'm old. I better rest up, she says. Rest up for what, eh? The Home?"

"Children nowadays," Minnie said, reaching the top of the steps.

"This one won't let me smoke in the house since she moved back from Toronto."

To her great delight, Minnie realized that she had found someone with whom she could have a nice long chat.

"Do you mind if I sit a spell, Mrs. LeBlanc?" she asked, pointing to an empty lawn chair.

Mrs. LeBlanc shrugged. "Call me Lila."

To Minnie's further delight she did not even have to bring up the subject of Sandy Whyte. No sooner had she sat down then Lila pointed to The Oaks. "I almost called the police on that bunch yesterday," she said.

"You don't say." Minnie nodded. "And why, may I ask?"

Lila LeBlanc shook her head and looked disgusted. "The other morning there, I'm outside for my first cigarette in the back — there's nothing to see out here that early so I go to the back steps and listen to all them darn birds" — here she took a long drag on her cigarette — "but I'm out there at the crack of dawn and I see him, I swear to God, crawling around his yard, waving a bottle of beer at me."

This surprised Minnie. "Was he drunk?"

Lila nodded and exhaled. "Stuff's been goin' on in there for years," she said. "Ever since the old lady got sick that last time. Maybe that's why she got sick. Poor old thing."

"Drunk," Minnie repeated. "You don't say. And what time of day was this?"

"Before seven. Seven *in the morning!*"

Minnie fell back in her lawn chair. "You don't say."

"He waves that bottle of beer at me like he wants me to go over and have some." She jabbed her cigarette towards The Oaks. "Just look at them windows — every blind in that house is always pulled down tight. They's in there drinking and oh my God only knows what!"

Minnie looked over at the Whyte house and imagined Sandy, naked and drunk, careening down the hallways with a bottle in his hand.

"Who's in there with him?" she asked.

"I dunno what-all hangs out there with him. But, my God, yesterday afternoon they was drunk and screaming at each other — you could hear them down at the bridge!"

"What were they fighting about?"

The old lady shrugged. "I told my daughter when she come home from work, but Mavis, she says to mind my own business. 'You didn't hear it,' I says to her. 'It'd wake the dead.' But they was at it Mrs., oh my God, they was at it like cats and dogs." She ground out her cigarette in the ashtray on her lap and opened her pack to take out another. "I used to be able to smoke in my own kitchen," she said bitterly.

But Minnie wanted to know who was attending Sandy Whyte's wild parties. "Are there cars in the yard?" she asked. "Where do the people come from?"

"One I know is a kid that's always hanging round. I see him there in the back, oh my God, lotsa times. And he's a bad one."

Minnie was keeping an eye on the street in case her sister came along. "Who is he?" she asked.

"I don't know. He's got that damn long hair like my grand-son in Moncton. And that one — the cops is always at the door for that one! They're bad kids. You can tell by the way they walks, like they think they's big. I look out some mornings and see him walking out the backyard and up into the woods. He either gets up and out of there damn early or he's been up all the night doing wild things with the rest of them."

"Why would he be going up in the woods?"

"Drugs," Lila said, nodding her head. "The woods is fulla drugs. They sneak them in from the States."

All through their conversation, Minnie was studying the side of The Oaks. The Whytes had always thought they were as good as royalty. When her sister had started going out with Sandy, Minnie knew that nothing would ever come of it — she had never heard of a Whyte who married outside the blood. Even old Mrs. Whyte, who had come from somewhere on the other side of Moncton, had been connected somehow. Hadn't her mother been a cousin of old Erminda Whyte's, Sandy's grandmother? Sandy Whyte would never have married Margaret in a million years.

And, besides, everybody knew that he had never been interested in girls to begin with, the filthy thing.

"Young people nowadays," Lila LeBlanc was saying, "they always gotta have something. Drugs or that damn crap they call music. They don't work — they don't know how to work. Not like my Roger. He was in that butcher store ten, twelve hours a day."

"Do you suppose," Minnie began, wanting to edge her way into the darkest rumours about Sandy Whyte, "do you suppose that there's some kind of hanky-panky with Mr. Whyte and that boy?"

Mrs. LeBlanc looked straight at her and gravely nodded her head. "I told Mavis's boy when he was just little, I told him, 'If ever that man next door tries to give you a candy bar or something, you're to say "no" and come right back home and tell me.'"

"I thought as much," said Minnie.

"You know what I'm saying, Mrs.?"

Minnie nodded sadly. A moment passed before she sighed and said, "My poor sister."

"That poor girl smartened up damn quick, didn't she? It was all a front, taking that poor girl out. We all knew that. Goddam sin," she said, "excuse my English. But we all knew. She's no fool, your sister."

"She's very active in our church." Minnie nodded. "She works on that anti-abortion hotline. I don't know how she does it."

"Good for her. These damn kids nowadays, they're all at it from the time they're twelve, thirteen. Stupid girls, they get all knocked up, oh my God, then they just run off and cry to some doctor and bang" — she slapped her hands together — "he picks up a knife and sends their poor little bastards off to Limbo."

Minnie made a clicking sound with her tongue. Both women sat silently for a moment, watching the side of The Oaks. "If any women had gone there in the last little while," Minnie began carefully — she did not want to raise Mrs. LeBlanc's curiosity about her sister — "you would have noticed, wouldn't you?"

"The only woman who goes near that place is that Gloria Maurice when she comes to clean."

"Oh. And has she ever seen anything suspicious?"

"Her?" She made a circling motion in the air beside her head. "She's crazy, always was crazy. Poor Rose Maurice — her mother — it isn't fair. Her whole family turned out no damn good."

Minnie nodded, although she was not the least bit interested in the Maurice family. "I guess," she said, "that even if that girl saw anything that no one would believe her."

"Nobody from our church, that's for damn sure. The only one of Rose's kids that could have amounted to anything was the second boy, that Danny: he led the whole high school in shop. But that bad brother of his made him go and lose his arm! And now her youngest boy's home from Toronto. With his boyfriend!"

"You don't say."

Lila nodded, "Mavis saw them and she told me he's got that AIDS, says you can tell just to look at him."

"Oh my God, you don't say!"

"And with all that wild carrying on next door — you can't tell me that *he* won't come down with it before you know it!"

Minnie broke out in a sweat that had nothing to do with the humidity. Suddenly she realized that Sandy Whyte's disgusting lifestyle could expose her sister to much more than a broken heart.

Hal had been dreaming that he and Raymond were back in Toronto, living in a hospital, when the dream turned and suddenly they were swimming in deep water towards the Dune.

"This water is really wet," he said, and then he was waking up wet and confused. Raymond was standing naked beside his bed and peeing on him.

"Raymond!" He pulled the chain on the light. "Raymond! What the hell are you doing?"

"It was the rum and Coke," Raymond said.

Hal threw off the sheet and jumped out of bed. "Are you awake?" he said. "Raymond, you're pissing on me."

"But I figured you'd understand."

"Understand what? Jesus!" He stripped the sheets off the bed and balled them up, keeping the wetness in the centre. The pee was bright yellow, all that vitamin C. Hal rubbed the sheets against his body, wiping himself dry. His pubic hair was matted and sticky.

"I didn't have time to go to the bathroom," Raymond said, very matter-of-factly, and went back to his own bed.

Hal stood holding the wet sheets and looked over at him. Raymond had closed his eyes and curled up as if nothing had happened. Had he been sleepwalking? Hal didn't think so. There had been nothing malicious in Raymond's voice or, Hal thought, in what he had just done. Raymond sounded hurt, as if Hal had not understood.

He turned back to his own bed and felt the mattress — it was barely damp, thank God. He dropped the sheets on the floor, slipped into his bathrobe, and went to the bathroom to wash off. Raymond's parents were snoring loudly as he passed their door. Well, at least they hadn't woken up.

His chest and stomach were tacky with urine. He filled up the sink with hot water and soaped a wash cloth. Gloria had left her watch on the counter; it was two in the morning.

Raymond's behaviour was starting to make horrible sense. Hal was afraid that the disease was edging its way into his brain

— his inhibitions were disappearing. That was the only thing that would explain his behaviour: his nudist routine on the beach in the afternoon, his cruelty to Mama and Gloria on the veranda, his forgetfulness, and now this. It would be easier if Raymond were simply being mean, but Hal was afraid that this was not the case and that things were going to start getting worse, and probably very quickly.

Moving quietly, he went back to the bedroom to get the sheets. Raymond was sleeping, his snores growing louder and converging with the snorts from Mama and Pop down the hall. Hal looked at him for a moment — the stronger line of his nose, and the higher bones of his cheeks: the disease was honing his features into a new sharpness. The gauntness was handsome in a terrible way. And yet, despite the fact that his face was losing all softness, Raymond looked more like a boy than like the man who had smiled at him at Clive's memorial service the day they met. He looked so guileless that Hal could not bear it; he picked up the sheets and turned off the light. He made his way down the dark stairs towards the laundry in the basement.

In the downstairs hall, he bumped into Junior, who was on his way to the veranda with two bottles of beer. He looked pretty drunk.

"Can't sleep?" asked Junior.

"No, I was asleep. It's Raymond."

"What?"

"Let me get rid of these first." He took the sheets down into the basement and shoved them inside the empty washer, then he threw in a handful of soap and turned it on. How could he explain this to Junior?

In the dark of the veranda, Junior handed Danny a beer. "One of those fairies just pissed the bed," he said. "Tell me we're not gonna catch this friggin' thing now."

"What?" Junior had taken so long to get his drink that Danny had fallen asleep waiting. "Who pissed the bed?"

"I dunno. But fucking P.U. — the sheets smelled pretty rank."

"Who?"

"Let him tell ya."

"Who?"

"*Who?* You a fucking owl or something? The bookstore fairy." Junior was annoyed because he had tried phoning Ginette from the kitchen and there was still no answer.

Danny was completely confused. He shrugged and sipped on his beer. Neither of them spoke again until Hal came out.

"So," said Junior. "Did he piss his bed or something?"

"No." Hal shook his head and stood awkwardly. "I woke up and he was standing there peeing on my bed."

"Jesus Christ," said Junior. "What'd you do to him?"

"I didn't do anything. I was asleep." Then he sat at the top of the front steps a short distance between the two brothers. "I think Raymond is getting dementia."

"You mean he's nuts?"

"Well, he's losing his inhibitions, that's for sure."

"But he always was nuts."

"Junior," Danny warned. "S'what I thought at the beach." He nodded. "Something's wrong somewhere. Something's not working. He nodded again, then drank from his beer.

"Dandy," Junior said, "just friggin' dandy!"

"So," Danny asked, "what'll we do?"

"My cigarettes are upstairs — can I bum one?"

"We'll do something," Danny said. "Hal? What'll we do? Here." He held out his lighter.

"Thanks." Danny's cigarette's were stronger than his, and filterless. He coughed a little as he handed the lighter back, and sat down again.

"I want to phone our doctor in the morning," he said. "I need his advice."

"Good plan," said Danny. "Yep, that's a good start." He didn't know why he said this — he had no faith in doctors of any kind.

"Can someone get him out of the house so he doesn't over-hear me? I'm not quite sure what I should do next and the doctor …" The cigarette was too strong and he was feeling light-headed. He decided not to smoke it any more.

Danny was nodding, "So you don't want him to know?"

"Not yet. Not until I've had a chance to talk to the doctor."

"And where should we take him?" Junior asked. "I'm not going to that friggin' Dune again."

"No just for like, half an hour. Just take him downtown or something."

"We'll take him for a little drive," Danny decided.

"Thanks. Thanks." He stood up. "Look, I'm going back to bed. Thanks for the smoke." He tossed the cigarette out towards the street. "Goodnight." And he went back upstairs.

"We're taking your car," Junior said after a minute or so had passed.

Danny shrugged. "Sure."

"'Cause I don't want him freaking out and pissing in mine."

"Poor little bugger," Danny said.

"Isn't that something fags do anyway?"

"What?"

"Piss on each other?"

"Oh, Junior, grow up."

They sat quietly for a long time and then Danny said, "Yeah, we'll take the poor little bugger for a drive. Even if we just go down to the end of the wharf."

But in the morning, when Hal wanted to phone Dr. Louie, both brothers were still sleeping in the attic. He called their names half a dozen times as he stood looking down at them sprawled on the mattress. "Useless," he muttered, "utterly fucking useless." He went to the bathroom. Now what?

Mama found the clean, wet sheets in the washer first thing and she sent Gloria to find out what had happened. Hal was in the bathroom, and when she looked into their bedroom Raymond was just getting up.

"Good morning! How'd you sleep?"

"Okay. Hal crawled in with me in the middle of the night." He grinned. "And Mama thought she could keep us apart with these stupid twin beds."

"Why's his bed stripped?"

Raymond looked over at the bare mattress; the trace of a memory flickered through him before he could catch it fully. "I don't know. Maybe he had an accident."

She decided not to tell Mama anything. The last thing that Hal needed was for her family to think that he was a bed-wetter. When she came downstairs and acted as if she had forgotten what Mama had sent her to find out, Mama got mad and they had an argument when Gloria started looking for some lobster cutlery.

"We don't need any lobster tools," Mama said. "We're gonna have cold pack."

"Oh, come on," said Gloria. "Raymond and Hal didn't come all the way from Toronto for friggin' canned lobster."

"No," said Mama. "All we got is one nutcracker and a couple of plastic lobster diggers. They look crummy. You're the one who's so hot on setting a fancy table for this damn lobster supper tonight. We're having cold pack."

"Well, I'll get us some cutlery," said Gloria. "Silver ones."

Mama had been kneading the dough for four loaves of bread. Her floured hands slapped down on the board in exasperation. "And where are you gonna get them?"

"At Sandy Whyte's place," she said. "I'll borrow them."

"But he's out of town, Smarty Pants."

"Well, I've got a key," Gloria announced. "And he won't mind — if he even finds out. I know right where they are, too. They're in that big old sideboard in the front hall."

Raymond and Hal were standing in the kitchen behind her.

"You-all goin' down ta the Whaat plantation?" Raymond crooned.

"Yeah, you wanna come?"

"We'd love to. Wouldn't we, Hal?"

"You go," Hal answered. "I'll help Mama here."

Despite the fact that Mama seemed out of sorts — she was pounding the dough with a vengeance — Hal wanted to talk to her about the sheets, and he knew that this was a good opportunity to call the doctor. He had just come down from his second trip to the attic; Junior and Danny were so unconscious that he couldn't even shake them awake.

"I don't think I'll bother with my purse," Gloria said, picking up her keys from the counter. "Come on, Raymond."

They went out to the car, then headed down the street.

"Mama," Hal said, "I need to talk to you. I have to call Raymond's doctor."

Not five minutes later, just after Gloria had switched on her signal light and was slowing down to turn into Sandy Whyte's driveway, Minnie waved goodbye to Lila, backed out of Mrs. LeBlanc's yard, and smashed into Gloria's left fender.

EIGHTEEN ✢

Deep in the night, Chaleur's mind separated from his body and drifted upwards into the stale air above the bed. It roamed about the top edges of the walls, trying not to look down on the flesh that was becoming as dry as parched bone. As long as it could still move about without creaking, he knew that there was lubrication somewhere and that would keep him from turning to dust. At times, the crack in the ceiling seemed about to open up, promising that he might catch a glimpse of stars like the ones he had seen above the woods. Once, somewhere at night, in a clearing, he had seen dragonflies silhouetted against an almost full moon. Moon and insects had seemed near enough to reach out and touch. He must have been very little then. His mind hovered below the crack, waiting for it to split wider, but it would not; the moon would not shine down on him. He knew that Annette had escaped through the woods and was waiting for him there.

A few times his stomach rumbled and his mind was dragged downwards, in front of the television on the old dresser. The dresser looked grumpy and he was afraid that it might advance towards the bed — he had to keep it away from his body. Occasionally it seemed that a hand would touch him and he would shut his eyes and pretend that it was his father's. Everything hurt.

After watching the boy late into the night, Sandy had fallen asleep on the floor and was awakened at mid-morning by the rasping noises from Chaleur's throat. His head was beneath the bed and, at first, he thought the sound was a snake's dry rattle above him. He peered about him, unable to focus in the dim light. The floor was hard as rock and he seemed to be in a cave. But then Chaleur shifted slightly, creaking the bedsprings ever so little, and Sandy remembered where he was. He crawled backwards and sat up on his knees. When he peeked up, he could see the boy staring hopelessly at him. His eyes were red-rimmed and frightened and his lips were cracking.

"I'll get you some water," Sandy said kindly, putting his hands on the edge of the bed and pushing himself upwards. His legs were stiff. He went to the bathroom and returned with a basin of cool water, and a clean wash cloth. He dipped the cloth into the water and then, cradling the sweet head and holding it up, he opened the suffering mouth and squeezed a bit of water into it. He thought of his mother's flowers parched and dying in the heat of the living-room window. "Just water them, Sandy," she said, "and they'll come back." And sometimes they did. He would nurse the boy back to health and untie his limbs, and then —

But there was a loud noise from the front yard: a thump like ridiculous thunder followed by a long, sad metallic scrape. A car horn blasted and a woman's voice began screeching. Other voices joined hers, and suddenly there was a godawful row.

"I'll be right back," he said, dropping the wash cloth on the pillow and hurrying into the hall. He stopped and shut the door behind him.

Chaleur was certain from the noise that the crack above him had begun to split, but it was not moving; it flowed across the ceiling like a dry creek bed. Yet it seemed he could smell wetness nearby. If he could only move his head a little more, a fraction of an inch, he might be able to catch the wash cloth between his teeth and suck the coolness into his stony throat.

When Sandy looked out through the front windows he could see two cars on the street at the base of his driveway; there must have been an accident of some kind, but the front hedges were obscuring his vision. Old Mrs. LeBlanc was standing in the middle of her yard, as still as a statue, holding a cigarette. A thin man was wandering on the lawn, looking up at his house. It was unfathomable, like an allegorical painting. And then, to his horror and surprise, Gloria Maurice was walking up his driveway very quickly and, snapping at her heels, was that fool sister of Margaret's. From the way that Gloria was holding out her hand, Sandy could tell that it contained the key to his front door.

"Oh dear!" He let the curtain slide back and then, turning quickly, he walked out into the hall and started down the stairs. He had barely reached the front hall when the door opened.

"Gloria," he said, as they stared at each other in surprise, "what do you think you're doing?"

The poor girl looked stunned. "I thought you were away," she said.

Behind her, Minnie was saying, "I don't care if you had the right of way, you stupid girl! Don't you dare hide out in there!"

Gloria was looking at Sandy in complete confusion. "I was just going to borrow your lobster silver for supper," she began, when Minnie grabbed her by the shoulders and said, "Don't turn your back on me, Missy!" And pointing out the front door, she waved her hand wildly. "It was not my fault!"

"I have to use your phone," Gloria stammered and, lowering her eyes, she brushed past Sandy and started for the kitchen.

"She came out of nowhere!" Minnie said to Sandy. "And she was way over the speed limit!"

"I was not!"

"Ladies…," he said.

"I'm calling the police," Gloria said, moving down the hall.

The police! Sandy looked towards the stairs and then, fearing he might give himself away, turned back to Minnie.

But she was storming past Sandy in her pursuit of Gloria, saying, "Call the police! They certainly won't side in with the likes of you!"

Sandy looked anxiously up the stairs again, and then followed the two women into his kitchen. "Ladies, ladies, please calm yourselves."

The front door was left wide open. Raymond, who Gloria had already told to "stay out of this" because he had told Minnie first to "shut up" then to "fuck off" after calling her a "fat old bitch," wandered into the front hall. He stood quietly, listening to the sharp, insistent voice of the woman who had hit them — "Call the police! It's nine-one-one! Here, give me the phone!" — and to Sandy Whyte's protests — "Ladies, calm yourselves. Shouldn't you move your cars? Aren't you blocking traffic?"

"Not till the police get here," Gloria was saying. "That's what my brother Danny always told me."

"Your brother!" Minnie replied. "As if anyone in your family knew anything!"

Raymond looked about. An oak mirror and hat rack hung on the wall to his left above an oak bench with a hinged seat. The walls were panelled in darkly stained oak, and the arches were oak as well. Everything was built to inspire awe, thought Raymond, and it was all hideous. The house had impressed him once, but he was no longer a little hick. Even the grandfather clock with its two faces — one for the time, the other for the phases of the moon — looked stumpy and worn out. There was an oak sideboard on the wall near the stairs that was carved with Gothic arches and vines; the knobs on the drawers were clusters of grapes. It was ugly enough to be interesting. "Cool," he whispered and went to it. Inside the drawer was a box containing the silver lobster cutlery, each piece monogrammed. He tucked it under his arm because, in the confusion, he didn't want Gloria to forget what they had come for.

He went to the foot of the stairs and looked up. He had been here once before, as a boy. He hung around Sherri Dobbins for two months only because he knew that her family would be invited to the Whyte's annual Christmas party. She was plain and unpopular and she bored him to death — he still felt guilty for using her — but it had been the only way he could think of to get into this house. There had been schoolground fag jokes about Sandy Whyte, and Raymond — without really understanding why — had needed to see where he lived. His excitement on entering the house that time had been in equal measure to his fear. As soon as he could, he had wandered away from Sherri and her mother. Sandy Whyte himself had been nowhere to be seen, and Raymond had decided to go looking for his bedroom because he imagined that it contained secrets. When old Mrs. Whyte caught him at the top of the stairs, he had pretended to be looking for the bathroom.

This morning, he snuck up the oak staircase for a second time while his sister and Minnie argued over the phone in the kitchen.

The stairs were not nearly so grand as he remembered them; they were neither as high nor as wide, and the worn runner was pure 'fifties, and all wrong for the age of the house. At the landing he stopped and looked about: everything was so tacky. The walls needed repainting — the colour was a hideous beige that might, at one time, have had a bit of pink in it. Gloria could scrub it for a month and it would never look clean. The varnish on the oak wainscotting was stripped in places, worn away, and needed refinishing. The only picture hanging on the stairs was a photograph of old Mrs. Whyte in a mattless dime-store frame. Sandy Whyte was a poor excuse for a fag, Raymond decided; he had no fashion sense at all. If *he* owned this place, he would sponge-paint the staircase walls into something spectacular.

At the top of the stairs, there was a miserable old print of *Samuel in Prayer*. "Oh, pul-eeze," Raymond whispered in disgust. Protestants were as hopeless as Catholics when it came to this kitsch. The top stair creaked under his foot and he giggled, imagining that he was Lucille Ball sneaking around after Ricky had told her to mind her own business. "Rickeee," he whispered, twisting his face into a bawl; "Rickeee." He moved into the hallway and looked about.

"Oh, you're plucky," he told himself, but his boldness began to fade when he heard a sound.

It was low, and sad, a moaning, and so eerie that for a moment he wondered if he had imagined it. But there it was again, and it seemed to be coming from the back of the house. All the bedroom doors were opened but one, and he moved towards it. *It's probably a cat*, he thought. Reaching the door, he placed his ear against the wood. There was strange throbbing sound, which he listened to very carefully until he realized that it was his own heart beating in his ear. He rolled his eyes at his own gullibility and stood quietly, his head cocked. The moaning sounds were faint, but they seemed to be close at hand. Someone was in there, he was pretty sure, because he could hear what seemed to be laboured breathing. His first thought was that old Mrs. Whyte had never died and she was locked away, like someone from *Jane Eyre*.

Downstairs there was a commotion of voices, and the fat woman was loudest. He knew that he did not have a lot of time.

Raymond made a little scratching sound on the moulding and heard a faint rustling from behind the door. He could not decide whether to go in or not. Then he decided that if he pushed on the door and it opened that he was supposed to go inside. He pushed and the door opened a crack.

"Avon calling." Raymond giggled and slipped inside.

The room was dark and bad-smelling, and Raymond peered about. Someone appeared to be in the bed. There was another sound, barely audible, and he moved towards it.

"Hello?" he said.

And then, as soon as his eyes became accustomed to the darkness and he could see the shape on the bed more clearly, he stopped, frightened. On the bed, a strange face had turned towards his, and a rattle of broken air passed through its lips. Raymond became confused and took a step backwards. He felt the way that he had yesterday on the Dune when the little house had wavered and disappeared. Something was shifting in the world around him and his mind was losing its bearings. He did not know what to do, and so, for a moment, he did nothing.

The boy on the bed seemed to be tied there and he was trying to speak. "El," he whispered and the fingers of one bound hand motioned feebly towards Raymond.

But his feet were frozen. He was thinking of the little house, how it had wavered, and he believed that if he moved his eyes or turned in the slightest way that this vision would disappear, too. And, because the smell from the bed was stale, like old urine, he thought suddenly of Gloria asking him about Hal's bed sheets, and he remembered getting out of his own bed last night and peeing on them. Had he really done that? Why had he? Because now he was certain that he had. He realized that something terrible was happening inside him. Because it was not possible for a boy to be tied to a bed in a house in this town — his home town could never be *this* interesting. He knew that his mind was playing tricks on him again. This was *it*. This was the start of *It*.

"Help me," the voice croaked so faintly, and Raymond finally moved. He walked very slowly towards the bed and stared at the boy. There was a wet rag lying beside his face on the pillow.

"I know you're only a mirage," Raymond whispered. "It's the heat."

And the boy almost shook his head and tried to raise himself.

"This is awful," Raymond whispered. "I wish I could help you, but I don't know where you really are."

The boy moaned again. Raymond set the box of silver on the bed, picked up the wet rag and, folding it into a thin band, laid it over the boy's forehead. "I know you are real. A mirage is really something, somewhere. I'll find you," he promised, and he carefully studied the boy, trying to memorize all that he could see: the long dark hair, the sallow cheeks, the clothing that he would need to identify. Gently he touched the boy's shoulder — it felt so warm, so real.

"I will."

And he picked up the box and left the room. Downstairs, he slipped quietly out the front door.

Chaleur had no tears left to cry. Ten minutes later, he was not sure if someone had come into the room or if he had been dreaming. He went back to the ceiling and waited for the crack to split open.

Out on the street, a small crowd had gathered. Cars were slowing down as drivers gawked at the accident, and a group of neighbours was standing on the sidewalk, talking and drinking coffee. Gloria kept close to Sandy, who kept glancing nervously back to the house. "Why is she being so mean?" Gloria said quietly.

"Don't pay any attention to her," he whispered.

"Everything's ruined," she said. "I've gotta go get lobsters — I gotta get *ready!*"

"This should only take a few minutes," he said hopefully. "It wasn't a major accident."

"It was to me!"

"But no one was hurt."

Minnie was recounting her version of events yet again when the policeman drove up. By this point, her story had expanded to the point where she was certain that Gloria had been travelling at fifty miles an hour. "A speed demon," she kept repeating.

"Thank heavens," she said, waving to the policeman. "Finally! Look at what she did to my car!"

"And your name is?"

"Mrs. Arthur Snow."

"And that's your car?" the policeman said, pointing to Gloria's.

"Certainly not — that's my car."

"It's my car," said Gloria.

The policeman looked over at her. "You're Pop Maurice's kid."

"Yes. Gloria."

"She must have been doing *sixty*," said Minnie.

The policeman studied both cars from a variety of angles. "Were there any witnesses?" he said.

"Well, I saw the whole thing," declared Minnie.

"Minnie, you're hardly a witness," Sandy moaned.

"Well, if I'm not, I don't know who is."

"You were one of the *drivers*," he said.

The policeman came over. "Mr. Whyte, did you see it?"

"No, Francis," said Sandy. "I was inside the house. But if Gloria were going as fast as Minnie claims she was, wouldn't there be more damage?"

"How fast were you going?"

"I had almost stopped," Gloria answered, trying not to cry.

"Liar," said Minnie. "You little liar."

"I was turning in! How could I have been going that fast if I was turning in?"

"But look at the damage to my car!"

"Could I see your licences, please?"

"Oh, no," said Gloria. "Mine's home in my purse. I can call someone to bring it."

"So's mine," said Minnie, and when the policeman looked at the purse on her arm, she said, "In my *good* purse. I just picked up this old thing because I was only going to visit Mrs. LeBlanc."

At that moment, Lila LeBlanc ground out her cigarette on the lawn and stepped forward. "I saw it all," she said.

"Yes?" said the officer.

"Mrs. Snow was at my place. She jumped in her car, backed out without looking, and ran straight into that Maurice girl."

"Lila!"

"That's just the way it happened." And she turned away from Minnie and stepped back into the crowd.

Sandy was furious at Minnie's stupidity and decided that he would make things as unpleasant for her as he possibly could. In the cheeriest voice he could muster, he said, "Minnie, I didn't know you drove any more these days. I thought Margaret did all the driving in your house."

"She *prefers* to drive," said Minnie.

"And yet you still keep up your licence. Isn't that smart?"

Minnie's jaw fell open slightly, then she shut it.

Raymond had been watching all of this from the low stone fence in front of The Oaks. He had tucked the box of silver under the hedge behind him. "She was driving without a licence!" he called out.

"Raymond, be quiet," Gloria said firmly.

"Oh, I'm sure that Minnie has it at home," Sandy said. "She can just show it at the police station later. You'll do that, won't you, Minnie?"

Minnie's eyes darted about in confusion. "I refuse to speak to the likes of you," she said. "Officer, do you have any idea what goes on in his house?"

"Mrs. Snow," said the officer, "do you have a valid driver's licence in your other purse?"

Sandy turned to Gloria and, to her great surprise, he winked at her.

Raymond wondered if Sandy Whyte was aware of the mirage in his bedroom, and was thinking about going over to ask him when suddenly Minnie bolted. She ran and opened the door of her car and tried to get it started. When the policeman ordered her to get out and Minnie started to cry, Raymond lost his train of thought. Suddenly, everything seemed to be going well: he smiled when the policeman radioed for a tow truck to impound Minnie's car, and he clapped when Minnie was driven off in the cruiser. The small crowd drifted away. As Sandy trotted back to his house, Raymond studied him carefully.

Mrs. LeBlanc turned to Gloria. "If she wants to talk to me again," she said, "she can come with her good purse next time." Maybe Gloria Maurice was nuts, but in the end you had to stand by the people who went to your own church. She walked back to her chair on the front porch.

Gloria stood looking at the crumpled fender. She would have to explain it to Pop, which would be bad enough, but she knew that Mama would tell her it was all her own fault because she couldn't be satisfied with canned lobster. She was not sure if Mrs. Snow's sister's insurance would pay to have it fixed — the policeman had told her to call her own company when she got home, which was the last thing on earth that she wanted to do. The day was a disaster: there would be no lobster silver, the fancy lobster supper was spoiled, and the family reunion would not be as special as it could have been.

"Raymond, come on, let's go home."

Slowly she went around to the driver's side and got in the car.

When Raymond jumped in beside her, she did not notice the box on his lap as they drove up Main Street and turned left on Dorchester.

"It's all ruined," she said.

"No, it isn't. They arrested the old bitch."

"Raymond, they just drove her home."

He had opened the box and taken out a long, elegant lobster pick. "Not my taste," he said, "but it is good silver."

Gloria took her eyes off the road and looked over at him.

"Where the hell you get those?" she demanded.

"They were right in the sideboard. Just where you said they'd be."

"Holy God, I better phone Sandy Whyte right away," she said, and turned safely into her driveway.

NINETEEN

S he was angry enough when Minnie came snooping around her bedroom door, but after her sister picked up the receiver to nose in on her conversation, Margaret's blood had really started to boil; she knew that if she did not get out of the house right away that she would say terrible, hurtful things. So she had stormed out the back door and gone around to sit in the shade of the far side of the house. When she was a little girl she had hidden there: in the corner between the living room and the sun porch there was a little nook where she could not be seen from inside.

"Hopeless," she hissed. "She's hopeless hopeless hopeless!"

Minnie's sway over daily events was turning into a reign; Margaret was living with a monstrous baby. She wanted to scream at Minnie, slap her fat cheeks, push her down the stairs. But there would be no satisfaction in doing these things, only the consequences. She was going to have to talk with her sister and lay down the law, an ordeal she dreaded. "Humph," Minnie would say, "you're high and mighty all of a sudden." Or, worse, she might cry.

"Don't you dare cry," Margaret hissed, as if her sister were standing in the mock orange beside her. "You can turn off the waterworks right now! Listen to me!"

She would go inside right now and do it. It would be un-pleasant, but she would do it.

But couldn't it wait until tomorrow, after she saw Annette? No, it would be better to put Minnie in her place first and give her a day alone to stew it over.

"Listen to me," she whispered, "listen to me now!" She whis-pered it over and over.

When she heard her car start in the driveway on the other side of the house, and she saw Minnie driving down the street, she was as confused as she was annoyed. What was Minnie up to now? Margaret knew that she would not go very far — she'd given up her licence because driving on the highway frightened her. Whatever she was doing, it must be another one of her lit-tle tricks and Margaret was not about to fall for it. She stood up and went back inside to wash the dishes.

When she wiped off the kitchen table, the dishcloth stuck to the bits of marmalade that had fallen from Minnie's fingers.

"Hopeless."

She scrubbed and cleaned, wondering where on earth her sister could have gone. Minnie never went anywhere on her own any more. She ran through the litany of her sister's demands:

Will you drive me to the store?

Will you take me up to the hairdresser's?

Will you pick me up some chips when you're out?

But what if Minnie herself was nearing a breaking point?

What if Minnie was asserting her independence? If so, this was a good thing. Yet, even as she thought this, Margaret knew it was wishful thinking. All that Minnie would ever assert was their dependence on each other. What did it matter where she was? Margaret should simply be grateful to be left alone and to have been spared an unhappy confrontation for the time being.

Fifteen minutes later the kitchen was as neat as a pin, the dishes were dry, and as she opened the cupboard to put the plates away, she heard chirping. *My goodness*, she thought, *it's so quiet in here I can hear the birds out in the yard.* She went to look.

There were sparrows on the back steps, but when she began to ease open the screen door, they flew away. She sighed and watched them dart into the trees. When she was a little girl, she had stood here with her mother, watching a baby robin learn to fly. They had watched it all morning and her mother had taken a snapshot of it perched on the railing. In the black-and-white picture, the tiny bird was virtually unnoticeable; it was overwhelmed by the chipped paint on the steps, the garbage can, the towels on the line, the garden tools. "Here's a picture of your cute little robin," her mother had said when the film came back from the drugstore. She didn't understand why Margaret had been so disappointed. It wasn't a picture of the robin at all: it was a picture of a cluttered-looking back porch badly in need of painting. Her mother had entered it in a photo contest at the newspaper and complained bitterly when it did not win. "That robin of yours was much cuter than this," she had said when the paper printed a photo of a kitten dressed in doll clothes.

Margaret had always blamed the war and Minnie for the changes in her mother. She had become whiny and stubborn when Margaret entered adolescence and Minnie's prattle began to dominate their lives. But maybe her mother had always been foolish.

She closed the screen door very gently.

It had been a long time since she had been alone in the house and it was lovely in the quiet. The television was not blaring from the living room, there was no one sitting behind her constantly asking silly questions: it was like a little vacation. Even the heat did not disturb her: when she got out of bed this morning, she had decided not to wear pantyhose, and the dress she had put on was an old one of light cotton. After she put the dishes away, she walked through the downstairs, tidying things up, and she started to hum. She picked up some magazines from the living-room floor and straightened the cushions on the couch. She began to sing in a slow, wavering voice.

"Jesus bids us shine
    With a pure, clear light,
Like a little candle
    Burning in the night.
In this world of darkness
    So let us —"

She was standing in the dining room, looking at Minnie's plastic flowers in the centre of the long oak table. She was tempted to throw them away right there and then, but she knew that it would cause an unnecessary row. She glared at them; they were so artificial they looked smug. The tiny bunny stuck in the middle of them, however — that could go. It was too shabby. She reached into the dusty bouquet, grabbed it, pulled it out, and squashed it in her hand. Tomorrow, or the next day, maybe she would replace the flowers with real ones — that would be the way to do it. Suddenly she wondered if they would remind Minnie of the Fool and his garden. They never talked about Arthur, had barely mentioned his name for years now. Did Arthur Snow haunt her sister's life the way that their father haunted her own?

And then her day was destroyed all over again — because she knew that her father had crept into her dreams again last night.

She was trying to turn away from him and climb off the table, but the room was filling up with water — a flood? — and it was very deep.

That was all she remembered, a moment, nothing more, but her heart sank. She slipped the crushed bunny into the pocket of her dress. He had no business coming back to her as she slept. She banged the table with the side of her hand.

"Why can't you all leave me alone!"

It was so quiet in the house that the sound of her own voice startled her.

Quite slowly she sat down in the chair where her father used to sit. She examined the room; the walls had been darker then, a kind of green. The buffet had been against another wall. She tried to imagine herself, age four, standing near the table's edge. She rubbed her hands where her little feet had been placed; she traced a circle where her little panties had been pulled down, a stray piece of dirty laundry draped over her shoes. She looked up to where her face would have been and sat, clasping and unclasping her hands. "Right here," she said. "Right here." It was here that she had been caught up in such a darkness that it still clung to her all these years later. Why were there no words she could say aloud that might break the spell? "Abracadabra," she whispered, and sat fiddling with her hands for a few long moments.

History was history; it was fact. She knew that there were no words and never would be words powerful enough to stop her father before he had ruined her. The past could never be changed.

She was staring ahead of her and moving both hands over the table top; there were fine scratches on the surface and she felt them with her fingertips, as if trying to decipher them. Had she made these little marks? Had her shoes made them? She tried to remember her little-girl shoes, but couldn't. The only image she could muster was of Shirley Temple in patent-leather taps.

She would never be able to look inside her own father's head and understand why he had done such terrible things. She could read books, looking for something familiar — "Yes, it was just like that, yes" — and try to piece together the psychology of the man who had been killed by a stray bottle when he was half the age that she was now. But that would not be her true father, it would be an invention of him, and she knew it could never bring her any satisfaction.

Her hands stopped moving and she patted the table top twice with her fingers. Her father. To the rest of the world he existed as a name on lists as meaningless as a dry leaf in a drift of leaves. He was dead, and the only person who ever thought about him was the daughter who had hated him all her life. In order for him to disappear, she would have to give up the ghost.

Somewhere, tucked away inside the folds of her brain, she imagined there was something like a dark little room that contained this table. With it were the circles of her panties, the doll her parents had given her, the deaf ears of her mother — and sitting in the middle of that room was Wayne Saunders.

The little table she had hoarded away was no longer this one — oak grain, four-by-five feet, the extra leaves tucked away in the front closet. In that room it evolved; it shrank and grew, it broke free of its moorings as she slept and floated through bits of memories. It was as potent as myth and of no importance to anyone but herself. If she were to throw out this table, the one she was sitting at this very moment, or if she were to set it on fire, the other one would still be inside her; it would drift to the surface of her nightmares, bearing the burden of her father.

Everyone must have these secret places. What would her sister's contain? The husband who had run away? The marbles that had bounced off her head when she opened her bedroom door? The older sister who had carefully prepared that ambush simply to torment her? Yes, no doubt Margaret herself was tucked away in Minnie's dreams. We were, none of us, solely ourselves. We were also the visions of ourselves carried around like baggage by everyone we met. She would be in Sandy's dreams too. And she had been in her father's.

When that bottle had slammed into his head, as he slipped through unconsciousness and into death, had her five-year-old self slipped out of that room, kicking and screaming, "Ruined, ruined, you ruined me, Daddy!" Or had he hidden her in another kind of place where his dying soul had run for solace? "Poor Daddy, oh my poor Daddy," her little five-year-old arms rocking him as he left this world.

What memories did Sandy Whyte have of her? What memories were being planted right now into this young girl, Annette?

She patted the table with her hands.

There was the sound of a car in the driveway and when she turned to look through the dining-room door and out the kitchen window, she was stunned. A police car was coming to a stop — it seemed as slow and as large as a warship. Something must have happened to Minnie. She pushed herself away from the table and walked quickly into the kitchen. But no, there was Minnie in the front seat. She was sitting with her head down, nodding slowly. Margaret knew she should go outside and find out what was happening, but the bold strangeness of the police car kept her rooted to the floor beside the sink, her mouth hanging open. After a minute, the policeman started his car again, and Minnie got out. She was downcast and, with her arms held tightly against her sides, she hurried to the back door. When she came in the kitchen, Margaret asked in amazement, "Minnie? Is everything all right?"

And Minnie ran to her, and buried her face on Margaret's shoulder and wept.

"What is it? What is it?"

But Minnie just kept shaking her head into Margaret's shoulder and sobbing unintelligibly. Margaret put her arms about her sister's shoulders.

"Minnie, you have to tell me what's wrong."

Minnie lifted her head and sniffled and said, "They laughed, they they they they all laughed," and she buried her face again into the wet stain she had made on Margaret's dress and wept some more.

"There, there," Margaret said, "there, there."

"And the policeman was was n-n-nasty."

"Come inside," Margaret said, taking one arm away and starting to lead her with the other. "Come inside and sit down. Would you like some tea?"

Minnie nodded her head and rubbed her nose.

"Here," said Margaret, reaching for the Kleenex on the counter. "Here. Just come inside and sit and I'll make us a cup of tea."

Minnie nodded again. "And a cookie?"

"Yes, dear."

It was not easy at first to understand exactly what had happened. Minnie would begin to explain, but then she would work up a full head of steam and become hysterical, ranting and raving about the police and Lila LeBlanc and Sandy Whyte and his cleaning lady, until her shouts turned to stutters and her stutters to whimpers and she was weeping again and incomprehensible. Margaret finally began to figure out what had taken place in that awful hour. Minnie had caused a minor accident; she had been caught driving without a licence and would be fined. Margaret's car had been damaged and towed away — the policeman had said it was not to be driven until the signal light was repaired.

Somehow, through Minnie's hysterics, it seemed that all of this had something to do with her fear that Margaret would go out with Sandy Whyte again and get sick and die. Somehow, Minnie felt that she had been acting on her sister's best behalf.

"Don't see him again, please, please. You can't ever talk to that man again."

"Minnie, I'm going to have to."

"Why?" Minnie raised her face, wet with tears and snot; it glistened in the sunlight, it sparkled.

"Because I need to go out of town tomorrow and it looks like I'll have to borrow someone's car."

"Don't borrow his, you'll get sick."

"Minnie, that's being silly."

"Where do you have to go?"

"Not very far. I promised a friend that I would take her somewhere."

"Can I come?"

"No, I'm sorry. It's a personal matter, and——"

"You're so mean to me, just like everybody else all my whole life!" And she was crying again.

Margaret sighed. "Minnie, I'll just be gone for the day. Now look —" She had the urge to punish her sister, to say something cutting, but then, quite simply, she realized that, for Minnie, life was punishment enough.

"Look, when the car gets back, we'll go somewhere for a drive. Maybe down to Albert County. We can take a picnic."

Minnie shrugged.

For the rest of the afternoon, she remained in her favourite chair and cried. Margaret had seen her sister sob countless times before, but it occurred to her that Minnie had only really cried twice in the past: the day Arthur left her and the night their mother had died. All those other tears had been false and had not come from the deep spring where these bitter ones had been stored. These were the tears of a woman who had been publicly humiliated, the tears of a buffoon who knew that she was a buffoon; they were true and deep, and they cut Margaret to the quick. A mother could comfort her child and help her, could make promises that need not be false, but there was nothing that could ease the pain inside poor, dumb Minnie. She was suffering and there was nothing that Margaret could do.

It had been so easy to be pulled into the orbit of Minnie's world — she would, after all, try to make you feel guilty for going to the bathroom successfully. But Margaret knew that her sister could not exist on her own; her desperation was that of a lonely child. Minnie would continue to screech and eat and lie and exasperate her, but Margaret knew that she would never leave Minnie. The only thing that she could do for Minnie was love her, which, because their bond was of blood and beyond all reasoning, she did.

Late in the afternoon, she called Sandy from the upstairs phone. It took him quite a while to answer; she was about to hang up when he did. He must have fumbled with the receiver because it dropped; a moment later, he was on the line.

"Yes?"

"Sandy, it's Margaret. I'm sorry to bother you."

"Oh." He sounded out of breath.

"I'm calling for two reasons. First, I am sorry about Minnie's behaviour this morning. I hope she didn't say anything too terrible."

"Think nothing of it." His voice was nervous-sounding, and cold. There was a scratching noise in the background.

"That's very kind of you."

"Think nothing of it," he repeated.

"Secondly, I need to ask you a favour."

"Yes?"

"I need to borrow your car. I have to go somewhere tomorrow — it's rather important — and, as you know, mine is out of commission."

"Oh."

"It's an imposition, I know, but I didn't know who else …" Her voice trailed off into an awkward pause. The scratching continued.

Finally he spoke. "When will you need it?"

Hadn't she said that? "Tomorrow. Friday. I won't need it for long. I could come over tonight after supper. Say, around seven-thirty? That way I wouldn't have to bother you early in the morning. I'd have it back to you late afternoon. I'm sorry to ask but, you know, I can't even get into the city to rent one or I would do that. And you were so thoughtful last Sunday. I hope you don't think this is out of line or …" She felt that she was starting to babble, so she stopped.

"No, it's not."

She was waiting for his response.

"Well, I don't know," he said.

"Were you going to be using it?"

"Um, I hadn't any firm plans …"

"So it's all right then?"

"I suppose …"

"Thank you, Sandy. I'll see you in a couple of hours." And she hung up. A few minutes later, she went downstairs.

"Minnie," she said, "come into the kitchen and help me make us some supper."

Minnie nodded, and she did.

Sandy would not have answered the phone. He was in the bathroom, running a basin of clean water, when it started to ring; but then he heard a noise in the hall and he dropped the basin and ran. The boy had almost reached the telephone in Sandy's bedroom; he was leaning against the door frame. When Sandy reached him, the boy dived forward, knocking the phone onto the floor as he fell to the rug. Sandy covered his mouth with the wash cloth he still held in his hands. The boy was so weak that it was no effort to hold him firmly until he got Margaret off the line.

He had untied him less than an hour before. Worried that the boy's limbs would atrophy, he had cut the ties from the bed-posts with a pair of scissors and then, unable to untie them, sheared through the thin, tight knots, being careful not to scratch the boy's skin. He was confident that the weak body could not struggle and, if he did, Sandy felt that he could threaten him with the scissors. He sat on the bed and, holding the boy in a sitting position, cradled the weak head against his neck and held a glass of water to the boy's lips.

"Da," the boy kept saying. "Da." It was baby talk: Sandy knew that the boy was delirious. He wondered if his own mind wasn't beginning to snap: after the police had taken Minnie away this morning, he had hurried back inside and found a wash cloth neatly folded on the boy's forehead — he could not for the life of him remember having put it there.

"Daa," Chaleur said faintly. He was aware that the ties were gone because his arms and legs felt light suddenly, as if they might float up above his head. Nothing seemed to be making any sense; he seemed to be drifting slowly through a vast, torpid whirlwind.

It was a long time before he could feel his toes and the ends of his fingers.

Sandy knew that he would have to restrain the boy again as soon as he showed signs of health. It was a shame that he could not find a balance and keep him in this lovely, fragile state. After giving him a drink, he reached down beside the bed and picked up the book he had placed there. He spread it open across both their laps.

"This," he said, "is the most beautiful painting in the world."

Chaleur could hardly focus on the confusion that seemed to be taking place in his lap. Suddenly there were lots of little people there, walking about; everything was green and red and he was remembering someone — his father? — carrying him away from a room filled with people and taking him up the stairs to bed. There were white bars on the crib to stick his feet through, and when he wet himself it was warm and nice.

Sandy felt the hot dampness against the back of his hand.

"Oh, dear," he said, quickly picking up the book and dropping it on the floor. He lay the boy back down and stripped off his pants. "I'll wash you up, get you nice and clean."

It was only a few minutes later when Chaleur crawled off the bed. He knew that it was important to be quiet because he was in a horror movie. It took him a little while to stand up and he tried to move like he was a bird — not a crow or an owl, but something small and light — then he might drift out the door and find his way outside. When he heard the water running, he thought he had made it to the river, but then he saw the old fart's back in the bathroom and eased his way past the door. There was such a long way to go, and he had no pants on.

Then the telephone started to ring and he knew that his only hope was to find it first and ask for help. He hoped his body would be the arrow that he could shoot across the room towards it, but he had missed and fallen, endlessly, into a pit.

After Sandy hung up the receiver, he picked up the edge of the braided rug and dragged the unconscious boy back to his mother's room. He washed him and changed the bed. When he tied him this time, he used his mother's old stockings and secured the boys arms to the metal frames at the side of the bed, carefully making sure that, although the boy could move his hands a bit, there was no danger of one hand being able to stretch across to free the other. This took considerable time. He gagged the boy's mouth with the cloth.

Why had he not been able to think quickly enough to say "no" to Margaret? But he was afraid that "no" would make her suspicious. The gag was secure. She must hear nothing.

He took the soiled clothing and sheets downstairs to the shed and threw them in the washing machine. With *The Great Masters of Europe* under his arm, he walked towards the front of the house.

When he passed the sideboard in the front hall, he glanced to make sure that his car keys were in the little bowl and saw that the top drawer was open. He stopped to shut it, but then opened it instead.

The box containing his mother's lobster silver was not inside.

He stood, dumbly, staring at the empty drawer the way a child stands looking in shock at the family heirloom he has just shattered.

"I've been robbed."

Then he remembered Gloria saying something this morning about wanting to borrow the silver. He was sure that she had, but in the confusion of stupid Minnie's screams and Gloria on the verge of tears, the both of them roaming about the downstairs like wild things, he could hardly recall what anyone had said, exactly. He had never left either of them alone for a moment, and no one else had been in the house.

When was the last time he had seen the silver? It hadn't been used for years. But Gloria had polished it in the spring — he was certain. Had she misplaced it? He slammed the drawer shut, then tore through the others, searching the entire sideboard.

No, the lobster silver had vanished.

Someone had been in the house.

He thought of the wash cloth lying across the boy's forehead like an Indian's headband.

He was being watched. Someone was watching him and toying with him. Someone knew about the boy. But who? Gloria? Minnie? That young man, Gloria's brother? What had she called him? Raymond. But Sandy had been with Gloria and Minnie the whole time, and Raymond had never entered the house. Wasn't he sitting on the wall by the driveway?

Sandy slowly closed the sideboard doors and shut the drawers. He was squeezing the book so tightly against his side that his arm was sore, so he took it in his hands and turned towards the stairs. He could not hear a sound from the bedroom.

Everything had gone so wrong, had turned so sour. The world had seemed so beautiful when the boy had appeared: now it was mean again. He was so saddened by the boy, who had done nothing but prove that behind every tree, beneath every stone along the way, there was humiliation. It had always lain in wait for Sandy when he had done nothing, and when, just this once, he had reached out and taken something, humiliation was descending on him with even more force and fury. Everything was rotten. Corrupt and rotten.

He thought of his father's body in its concrete coffin — preserved, the old man thought, until the Great Judgment. Sandy was as big a fool as his father had been: the rot did not attack from outside — it was there all along. By now there would be nothing left for the worms to feast on and, if the concrete had them trapped inside, he imagined that they would simply have devoured each other: his father's bones a meaningless landscape for their puny lives.

On Judgment Day, the old man's body would be as rotten as all the others. The preservation of the flesh had meant so much to him, but it meant nothing to God. Nothing did. When all the world went up in flames, God would not stoop down to rescue the cantatas of Bach or the paintings that glorified him. He would not save the meek whose sole, sorry purpose was to run untrampled across the great lawns of heaven.

With a sinking heart, he knew that the boy could not stay. It was only foolish sentiment to keep trying; it wasn't working. But after the last two days, how could he simply untie the boy and let him leave? They would come for Sandy, the world would point at him and spit, and the rest of his life would be terrifying. He couldn't bear it.

And if he killed himself? But that would be it — it would be over, and despite its miseries, he was not ready to give up his life.

He could save himself. To the blind eye of heaven, it would make no difference when the boy died. It would not matter if he died in a flophouse somewhere, or in drunken old age, or if, tomorrow, his beautiful body lay in the woods near the side of a road. If he were to die now, at least he would have lived his whole life in a body so fair and fine that it seemed to cheat corruption until the very end. Sandy wished he had held the cushion to the boy's face a few minutes longer.

He saw himself carrying the boy downstairs at night, placing him in the trunk of the car, driving off somewhere to hide him. No one could possibly miss this boy. His family would probably breathe a sigh of relief to be rid of him.

If he hid the boy in the woods no one would find him for a while.

And the cushion, if he used it to smother him? It would have to be burnt. He could burn it in the fireplace late at night.

But they would find his footprints in the ground, they would track them to the car, bloodhounds would follow him to his door.

The sandwich that he had eaten at suppertime suddenly erupted in his stomach and gushed upwards into his throat. He covered his mouth with his hand and swallowed. He stood, both hands over his mouth, and started to tremble.

How was it possible that suddenly he was planning these terrible things? And yet, what choice was there? It was hardly a decision: it was the only way to keep himself from being buried alive. After all, he knew that if the situations were reversed that a foul-mouthed boy like this one would not hesitate to kill him.

He was feeling a little dizzy and his heart was racing. Still holding his hands over his mouth, he sat down on the bench inside the doorway and waited for Margaret.

TWENTY

Mama had rammed two balls of dough into each bread pan. She was trying to make the double loaves even, but one half of every loaf was smaller than the other. Hal was standing too close to her and talking too carefully. She knew that he was trying to be as considerate as possible, but she wanted him on the other side of the pantry door, on the other side of the kitchen, on the other side of the world. Only once before had she been in such close quarters with an outsider who wanted to become a member of the family, and that had been Ginette on the night that Junior brought her out for supper. She had helped Mama do the dishes and they had talked about hairdressers. That was the kind of conversation Mama wanted to have with her prospective in-laws. The fact that she was even thinking of Hal as an *in-law* upset her: it wasn't normal. Besides that, she barely knew the man — had not even known he existed until Tuesday, for heaven's sake — and here he was, two days later, touching her shoulder and telling her that her son was losing his mind. "I hope I'm wrong," he was saying, "but he's acting so strangely."

And you're the reason, Mama thought, *people like you who took my boy away from me.*

He thought he should call a doctor, he thought he should explain it all to her first; but what on earth made him think that he could stand so close, talk so confidentially, touch her shoulder with his hand as if he could comfort her? Touch her shoulder in a way that none of her own children had touched her since they were little? On the day he arrived she had made a big show of telling him that the strawberry-rhubarb pie was for him: it had been a gesture to make him feel welcome, and now she wished she had not been so foolhardy. He was speaking to her about her son as if he had a right to. Beneath his unwanted hand her body had started to churn, her insides stirring and plopping; eruptions of gas that felt as solid as cannonballs were slowly rolling through the fleshy canyons behind her apron, inside her dress, deep in her bowels.

Mama's body grew so tense beneath his hand that Hal thought she was about to cry. "I'm sorry," he said. He knew that more than anyone else she understood the frustrations and the joys of caring for Raymond; in their very different and separate ways, they shared them. When Hal used to visit his own mother, she had never held him, barely touched her lips to his cheek: "Mind my hair, Harold, I just had it done," "Don't crush my sweater, it's fresh from the cleaners," "Harold, be careful with my face! I just put it on." *Careful. Careful. Mind. Don't.* Unlike his own mother, Mama had hugged her son as soon as he came in the door; her feelings for him compelled her arms to draw him close. As he raised his hand to comfort his lover's mother, Hal realized that she understood why he wanted to touch her son. She was standing so still and tense, her four perfect loaves of bread in a line on the counter in front of them, that he could not contain the sadness and tenderness he felt for her.

But when he said "We both love him," and tried to put his arm around her, Mama clenched her fists as tightly as she had been clenching the cheeks of her bum.

"No!" she cried, banging her hands on the bread board. *"Nonono!"* as she pushed past him and bolted towards the stairs.

Pop was sitting in the bathroom, trying to make out the words as they drifted up through the water pipes from the pantry below, but that man's voice was too low and quiet — it was hard to follow. When they were first married, Mama had made Pop whisper when they did the dishes: his mother-in-law would sit on the toilet after supper and eavesdrop on their conversation. "Shh," Mama would say quietly, lifting her eyes to the ceiling, "the Queen's on the throne." Pop figured that fellow was talking to Mama about Raymond, but he could only hear every second or third word. Something about brains, then something about doctors, something else about Raymond being mean. Pop leaned towards the pipe beside the toilet, wishing he could hear his wife's response. Was she saying anything or was she so used to talking secretly in the pantry that her words were instinctively hushed, inaccessible through the plumbing?

Then he heard her cry out. She was upset. That little bastard had said something to upset her!

Pop stormed out the bathroom door just as Junior was coming down from the attic. Mama and Pop crashed into him at the foot of the attic stairs.

"Move!" Mama hurled herself past them and lunged into the bathroom, slamming the door behind her.

"What in hell —"

Pop's face was as red as a fireplug; he was starting to shake. Junior's first instinct was to run — this kind of anger usually meant that Pop had caught him doing something wrong. He tried to sound as casual as possible.

"What's up, Pop?"

"He said something to her, he said something to upset her!" Father and son stood looking at each other, each hoping the other one would do something. There was a faint grunt from the bathroom, and then the tinny noise of the portable radio from the shelf over the toilet paper.

"What'd he say?" Junior asked, not knowing for sure who he was talking about.

"How in hell should I know?"

Danny had gotten out of bed just after Junior; his bad arm was tingling and he shook it as he came down the attic stairs. "What did you say, Pop?" he asked, yawning.

Pop glared up at Danny. "Wasn't me, goddammit, wasn't me!"

"Who then?"

Junior looked at Pop. "Was it Raymond?"

"Raymond? Raymond and Gloria took off somewheres in the car. No, it was that piss-assed friend of his, that whatsisname!"

"Hal?"

"That bastard!"

"The little prick!" Junior said.

Danny wiped the sleep from his eyes. "What did he say?"

Pop looked away from him. "How the hell should I know? He mumbles."

"Well, what did Mama say happened?"

"She didn't have time to say anything."

"Is anyone going to ask her?"

"Don't bother your mother right now. She's busy." As Pop

spoke, the thin, flat sound of the bathroom radio was cranked up another notch. They all turned to the bathroom door. Mixed in with the radio and a blast from Mama's bowels was a plaintive, almost inaudible sob.

"Damn him," Pop muttered, shaking his head.

"Well, where is he? Is he downstairs?"

"Kitchen." Pop scowled.

Danny was awake enough now to know that whatever had happened could get much worse than it already was. "Stay here. I'll go find out what he said." He sighed and went down the stairs while the other two listened from the upstairs hall.

There was no one in the kitchen, or the pantry. Danny walked through the downstairs rooms and looked out on the veranda. No one. He circled back through the house, even glancing in the front and hall closets, and looked out the kitchen windows to check the backyard. It seemed to be empty, but maybe he should go out to make sure. Gloria had left a pair of shoes on the floor in front of the cellar door, so he knew that Hal couldn't have gone down there and closed the door behind him. He went outside and walked around one side of the house. This was why he spent his days off tinkering with the washers in his apartment building, cleaning the dryers, having a drink in the furnace room. Every time he came home it was always one damn thing after another. He stood out in the front yard, looking up and down the street. A couple of neighbourhood kids pointed at him and giggled because he was wearing his housecoat. Raymond's boyfriend was nowhere in sight. What could he have said to Mama? Then he remembered that Hal had come down to the veranda late last night and said something about Raymond acting funny and calling his doctor. It must have been that. He cursed himself for sleeping in.

He turned around when he heard the screen door open, but it was just Junior who had come out onto the veranda and was standing there, scratching his big belly.

"Where'd the little fruit take off to?"

"Your guess is as good as mine." He walked slowly up the steps, shaking his head and looking about. "What the hell happened?"

"I don't know. Pop's trying to get Mama to come out of the can, but she won't open the door. Where'd Gloria and Raymond go?"

"How should I know? Maybe she was taking him out for a drive so Hal could phone the doctor like he wanted."

"Oh, right."

Danny walked past him and went back into the house to get dressed. He'd pack his bag while he was at it; as soon as he made sure that everything was okay, he wanted to go home to his apartment, where there was a little peace and quiet. The tingle in his missing hand was turning into a throbbing pain.

When Raymond and Gloria drove back into the yard, Hal watched them through a screen of green lattice and dwarf hemlock bushes from his hiding place beneath the veranda. He had not meant to hole up under there, it had just happened somehow. After Mama had shoved past him, he had stood very still in the pantry door, unable to move. He had not realized that he was stepping over some terrible line with her until it was too late. When Mama shoved him aside, he felt as if he had been pushed out the door like an unwanted and potentially dangerous stranger. The blood drained from his face and he felt his stomach go weak. Then he heard Pop and Junior talking angrily upstairs — Pop sounding like he wanted to form a posse — and he knew then that the whole Maurice family was out to get him and he that he couldn't deal with anything until Raymond came back. He hurried outside, hoping that Gloria would bring Raymond back soon and he could grab him before Pop or Junior did. He would grab Raymond and say —

And say what?

I was trying to talk to Mama about your dementia and she hit the roof?

When he ducked down beside the veranda to avoid Danny, he saw the open space between the lattice and the corner of the house. When Junior came out the front door, he crouched down lower beside the hemlocks. When he heard Junior call him a fruit, he crawled through the opening.

It was musty under the veranda, and filthy: the ground more like dust than soil. Hal snuck in a few feet and leaned against the old stone foundation, hugging his knees to his chest. He could hear Junior moving on the veranda floor just over his head. *This is ridiculous*, he thought.

Danny went into the house and Hal waited for Junior to follow him, but then he heard the springs creak on the old cot, and he knew that Junior was lying down above him and he was trapped. What could he do now? Junior would see him if he tried to slip out.

He settled back and looked around. The dwarf hemlocks blocked most of the light on the sunny side of the veranda. Just a bit of it came through and speckled the dirt on one corner of his hiding place. There were little rocks scattered about and a few old bottles. A chipmunk darted under the edge of the lattice frame, then stood watching him; when Hal stared back, it turned and scurried away. How could he get out of this mess? He knew that every moment he sat doing nothing he was making his situation more difficult, but he couldn't move. After ten minutes, he felt that escape had become impossible. He would have to stay under the veranda until he was sure the coast was clear — that might take, how long? Ten more minutes? An hour? All day? Thank God he had his cigarettes with him.

But just as he was thinking this, he heard the click of Junior's lighter and he knew that if he used his own that the sound would give him away. He would not be able to smoke until the veranda was deserted.

A police siren wailed from down the street. He felt homesick for Toronto: sirens and traffic, streetcars slamming up and down Broadview Avenue, car alarms going off outside their apartment at all hours of the day and night — their beautiful little crummy apartment filled with books and paintings, with the mismatched furniture they had pooled when they moved in together, and the mess from Raymond's latest design project spread all over the place. He yearned for everything that he had wanted to escape by coming down here. He longed for the day, weeks from now, when he might be able to think back on this nightmare and find it funny. It might even sound like one of Raymond's stories about growing up in Membartouche. Those stories had made him believe that life was still worth living because he had fallen in love with a man who could tell him stories and make him laugh. What a mistake this trip had been! He had to get Raymond back home.

He sat very still for a long time. He watched dozens of ants moving about in their haphazard, purposeful way, and a beetle manoeuvre around a small line of rocks. A robin flew into the bushes and perched there for minutes. He watched it watch something on the far side of the driveway. Danny came out onto the veranda above his head.

"Well?" Junior asked.

"She's out of the bathroom, but she's not talking."

"Did you tell her the little fruit's fucked off somewhere?"

Hal waited for Danny to answer, to say "Don't call him a fruit," but there was just the sound of the screen door shutting. He looked up at the floorboards above him: on one of the brace beams just over his head there were faded letters printed in blue chalk. The messier ones spelled out "Gloria," and beside them, neatly printed, they spelled out "Raymond." At that moment the car pulled into the driveway.

As he watched Gloria and Raymond walk towards the back door, he thought he should try to sneak out and follow them, and he was starting to shift to his knees to crawl towards the opening when Junior said, "I'd wait out here if I was you. Pop's on the warpath."

He saw Raymond and Gloria's legs approach the veranda and heard the cot springs squeal as Junior stood up.

"Why?" asked Gloria.

"Who the hell knows? Your little friend said something mean to Mama."

"Hal?" Raymond asked. "What did he say?"

"Beats me."

"Where is he?"

"He took off somewhere. Hey, what in friggin' hell happened to Pop's car?"

It was a long time ago now, that sorrowful night two days before Christmas when Mama and Pop had just bailed Junior out of jail and the three of them were back at the house, sitting silently at the kitchen table. Danny and Gloria were upstairs, playing cards and talking quietly. Pop had exploded in the car outside the jail, and had ranted all the way home through a snowstorm. There was little else left for any of them to say. Yet it didn't seem right to come back home and simply carry on with Christmas — the three of them were compelled to prolong the agony by sitting in silence, staring at the plastic gumdrop tree that Gloria had decorated and left on the table in front of them. The quiet in this house always seemed to be fuelled by anger and filled with guilt. Mama couldn't stand it any more and said, "Well, Raymond's been spared all this, thank God. He'll have a nicer Christmas up in Toronto with his girlfriend." She knew that the girlfriend part wasn't true. She had said it to comfort herself — and God knows she had needed some comfort that night. But Junior, not content with being arrested for stealing, had opened his big trap and said what she had always suspected to be the truth.

"Mama, come on. We all know that Raymond isn't with a friggin' *girl*."

And she hadn't been able to let it rest at that; oh no, she was so angry at Junior that she just had to oppose him. "And how would you know that, Mr. Smarty Pants?"

Junior looked square at her. "Because Raymond is a, you know, one of those homosexual fellows." Halfway through the sentence he had seen the look on her face and dropped his eyes, chastened, to the little fence around the gumdrop tree.

Pop stood up. "Haven't you upset your mother enough for one night?" he said angrily as he fled the room. That is how Mama discovered that the whole family had known what she suspected all along and, like her, had said nothing about it. What else did everyone know? She had looked at Junior, seen the sad way he raised his eyes from the table to watch Pop's departure, then glance back to her, then to the gumdrop-tree fence, and she knew that he suspected other secrets. When she and Pop had their tenth anniversary, ten-and-a-half-year-old Junior had looked up quizzically from his piece of Tom and Jerry cake and asked, "Hey, when was I born anyway?" "Just eat your cake," Pop had said and their anniversaries had gone unmarked after that.

She had left her son alone with the Christmas decorations and gone upstairs to Pop because she was afraid of what he might rightfully say, the questions that were his to ask.

While Mama sat alone in the bathroom, her mind raged over the secrets she had kept from her family, and those that they all had kept from her. Unspoken agreements between herself and Pop. The web of mysteries that everyone tangled about their lives and the lives of their children. Secrets that people did not talk about because talking about them only created more tension and upset. She thought about the Melanson boy with his Davy Crockett jacket who had made love to her on the beach one night in August over forty years before. He was a cousin of Fred Melanson's and was staying at his uncle's cottage that summer. Her hands had clutched the fringe of his jacket while she lay beneath him on the beach, thinking a terrible secret thing, thinking that Pop would never own anything so smart as a brown suede jacket with fringe. Her mother had been making snide remarks about the way Pop dressed since she first laid eyes on him. Mama knew that wasn't the reason she had argued with him and gone for a walk to see the sunset with the Melanson boy from Away, but the Davy Crockett fringe between her fingers made her heart feel sick. After the boy had gone back to Montreal, Mama found out that she was pregnant. And Pop, who would never wear anything in his whole life that did not look like work clothes, had married her.

She had not listened to what Hal was saying because she didn't believe that he had any right to say it; those things were none of his business. She had not reacted to his words but to his assumption that, so far as Raymond's life was concerned, he was on an equal footing with her. But now, what he had been trying to say to her started to filter through her upset and anger.

Raymond was sick — well, she knew that the moment he walked in the door; in fact, she had known about it, secretly worried about it, for months. Raymond's arrival had only confirmed the worst. Hal had been trying to let her in on something that she assumed was hers and hers alone. But she had given him permission to do that herself; she had given him permission when she had presented him with that damn strawberry-rhubarb pie.

Pop's angry voice through the bathroom door distressed her terribly. She would rather avoid all of this and just try to carry on as if nothing had happened, but her son was sick and she knew that she had to set a few things straight.

Raymond and Gloria stepped into the house and into an uproar. Mama was in the pantry, angrily scraping flour off the counter, while Pop paced back and forth behind her, hissing "What'd he say? What'd he say to you?"

"Just stay out of this, Pop. It's between Raymond's friend and me."

"What'd he say?"

"I said, 'Just stay out of it!'"

Danny came down into the kitchen with his overnight bag and announced that he was going home to celebrate the reunion by himself.

"No," said Gloria, "you can't do that!"

He mumbled something about not being able to live in a nuthouse. Then Junior came in from the porch to tell Gloria that he'd crawled under the car and didn't think there'd been any damage to the frame but they couldn't be sure till it was up on a hoist.

"What's all this?" Pop said.

"Oh, no," Gloria moaned.

Mama said, "What now, Gloria?"

"We got the lobster tools from Sandy Whyte's place, but the car got hit."

"What?"

"They arrested her," Raymond piped up.

"They arrested you?" Mama asked.

"No, that foolish Minnie Snow ploughed into me when I was driving into Sandy Whyte's driveway. The cop took her home 'cause she was driving without a licence."

Mama slammed a loaf pan against the back of the counter. "Gloria, you and that damn lobster are gonna be the death of me, as sure as there's shit in a cat!" She shook her head. "Let's go take a look." And they all trooped out to the driveway to inspect the fender.

When he saw all the males in the Maurice family down on their hands and knees in the driveway a short distance away from the side of the veranda, Hal was afraid that one of them might see him, so he eased his way deeper into the shadows. He had been about to light a cigarette and he held the lighter in his motionless hand.

"She sure clipped you," Pop said. "We'll have to take it into Romeo's for an estimate."

"She was crazy as the birds," Gloria pleaded. "She came at me like a bat outta hell." In all the excitement, she had decided not to phone Sandy Whyte to tell him that Raymond had borrowed the lobster silver. She would take it back tomorrow after things calmed down.

"Why don't you drive the damn car down now?" Mama said. "I'll go call Romeo and say you're on your way." Without waiting for an answer, she went back into the house.

"I'll go with you, Pop," Danny said. Junior, Raymond, and Gloria went up onto the veranda. Raymond was looking about with a very confused expression, and for a brief moment he wasn't really sure if Hal had come home with him, or if he was still back in Toronto. *Maybe*, he thought with horror, *maybe I never actually moved away. Maybe my whole life was something I cooked up in my sleep.* If he asked Junior and Gloria, they would think he was nuts.

"Junior," Gloria said, "Danny can't go back to Moncton. Everyone has to be home with Raymond and Hal for the lobster reunion." As she said it, she realized that her big family celebration was about as ridiculous as an idea could be under the circumstances.

"Why don't you take that friggin' lobster supper and shove it up your big fat arse!" Junior said, opening the door.

"Where's Hal?" Raymond asked, relieved that Gloria had mentioned his name.

"We don't know," Junior answered. "He vanished into thin air, just like a little fairy."

"Did anyone look in the attic?"

"We were upstairs when he took off. I didn't see him fly by."

"Are you sure?"

"Well, why don't you whiz right on up there and take a look for yourself."

Beneath them, Hal had his lighter ready when he heard the screen door open; he held it to his cigarette primed to synchronize its click with the bang of the door.

Gloria was ready to cry. She was so stupid. Stupid to think she could talk her mother into fresh lobster, stupid to think that her family would want to get together and celebrate anything, stupid to think that they could be happy again. And they had been happy once, she remembered it. Those feelings could never leave her; they sustained her during the days she scrubbed and washed and dusted her way through other people's houses, during the silent meals with Mama and Pop, the nights she lay alone in bed wondering why on earth anyone had to grow up and get fat and face the terrible sadness of being an adult. Why was everything so unfair? When she was little her brothers had protected her, had kept the meanness of the world away. She had believed for so long that the one and only place where she could really and truly belong was with her family, but that feeling was as stupid as all the others. She was alone on the veranda, knowing that there was no place in all of Membartouche that wanted her, that needed her to do anything other than clean house. And she knew that if she refused to do that for them, no one would even care; they would just go out and hire somebody else, the way Mrs. Crossman had done after her yappy Pekingese dog, Brandy, broke a Royal Doulton figurine and she blamed it on Gloria. The reunion that she had yearned for so deeply had turned into the worst week of her life. Almost everyone was mad at everyone else, and when she thought about the sound of Minnie Snow's car smashing into hers, she wanted to sit right down on the floor and bawl. What else could possibly go wrong?

Then she looked down and saw a thin curl of smoke rise from a crack between the boards in the veranda floor.

"Holy Mother of God," Gloria cried, "the house's on fire!"

Junior heard his sister holler about something, but at that moment the phone in Halifax stopped ringing.

"Hello?"

Her voice sounded tired, but just as pretty as ever. "Ginette, it's Junior."

"Yeah?"

"I been trying to call you."

"I been out. I've been working. Unlike *some* people."

"How are the kids?"

"Fine. Whatta you want?"

"I miss you."

"So?"

"Aw, come on."

"Junior, you used up all your excuses."

"You're talking like we broke up. Did we break up?"

"Well, I left you."

"I'll do anything you want."

"Junior, I can't talk now, my kids are here. Call me tonight."

The line went dead — she hung up without saying good-bye. That was a bad sign. But she wanted him to call back, that was a good sign.

He sat on Mama and Pop's bed with their phone on his lap. The house was quiet — Gloria hadn't hollered again. His sister was driving him nuts.

Ginette wanted him to call her back. That had to be a good sign. He put the phone back on Mama's dresser and smiled.

"Sssh!" said the voice from beneath the veranda floor. "Sssh! Gloria?"

"What? Who's that?"

"It's me, it's Hal. I'm just having a smoke."

"Under the veranda?"

"Yeah."

"How come?"

"I don't know. It just happened."

"You gonna stay there?"

"No. Hang on. I'll come out."

He looked very sheepish after he crawled out from between the hemlock bushes and stood up. Gloria looked down at him from the side of the veranda. "What were you doing under there?"

He dusted off his shorts and his legs, and shrugged. Now that his ordeal was over, it seemed foolishly insignificant. "Your father and Junior were really mad. I guess I, well, I guess I was … concerned." He shrugged again.

"They wouldn't hurt a fly," she said. "Big talkers."

He didn't want to sound like a complete sissy. "It's just that, well, Junior's big and he's been to jail and——"

Gloria snorted. "He went to jail for stealing a bunch of dumb things nobody wanted anyway." She was still mad at Junior for where he told her to stick the lobster supper, so she went on. "And he got hauled in a couple of other times, but that was just for shooting off his big mouth when he was drunk. And he got caught once walking out of the liquor store with a bottle in his pants —" Suddenly she felt bad about the things that she was saying about Junior. "He wouldn't hurt a fly," she finished.

Hal nodded and looked out towards the street.

"Why were they so mad?" she asked after a minute.

"I upset your mother."

"How come?"

"I told her I was worried about Raymond."

"His spots?"

"That too."

Gloria felt that the distance between them was too big; she crouched down and rested her chin on the veranda railing. "Then why is she upset at you? Did you say something mean?"

Hal shook his head. "I just told her how I feel about Raymond."

"Oh, Mama can't talk about stuff like that," she said, shaking her head, "mushy stuff. No one around here can. Oh, maybe Danny sometimes."

"It's hard for Raymond, too."

She nodded. She turned to look at the door, as if she was

worried it might suddenly open. "We better go find her, get things straightened out." Hal nodded and walked around to the veranda steps. She stood up and watched him. When he was beside her, as she was opening the front door for them both, she turned and whispered conspiratorially, "We'll just say you went for a walk so you both could get cooled off."

He nodded his head and followed her into the kitchen.

"Mama, guess who I found wandering up the street?"

Mama was washing out the bread bowl. "There you are," she said, then she turned back to the sink. "Why don't you talk to that doctor first thing while I finish this up and make us some coffee. Gloria, would you be so kind as to go and find Raymond and keep him busy for a few minutes."

"What'll I tell'm?"

"As if you ever had any trouble coming up with something to say."

"I know. We'll plan the lobster supper. That is … I mean, we got the silverware and everything. Unless you're still bent on cold pack."

Mama grabbed a dishtowel and lifted the bowl from the drain board. She shook her head. "Hal, you're the company, you settle this. What would you rather have — lobster in the shell or cold pack?"

Hal looked from Mama to her daughter. Gloria started to bounce quietly on her toes. "*Shell*," her mouth formed soundlessly, "*Shell shell shell.*"

"In the shell," he answered.

"Well, that's settled," Mama said. "Now you better make your phone call."

When Pop and Danny came back with the car an hour later, Gloria was waiting on the back steps. She got up and walked over to them. "Don't bother getting out," she said. "Mama wants you to drive me down to the wharf so I can get the lobster."

"I'll go call the insurance guy, Pop," Danny said, getting out of the car. He held open the door for Gloria.

"Danny, promise me you'll stay for supper."

"Maybe."

"Please, please, pretty please!"

"Yeah, all right." He had never been able to say "no" to his sister.

"Thanks," and she kissed him on the cheek and jumped into the front seat. Pop started the car and backed out of the driveway.

Raymond and Hal were sitting beside each other on a reclining lawn chair under the lilacs; Danny lit a cigarette and watched them out of the corner of his eye. He watched Raymond lean over and pull a forget-me-not from a clump beside the chair; he appeared to be studying the flower, touching the tiny petals with his fingertips. Danny sat down on the back steps.

Raymond twirled the stem between his thumb and forefinger. Hal was just getting ready to speak when he said, "I'm getting worried that some of the things that happen aren't really happening." He lowered his head and sniffed the flower. "Or what I think is happening isn't really what's happening."

Hal was relieved — it was as if Raymond were giving him permission to talk about phoning Dr. Louie.

"I peed on your bed last night, didn't I?" Raymond said.

"Um, yes. Yes, you did." Hal looked at him and then lowered his eyes.

"I'm sorry."

"That's okay."

"I probably was half-asleep, but I think there's something else."

"Yes?"

"Well, I wasn't trying to be funny or anything. I remember waking up, and thinking that I had to pee, and then it just seemed to make sense. Maybe I just knew that you'd have to sleep in my bed after. But …"

"Yeah? Go on."

"Do you know how bad it is? Do you know what I just saw at Sandy Whyte's? Thought I saw."

"What?"

"A mirage."

"The little house, like the one at the Dune?"

"No. This one was so close that I touched it. It was in the room with me, and I touched it."

"A mirage. What are you talking about?"

Danny had started to get up to call the insurance agent, but he decided to sit quietly and listen. He settled back down on the steps.

"I went upstairs to look around and found him in a bedroom."

"Sandy Whyte?"

"No, he was downstairs with Gloria and that crazy bitch."

"Who did you find?"

"A beautiful boy tied to a bed." He lay the flower across his knee.

"What are you talking about?"

"There he was, all stretched out like a saint on the rack."

"Raymond, what are you talking about?"

"The mirage. The boy at Sandy Whyte's. I touched him."

Hal was thinking of the face in the window as they drove away from the Whyte place. "Raymond, it's one thing to imagine a little house in the distance and another to touch someone that you say is tied to a bed."

"I can't tell the difference any more. I'm turning into Clive, aren't I?"

"I hope not, babe." He held Raymond's hand.

"But I think so." Raymond thought that if he said it like Tallulah Bankhead it might not sound so bad. "It's dementia, darling."

Hal squeezed his hand. "I called Dr. Louie this morning. He thinks we should go home early."

Raymond had been talking so quietly that Danny could not be sure that he had heard him right.

Although Mama had taken Pop and Junior aside and read them the riot act and although they tried to act as if everything was fine, it was still one of the saddest suppers that Gloria could ever remember. Raymond said he wasn't hungry and went to bed; he was running a bit of a fever and Hal kept going upstairs to check on him. Hal had phoned the train station to change their tickets; they would leave after the weekend. Danny tried to talk a bit but he seemed somewhere else. Junior kept looking at his watch and Pop hardly ever lifted his head.

Mama sat straight up in her chair and ate as carefully as possible. "This silver is pretty nice," she said. "Gloria, you won't forget to thank Sandy Whyte for us."

"I won't."

There was very little talk after that, just the crunch of the nutcrackers, the sound of the lobster shells cracking, the sucking sounds of people taking the meat out of the legs, the little ding when someone's empty shell hit the side of the big bowl in the middle of the table.

"Well," Mama said afterwards, "that was good lobster, Gloria. Thank you. That was a pretty good feed of lobster."

TWENTY-ONE ✜

S andy and the boy were getting ready for bed. They should have been asleep long before, but they had been outside, playing after dark. Sandy's bedroom was a schoolroom now — the wall was filled with a row of tall windows — and they were standing beside the big bed at the front of the class. Sandy watched the boy pull a long white nightshirt over his head.

Suddenly Father stood at the door, his voice stony and fierce.

"Have you said your prayers? Have you said 'Jesus Tender Shepherd, Hear Me'? Are you listening to me, Sandy?"

Neither he nor the boy could stop giggling, and Sandy felt buoyed by the wonder of this, of the boy's laugh, at the same time that he was afraid of his father's growing anger. He and the boy were friends, conspiratorial laughter cementing their friendship — but suddenly his father was between them with a strap in his hand.

Then Sandy was confused and sticky with sweat under the thin sheet. Awake.

He could hear the boy's rasping breath from his mother's bedroom. He wished that he could just go and lie down beside him. Seconds before, in a dream of this very room, the boy had been kneeling nearby in a soft, white nightshirt. Sandy pulled a pillow over his face and whispered to himself.

"Jesus tender shepherd, hear me
Bless thy little lamb tonight
Through the darkness be thou near me
Keep me safe till morning light."

He shoved the pillow away and sighed.

He could never believe in Jesus the way others did: he could not fathom their faith, found it suspect. There was nothing about any of them to indicate that they lived their lives in the presence of anything so glorious as the claims they made for Jesus Christ.

In most paintings, Jesus was dull and weak-looking, holding one hand aloft as if he were saying "Hear ye, hear ye" like some bland Rotarian at a banquet. The only pictures of him that interested Sandy were the crucifixions, the descents from the Cross, in which Jesus wore only a little strip of cloth about his waist. Sandy could sit in the same room as his parents and look at pictures of a nearly naked man and their only concern would be that their son might turn into a Catholic. Some of those paintings, especially the Gothic ones, were terrible: Jesus was so frail and rotten that it looked like you could pull him apart, like twisting the drumsticks from a roast chicken. But in others he was young and had muscles, and Sandy could imagine himself in a *pietà* with naked Jesus sprawled out in his lap.

But there was so much guilt attached in thinking these things — it was Jesus after all — that eventually he avoided crucifixions and descents. There were better pictures to look at, statues of Apollo and David, Laocoön and his sons. Because, other than the sight of his naked body and despite everything that other people seemed to believe, Sandy did not think that Jesus was all that interesting. The boy Jesus at the temple in Jerusalem was not so appealing a story as the boy Samuel at the temple in Shiloh. His mother had read that story to him countless times from *Bible Bedtime Stories*. It was special because of the picture of Samuel hanging in his room.

A voice had called to Samuel in the night and he sat up in bed, saying "Here am I." He went to Eli, his kind old teacher, and the old man said, "I did not call you, go back to bed." But once he was tucked in, the voice called again, "Samuel! Samuel!" and he was off again to Eli's bedroom. This happened three times until it occurred to old Eli that God was calling the boy. The next time the voice called him, the boy stayed in bed as the old man had told him and listened for the voice of God. And the Lord said, "Behold, I will do a thing in Israel, at which both the ears of everyone that heareth it shall tingle." Sandy remembered that because the word "tingle" had made his scalp do just that. But the thing that God was going to do wasn't in the picture book. It was only later, when Sandy graduated from *Bible Bedtime Stories* to the real thing, that he discovered God's message to the boy was that he was about to destroy Eli and all his family.

The boy Sandy had lain in bed, wishing that God would speak to him, wishing that God would say "I am not pleased with your father and I will destroy him."

The night crawled along. He wanted it to end at the same time that he dreaded the following day. He knew what had to be done with the boy, and he was afraid to think about it.

The house was filled with little noises: scratches and scurryings in the walls, rustling above the ceilings, floorboards and stairs creaking in the hot, damp air. There were mice, there were pigeons, there were probably all manner of bugs: flies and silverfish, wasps in a nest somewhere under the eaves.

Would sleep ever come again? What time was it?

Better not to know.

He rolled to the side of the bed away from the clock. He considered checking on the boy, but that would only sadden him and make the night longer.

It was hard now to remember a time when the boy had not been in the house; it was as if this last week had taken the place of all the years that went before. If only the boy could see Sandy's side of things — could that ever be possible? If only he could even dream again about the boy and have the two of them be happy.

He sighed and slid his hands under the sheet. The pigeons were starting to make noises above him — soon the sun would be up and the terrible heat would be worse. Margaret would be leaving soon with his car on her mysterious drive; she had promised that it would be back in the yard by late afternoon. Twenty-four hours from now it would all be over, somehow.

He wished that he and Margaret had stayed friends, that there had never been a time when they had tried, impossibly, to be more than that. He wondered why on earth she would move her membership to a Holy Roller church — what did she make of Jesus these days? Did she stand there, shrieking his name like a lovesick hysteric? She had always been a smart woman, it just didn't seem like her. Going to a place like that must have been her foolish sister's idea, that damn Minnie.

And then he thought of Minnie and Gloria that morning, and the wash cloth on the boy's forehead and the missing lobster silver, and fear and mortification rushed through him. He kept blushing, the blood of embarrassment rushing to his cheeks again and again. For the next hour he lay as still as possible, hoping that sleep would return and overwhelm his shame.

When he finally fell back to sleep, he carried these terrible feelings with him. He found the boy in the attic. "I've been waiting for you, Sandy," he said, and that was when Sandy understood that the boy had always been here. He had slipped about the house at night while all the Whytes were asleep; he had been watching them for a long time. He showed Sandy how to glide between the walls and take food from the pantry, then he went away leaving Sandy in a dark place, unable to move.

He was shoved into something dusty and cramped. The iron taste of blood was seeping into his mouth. He knew that he was in two places at once, and yet both were the same dreadful space: he was shut up in the wall behind the pantry shelves and he was also in his father's coffin, embedded deep in concrete. He could move his hands only a little; when he tried to raise his arms, he could feel small chunks of plaster and lathe scratching his skin. He held his breath, trying not to panic. Then he was aware of a conversation, of two people talking from the other side of the wall. He listened, quiet as a mouse.

Father and Mother were having morning coffee in the kitchen — their voices had sounded this way when he was a little boy lying in bed and they were already downstairs, eating their oatmeal, their talk and the clatter of dishes drifting up to him on the second floor. He listened very carefully; despite his imprisonment he was excited to be finally able to make out what they were saying about him.

"What's wrong with the boy?" his father was saying.

"Do you know why you're so hard on him?"

"He doesn't use his head."

"No. You're just alike you two. You're just alike."

His father's sigh was so deep that Sandy could feel it through the wall, a gust of stale air. When his father shook his head, the weight of the movement caused plaster to fall about Sandy's shoulders. His face was pushing against the lathe, he could feel the hard curls of plaster on his cheek. It was both dry and wet; it scratched and it stuck. It was plaster and it was concrete and it was starting to pour down on him in a thick rain. Inches away were the tongue-and-groove cupboards stocked with flour and sugar, jars of preserves and jams, his mother's oatmeal cookies in the big beige tin with the red-checker lid. But he was pinned, trapped. His face was itchy and he could not bring his hands to scratch it.

"Like two peas in a pod," his mother was saying. "For heaven's sakes, you even walk the same way!"

"Jesus Christ!" his father shouted, banging his fists. Then the pigeons were flying in the walls and they woke him.

At first, he was upset because the boy had not slipped back through the walls of his dream to free him, but then he realized that this was foolishness. Dreams were nothing but images set in motion by electrical sparks in his brain. They meant nothing. And yet, he cherished the memory of the boy laughing beside him in Samuel's nightshirt at bedtime.

And it was then, as he thought of these things, that Sandy admitted to himself how much he wanted to touch the poor, condemned boy. Touch him, hold him, feel him — do with the boy's sweet body what he had only ever done with his own useless one when he was alone. If that were possible, the boy could live.

He could go in there right now and lie down beside him; he could kiss him, feel the boy's skin against his own — he could finally know what another body stretched out against his would truly feel like. As he thought these things, Sandy's right hand gripped his growing penis in a comfortable, familiar way. He lifted his left hand, pushing the sheet upwards in a tent above his groin — he had never been able to watch himself masturbate, not even in the dark, and the tenting would prevent staining on the top sheet. He imagines the bedroom door opening before him and his moving to the boy's bedside. He unties the boy and lies beside him. "Here am I," he says, and the boy lifts himself smiling into Sandy's arms. "Here am I."

And then the space inside the little tent he makes with his hand seems to grow and the movements taking place there become a vast, expansive thing. He and the boy are walking along the great plains under the dark, sheeted sky, their arms about each other's waist. The air is sweet and the ground beneath their feet is smooth and muscled as the arms of a labourer. They talk quietly and walk into the lovely dark for hours. There is no rest of the world; there is only this moment, this journey, this universe of velvet warmth.

"I will never leave you."

"Here am I."

Stars are beginning to appear — if he keeps his eyes closed tightly he can see them arrive and explode like tiny pinwheels, a constant sensation of wonder that he sustains by slowing the movement of his right hand. The pillow is the boy's flushed cheek against his own.

"Here am I."

They are kissing against the sky, a kiss as large as the sky itself; Sandy's tongue moves over the boulders of his teeth, gleaming white in the silver glowing from above. There are cities in the distance, emptied of all life and waiting for them, hundreds of little rooms to be filled with love, hours of twilight, of dusk and dawn and the heat of the day and the cool breezes of night, and all shall be well and all shall be well, and all manner of thing shall be well.

And then, just a moment before his body quivers and shakes, when it is too late to slow himself and stop, his father and mother both turn their accusing faces to his, the boy hurtles back to his prisoner's bed down the hall, and Sandy knows that he is grey and old and pathetic, with only the tiniest drop of sperm dribbling like half a tear over his pale, wrinkled thumb.

Chaleur wanted to die. When he slept, the pain woke him moments later. Time was confused and lost; he was stranded hopelessly and his universe was a body filled with torment.

His dreams were scattered, fragmented bits and pieces of suffering. Annette standing by the bedside telling him that she would not set him free; Rory and his mother fighting near the dresser, not even turning to look at him; the cornflake baby floating back and forth in a bubble along the ceiling crack — its face old and terrible. A strange man as skinny as a rail touched his forehead and then ran away. Over and over again, Grandmère was in the same bed with him, and he was her and she was him and both of them were tied up and hurting. He dreamed that he was in this bed, dreaming that he was in this bed, and then the pain would wake him up and everything would hurt and he would moan into the gag about his mouth.

Everything hurt, everything ached. He wanted to pull out every tooth in his head, to cut off his hands and his feet; he wanted the steady throb in his head to be the ticking of a bomb — because maybe, maybe, if his skull were to blow wide open, if his body were to shatter, if the room were to go up in flames, then the pain might go away.

In a horror movie, you were tied up and tortured by Freddy with his knife fingers or Jason with his hockey mask — somebody who looked scary. All that he had was a stupid old faggot with grey teeth who tried to look scary by putting a shower cap on his head. He was in a horror movie that wouldn't scare any-body. It was a bad joke. His whole life had been a bad joke.

There was no hope. He knew that no one was looking for him, that nothing mattered, that no one cared. If they did find him, save him, they still wouldn't care. They might make a big fuss, but a couple of days later Rory would start calling him names again and his mother would do nothing about it, his stu-pid brother would still be perfect, and Grandmère would still be tied to a bed in the Home. His dad would always be dead.

And Annette?

If he were to die, he was sure that she would cry. He imag-ined her standing beside the river up in the woods; she was look-ing into the water and crying.

Maybe if he were dead, all of them might feel bad. They might feel almost as bad as he had felt his whole fucking life. He had not asked to be born anyway. No one had. You were alive because two people had screwed each other. Maybe they had a baby and maybe they didn't. Maybe they killed the baby before it was born. If you were alive, you were just a cornflake baby that hadn't been cut out.

He tried to work his way through one of his favourite songs, but he couldn't. He would imagine the beginning, the guitar first and the drums, then he would start to move through the words, ready to be carried off by them, but he would get snagged by a phrase, stuck inside the ache in Axl Rose's voice. The ache would fill him and he would swirl around in it; that hurt was now his hurt, over and over. There was nothing else.

And he wanted to die right there, where he was the nothing of pure ache, a pain that was beautiful because it was his and someone else was singing it.

TWENTY-TWO ✣

Raymond lay on his twin bed in the sweltering evening heat, feeling lost; the neighbours' children were playing hide-and-go-seek in the yard next door and their excited shouts filled the little back bedroom with sadness.

A little boy's voice called out, "Ready or not, here I come!" and Raymond wished it were his own. He had been so good at hide-and-go-seek that even Junior never said he was too little to play. He had always been able to hide in plain sight, right under the nose of whoever was It; he could lie down in the middle of an empty yard and never be seen; he would be so still that they would walk right past him, back and forth, over and over until his brothers would bust a gut laughing and Raymond would feel the thrill of belonging. Junior and Danny wanted him to play so badly that he could convince them to let Gloria play too, even though she was always the first to get caught.

The voices outside made him realize that the game he had played so long ago had never ended. It had been going on without him and without Gloria and his brothers all this time; they had grown up and it had left them behind.

He wished that he and Hal had never left Toronto, that he had gone on keeping his real life separate from his family. Coming home had been a mistake. He and Hal should have stayed put. They were familiar with death now; he should have realized that death was their new family; there was no room for any other. He felt certain of this even though he knew that he could never truly be certain of anything else again. He had started to see what wasn't there. A house on the Dune. A boy in a bed.

As the room grew darker, he tried to remember every detail of his walk up the stairs at Sandy Whyte's: he had stood outside the door, he had gone into that stale bedroom, he had seen the boy on the bed. He retraced his steps over and over until his memory lost its flow and broke into two images as solid as paintings. The first was the boy's body tied to an old iron bed, all milky white limbs and ragged breathing. When his face turned towards Raymond's, his eyes were red and sad. In the other, the boy's face hovers below him in close-up, a face like those of the handsome young thugs Raymond had crushes on in high school.

He had promised the boy that he would search for him, that he would find him, but the more he thought about that handsome face, the more he knew that the boy was tied up only in his head. There could be no real boy in the real world. Raymond broke out in a sweat; he was afraid. What little future he had left was starting to swallow him up. He was failing, he was slipping away from the world. Soon he would be lost, buried in madness and night sweats while the real world went on outside the window. He would be Clive, half-blind and all madness, screaming from a place no one could understand.

The children's voices receded as he silently ranted at the darkness pulling him closer. His body hurt; the pain was the darkness itself and he was a black hole collapsing inward.

The boy had seemed so real. Hadn't Raymond touched him? No, the whole thing was impossible. It was craziness. It was dementia, darling. But if he knew that, couldn't it help him hang on to what was real? He did not want to become Clive, become so far gone that he would drive all his friends away.

The last time the police had phoned Raymond, Clive had been picked up on Queen Street at seven in the morning. "He resisted arrest," the officer said.

"Arrest! Why were you arresting him?"

"Mr. Maurice, all that your friend had on was a jockstrap and he was screaming at people. He shoved an old lady. No one's laying charges. Just bring some clothes, and come and get him."

Out of loyalty to Clive's old self, his friends were trying to keep him at home. He was horrible there, but he was worse anywhere else. In the end, the skeleton that smashed its way through the hospital window was fuelled only with rage. Raymond did not want to be Clive escaping into six storeys of air.

In the cab going home from the police station, Clive had ranted, "Fucking pigs! The human body is a beautiful thing. God's own image, for chrissakes." And he had tried to get undressed.

Raymond thought of a place where he and Clive could be quiet together and talk: the cab faded and he imagined Clive lying beside him on the sand near the end of the Dune.

"Clive," he said, "our goose is cooked."

"You've got Hal," Clive whined. "I'm all alone."

"Don't be crazy. I'm all alone too." Where was Hal now?

"Raymond?"

Raymond reached out his hand on the sand beside him, and touched Hal's hand. "He's right here."

"Raymond?"

He opened his eyes. Hal was sitting beside him on the edge of the bed. Had he been there for a while? Clive had been dead for a long time now, and it was dark out already.

"Raymond? Knock knock." His voice was so quiet. "You there?"

"I'm here." He nodded. "I'm vague, but I'm here."

Hal switched on the little light beside the bed. "Last call for lobster."

"I couldn't." Then he groaned. "This must be the end. I just said 'No' to lobster. It's like turning down sex with John Travolta."

"He's downstairs waiting — should I send him home?"

Raymond snorted. "That's so lame — why am I even laughing?"

Hal shrugged. "Look, can I get you anything?"

"All I want is my old unsick self back," Raymond said.

"I never knew him."

He sighed. "Ice water'd be nice."

"I'll be right back." Hal picked up Raymond's hand and squeezed it, then he went downstairs.

Raymond wished that he had been able to have one final, sane talk with Clive. One last little joke. It was hard sometimes to remember the old Clive, and he did not want people to think that way about him after he died.

If only the boy could be real, because if he were, then Raymond would not be losing his mind so quickly. But why should some poor boy be tied up just to help Raymond prove to himself that he wasn't crazy? "I don't care," he whispered. "Why the hell should I care? I don't want to be crazy, I don't want to be sick, and I don't want to die. Fuck him. Whoever he is."

On his way to the kitchen, Hal ran into Gloria.

"Why don't you take a break," she said. "Junior and Danny are going down to the Club. I'll sit with Raymond for a while."

"I'm okay."

"I know you're okay," she said, "but you can be alone with Raymond anytime." As soon as she said it, she winced. "I'm sorry, that didn't sound very nice."

"That's all right," Hal said. "I know what you mean. He wants a glass of water, you want to take it up?"

She nodded.

"Where are your folks?"

"Mama and Pop went out for a drive. Danny and Junior are outside."

Hal would rather have gone for a walk by himself, but he thought it would be better to try to be with Junior and Danny. After Mama had forced herself to deal with him, he thought that it was the least he could do. They were just getting ready to leave when he went out to the veranda. "You guys going to the Club?"

"Yeah," Junior said.

"Okay if I come along? I could use a drink."

Junior shrugged and walked down the steps. Danny nodded and waved "come on then." Hal joined him and they followed Junior down the sidewalk. They walked past a few houses in silence before Danny said, "Club's not much, you know."

"Oh, that doesn't matter," Hal replied.

But Danny was right. It had no windows and was dim and dark inside, the air thick with spilled beer and stale ashtrays. The walls were grim-looking wallboard, and the low drop ceilings were yellowed acoustic tiles. It was a dive, a place for drunks to hide out. When they arrived, the place was half-full; most of the people looked like they had been there all day drinking. A crappy band was playing covers of old country songs, songs that Hal had been avoiding on radios for the last twenty years.

No one said anything for a long while, until, finally, Danny asked, "So what's all this about Raymond seeing somebody all tied up down at Sandy Whyte's place?"

"Oh, Christ," said Junior. "What now?"

Raymond had not moved since she came in, he was all curled up in bed with his eyes closed. Gloria put the glass of water on the night table.

She sat in the chair at the foot of the bed, but that seemed too far away, so she moved it up closer. The window was open, but there wasn't even the trace of a breeze. The heat would have been unbearable if Mama hadn't put a fan beside the bed. Gloria sat there, thinking about how this was the last time that Raymond would ever come home. His funeral would probably be away up in Toronto.

"Stop it," she hissed at herself. "Just quit it!"

"Stop what?"

"Sorry, Raymond, I thought you were asleep. I was talking to myself. You feeling all right?"

"I'm really tired."

"It's night time."

"Yeah, but it's a different kind of tired. I'm dying, you know."

"Oh, Raymond, don't say that."

"Why not? It's true."

"I know it's true. I brought you some water."

"Where's Hal?"

"He'll be back. He went out for a drink with Danny and Junior."

"Oh." He thought that Hal must be desperate to get away

from him if he would agree to go out with his brothers. *Running away from me already, the little shit.* He would not talk to Gloria about the boy in the bed; he did not want to scare her into running away too.

"Did you ever think about coming up to Toronto to visit sometime?"

"What? Yeah." Gloria had never really thought about going; she was thinking that she wanted to hold his hand, but was worried that he would think that was too corny.

"I'd like you to see where I live before I die."

"Will you quit talking like this is gonna happen tomorrow?"

"But it could."

The whine in his voice made her want to say that most of the time it wasn't easy to be alive either, but she didn't.

His mind started wandering, planning her visit. Would she be interested in the Museum? Not really. Nor the Art Gallery. But she'd want to go to the top of the CN Tower. In all the time he'd lived in Toronto he had never once bothered to go there. Why not? The view was probably fabulous. Maybe they could even see his apartment through a telescope. They would get Hal to stay home, and arrange a time so he could go to the window and wave at them. He could see Hal standing there beside the drafting table, looking at his watch and waiting because Raymond and Gloria were early. They had gone down to Broadview and caught a streetcar right away. They were fifteen minutes early and Hal was not even dressed. "Don't look yet," he said to Gloria. "He's buck naked."

"What? Who?"

"Oh."

"Are you asleep again?"

"Maybe."

She smiled. "Remember the summer we played softball every day like we couldn't get enough of it? And one night you went to sleep on the chesterfield and when Pop woke you up to take you to bed you said, 'Wait a minute! It's my turn to bunt!'"

"I was still asleep, I guess."

"And dreaming that you were playing ball."

Neither one of them said anything for a while. Gloria didn't want him slipping away from her, so she decided that she didn't care if he thought she was corny. She held his hand. His hand squeezed hers and they both sat very still.

"This is nice," he said.

"Umhum."

They didn't speak again for a moment and he was planning her visit to Toronto again, wondering about which parts of the Museum to show her and where to take her for dinner. He imagined her reaction to sushi. "It's just raw fish," he said. "Go ahead and try it."

"What the frig are you dreaming about now?"

"I'm not dreaming, I'm just crazy."

"Raymond, you're not crazy."

He hugged her hand again and sighed. It was one thing to know that you were going to die sooner rather than later — you could trick yourself into thinking that sooner would be later; but it was another to realize that you were losing your mind in the process. He wanted to talk about it, but he thought that it wouldn't be fair to Gloria.

"Are you always gonna live with Mama and Pop?"

"I dunno. I guess so now, eh?"

"No guy ever?"

"You mean, like a boyfriend?"

"Yeah."

"I'm too fat."

He squeezed her hand tightly. "That's stupid."

She shrugged.

"You don't really think that, do you?"

"Maybe. I used to blame guys, but now I think maybe it's my fault. Maybe I like it here and so I never tried very hard. I had a big crush on one of Junior's friends once, but he went to jail for armed robbery so I figure I'm lucky."

They had never talked about this. When they were teenagers he had wanted to talk about the guys that he had crushes on, but every time he started to, he chickened out. The closest they ever came was talking about movie stars.

"Poor Mama and Pop," he said. "None of us did so hot in the marriage department."

"You."

"Oh, come on."

"Well, it's not like Danny or me ever brought somebody like Hal home. Danny's too shy to even meet girls." If Raymond were not so sick she would have told him about the woman in Danny's building that he had gone out with that time. But it was a sad story, and there was no way to make it sound any different. Some stories could not be funny no matter how you told them. Her hand was getting cramped; it was starting to fall asleep.

"What about Junior?"

"Aw, he and Ginette's always fighting."

"Do you like her?"

She shrugged. "Not like a best friend or anything."

"Does she have big boobs?"

Gloria laughed. "Whatta you think?"

"I think knockers. Great big honking knockers."

She pulled her hand free and gave him a little poke.

"Keep holding my hand."

"I can't get comfortable."

"Why don't you just lie down."

She did. She crawled into bed and lay down next to her brother. Put her arm around his waist. He felt so light and frail beside her, as if she could pick him up in one hand and twirl him in the air.

After a while Raymond said, "Tell me a story."

"I can't tell stories very well."

"Yes, you can. Just tell me one."

"Like what? Nancy Drew?"

"No. That's not what I mean. Tell me a story from when we were kids."

She thought for a moment. "Like when?" she asked because suddenly she couldn't think of anything as important as being with Raymond right now. "The time we danced the hula?"

"No. Tell me about the Virgin Mary."

While they were doing the dishes, Mama had asked Pop to take her for a drive. "I need to get out of this house for a little while," she said, "go somewheres quiet."

"All right." A minute later he said, "We'll have to take Danny's car." After Danny had talked to the insurance agent, Pop had taken his car back to Romeo's.

"Danny won't mind." She scrubbed out the dish pan while Pop put the last piece of Sandy Whyte's silver back in its box. He went to get the key from Danny.

They drove to the beach, but it was crowded there and Pop just turned the car around and headed back through town. Mama shook her head; she didn't care for tourists much: as soon as the good weather came, they took over the place, driving up prices at the grocery store and jamming Main Street with so many cars that the town had to put up a traffic light.

Pop drove past their street, and kept going west on Main. When they got to Sandy Whyte's place, he slowed down and said, "That must be where Gloria got clipped." They both stared at the shoulder near the driveway as if it might reveal something.

Sandy Whyte's car was coming down the drive; if he were going out of town, it was pretty late in the day to get started.

Just before they came to the bridge, Pop turned left onto the River Road. The sun was going down and the water at the mouth of the Membartouche River was as smooth as a mill pond.

"Herons," Pop said, nodding his head towards the water.

She nodded. "I count five of them." Four were spread out, fifteen or twenty feet apart in the shallow water just up from the bridge; the fifth was standing by itself near the other shore. For a long time there had been no herons in the bay, but they had been coming back now for fifteen years or so. They nested on the island. She had been out with Pop in Alphonse's boat one day when the weather turned and it was suddenly rainy and rough. As they came around the island, heading home, she had seen the herons sheltering high in the branches of spruce trees; it was as odd as seeing a horse on top of a fence. There was something exotic about blue herons, they weren't like gulls or crows; it was as if they really should be somewhere else, like Japan or China. They weren't plain enough to be local.

Almost a mile up River Road, after they went over the overpass above the four-lane and past the last house, Pop turned onto a dirt road that ran along beside the old railway bed.

"Been a long while since I was up in this neck of the woods," Mama said. "Not since they tore down the Iron Bridge."

Pop grunted. "Goddam government." The old railway bridge had been gone for twenty years.

The road was bumpy and the car stirred up a lot of dust, so he lifted his foot from the gas and coasted along for a minute, then slowed down and parked by the side of the road. Mama had rolled down her window; it was very quiet when he shut off the engine. He would have been content just to sit in the car, but she opened her door, so he got out too.

It was still hot, but the air was a little fresher up here in the woods. They waded through the little dry ditch filled with Queen Anne's lace and up the embankment to the rail bed. Purple vetch clung to her ankles.

"Watch out for burdocks," he said.

"Oh, they're not too-too bad here yet." The rail bed was just a worn path through thickets of weeds; they walked to the end, where once the bridge had started. Before they were married, they had sometimes walked along the tracks from the station to the Iron Bridge.

"Used to be good strawberries here," she said.

He nodded. They were both thinking of a day when Gloria and Raymond had helped her pick a couple of pails full while he sat down on the bank with Junior and Danny, fishing for trout.

Everywhere else along the river the woods sloped down to the water's edge, but here, where the trains had run, the approach to the bridge had been built up and they were standing high above the river. They could look upstream to where the river turned east and cut across the top of their street; downstream, they could see as far as the big bend before the waters widened under the four-lane and opened out into the bay. The water was smooth, but even in the fading light they could tell that it was moving quickly. A branch of silver birch went gliding by below them; it would be carried out in the bay with the tide and then washed ashore on a beach somewhere. The bridge had been torn down, but its five heavy stone pilings still rose up high from the river, like a line of towers, their big stone blocks like castle walls. When the Iron Bridge was here, Mama had not really noticed them; now they made her think of ruins she might have seen in a TV show about Europe.

At the end of the railway bed a line of stone blocks had been put up like a little wall to keep people from walking over the edge.

"Four trains a day," she said, shaking her head. "Hard to believe."

"Goddam government."

It was right here, walking along the rails to the Iron Bridge, that she had wanted to tell him the truth about the boy in the Davy Crockett jacket. But she was scared that he would not want to marry her any more after he heard it, and she was afraid to disobey her mother's warning.

"Keep your big trap shut," the old lady had said. "What he doesn't know won't hurt him."

She had managed to tell him only half the truth. "I'm going to have a baby," she stammered.

They could hear traffic from the highway faintly in the distance. In the twilight, the line of spruce on the far bank was dark and jagged against the sky.

"I wish today had been easier. Poor Gloria, she was counting on that lobster."

"Most you can say about today is that we won't have to live through it again." He was scanning the water below them, looking at nothing in particular.

As it got darker, the woods seemed to close about them in a tender way. The old pilings of the bridge became dark shadows on the river. Mama could smell spruce in the air. Something big moved below them in the alders down near the bank — a deer probably. All sorts of animals would be getting ready to go out on the prowl.

"Albert," she said after a minute, and he knew that she was going to say something serious because she never called him that.

Without looking at him, she went on, "I think we should tell Raymond and his friend that if things go bad for them they can always come home."

Pop wanted to argue with her, wanted to tell her that he didn't want that boyfriend of Raymond's around after Monday. He didn't want to have anything to do with this AIDS business at all. But all he did was shrug. Pop hoped that Raymond and his friend would just disappear and leave them alone.

"Well," he said after a minute, "one good thing. Weather's gonna break."

She was staring down into the darkness. "Funny to think, isn't it, that where the train used to go is just air now."

He spat over the edge.

"We were more isolated back then," Mama said, "before airplanes and everybody having a car. But I felt more a part of things. The trains made me feel connected. How do you figure that?"

Maybe Lavinia's piano lesson with the nuns had gone on longer than usual, because it seemed to Gloria that it was quite late when they set out for home from the convent through the graveyard. It must have been September because, even though she was sure that it had been a school night, it felt like summer. Gloria knew it could not have been the spring, because the two of them had played together the whole summer vacation. She doesn't remember why they decided to walk all the way to the top of the field; there was a small stand of spruce trees up there, beside an old oak. Back then, Gloria thought that the oak tree was practically magic because there were no trees like it in her yard. The leaves were mysterious-looking, much better than maples, and the acorns were so cute. They started to collect some so that they could make acorn jewellery. Lavinia said, "Mine'll be a rosary." Everything she did was holy.

The first strange thing that happened was that they saw a rabbit hop right past them into the trees. In Gloria's mind, it was white, but whenever she saw rabbits in the woods — which was not very often — they had been brown. Even though it was very close to them, just a couple of feet away, she had seen it only for a second, so she couldn't be sure any more.

Lying next to Raymond, she could see the moon through the top of the window, and she thought that maybe the rabbit had been that colour — soft and milky, glowing in the darkening light. Well, whatever colour it had been, she and Lavinia decided to follow it and started crawling under the spruce boughs on the dry brown needles.

How long had it been before Lavinia pointed to a light shining up ahead? A minute maybe. Maybe more. What Gloria was sure of was that she started to get frightened.

They came out from under the trees in the middle of a little grove. And there, at the other end of it, was the lady. Gloria thought that she was very small, like a little girl. The light in the grove was like a TV set in a dark room — it flickered all around on the evergreens, and must have been coming from the lady herself. She was wearing a blue dress that was the same colour as the ceiling in the convent chapel where the nuns got married to Jesus.

They stood up, and as soon as they did, the lady smiled. Then she went away. Whether she disappeared into the woods or just vanished, Gloria cannot remember. One moment she was there, and the next, she was gone. Although she had smiled, it was so sad that Gloria knew it was the kind of smile that had nothing to do with happiness.

And that was when Lavinia fell down on the ground and started to shake all over like someone having a big fit. Gloria stood, looking down at her, scared out of her mind, thinking that this was something terrible that only grown-ups should know about. Lavinia's hips twisted violently and her bum banged up and down. Her little hands were pounding on the brown needles as if something were trying to hurt her.

"What did you do?" Raymond asked.

"I waited till she was finished having her fit."

He snuggled closer to his sister. "And that's it?"

"Pretty much." she said.

When Lavinia came to, she cried and then started smiling; all the way home she kept talking about how lucky they were. Gloria didn't know before that being lucky could be so scary.

She had seen the lady for such a short time, seconds really, and over the years her image had become both sharp and vague. She seemed to recall a detail of the blue dress — it was a line of little gold squares with a star inside each one — but then, that could have been on a statue in the convent chapel. The clearest memory was that smile, lingering there in the spruce grove.

Raymond turned his head towards her. "Do you think she was real?" he asked.

"I don't know any more." She shrugged. "No, that's not right. I pretend to myself that maybe it never happened, but how can that be? I remember her."

He nodded, squeezing her hand. "Do you wish it were true?"

"I'd be happiest if it never happened. It felt like the whole town was mad at me after. Like that mean old nun, remember?"

"Which one?"

"That day we had no school, so you and me went over to play with the kids at Ste. Anne's."

"Oh, that sour old bitch! 'Don't play with the bad girl, children, she makes up lies about the Virgin!' I can still see her." And then suddenly he exclaimed, "I told her to kiss my arse!"

Gloria laughed. "That's right. You told that miserable old nun to kiss your arse. You even waved it at her. Stuck it right out and waved it right at her."

He wiggled his bum against her side. "Kiss me arse, kiss me arse!" he chanted, and Gloria laughed, her big body shaking the bed.

"Somedays" — she sighed — "somedays I wish I'd said that to half the friggin' town."

They were lying with their arms around each other and, in a minute, he started to snore.

When Mama and Pop looked in a little while later, Gloria was sleeping too.

Junior and Danny were well into their sixth beer, but Hal was slowing down, nursing his third. He had told them Raymond's story about going into the bedroom at Sandy Whyte's, and he had told them about their friend Clive. He said that both he and Raymond were worried. "But it's a weird thing to imagine, someone tied up like that."

Danny drummed on the table a couple of times with his fingers. "I dunno," he said. "Every time they catch a real screwball it seems to me that all the neighbours always say he was the sort of quiet guy who wouldn't hurt a fly."

"What are you talking about?"

"Maybe the poor little bugger did see something."

"Come on," said Hal. "It doesn't make any sense."

"That's right," Danny said. "Either way, it makes no sense either way, so I figure chances are that he could've seen something."

Junior grunted. "Well, we are talking about Sandy Whyte and if he did something wacko it wouldn't surprise me at all."

"Because he's gay?" Hal said, a bit too defensively.

"Don't be an asshole." He pushed back his chair. "I gotta take a piss."

Danny watched Junior walk to the bathroom, and shook his head. "He's phoning Ginette," he said.

"His girlfriend?"

Danny nodded.

Hal wondered why Danny didn't have a girlfriend; he was a good-looking guy really. "What do you think the chances are that right now somebody's tied up at Sandy Whyte's?"

Danny shrugged. "Fifty-fifty."

"Junior——"

Before Ginette could say anything else, Junior wanted to tell her everything that was on his mind.

"Ginette, I want us to get married."

She was lighting a cigarette. He could hear her little silver lighter snap shut. "Jesus Christ, Junior!"

"First I'd get a job."

"Doing what?"

"I've been thinking about this. There's a friend of the old man's who has a garage. He thinks he can use me." He listened while she took another drag on her cigarette. Why didn't she say something? "So what you think?" he asked.

She took another drag, then she said, "I'm staying in Halifax, Junior. I gotta job, started last week."

"Ginette, I'll come down. I'll find a job there."

"There's no jobs here. Besides, why should I believe you?"

"'Cause you're all I think about. But I gotta show you that I'm, you know, worthy like."

By the way she exhaled, he could tell that she was shaking her head.

"Junior, why d'you think it'll be any different this time?"

"'Cause I want it to be. Jesus Christ, Ginette, it's our last chance. I gotta try."

"You big Jesus asshole," she said. "I'm sick of trying. I've got kids to look out for."

"But you know I love those kids."

"Just 'cause you're a big kid yerself. You and your friggin' dumb titty magazines."

"I'll never bring another one into the house."

"Right."

"Swear to God."

"Junior, it's after midnight. I'm tired."

"What's your job?" he asked.

"It's not much. Waitress. It's a bar. Tips is good."

"They need a bouncer?"

He had meant it as a joke, but when she said nothing he could tell from her silence that he had hit the nail on its head.

"They do, don't they?" He laughed.

"Jesus, I dunno, Junior."

"How are the kids?"

He couldn't believe his luck. He had hit the nail on the head.

"Well, I know what we'll do," Danny said. They were walking up the street after the Club closed; the night was so quiet that they could hear a truck driving on the highway above the town. They were all pretty drunk.

"What?" said Hal.

"We'll go in, me and Junior."

"In where?"

"Sandy Whyte's."

"Frig right off!" Junior said.

Danny shook his head. "We'll plan it tomorrow, go down after dark."

"And why?" asked Junior.

"Reason number one: we gotta give Raymond the benefit of the doubt, right?"

"And reason number two, arsehole?"

Danny stood as still as he could and raised his hand in the air, "Reason number two" — he couldn't help himself, he started to laugh — "Reason number two: the Sheik rides again."

"Frig off, you clown." Junior gave him a shove.

"You're nuts," Hal said. "What if you get caught?"

Junior glared at him. "I never get caught."

Danny laughed. "Then how come you went to jail, Sheiky?"

"I never got caught breaking in. I only ever got caught stealing. There's a difference."

TWENTY-THREE

E ven with the Coles Island shortcut, it was always a longer drive than Margaret remembered, and Sandy's old car slowed down to a crawl on every hill. Because the heat had not yet broken, it was not a pleasant trip: the scenery was washed out, pale and smudged in the humidity.

"It's a shame," she said when they stopped for gas on the top of Steeves' Mountain. "Normally that's such a pretty view."

Annette shrugged and climbed out of the car.

They were ill-at-ease with each other; they had been able to talk only in fits and starts, and this annoyed them both and made things worse.

The man from the service station checked the oil and told Margaret that the car had none.

"Dry as a bone, Mrs."

"Fill that up then, too, please."

On the lighthouse steps the day before yesterday she and Annette had been much more comfortable. She knew that it was their destination that was making them both feel miserable; neither one was capable of saying anything that might allow a conversation to develop. Annette was nervous, and Margaret did not yet understand what was going to happen — she believed that she was exactly where she should be, but she was worried.

When they had pulled into the service station across from the Lookout, Annette had been pretending to sleep; Margaret knew it and Annette knew that she knew. While the man was checking the oil, she wandered away from the pumps towards the highway, where she lit a cigarette.

An hour earlier, when Margaret had stopped the car beside the park, Annette was already waiting, and there was something about the way she was slouched on the bench and the way she walked to the car that bothered Margaret. She moved too slowly, she looked bored, and she was wearing too much make-up.

"I hope you haven't been waiting long," Margaret said, even though she knew that she was right on time. Eight on the dot.

"That's okay. I couldn't sleep."

The tone of her voice made Margaret stiffen slightly. It wasn't ungrateful, but it wasn't grateful either. It was dismissive somehow.

There had been very little traffic on Main Street; the town felt deserted. As they drove over the bridge, Margaret said, "Any word yet?"

Annette had shaken her head. "I'm just about nuts. If he hasn't called when I get back, I'm going to the police."

"And his family?"

"That bunch? Don't make me laugh. Is it okay if I smoke?"

Although Margaret thought it certainly was not, she nodded her head. "We'll just have to remember to clean out the ashtray before I take the car back to Sandy."

"Is the problem with your car very serious?"

Margaret shook her head. "No, I don't think so. It just wouldn't start." She had not explained the true reason for the borrowed car because she did not want to discuss Minnie's humiliation. If Sandy's car hadn't been so untidy, she wouldn't have mentioned it at all.

The ashtray was jammed with bits of rolled-up paper, and Margaret was annoyed when Annette dug them out and carefully dumped them on the floor. She furiously rolled her window down all the way, and Annette quickly rolled hers down too, and turned away from Margaret so that the smoke could go outside.

Margaret felt that the car with its curious smells (old aftershave? sweat?) and its clutter of papers and pencils on the dashboard and floor was as imposing as Sandy himself might have been sitting between them. It made things uncomfortable.

Last night she had wanted to have a serious talk with him; on her walk to his house she had hoped that he would invite her in for a cup of tea. But when she saw him, his behaviour had been so peculiar. He had not been cold, exactly; he had been — well, "peculiar" summed it up.

She had walked up the steps and was about to ring his bell when he pulled the door open — he must have been standing just inside in the dark and waiting for her. And then he said, "Isn't it a lovely night?" and stepped past her, shutting the door behind him, so that their brief conversation took place on the veranda.

Isn't it a lovely night? What could he have been thinking? It had been a horrible night, so wretchedly hot. It was such a strange thing to say, and he had tried to sound so buoyant. She could not help but notice the wet circles in the armpits of his shirt. She could smell them — his sweat was as strong as urine. Had his eyes always darted about so nervously? She supposed so, but she had never noticed it so much — and he had looked very pale. Ashen, she thought.

"I really appreciate this, Sandy," she had said after he gave her the keys. "I really do."

"Maybe you can come to me in my hour of need," he said, and his voice was suddenly forlorn, as if that hour were fast approaching. "I'm afraid there's not much gas in it. Well, I have some things to do, so I won't keep you." And he left her standing there with the keys, staring at the closing door.

Margaret reached into the ashtray and removed Annette's two cigarette butts. She wrapped them in a Kleenex and opened the car door.

"Where are you and your daughter off to today, Mrs.?" the man asked her when she stepped out of the car and moved towards the trash can.

"Oh," she said. "Just a drive."

She stood watching Annette smoke her cigarette. Her daughter. How strange, and yet she supposed that was the logical thing for him to think. Right now, the most familial thing about them both was the tension between them. Her daughter. Smoking a cigarette. With that junk lathered around her eyes. Margaret sighed, thinking that Annette looked just like the sort of girl who would be on her way to an abortion clinic. Did she look like the sort of woman who would be taking her daughter there? She yearned to know why the two of them had been brought together.

Even though she was turned away from the gas pumps and looking out at the highway, Annette knew that Margaret was watching her. The traffic was steady and loud, and she found herself wondering what would happen if she ran out and jumped in front of a car. Would it have time to stop? Probably not. Everything would be over in seconds. She wondered what else would have to happen to push her over that edge, ending her life with the screech of tires and a thud. Any one of these cars could kill her. This was not something that she wished, it was simply a fact, and the only reason she was thinking it was that she was feeling so miserable. When she had called Chaleur's place late last evening, Ralphie had answered. She could hear his mother and Rory arguing in the background.

"Ralphie, is Chaleur there?"

"Nope."

"Has anyone heard from him?"

"Nope."

"Can I talk to your mother for a minute?"

"I don't think so." The shouting had grown louder in the background. She could not make out very much — both of them seemed to be shouting "Oh yeah? Oh yeah?" like enemy wrestlers being interviewed on TV.

"Okay. Do you have any idea where he could be?"

"Nope. But he's in big trouble when he gets back."

Annette realized that, for a change, there was nothing smug in Ralphie's voice. "Well, okay then," she said, ready to hang up.

"Annette?"

"Yeah?"

"Think he ran away?"

"I don't know. I don't think so."

"I didn't mean to ruin his poster."

"Okay, Ralphie. I'll tell him if I see him."

Afterwards, she wished that she had said "when I see him."

In her dream last night, Chaleur had mocked her, called her names. He was holding a baby on his shoulder wrapped up in an old blanket — it was not her baby because in the dream the abortion had happened a long time ago. So she knew that he had a new girlfriend now. She could not remember where they were, only that everywhere she went Chaleur kept jumping up in front of her with that baby and, when she tried to run away, he would still be there, laughing and shouting those awful names. When she finally saw the baby's face, it was all squished up, like a bag of snakes. It scared her so much that she woke up and lay worrying that the dream had been real. Then she started worrying that every night from now on would be filled with terrible dreams. Maybe the cornflake baby knew what she was planning and was starting to send them to her. She knew that it was not really a baby yet, it was still a part of her, but if she and Chaleur were married and ready for a family, she knew that she would be thinking of it as a little baby already, with pink skin and little eyes the colour of Chaleur's, and she was trying hard not to do that.

She had crawled out of bed at six and thrown up; when she saw her face in the mirror, it was so tired-looking that she had put on more make-up than usual. From the way Margaret looked at her as she climbed into the car, she knew the woman thought she looked cheap. But what did she care what other people thought?

Margaret watched the unhappy girl walk slowly back and forth along the gravel shoulder. She wished that she could go over and put her arm around her in a consoling way, but she didn't know how to do that sort of thing. She was like her mother that way. Yesterday she had been able to hug Minnie because her sister had come to her.

She sighed and looked across the highway to the Lookout, longing to see the view in a pure, clear light. She was troubled by the cars zooming past; she hated the huge, filthy transports loudly roaring up the mountain in the slow lane. She knew that the land below her was green, with farms stretching around the little villages — Boundary Creek, Coverdale, Salisbury, and, beyond them, Colpitts Settlement and The Glades — all those places where she used to go for Sunday drives. Down there were daisies along the roadsides, and purple vetch, and the rich scent of wild roses. In the distance were sugar woods — she and Minnie had been taken there as children: they had poured hot syrup onto the snow and seen a falling star. There were forests of evergreens and pastures of fat cows. Pink with mud, the Petitcodiac River curled through the rich land. The brooks and creeks were all named for the farmers' lands they crossed: Hopper, Stiles, Babcock, Leeman. Abandoned fox farms were down there, and miles of snake fence, old wood so grey that it was burnished silver. All this was stretched out below her, but she could see nothing through the sickening haze that was as ugly as the sound of the tractor trailers. The land was invisible, but she knew it was there.

Without looking at each other, both women went back to the car at the same time. Margaret paid the man.

"Have a nice drive, ladies," he said, tipping his baseball hat.

Margaret pulled out on the highway, shaking her head. "That beats all," she said.

"What?"

"He thought I was your mother. Why, I'd have been pushing fifty when you were born."

Annette looked over at Margaret. They both giggled nervously. It was their first moment of affinity all day.

While they were driving through the woods, just after they had passed Coles Island, Annette said, "I called his family last night."

"Yes?"

She shook her head. "His parents were fighting. I talked to his little brother. He sounded almost scared." She was looking out the side window; the trees were suddenly sparse and thin, with lots of dead wood. There must have been a fire here, not this year but last, maybe, or the year before that. "Poor Ralphie. I felt sorry for him for the first time ever."

Margaret worried about this irresponsible boy. Why could she not form a picture of him in her head? When she tried to imagine what he might look like, his face kept changing and she could not focus on a clear image. She had been able to see Annette as she talked to her on the phone — why not this Chaleur? She tried to picture his face, but she could only hear something, like singing. There was a kind of mystery surrounding him, as if Annette had been impregnated by a ghost. She wondered if, like her own father, he had appalling desires for the baby. Margaret thought that the young man sounded no better than his family. When she met him, she wanted to give him a good talking to.

"It does make you wonder why people like that have children," she said.

She had meant the remark to sound casual. Non-committal. Just a means of extending the conversation a bit. Instead, she stopped it cold.

Annette stared at her. People like *that*. People like Margaret were always saying *things like that* about people from the wrong side of town, as if only the right side had any business having babies. Is that why she worked for the abortion clinic? Because she thought people like Annette were low-class? *Fuck her*, Annette thought, and she lit another cigarette, not caring if her smoke went out the window or not. She dropped the package onto her lap, but it bounced and fell down the space beside the door and slipped under the seat.

Margaret knew that her remark had come out wrong, but she did not know how to take it back. It sat in the car with them, like a bad smell. Annette probably thought she was talking about class, but she wasn't. Of all the people who should never have had children, her father and mother were at the top of the list.

"My father … " she began.

"Yeah?"

But Margaret, who had never told the story of her father to anyone in her life, had no idea how to begin telling it. It was so dirty. "Nothing."

They drove on in awkward silence. The oppressive heat seemed to increase the further they went, making them both feel worse.

After a while they passed a restaurant beside the road. "There was always good pie in that place," Margaret said. "Cream pie especially. Maybe we can stop off on the way back and have a little treat."

"Sure."

"A big slice of coconut cream pie might be nice."

Annette shrugged. She hated cream pie. Did Margaret think she was a baby? Maybe it would have been better if she had borrowed her sister's car and driven to the clinic by herself.

Just before the short cut ended and they turned back onto the highway, they passed a tall single pine on a hill overlooking a little field; Margaret remembered Cindy from the church pointing it out to her when they drove up to picket the clinic. "That tree is exactly halfway between our door and where we're going," Cindy had said. "Bob and I measured it on the speedometer." Bob and Cindy had made this drive many times — she certainly hoped they weren't making it today. She was feeling very uneasy; she sensed that God was watching and judging her every move, racking up points on either side of a thick black line. What if she was not doing the right thing?

The last leg of their trip was along the river, where at least they were driving in the shade of trees overhanging the narrow, twisting road.

As they drew closer to Fredericton, Annette worried more about the clinic. She tried to calm herself by going over the details that Margaret had explained to her yesterday on the phone: they would examine her and ask her questions, then they would give her another appointment. She would still be pregnant when she left. These things made her anxious, but they did not scare her. What was frightening her was the uncertainty of what might happen on the way into the clinic. She had seen protesters on television, and she did not want to have to walk past them, to have them scream at her. The idea of someone saying something mean made her think of her dream again, and she wondered if the clinic was where Chaleur might be. What if he had hitch-hiked there and would be waiting for her? If he were there, would she be so glad to see him that she would just run away with him and leave Margaret standing alone? If she saw him, would she be able to walk into the clinic?

Margaret was worried about arriving at the clinic as well. They would be there within the hour and something was telling her that this was wrong. Her fingers were sweaty and slippery on the wheel. The road was narrow here and, as they were going around a corner, she lost her grip and the right side of the car skidded on the gravel shoulder. They almost plunged into the ditch.

She pulled back onto the highway and swerved across the centre lane.

"Oh!"

"What? What's wrong?"

"Nothing." She could not let Annette see her distress. "I'm going to pull over there," she said. "I need to stretch my legs."

On the other side of the road was a little rest stop beside the wide river: a gravelled crescent with a few picnic tables, a water faucet, and a blue plastic portable toilet. She turned in too quickly and almost lost control of the car again. Was God angry at her? When she braked, the rear end skidded noisily in the gravel.

"There's a thermos of iced tea in the back," she said after the car stopped. "Would you like some?" She hoped that her cheeriness didn't sound too forced.

"Yeah. Thanks."

Margaret looked over at the girl, who did not seem to be shaken at all. Annette was looking past Margaret, out the driver's window and through the willow trees along the bank, to the thin green finger of an island in the middle of the river. A half-dozen cows were standing there in the shade, and Annette was wondering how they had ever gotten there. On a barge? On the ice in the winter? Could cows swim? She imagined what it would be like to live all alone on a little island like that. She would build a cabin and cook fish on coals and wait for Chaleur to row across to her in a little boat.

Margaret took the cups and thermos to a picnic table and poured them each a drink. The ice cubes had not melted and the tea was strong and cold.

"Thank you," Annette said, taking her cup and drinking. "Oh, it's real."

"Umhum. That old instant tastes like Kool-Aid to me."

They were standing in the shade of a willow, leaning against the table, looking out at the river. The thickness of the air seemed to be preventing all movement: no breeze stirred the trees, the cows on the island had not budged, even the water looked still. Neither woman moved for a few moments, and then, when Annette spoke, her voice was as quiet as the day itself, as if her words were a part of the stillness about them.

"Do you remember your dreams?" she said, without taking her eyes from the river.

Margaret looked at her. "I beg your pardon?"

"Like I had a scary dream last night. I don't think I have them all the time, but I hardly ever remember them. Do you remember yours?"

"Sometimes." Margaret felt her arms tingle. She knew that something was about to happen. *Have we gathered at the river?*

"Good ones or bad ones?"

"I don't know, dear. Both, I suppose." Because her hands were starting to tremble, she carefully placed her cup on the table and then folded her arms.

"Do you have bad dreams a lot?"

Margaret turned back to the river; its surface was so smooth it looked solid, as if she might be able to step out onto it. "Well, yes, yes, I suppose I do," she said

"Last night I dreamed Chaleur was after me with a monster baby. Sounds dumb when I say it, but it was awful."

Margaret said nothing; she sensed that God was revealing himself.

"My bad dreams before were not that bad. I mean, they were like about being locked up and missing an exam at school or something. I can't remember many good dreams — like when I can fly and that? — and when I try to remember them, it's like the dream keeps moving further away."

Something dark and flat was floating from upstream, moving slowly towards the little island. Margaret watched it, and thought that, despite the calm surface, there were strong currents deep in the river.

Annette had finished her tea. There was a faucet a few yards away, and she started to walk towards it to fill her cup with water. "What do you dream about?" she asked.

The question made Margaret's arms jump and her body shudder; Annette did not see this, and she could barely hear her when she said, "I dream about when I was a little girl."

Annette called back over her shoulder, "You're a little girl in your dreams?"

She whispered the words that she had not dared to say in the car. "I have nightmares about my father."

Annette had turned on the faucet and did not hear what Margaret had said at all. She was wondering how old she was in her own dreams, and she wanted a smoke.

The object was gliding closer. Margaret left her cup behind her and stepped past the willow to get a closer look.

Annette went back to the car to get her cigarettes. She knew they were under the seat, and she crouched down beside the open door, feeling for them. The car was filthy and filled with junk: her hand brushed against forgotten papers and old Kleenex. She could just touch the package with her fingers, but she could not get a grip on it.

As Margaret drew near to the edge of the river, she saw to her horror that the object floating downstream was a table.

It was moving slowly, forty or so feet from shore, between her and the little island; its dark wooden top was level with the smooth surface of the water. As she watched, she prayed that it would be a large board or a small platform of some kind. As soon as she had reached the bank, it halted for a moment, then slowly began to swing around towards her in a menacing arc. One corner slowly lifted out of the water and pointed at her. She could see the wooden apron board and a few inches of the top of one leg: it was an old-fashioned kitchen table — the lathe work on the exposed fraction of leg was like a post on her front-stair banister. It stopped drifting, and lay in the same position halfway between Margaret and the island. Then the accusing corner rose up higher out of the water — one of the legs must have caught on something in the river — the corner murmured slowly up, then down, and then it was very still. It lingered there.

It's waiting for me, she thought, and all she wanted was to run back to the car and speed away. The yaw of the table was a taunting mouth on the river's surface, calling to her.

Annette had managed to fish the cigarettes out of the mess under the car seat and, when she stood up, Margaret was nowhere to be seen. She looked about and, seeing the little blue toilet in the trees, assumed she was inside. Lighting a cigarette, she looked down the highway; the clinic was less than an hour away. If only Chaleur had not come over that Saturday night, none of this would be happening. She cursed him, and then she felt bad and told him that she was sorry. Then she cursed him again. *What do I have to be sorry about? You took off.* She did not see Margaret move down the bank through the willows and the long grass. She did not see her step into the river.

For a brief, foolish moment, Margaret half-expected her foot not to break the surface, as if she might be able to dart across it to the table as weightless as a water spider. But her foot sank down to the weedy bottom as she began to wade from the shore. What miry secrets were locked in the tangle of the river bed? Yet the water was refreshing in the heat; when it filled her shoes, the wetness was comforting. As she waded further, the underwater plants felt soft and caressing against her legs. A few yards from shore, where the water was as deep as her thighs, her feet stuck in the muddy bottom and she staggered and fell. Annette heard the splash, but did not turn to look. It was quick and far-away sounding, and she thought it was a fish.

Margaret's head went under, but even in her panic she did not swallow any water. She pulled forwards with the flat of her hands and paddled her feet downwards until they were back on the bottom. In a moment, she was walking again, the water up to her waist, and she was almost halfway there. Her feet were sinking into the soft mud — soon she would have to swim. Then the river bed sucked first one shoe, then the other, from her feet, but it was easier walking without them. She remembered buying them at Eaton's; she had almost tried on a pair of lovely red leather but had bought these because they were more sensible. The corner bobbed up again. *God has a purpose for you, Sister.* She planted a grim smile on her face as it beckoned. *Thou preparest a table for me, Lord.* Her dress was soaking; the water was just below her breasts now, too deep for walking, so she kicked up with her feet, freeing them from the mud, and began making long, smooth strokes with her arms. And it was then, as the current began to carry her downstream of the table, that Annette looked out at the river and saw her.

"Holy shit," she said aloud. *What the fuck is she doing?* She dropped her cigarette on the gravel and ran towards the river's edge.

"Margaret! Margaret!"

Her voice skimmed across the surface of the water so clearly that Margaret imagined the girl was right behind her. *Goodness and mercy shall follow me.*

But it was then that the table rose one last time, curling around in the water, before it broke free.

At first Margaret thought that she was moving faster — it was looming so close — but a split second later it was further away. *No!* She tried to swim faster, but in her desperation her movements became frantic, and she broke her stride and started to flail. She was less than ten feet away when it went sailing past her. *Stop!* It had moved into the thick of the strong current and was picking up speed. It had been so close!

The world was suddenly very small and immense at once: it contained only Margaret and the river, and it was frightening and filled with panic. The flat noise of water in her ears smothered the sounds, the clear ripples, of the river. Annette's screams on the far shore were lost as the thud of her heart grew louder and then, like an old car running down a grade, began to drum faster. Her arms were swinging uselessly; she could no longer tell if her legs were moving at all. She was swallowing water.

I'm going to drown!

Water pressed in from all sides, as if the entire weight of the river were focused on her. The pounding in her ears and the pounding within her chest were rising together now, driving her towards something. What? God's anger? If Annette had the abortion, both of them would be guilty. She felt all of God's furious heaven inside her. Black clouds rolled through her veins with thunder. Her soul would never be washed in the blood of the lamb. God's love was frightening. It was the terror at the centre of the earth. The rage of tornadoes. The cold lash of freezing rain that cuts into the forehead and draws blood. She had taken God for granted, had worshipped him without worshipping him, prayed to him without really praying to him, been baptised without truly being born again. His power was so great and his fearsomeness so full that she was afraid.

God spoke through the river. "You doubted me," the waters said.

Sorry. Sorry, sorry, sorry, sorry.

The river was flowing through her now. They were one and the same. Her arms stopped moving, and floated out and up behind her, like wings. *Forgive me.*

And then there was a gradual quiet, a stillness. *If I relax into it, it will be easier, easier than fighting.* She rolled over onto her back and floated with the stream. Her eyes had been closed. She opened them. Vague shapes moved above her through the water. *Breathing water now. A fish.* Her eyes closed. The river was slower, a bedtime story.

She suddenly felt very content and safe. She was in a car that was slowing down to stop in a yard in the country. The man driving, the man beside her, was her husband. This was their yard. The journey that they had been on was clear to her — it seemed to stretch on and on backwards through her memory. Details of their life came to her: walking to church together, a chicken dinner in the evening light, a bracelet, a wedding cake, kissing the small of his back. They had been married for years. They were very happy. *I did not know this was possible. This happiness.* One of them was saying that. Which? She smiled and turned to him as the car stopped, wanting to touch him. They had been together for such a long time, but she could not remember who he was. She laughed, knowing that this would make him laugh, too, this momentary lapse of memory. "Darling," she said, trying to see his face. "Sit up," he said gently, and she sat up.

She was sitting on the sandy river bed in shallow water.

She coughed a few times. That man, who had he been? She had loved him. Still loved him. She could see the rich weave of the fabric of his suit coat, a navy wool as brilliant as the clear night sky. Stars could settle on his shoulder. She could vaguely remember having helped him pick it out. How long had she been married? She had travelled quite a distance downstream and, at first, she could not tell if she were on the island or the mainland. But then, to her delight, she saw that she was on the island. *Maybe my husband is here*, she thought.

She got to her feet and began to wade to the shore.

The island was very narrow — scarcely a hundred feet across. She was no longer frightened, because the warmth of her dream still comforted her, and, of course, because she had almost drowned and now was safe on dry land — although, at first, that did not seem as important somehow as the dream of her husband. She had loved and been loved — something that she had never thought possible had been so real that it was suddenly imaginable. There was a little clearing on the shore bordered by willows and silver birch. A squirrel chattered in a tree. "Why, hello," Margaret said, looking up at him. "You must be the king of this place."

The squirrel laughed and flicked his tail before jumping to another tree and disappearing.

She sat down in the clearing and tried to reason through her experience in the river, but nature kept interfering. There were flowers everywhere: cowsills, violets, forget-me-nots; the grass was soft and did not cut her feet. The wetness of her dress felt good in the heat of the day. Why were the trees that grew on an island more wonderful than those on the mainland? They were not so ordinary, they were special. When the river flooded in the spring, all of this was underwater — she had driven by in April and seen the trees growing out of the water — how amazing it was that all of these flowers were not washed away. There was a cow path leading from the clearing to the upper end of the island.

How long had she been in the water? And that strange dream that still seemed so real, how long had she been dreaming it? Moments? Hours? It did not matter, really; all that mattered was that a kind of happiness seemed possible. She looked at her watch — it was filled with water, so she threw it away.

Annette would be worried about her, so she stood up and started to walk along the path.

Annette was both relieved and pissed off. Margaret was safe, but they were driving back home and had missed the appointment at the clinic. Annette would have to reschedule it, and drive up here again.

When Margaret's body had disappeared downstream, she had been sure that the old lady was dead and had stood there help-lessly for a few moments. Then she had run to the highway and tried to flag down a car. If a Mountie had not come by, she did not know what she would have done — no one else had stopped.

"There's a lady in the river. I think she's drowned!"

It seemed to take for ever: the Mountie taking down infor-mation and talking on the radio, Annette pacing back and forth by the riverside. And, because she was pregnant and sixteen and on her way to an abortion clinic, she felt guilty and uncomfort-able talking to the police, as if the whole thing were her fault. She imagined Margaret's dead body washing ashore and she imagined herself in a reform school. Each minute was endless and filled with fear.

But it was less than half an hour before another policeman appeared on the river in a motor boat, and, just as he did, Annette saw Margaret walking through the trees on the little island. The cows all turned to stare at her.

"There she is! She's all right!"

The Mountie had been talking on his car radio and he came down to the riverside with a bullhorn.

"Miss Saunders," his voice boomed across the water. "Are you all right?"

Margaret waved. When the second policeman came ashore from his motor boat she extended her hand to him. "Hello," she said. "Thank you."

While the little boat ferried her to shore, Annette's relief was replaced with anger. Now that Margaret was safe, she had missed her appointment for nothing and the whole miserable day had been in vain.

"Your friend thought she had lost you," the Mountie said when she was back in the little park.

"No," said Margaret. "But it was touch and go. Thank you."

By the time the police left them, it was too late for the appointment and besides, as Margaret said, she looked like the wrath of God. Because she had lost her shoes in the river, she asked Annette to drive Sandy's car back to Membartouche. Deep in the woods of the Coles Island short cut, when they were miles from anywhere, the rear left tire went flat. There was no spare in the trunk.

"This is the longest day of my life," Annette grumbled as she stood by the side of the road, sticking out her thumb to hitch-hike to a garage they had passed a few miles back.

"I'm sorry, Annette," Margaret said. "But I'm sure everything is going according to plan."

"Some plan," she muttered just as an old truck came to a stop up the road. "I'll see you as soon as I can!" she called over her shoulder as she ran towards it.

"Take your time, dear."

Margaret had been standing beside the rear of the car. She stepped across the ditch and sat on an old log. The grass was prickly and sharp on her feet: it tickled and it hurt. She had not said anything to Annette about her experience in the river because she did not know what to say. She sat watching the butterflies and listening to a lone crow call from the woods. The man in her dream was someone she had known for a long time, but she did not know who he was — how could that be?

She could not say how much time had passed before Annette returned with a man driving a tow truck.

At the garage restaurant she treated them to lemon meringue pie and she bought a pair of flip-flops. Annette was sullen again and Margaret was lost in thought. They ate quietly.

Then, with her new sandals in place, she drove the rest of the way home. Beside her, Annette slept and pretended to sleep. The look on Margaret's face bugged her, it was so smug. But she was relieved that the old lady never mentioned the clinic — she would reschedule the appointment and drive up there with her sister.

"You don't mind walking from Sandy Whyte's place, do you?" Margaret asked as they turned off the highway.

Annette shook her head; she would walk from here if Margaret stopped the car. All she wanted right now was to go to bed and cry.

It was after dusk and they were going over the bridge onto Main Street. The tide was out and the sandbars were ribbed and stretching out towards the calm water of the bay. As soon as it started to rain, Margaret knew that the man in her dream could be no one but Jesus.

TWENTY-FOUR ✣

On Friday morning Sandy glanced into the bedroom: the boy was asleep and beautiful, but he must not let beauty sway him. This sour little ruffian on his mother's bed was not the boy he loved; that boy lived only in his dreams. The cushion to smother him was sitting on the chair by the dressing table, as innocent as a knife. He sighed and turned away. If only the boy would simply die of his own accord — a bad heart, a deadly seizure — it would not be so awful and Sandy would not be as responsible as he would be holding a pillow over that sleeping face.

He went downstairs and started the oatmeal. When Margaret returned with the car, he would have to act. He spent the morning making his plans: he would wrap the body in something that could not be traced — there were unused sheets in the linen closet, still in their plastic covers: would one of them do?

He would park the car near the back door after Margaret brought it back — if he got out the hose and washed it, nothing would look suspicious. Then, after dark, he would deposit the body in the trunk and drive up the coast. One good thing about this miserably hot weather, the dirt roads would be packed hard and he would leave no tire marks. He studied a map from his box of files on Membartouche, looking at side roads, wood roads off side roads, and made his plans, writing notes and lists, then burning them in the sink, turning on the taps to flush the lacy black ashes down the drain. He planned and revised over and over again; planned everything, of course, except the actual killing. He felt that he was wasting time — *Just go and do it!* — but he needed to believe that things were under control, that something was being accomplished. When the time came — when his vehicle was returned — he would simply have to walk upstairs, pick up the cushion, and be done with it.

It was mid-morning before he remembered that the boy's pants were in the dryer. What other traces were in the house to be gathered up? There was an empty knapsack tucked away in the shed. And the boy's glasses. Evidence.

Chaleur was a baby now; he had peed the bed and there was a tiny bit of runny poop on his bum.

"Da," he moaned.

Sandy stood inside the door with clean underwear and jeans — the room smelled disgusting. *This has gone on long enough! Put an end to it right now!* He dropped the clothing on the floor and picked up the cushion, but then he began to tremble so violently that he sat down quickly, hugging the cushion to his chest. He did not want to touch the dirty boy.

The boy seemed oblivious to his presence, lost. If Sandy had never laid eyes on him, he would never have known the horror that dwelt inside himself; he hated the boy for making him feel this way, hated him as much as he hated himself. He needed to compose himself. He sighed and sat very still, trying to look around the room as if the trespasser did not exist. Would it be possible to even imagine a time before he had arrived?

It had been a mistake to bring him to this room — Sandy's own bedroom would have been better, or the maid's old room in the attic — any place but this. Mother had died in this bed. Sandy had found her in the afternoon, her mouth locked in a morbid smile that bared her teeth, as if her skull were starting to force its way through what was left of her flesh. While he was away at the post office, something momentous had occurred and the only witness had been the room itself. The room was filled with the past. Sandy had sat here eating his oatmeal while Mother cried into hers. As a boy, he had perched on the side of that bed on Sunday mornings and watched her as she sat delicately in this chair in front of her dressing table, fixing her hair for church. Beside him on the dresser, next to the pitcher of water and empty glass, were the familiar objects that had been there since the dawn of Sandy's time: the monogrammed toilet set — brush, mirror, and comb — the little white porcelain jar filled with hairpins, the family photographs in their tarnished silver frames: Sandy in a long white baby dress, Mother and Father at the church door after their wedding, Father as a young man. There was a slight film of dust on the dresser top; he noticed it when he lifted the hand mirror and saw an oval of polished wood. The pillow slid from his lap onto the floor.

If only Sandy could have lived in the time of those objects, that time before his own consciousness, the time from which he had been forcibly excluded. It would have resembled his early childhood, a world where days were spent laughing beside Mother's flower beds in the morning light, where there were long walks through apple blossoms, where lambs and deer slept gently in the green shadows of the fruit trees. No one was unhappy.

Without looking in the little mirror, he set it back carefully in the space reserved for it by the dust, and he picked up the photo of his father — a smiling young man, standing beside the back door with his sleeves rolled up. He had dreamed about this man last night. *What binds me to him? Was it only fear?* Had there ever been a moment of tenderness between them?

Father was inescapable. He was in Sandy's blood — he was his blood. If his father had simply been any man from anywhere, then they could have hated each other when their paths crossed and be done with it; but, because they were flesh and blood, father and son had to keep returning, each to the other, trying to understand who they were. The smiling man in the photograph was so young, so optimistic, a man that Sandy had never known.

"Two peas in a pod," Mother had said.

They had defined their relationship to each other in terms of their relationship to Mother: each was jealous of her love for the other. In a universe without Grace Whyte, where would he and his father have been? Was it her love for them both — for she loved them both, certainly, and from the bottom of her heart — that had prevented them from knowing each other? Had love prevented love? He knew now, after his mother's long, slow death, that love was not easy, that often it was wrapped in suffering.

His young father even looked handsome. It wasn't fair — Sandy had inherited this same face and never ever, not even for a moment, had he or anyone else considered him to be good-looking. Young Alexander Whyte's sleeves were rolled up over his forearms; everything about him seemed tanned and healthy. Whoever was taking the picture was someone that he cared for — that was apparent from his eyes, the shy way that he was smiling. These were not the mean, little eyes of the man who had begged his wife to join him in a concrete grave, of the father who had tormented and teased his son. Sandy had never known this man; the smile on Father's young face made him unrecognizable. Here, in his hand, was his father with his whole life ahead of him, although that life had ended years ago and his father was dead, buried, encased in concrete, and rotten.

"Da," the boy moaned.

He placed his father in a dresser drawer. Mother and Father smiled in their wedding picture; he picked that up and put it in the drawer, too. He went to the bathroom and got some clean sheets and towels, a wash cloth, and a basin of warm water.

Sandy lifted the filthy torso onto a towel and pulled the dirty sheet out from under it; he untied the feet and began washing the legs, lifting them gently and caressing them with the wash cloth. They were so beautiful that he began to cry quietly, a tear dripped onto the boy's thigh. Why did the body he loved house a being so unworthy? He put a clean towel under it and dried the warm skin; he pulled the underwear up the boy's legs.

Fucker, Chaleur thought, as he realized what was happening. *Stupid fucker.* The water was waking him, making him think more clearly. It must be daytime. He hated the stupid creepy hands touching him, but the clean water felt good, as if it were washing away the long dark night. If his hands were only untied, if only that. Then he would jump out the window. Fly away. Fall down into the bushes. And if he lived, there would only be broken bones. If he died, he would be nothing, just a song.

It was so hot in the room that Sandy left the clean jeans folded on the side of the bed. He tied the legs again and went downstairs with the stinking sheets. After he put them in the washer he went back to his maps and lists.

Why couldn't the boy simply die? Die and disappear.

This suffering was so cruel. If he must die — and what alternative was there? — better to just kill him and have an end to it. That was the humane thing.

At noon he was already sitting in the front room, watching for Margaret.

Even though he had not heard a car in the driveway, when the doorbell rang in the afternoon he assumed it was Margaret; he wadded up his latest list and stuck it in his pocket as he trotted to the front door.

There stood Gloria Maurice with a shopping bag.

"Mr. Whyte," she said, "I'm so sorry." Her eyes were downcast.

"Yes?" He was not going to let her in the house, so he stayed in the doorway, holding the door partly closed. She stood there stupidly for a moment, then she reached into the bag and he saw the box containing Mother's lobster silver. "Oh."

"I came to borrow it yesterday and then when that Snow lady hit my car and everything …"

"Yes?" He stepped out onto the veranda and shut the door behind him. Gloria was holding the box and looking at it, not at Sandy. "How…," he started to ask.

"It's my brother Raymond. When I was on the phone to the police he came in and took it. He knew where it was because I said so on the way here, I said, 'I know right where the silver is in the buffet in the front hall,' so when I was on the phone he just walked in and took it. He didn't mean any harm, like we were just going to borrow them 'cause we were having a special supper and …"

He was breathing a sigh of relief that he did not want her to see. "Oh."

"I know he should come and say he's sorry himself, but he's sick."

Conveniently, he thought, but he said, "I hope he's better soon."

"Thank you," she said. "But he'll never get better."

What else had the little thief taken? What had he seen? "He just came in and took the silver and went back out?"

Gloria nodded. "He's getting confused these days. I mean, things confuse him."

What on earth did she mean? He was about to reach out and take the box from her, but his hands somehow slipped behind him; he held them there, rocking back and forth on his heels and toes.

"And don't worry," she said quickly, "you can't catch it this way or nothing and, anyways, he was too tired to eat last night so he never used the silver. Mama washed it after dinner and I polished it for you this morning."

He didn't have a clue what to say and so he said exactly what his mother had trained him to say: "Well, I'm very sorry about your brother."

She nodded, "Thanks. Here then," and she handed him the silver. He took it with one hand and tucked the box under his arm.

"Well, no harm done. I didn't even know they were missing."

Both of them were breathing sighs of relief.

"And how was your dinner?"

Gloria shook her head. "It's been a hard week. When do you want me to come back and clean?"

She looked at him, but he turned and looked away. "I'll call you next week and we'll talk about it then."

"Oh." She nodded. "Oh."

At that very moment he had decided to give her notice, and Gloria knew it because she said, "Here then," and reached into the pocket of her shorts and handed him the key to his house. They both knew that notice would not be given in person, that he would send a letter or leave a message with her mother.

"Well, you'll be wanting to get back to your brother," he said, and as she was nodding he went into the house. He stood back a bit from the door and watched her through the diamond panes. Dozens of Glorias in bits and pieces moved down the steps and across the yard. When she was halfway down the driveway, he clicked the lock on the door.

He opened the box and there was the silver, gleaming in the rigid navy blue velvet folds. He closed it again and put it in the buffet, where it belonged. Safe. No one had been upstairs; he must have put the folded wash cloth on the boy's forehead himself when the cars crashed outside.

Yes, he was safe. A great weight had lifted and he felt giddy. There was time now; he need not be hasty. He was safe.

By late afternoon, Margaret had not returned and he was angry with her. Was she getting back at him for something he had said to Minnie? But what if something had happened to her — what if she had been in an accident? What would he do then? Without a car, what would he do? Where would he put the body?

He thought of the boy's body lying dead. First he thought of it all washed and clean, and perfumed on the bed. He was standing at the kitchen window when he thought this, looking out towards the orchard.

Then he imagined coming through a little grove of apple trees into a clearing and seeing the body lying there, raised up from the ground on a little platform covered with a white cloth. It does not move, it waits, it waits for him alone. It would not be horrible and sweaty like the boy upstairs, but cool and refreshing to the touch. Like the river on a hot day when he and Joey had taken off their clothes and waded in. Like a marble statue, like Apollo or David.

Like marble.

He had the sudden urge to touch that coolness: Grandmother Whyte's pastry marble was beneath the counter in the pantry; he got down on his knees and found it under a pile of old black cookie sheets and muffin tins. He set it on the counter, running the palms of his hands over its smooth surface. His fingers flickered — a pianist playing soft, inaudible runs; his mother's fingers fluting the edges of an apple pie. He had pressed a star-shaped cookie cutter into the rolled-out dough and helped her decorate the crusts: the Big Dipper, Orion, the Christmas Star surrounded with a wreath of pastry holly leaves. The marble was heavy when he lifted it, held it so cool in his hands, twelve by eighteen inches of white stone with delicate dark grey veins. He raised the marble, a bowl of water that could not spill, then turned it and held it to his cheek; he rubbed his face gently against it, then turned his mouth and began to kiss the coolness. He licked it, his tongue as delicate as a cat's.

And then Sandy realized that if the foul-mouthed boy were dead, the body would be relieved of the troublesome, stupid life that inhabited it; the cool, perfect body would be his then, his and his alone. It would be there beside him in the morning and he could hold it close to him at night. The crude trespasser would be gone and the body would be his heart's desire, even for just a precious little while. Yes. He could hold it and kiss it, be free to explore it and know it. It would not laugh at him or swear or torment him. It would be a loving and a sacred thing, a work of art he could hold in his own two hands.

He gently set the pie marble back on the counter and, as his eyes traced the beauty of its dark veins, he unbuttoned his shirt; he lifted the marble again and pressed it to his bare skin, rubbing it back and forth very slowly against his belly. He held it close to him. It was the lean muscle of his beloved's chest. He undid his pants and let them drop to the pantry floor about his feet.

He could scarcely believe his excitement.

Outside, a cloud bank was slowly moving in from the west and the temperature had dropped two degrees; but this went unnoticed inside The Oaks. The rooms were hot and airless. The only relief was in the thin marble slab that Sandy carried about with him.

By early evening, he decided that he could no longer wait for Margaret. He had been sitting in his father's big chair beside the fireplace, holding the cold stone on his lap. He went to his desk and wrote a note, telling her to leave the car keys under the mat, then taped it to the front door. That was all the explanation she was going to get from him.

He had to act right now, this minute.

He marched up the stairs.

He grabbed the pillow and strode to the head of the bed, holding it in his hands like a deadly gift.

The room was so quiet. A board creaked somewhere in the house, and the moment of silence afterwards seemed endless. *Now*, Sandy thought and he took a step closer. The cushion was steady; his hands were not shaking. He would do it.

"Rrrrrugh."

The boy's stomach rumbled.

"Rrrrrugh."

And again.

No last words, just the banal, useless rolling of gas in his stomach. *How stupid*, Sandy thought. *How pointless.*

Another board creaked from deep in the house. He cocked his head and listened carefully. Even the familiar sounds of the old house sounded new and important. The body lay so still. So perfect. Soon, soon, it would be his.

Sadness had made the face so much more handsome, so desirable. Sandy wanted to stretch out the agony of this moment, to make them both suffer as much as they could, joyful suffering. Things need not be rushed; he was always rushing. Whenever he masturbated, he usually felt so guilty that he needed to ejaculate as quickly as possible; those rare times that he stretched it out, it was so much better. This would be like one of those times. He would not rush things, he would move slowly and steadily, savouring each moment.

The boy watched the ceiling.

Sandy hugged the pillow to his chest. The body below him was sweaty and sticky and hot; soon it would be as refreshing as a pool of water. He began to speak to it.

"I used to go to the woods, too," he said. "Up past the pasture. Joey and I."

"Heu," Chaleur said.

But Sandy paid no attention. He was not speaking to this rude, nameless boy, but to the body that had also done these things. Somehow the living body must be aware of him before it became his alone. His left hand continued to hug the pillow to his chest, but he moved his right one down and began to rub it gently against his crotch. He was too excited, too nervous to become hard right away, so he continued to speak quietly. His words became one with the delicious sensations spreading beneath his hand. The river, the water against his bare legs, Joey floating on his back. In a few moments there was a growing stiffness under his fingers and palm. He continued to talk in a whisper, a slow chanting that found its own steady rhythm. The words were slipping out of him — Joey Mullins and the woods, how Joey had beaten him up and how no one had spoken to him after that, of the evil boys at university, his father's cruel words — his whole heart began to tumble out in bits and pieces. It was the lifting of a great burden: for the first time there was a witness to his life; this lovely body was his witness.

"I have been unhappy all my life," Sandy said. He wanted so badly to push the pillow onto the boy's face, to sit astride the marble chest and ride the body into heaven, but he must not rush things, he must be patient. There must be the prayer of confession and the sermon before the offering and the benediction. "I hated my father and he hated me," he began.

There were creaks in the floorboards downstairs. Rustlings from the pantry.

Like a song where love is the saddest thing and lost at the end of a long, sorry world, Sandy declared his feelings to the body. He told it how he had watched from the window, how he had yearned for it, how he had imagined it up in the woods.

Some of these words curled into Chaleur's ears and terrified him. They were about him, but they were for someone else, as if he were hearing them only because he was in the way, and he understood that this was how it had been all his life. He had always been convinced of his puniness, his undesirability — he did not blame Rory for hating him, he deserved no better — and now he realized why Annette wanted to kill the cornflake baby: it was his. No one had ever wanted him, no one since his father; and maybe he had only dreamed that his father had wanted him — he would never know.

"I have denied myself all my life," Sandy was saying, "I have lied about myself and lived a dreadful lie." He touched the boy's chest with his hand, "This is the truth." The rank, sweaty smell sickened him, but soon it would be fresh.

Chaleur was very frightened. He thought about Annette and his father, how they would never know each other, how he would never in his life know anybody, how he would never see anyone again except this crazy, crazy old man.

"*Agnus dei*," Sandy was saying. "Dost thou know who made thee…?" He was stroking the boy's hair. "*Agnus dei, Agnus dei* …" He giggled, then smiled sadly and his voice trailed off. He lifted his hand from the damp hair and wiped it on the pillow. His heart was racing. There was nothing left to say now; he was holding the pillow in both his hands, pressing it against the stiffness in his crotch.

"Daa …" Chaleur moaned. His voice was far away, like a baby in a distant room. Sandy stopped looking at the body and looked at the boy's face.

"And now I have to kill you," Sandy said as Chaleur turned his head and looked up into his eyes. Chaleur tried to speak, but when he opened his mouth there was nothing but a dry rattle.

It was only fair, thought Sandy, only fair that the boy be able to speak his last words. He turned away from the bed towards the dressing table and started to reach for the glass of water sitting there beside the pitcher. And that is when he heard the voice. It was loud and angry and it made him jump.

"Jesus Christ!" it boomed.

Sandy spun around. It was not the boy — the voice was like thunder throughout the house; it seemed to come from the house itself, as if it had suddenly begun to speak. He held his breath and listened for more, but there was no other sound. He turned back towards the dresser and gasped — standing there in the mirror was his father reaching for the glass as well! In his other hand Father was not holding the cushion but Sandy's baby picture. Sandy knew that this was his own reflection, but the eyes in the mirror were not his own, they were mean and little. While the voice reverberated in his head like a curse from a nightmare, he stared into his father's eyes. It was Father's voice, escaping from over the years, roaring through the plaster, reaching up for him from beneath the floorboards.

"Dad?" Chaleur moaned.

Chaleur's voice startled him and Sandy bumped against the dresser. The baby picture immediately slid forward, falling on its back with a soft plop. It was like a magic trick: one moment Father had been holding the photograph and then, like his son, he was holding the pillow, and then Sandy was standing and looking at himself. There was a buzzing sound in his ears and he leaned against the dresser to steady himself. The room began to shift. The little picture skidded off the dresser and fell to the floor. He looked into the mirror beyond his reflection and saw the boy lying there behind him, no longer the beautiful *agnus dei* but helpless, the descent from the Cross. Chaleur's eyes found his in the mirror. The boy's suffering was terrible — a painting by Grünewald, by Rogier van der Weyden: *Good Friday.*

I am my father!

"Oh dear."

He sat on the chair beside the vanity. "Oh my."

He dropped the pillow. "My my."

He looked at the boy's face.

Chaleur had heard that he was to die, and so every move that Sandy made was a step towards his execution. No one in the world could help him now; he yearned for the comfort of his dad, and sensed that his dad was looking for him.

"I will untie you now," Sandy said.

Chaleur was so weak that he had barely pulled on the stockings that bound him: the knots could be fumbled with and undone: there was no need of scissors or a knife. When he was finished, Sandy brought the glass over to the bed; sitting sideways on the edge, he leaned over, and slid his arm under Chaleur's neck and pulled his body towards him; he pressed the sweet head to his chest and poured water gently into the mouth.

The water rushed over Chaleur's chin, some of it slipped down his greedy throat, a spoonful but it seemed a torrent, as powerful as rain. He gulped and choked and the rain moved back a bit until he could drink some more.

"You should go slowly at first."

Chaleur nodded. And drank some more.

"I'll get you another glass."

A moment later there was rain again and he was drinking, lost in the happy delirium of water. Was Dad hiding in the rain?

Sandy seemed so big to Chaleur, so male, his face looming in so close, so hot and sweaty that Chaleur was in the woods with his father in the shelter of the old cabin.

"One kiss," Sandy said, lowering his head. His lips touched Chaleur's.

Chaleur opened his mouth to say "Dad" and, as his cracked lips parted, Sandy's tongue gently slid between them, exploring the deep, warm mystery of another. The sour taste, the sick taste — all was a part of sweetness. His tongue was Van Eyck's brush revealing the spires of Ghent, the green meadow grass, the saints and martyrs, and in that moment Sandy wondered if the boy and his body could be his — they both were forsaken except for each other; could their suffering make them one? Could their separate anguishes merge and mingle in the sad air above the bed? He kissed the boy's cheek.

Then his mother's ashes called to him and he stood up.

"Thank you," he said, and then, "Goodbye," and then he turned back to look at the bed as he left the room. "I'm sorry for the inconvenience."

He stepped into the hall.

The house was alive with whispers and voices. They both could hear them; there were creatures in the wood.

"What's he doing?" the voices whispered.

"Jesus Christ!" they hissed.

Foxes and wolves.

anny and Junior came down through the orchard after dusk, and, although neither one of them said anything to the other, both were thinking that this was the time of day when they used to play hide-and-go-seek. They had driven slowly past The Oaks after supper and could not see Sandy Whyte's old car anywhere in the yard. "Well, that's a relief," Danny said. Junior shook his head. "Unless it's in the back. Let's hope the old fucker's out for the night." They parked downtown by the post office and walked along the abandoned railway bed up into the woods; then they cut down through Whyte's old pasture into the apple trees. It was dark when they crept up to what was left of the old fence and sat in the shadow of the maples, looking at the back of the house. Except for a dim light through the drawn curtains and pulled blind in an upstairs bedroom window, the whole place was in darkness.

"Well, what do you think?" Danny whispered.

Junior was surveying the windows along the back on the ground floor. There was a double one in the middle — that would be the kitchen — and another in the shed near the back door. Off to the other side of the kitchen was a fourth. "That one looks good," he said pointing to it.

"What about that?" Danny was pointing at the window in the back shed. It was lower than the others and would be a lot easier to climb in through.

Junior shook his head. "That'll just get you into the shed," he said. "There's another door inside that'll be locked." He was squinting. "Shit, will you look at that? They've all got fucking storm windows on them."

"What about the cellar windows then?"

"Too small. It's not gonna be easy getting in."

"Look, if there's somebody in there tied to a bed," Danny said, "we'll be friggin' heroes."

"And if there ain't, it's break and enter and we're fucked." The whole thing was stupid anyway as far as Junior was concerned. Raymond was nuts to begin with and Danny was just as bad for trying to prove that he wasn't. "We'll never get the storms off without a friggin' screwdriver." He shook his head. "Well, let's go take a look," he said, standing up.

They checked out the LeBlanc house next door — the lights were all on, so no one could see out — then, sure that they were not being watched, they climbed over the broken fence and darted across the yard to the window. The bottom sill was a foot above their heads. Junior reached up, but the wing screws holding the storms were too high.

"Gimme a boost," he whispered.

"Give you a boost? With what?"

"Your hand, for chrissakes."

"I only got one."

"Aw, quit whining."

Danny leaned his back against the side of the house and bent his left leg a bit. "Put your foot here, Lard Arse." He pointed just above his knee, "You'll probably snap my friggin' leg in two."

"Aw, can it. Whose brilliant fucking idea was this anyway?" Junior put his hands on Danny's shoulders, lifted his foot to his brother's leg, and hefted himself up.

"Ugh, Jesus!" Danny hissed.

"Shuddup." He could see into the dark pantry. This would be a good way in: there was a counter inside that was almost flush with the bottom of the window. And the window itself was good and wide. He tried the wing screw on the left of the old storm window; it was as solid as a rock, the old screw rusted onto the wing.

"Well?"

"You'd need a pressure gun to budge this thing."

"Get down then. My leg's dead." Danny felt that Junior's body must be about as dense as lead, he was so heavy; the weight was like a tourniquet and his left foot was going to sleep.

"Hang on." Junior wanted to try the wing screw on the other side.

"You're busting my friggin' leg." Danny's hand was holding his brother's thigh just below his butt; Junior's gut was pushing the back of his head against the house, and the edge of a clapboard was digging into his skull. "Hurry up."

"Boo hoo, little baby, just hang on." The other wing screw seemed even tighter. He tried to get a grip on the edge of the storm, but it was flush with the frame and stuck in there like glue. "I'm coming down." He steadied himself, then put his hands back onto Danny's shoulders and jumped back. He hit the yard with a thud, lost his balance, and fell backwards onto his bum. Danny rubbed his leg, trying to get the circulation going again.

"I need something," Junior whispered as he rolled over and heaved himself up. "Like a dime or a quarter or something to get at the screw. Got any change?"

"Loonies."

"Too thick. Must be something around." And he started searching the yard along the edge of the house. This was the stupidest thing he had ever done. Who'd have thought that Sandy Whyte would have the storm windows on in a friggin' heatwave?

Danny limped over to check out the window in the shed. He stepped up on the porch, moving carefully because the thing was falling apart — there was a hole where someone's foot had smashed through. When he tried the wing screw, it was welded shut. He figured that you'd twist a dime in two before you could make the thing budge. "Shit." He shrugged and, as an afterthought, reached over and turned the knob on the door.

"Hey lookit," Junior hissed. He was down on his hands and knees, "There's money all over the place here," and he held up a couple of quarters.

"Forget it," Danny whispered opening the door.

"Well." Junior grinned. "Fuck me dead."

"Careful, the deck's rotten as an old arsehole." Danny stepped into the back shed. It was dark and he slowly swung his hand in front of him as he walked. He could hear nothing from inside the house. Behind him, Junior started to crash through a board on the porch, but jumped inside the shed door before he went through. He was not light on his feet and whole floor shook.

"Ssh!"

"I know, I know. Place is a fucking death trap." He reached into his pocket and pulled out the little penlight on his key chain.

"Here." The dim circle of light on the floor reflected on the white enamel of a washer and dryer — everything else was dark shadow.

"What's that?" Danny asked, pointing towards a lump on top of the dryer. It had a fluorescent stripe that caught the light. A knapsack.

"So what?"

"When was the last time you saw him go hiking?"

"Maybe he wears it around the house, playing Boy Scout."

Danny lifted it up. "Empty anyways." He put it back on the dryer.

"Check the pockets, Sherlock." Junior came over beside Danny and pointed the light on the knapsack.

"What's that say?" There were words in black marker on the flaps.

"Guns N' Roses."

"Well, I bet he listens to them all the time," Junior said.

Danny held the knapsack steady with his arm while he opened the little zippers and searched through them. There was something crinkly in one pocket. Danny pulled out a strip of condoms.

"The old skin dog," said Junior. "Heavy metal and Sheiks."

"Make you feel right at home?"

"Shuddup and see if the kitchen door's open."

It was locked.

"Move over," Junior muttered, shoving Danny off the mat in front of the door, then he bent down and lifted it up. The key shone in his penlight. "Bingo." He unlocked the door and they stepped inside.

Lila LeBlanc had been arguing with her daughter because Mavis had brought home a video from the drugstore about quitting smoking with the patch and insisted they all watch it together "like a family." She finally snuck out into the backyard to have a cigarette in peace. It was going to rain, which she supposed was a good thing for the farmers, but she didn't want to get wet when she had her smoke. That damn Mavis would make her go outside for a puff in a hurricane. She had just butted out her cigarette under her daughter's yellow rose bush when she saw two men come down through the orchard. She sat down in the shadow on the back steps and watched through the hedge. When she realized that the smaller man had something wrong with one of his arms, she recognized them both. What the hell were those fool Maurice boys up to? They arsed around for five minutes before they snuck into Sandy Whyte's house.

"Hum," she said, lighting another cigarette. She'd just sit here for a while and keep an eye on things.

All the downstairs was in darkness; it was unbelievably hot and stale inside the house. Junior and Danny crept into the middle of the kitchen; someone was talking upstairs — cocking their heads, they listened carefully.

"That him?" Danny mouthed.

Junior shrugged. He could not make out what the voice was saying; it droned on and on like Mama's Hail Marys. Despite himself, he was feeling the old excitement he had felt long ago when he had broken into the cottages near the beach. There was something about the feel of a place that you had not been invited to step inside that made his large body start to tingle. He was even getting a boner.

"Well, let's go up, take a look see."

Danny was starting to get cold feet. He sensed that this was all wrong; he'd known it as soon as he pulled the condoms out of the knapsack. He was suddenly afraid of discovering something that he did not want to know — like the time he had stood outside Marsha's apartment door and heard her call him a cripple and laugh. "But there's somebody up there," he whispered.

"Isn't that the whole point? Aren't we here to rescue some friggin' figment of Raymond's imagination? C'mon. There must be a back stairs here somewheres."

The closest door led into the pantry; at the other end of the room was the door to the hall and the rest of the downstairs. In the corner behind them, next to the shed door, was a fourth one, tongue and groove, painted white, with a step below it. He pointed the penlight at it and nodded. "There."

Danny opened the door and looked up. The stairwell was narrow with no railing and there was a little landing halfway up, where the stairs turned. The voice from up there was louder, but no clearer; it was fuzzy, like a radio announcer's when the dial is off the station. He did not want to go up.

"Move it," hissed Junior, but Danny moved to one side and ushered his brother ahead with his bad arm. Junior shook his head and, shining his little light on the step in front of him, started up. For the first time in ages he was doing something that he enjoyed; this was what he was meant to do. The first step was quiet, but the second step screeched under his foot; it was worse than fingernails on a blackboard. Junior froze, his other foot dangling in midair. Above them, the voice stopped. Junior shut off the penlight with the loudest click that Danny had ever heard. In that silence it was like a gun going off. The stairs were as dark as pitch. Junior was carefully lifting his other foot to the step above, praying that it would be quiet. If he were a cop now and someone caught him, everything would be all right, he would just be doing his duty. He suddenly realized what a fool he was — he had been playing for the wrong side all along.

Danny wanted to run out the door, but then he heard a second voice, a moan, and he knew that, no matter what happened, he had to believe in Raymond.

The little moan made Junior want to turn around. It sounded to him like someone about to get his rocks off. What if Raymond had seen someone tied up but it was just one of those kinky sex things? His boner was so hard that the head of it was tugging at his pubic hair. "Great," he thought, "there's fags upstairs doing kinky sex and I've got a friggin' hard-on."

The quiet seemed to go on for ever, but soon the voice started talking quietly again. Junior waited a minute until his lower foot was so sore he had to shift his weight. The next step was solid and he breathed a sigh of relief. He clicked on the light again and moved up another step. When he was at the landing, he turned and signalled for Danny to follow him.

Danny had not moved; he was looking at the steps, trying to remember which one had squeaked. He lifted his foot, placed it gingerly down, and hoisted himself onto the wrong one.

Skreek!

How could anybody be so stupid? Before he realized it, Junior glared down at Danny and said, "Jesus Christ!" His big face fell and his big hand shot up over his big mouth. Danny stood staring at him, unbelievingly.

There was no way whoever was upstairs could not have heard that. Both of them were ready to run out the back door as soon as they heard someone coming.

But there were no sounds from upstairs. Something small fell on the floor, and the quiet talking continued. After a couple of minutes Junior shrugged, pointed up the stairs, and nodded. They moved slowly ahead.

When Danny got to the top, Junior was waiting for him. They peered around the corner into the hall. Just down to their

right a light was shining through a half-open bedroom door —
the light that they had seen through the curtains when they were
out in the yard. There was movement in there; Junior knew that
they had to get a better look. He pointed to himself, wiggled his
fingers like they were walking, then pointed to the right side of
the hallway; he pointed to Danny, wiggled his fingers again, and
gestured to the other side. Danny nodded and moved across the
hall. Junior turned off his light.

They crept down the hallway, one on either side. The light
through the door revealed an open door beside it, the bathroom.
As they crept closer, walking on tiptoes, Junior had a better angle
from his side on what was happening inside the bedroom. There
were two people on the bed, and they were kissing. His heart
sank. He had been right — it was nothing but kinky fag sex and
they better get the hell out. But as he turned to signal to Danny,
Sandy Whyte got up from the bed and stood beside it. He had
his clothes on.

"Thank you," he said to the person on the bed, and then
"Goodbye." He was starting to walk out into the hall. Junior and
Danny were sitting ducks.

"Hide!" Junior hissed, and Danny, who was closer to the other
open door, ducked into the bathroom, but there was nowhere
for Junior to go. He backed up and flattened himself against the
closed attic door and held his breath.

Sandy Whyte stopped in the doorway and turned back to the
bed. "I'm sorry for the inconvenience," he said, and he walked
down the hall like a man in a dream, right past Junior, less than
a foot away without seeing him. It was just like hide-and-go-seek.

Sandy went to his room and picked up the cardboard box
very tenderly — pressing the heels of his hands against it, one on
each side, he held the ashes like an offering as he walked down
the front stairs. Mother was waiting for him. He could see her

surrounded by crocuses; tulips and daffodils were poking their heads through the ground.

"This is my favourite time of year," she said, "when it all begins again."

As he walked through the kitchen, he could feel the hard, tight knot of a bud in his chest; soon everything would be in bloom.

Lila had smoked another cigarette and wished that something would happen soon because it was starting to rain, a fine mist. She had sharp little eyes, if she saw those Maurice boys try to make off with something, she'd catch them.

Mavis came to the back door. "We've got the VCR on pause," she said. "How long you gonna be? Mikey's got a movie."

"Let the kid have his movie," Lila said.

Mavis sighed and stared at her mother. "Why I worry about you, I got no idea."

Lila had to cough but she held her breath until Mavis went back inside. The mist was turning into drops; one of them plopped on the end of her cigarette and fizzled. She cleared her throat, but could not escape from coughing. When there was movement at Sandy Whyte's back door, she covered her mouth with her hands so that she would not be heard.

Sandy Whyte stumbled into the yard. He walked over to the far side, then got down on his knees; he was all bent over, and she couldn't make out what he was doing. Lila stood up and moved into the hedge to get a better look, but, just then, there was such a commotion in the front — car doors slammed and a girl let out a godawful scream — that she hurried along the side of the house to see what was going on up there.

Danny's head poked out the bathroom door. Junior was waving at him. Danny pointed to the bedroom door, but Junior was shaking his head and waving frantically so Danny tiptoed back to his brother.

"What's he doin'?" he whispered.

"Sex, it's just sex," Junior hissed in his ear.

Junior was tugging him back towards the stairs. They could sneak out of this place before Sandy Whyte's little love bunny smartened up if Danny would only get a move on. But Danny shook his head and started back towards the door. Junior lunged for his arm to pull him back, but he reached for the wrong one and grabbed a handful of air.

Chaleur was trying to crawl off the bed, and for a moment Danny's heart sank because he thought that Junior had been right. Just sex. But the boy looked up at him, and Danny saw the red welts on the boy's wrists and more on his ankles. He could see the stockings that had tied him to the bed.

"You okay?" Danny asked quietly, stepping into the room.

Chaleur looked right at him and smiled. "Dad?" he said.

Junior was behind Danny and when he heard Chaleur's voice he thought, *Oh great, and the kid's a retard to boot.*

Danny could see that the boy was very weak. He turned to his brother. "Let's get him out of here," he said quietly. "We gotta get a doctor." He turned back to Chaleur. "Can you walk?"

Chaleur nodded, but when he tried to stand, his legs were soft and useless; Danny caught him before he fell to the floor and set him back on the bed. "He's weak as a baby," he said.

"Here." Junior handed the penlight to his brother and crouched down beside the bed. "I'm gonna carry you. Put your arms around my neck." And then he hoisted Chaleur up, holding him the way that he had held Ginette's kids when he carried them to bed, and turned towards the door. "Lead on there, Sherlock."

Danny went ahead to make sure that the coast was clear. The kid was weak, but he still weighed a ton. Junior was panting before he got down the stairs, and he thought that if he was going to be a bouncer he was going to have to quit smoking.

As he was being carried through the hall and down the front stairs, Chaleur knew only that he had died and was with his father, but Dad was bringing him back.

Sandy was nowhere to be seen. Danny opened the front door and waved his brother through. As soon as they stepped out onto the veranda, they were suddenly caught in a blinding light.

"Aw dandy," Junior said and he set Chaleur down at the top of the veranda steps. "Where to now?"

A car had stopped in front of them and, even though the headlights shut off, the only way to get away was back though the house. They were caught. Chaleur moaned very loudly, so Danny knelt down beside him, cradling his head in his good arm. Two women had gotten out of the car and were walking towards the veranda.

"Am I still dead?" Chaleur asked.

Danny touched the boy's chest with his stump, rubbed it gently to comfort him. "You're fine," he said. "You're gonna be just fine."

Annette saw someone half-naked lying down and two men bent over him. She was a few feet from the car when she realized that the body on the veranda was Chaleur. At first, she could not believe her eyes — the man bending over him had his arm buried in Chaleur's chest as deep as his elbow. *His heart has stopped*, she thought. *His heart has stopped and that man is massaging it with his hand.* She screamed and started running. And then, before she reached the steps, she had the strangest thought: *Horror movies are all wrong. In real life there's no blood at all.*

"Can you save him?" she said and then she saw Danny's arm. "Oh!" She burst into tears and knelt down on the step and kissed

Chaleur's face. "What happened?" she said. "Where've you been? I've been going crazy."

When Annette started running towards the steps, Margaret stopped in her tracks; her body had been singing all the drive home and suddenly there was an uneasy hush. *Be careful*, she thought, but her body pulled her forwards. She was moving up the veranda stairs when she heard Junior say, "How long's he been missing?"

"All week. What happened?"

"He was tied up upstairs," Junior answered, hoping it was really true.

"Jesus God!" and Annette flung her arms around Chaleur and kissed him again. "I knew you hadn't run away," she whispered in his ear. "I knew it."

Margaret looked stupidly about her. *What on earth was going on?* "Where's Sandy?" she asked.

"Inside somewheres," said Junior. Now that the women had arrived and the kid seemed to have been missing, he was convincing himself that he might be a hero. "Let's go see." The old guy wouldn't try anything and, if he did, he would be no match for Junior. "I better call an ambulance and the police," he said, but he didn't move.

Annette looked up at him. "Who tied him up?"

"Sandy Whyte," Junior said.

"How? Why?"

Junior shrugged. "Guess we'll find out."

Margaret looked down at the boy. So here he was, the famous Chaleur. He looked so weak and his features were so delicate, he did not seem either old or substantial enough to have impregnated Annette. If he got rid of that hair, he might be good-looking. Couldn't someone cover him up? All he had on was his underwear. Annette was kneeling beside him, holding him; as Margaret watched, Chaleur lifted his hand and touched her shoulder. His fingers trembled; it was as if he had never touched anyone before. The touch was so intimate that it embarrassed Margaret; she felt she should look away. But she couldn't.

She looked about her as if she were studying a picture. Annette and Chaleur, the one-armed man standing above them, the big man hesitating at the door — could she be a member of this strange assembly? She knew that as soon as she moved forward she would be: she was standing on the edge of a dream, knowing that her fear must not stop her from stepping inside of it and realizing something that she did not want to know. She was awake, but she was feeling the horror that came with the dreams about her father. Then she knew that she needed to lead that big man into the house.

As she stepped around Annette at the top of the stairs, her own body felt far away. "Where's Sandy?" she repeated, and her voice seemed to come from outside of her.

The man at the door shrugged again. "He came downstairs just a couple a minutes ago. He can't be far. Don't imagine he'd be armed or anything, do you?"

Armed? "Of course not." She shook her head and went through the door. Junior followed her. They stood together in the darkness then she turned on the hall lights and they went to look in the empty living room. "Sandy?" They went across the hall to the study. Nothing. They walked deeper into the house. Junior opened a closet door.

"He wouldn't be in there," she said, going on ahead to peer into the dining room. "Not here either." What was happening was a shock but, like a nightmare, it was all making dreadful sense: the confirmation of some dark truth.

"Sandy?" she called.

"You a friend of his?"

"We go to the same church," she answered, wondering if this was a lie. "I borrowed his car because my sister —"

At that moment Margaret and Junior each realized who they were talking to.

"Oh," she said, staring at him for a moment before turning away.

He nodded, then cleared his throat. They were standing in the dark kitchen.

"Sandy had the boy tied down." She had meant to ask a question, but it came out sounding like a statement of fact.

"Yeah. To a bed upstairs."

To a bed. She knew this already, had known it as soon as she entered the house. Chaleur had been tied here while she and Annette walked on the beach, when Minnie had her accident out front, when she herself came to the door last night to borrow the car. All that time, he was holding the boy captive. "All this week," she said, "a prisoner."

"All's I know is he was tied up. You know where the light is? I better find the phone."

"Try beside the door."

He fumbled around the edge of the kitchen door, looking for the switch. There. The kitchen was blindingly bright for a moment, and he saw the phone. The shed door was open — had he and Danny left it that wide?

"Do you suppose he's upstairs?"

"Check out there in the shed first," he said, picking up the receiver. He watched her walk slowly and peer out.

She turned around and whispered, "The back door is open."

"Careful," Junior called out from the kitchen. "Wood's all rotten out there." He dialled 911.

Lila watched the scene on the veranda from the corner of the house and then, curiosity getting the better of her, she walked across the lawn. It was one of the Maurice boys, all right, that Danny, and a young girl. They were bending over the hoodlum with the long hair that she had seen prowling around the house.

"You caught him," she said just as the clouds broke.

On his knees in the garden, Sandy had torn open the small cardboard box, shaken out the container, and pried open its lid with a quarter. He ripped at the plastic liner inside. When he took out the first small fistful, he realized that it was raining: his hands were wet and some of the ash stuck to his fingers in a fine paste. A part of it seemed to dissolve. He rubbed his hand on the grass, then reached into the container again. Some of the ash was a smooth powder, but there were also small, hard chunks, like nuggets. *Bones*, and he thought of Mother's knuckles, old and arthritic at the end, but how they had once been lovely and smooth, her long fingers so gentle touching his face. He flung the handful into her old garden and put his hand inside for more. The hard knot of the bud within him was pushing, straining to open. The petals were strong: they hurt him, they cut into his ribs. It would burgeon too quickly, there was not enough time. He dumped the container upside down, spilling ashes on the wet ground, and then he shook out the rest. He picked up handfuls, flinging them about him, then grabbed the empty container and held it tightly. He pushed it against the bloom; the petals were deep red, their edges cut into him like delicate razors.

All that remained of Mother was scattered about him, fragments of her clung to his skin and clothes. Five miles away, the dust of his father lay still and quiet, sealed away from the world for ever.

Something hard was stuck to the back of his hand and he picked it off. Bone?

No, a bit of tooth.

"No!" The moan was instinctive and loud, pure horror. Her bones had been hidden inside her, but he had seen her teeth, he had known them: her smile when she saw him all dressed up for Sunday school, that grimace on the final day when he had found her body. Teeth that his father's tongue had touched just as he had touched the boy's. He fingered the hard little bump, squeezed it between the tips of his thumb and forefinger. This was how everything ended, with nothing left to show for your life but bits of teeth, bone, and dust, meaningless unless they could be attached to the name of someone who had left something greater — a painting, a temple, a miracle. All that he had to show for his life was a kiss that he had stolen from the life he had spared, but no one would care. If he were remembered at all, it would be with loathing. He popped the bit of tooth into his mouth and swallowed it like a little pill.

The porch boards were soft and spongy, and there was a hole in the deck, so Margaret moved carefully. She could see Sandy near the old flower bed — he was on his knees, hugging something to his chest. As she watched he leaned and fell forward, his head hitting a little pile of dirt. Then he toppled onto his side and lay there curled up in a ball.

She did not know what Sandy had done to Annette's boyfriend, and she did not need to know the details: she understood them. She understood because she had known her father. Whatever had driven her father into her bedroom, into lifting her onto the dining-room table, that same thing had driven Sandy. Her father had haunted her all these years, a bogeyman, and she had hated him, despised him, thrown up walls against him, but now she needed to draw close to him.

She stepped down off the porch, and the moment her plastic sandal touched the grass the light rain became a downpour; it was like music quickening and driving into a stronger key. It was dangerous, but she would not be afraid; she could pass through it unscathed. The rain was filled with jeers and shouts, the pummelling of fists, bottles sailing through the air, marbles crashing to the ground — she was walking through it towards her father; Jesus was walking with her.

When she reached Sandy, her dress was soaking wet for the second time that day. She stood looking down, studying him. He was wearing his old Sunday suit, wrinkled and wet and ruined, and he had not shaved; his cheeks were covered with grey stubble and streaks of dirt. Beneath all that was something miserable beyond pity, like an ugly little animal whimpering at her feet. If she were only wearing leather shoes, she could have kicked it, and she knew that there would be such satisfaction in that moment, her hard toe hitting the mewling flesh, the pleasure of hearing tiny bones splinter. She could kick him with a lifetime of rage. But Jesus and the river had taken her shoes away.

"Sandy."

He did not even know that she was there. She crouched down beside him. "Sandy?" Her voice was very quiet. He looked up, but not at her. "Sandy, I know what has happened."

He knew that there was someone beside him, but the world was dark and he could not tell who it was. He was lost in panic. The petals were tearing at him; his whole body was straining to rupture. No one would care about his unhappiness, about the humiliation he had suffered all of his life. He had left nothing behind, a talentless, unmiraculous life. Until the end of time, until Membartouche slid into the sea, everyone who mentioned his name would remember only that he had died in disgrace. He started to cry. "I'm nothing," he whined.

There was something so pathetic about his wormy nothing-ness that she could not help herself — it would be like picking at a scab — she had to touch it. Her every move was slow and delib-erate; the scene of the crime was as calm as the eye of a hurricane. She moved closer to him and lifted his head onto her lap. It was as large and as heavy as her father's. She wanted to beat it with her fists, but Jesus was in her hands.

"Sandy!" she said. "Sandy!" He was sobbing now and trying to hide his face against her legs, but she needed to look at him. She held his head firmly in her hands and turned it like a giant ball. His eyes were squeezed shut, a child who hopes his own blindness will hide him from the world. "How could you?" she said, shoving the back of his head against her legs.

"Mmmph!" He opened his eyes but could not focus on her; they darted about wildly.

"How could you?" she said again, and, in saying it, she knew.

Sandy and her father lived in a world that was closed to them — they did not see how they could be worthy of such a world. Their happiness was impossible. She understood impossibility — her father had bequeathed it to her with his big, wounding hands. Impossibility bred impossibility and vengeance. If she was innocent of a crime as terrible as her father's or Sandy's, it was only because she had been spared the opportunity to fulfil it.

And just as she had in that hotel room thirty years ago, she lay her hand on his forehead.

"There," she said, wiping the rain and tears from his face. "There, there."

Were there hands touching him, or was it the weight of the rain? It was warm, a bath, and someone was washing him. No, he has wet the bed and they are upset. They will laugh at him. Everyone hated him. They would line up to spit on him. "I can't be forgiven," he sobbed.

Margaret wiped the wet from his cheek with the flat of her hand.

"I forgive you," she said.

And then, as his chest burst open with a pain as beautiful as a rose, he knew clearly where he was. A deer was leaning over him, a doe, and a strong young fawn was standing beside her. Mother and Joey Mullins had come to ask his forgiveness just as he could now forgive them. At that moment, all was forgiven. He jumped up from the garden and bounded after them into the greenwood. There was the thrill and power of his flight and the promise of lying beside them in the cool shade of the spruce and alders and then, suddenly, there was the warmth and comfort of a deep, deep dark.

Lila thought about going to get Mavis because all this was better than a movie. The Maurice boys were telling her that the kid with the long hair had been Sandy's prisoner, the girl got mad at her when Lila said she'd seen him sneaking around, and just after the police and the ambulance pulled into the driveway, Margaret Saunders came out the front door and announced that she was pretty sure that Sandy Whyte was dead.

"You killed him?" Annette said.

"No, dear, of course not. A heart attack, I think."

One of the ambulance attendants went back through the house with her. The rain was coming down in buckets and a wind had come up, driving it onto the veranda.

"Why don't we go inside and sit down," Lila said. She was thinking how good it would be to sit down in a big, comfy chair and smoke.

"We might tamper with the evidence," Junior said, shaking his head. "Eh, Francis?"

The policeman was shaking his head too. "How's the boy?"

The other attendant was looking into Chaleur's eyes with a little light. "He's dehydrated, but he's gonna be fine. We'll put him on an IV and get him to the hospital."

Annette was still on her knees, as close to Chaleur as she could be without being in the way.

The policeman turned to Junior. "Did you untie him?"

Junior was about to say "Yes," then he knew that he wanted to be honest and make Ginette proud of him. "No," he said. "He'd been untied but he was too weak to move, so I carried him downstairs."

"And how did you boys know that he was in the house?"

"My sister works here."

"She cleans," said Lila.

Danny glared at her. "Gloria was here yesterday with my kid brother and he thought he saw something."

"They were in a car accident," Lila put in.

"I know that," said Francis. "I was here."

"They didn't all know," she said gesturing towards Annette and moving towards the inside edge of the veranda, out of the rain.

The policeman sighed. "So you two broke in."

"Broke in? No, sir. Door was wide open."

"That's right," Lila said. "I saw them myself. They just walked right in."

"Where were you, Mrs. LeBlanc?"

"I want to go inside and sit down," she said.

"Just answer the question, please."

"I was outside, having my smoke."

Margaret came back out the door. "The man wants someone to go help him carry Sandy into the house."

"Why don't you go and give him a hand," Francis said, pointing to Danny, then he noticed Danny's stump and said, "Naw, let your brother go."

"I can do it," said Danny, and he left to help.

"Well," Francis said, scratching his head, "I guess we won't know what we've got here until this fellow is able to do some talking. I better get someone to come and pick up Mr. Whyte." He looked at the driving rain separating him from the police car.

"Use the phone inside," said Junior, leading the way.

Lila opened her damp cigarette pack and followed them.

Margaret sighed and watched Annette. In her purse was the phone number of the clinic they had never reached. "Here," she said, "I think you should have this. I've meddled enough. It's your decision."

"Oh."

"The number you called to get me? It wasn't the right one. Just throw it away."

"Oh." Annette stood up. "I have to see where he was," she said. "I won't touch anything, I just have to see where he was locked up."

In the ambulance to Moncton, Annette's shock started to give way to a deep, frightening anger. The old creep, what had he done? Who did he think he was? As they sped along the four-lane, rain streaking down the windows and thunder so loud it seemed to be crashing inches above them, she started to get mad at the two attendants sitting together, talking quietly to each other.

"He's so weak, can't you do something else?"

"It's simply dehydration," one of them said. "If he's been shut up in hot room with no water or food …"

"Can't you fucking do something?"

"The IV'll help. Don't worry, Annette, he'll be fine. He just needs to get his strength back."

Useless idiots. Annette was sitting beside the guerney, holding Chaleur's hand; she had always felt this protective of him —

it wasn't like he was a helpless kid or anything, but there was a part of him that she knew needed her to keep it safe. How could this dreadful thing have happened to him? They should live together; he needed her to look out for him. How had the old guy gotten his hands on Chaleur? What had he done to him? And what was she going to do about the baby?

She had named it a baby. Did that mean that she was going to keep it now? After all that Chaleur had been through, wasn't this the right thing to do? She didn't have to finish school and go into nursing right away; she could wait until the baby was born. She could wait. She had seen the room where Chaleur had been tied up — she didn't see it for long: as soon as she stuck her head in, she closed her eyes and came back down to the veranda. It was like one of those horrible pictures in a supermarket newspaper. It made her feel dirty; as soon as she had smelled it, she knew that it was none of her business. Maybe he would tell her all that had happened to him up there — when she started to imagine it, her blood started to boil. Wouldn't it be mean of her to have the abortion now?

No. Chaleur was going to be enough to look after for a while, she didn't need a baby too, not just yet. There would be time for kids later. There would be time for all that. She would talk to her sister and call the clinic.

"Where am I?"

"He's awake," she said, and bent down to touch his face. "I'm here. Everything's gonna be all right."

Chaleur nodded. Annette was near him and they were in an airplane flying somewhere. "Where we going?"

"To the hospital. They just need to check you out."

He was trying to remember. He had been lost in the woods and a crazy man had tied him up. No, the old man had tied him up in a house. He panicked. Was the old fart coming after him?

"He's gonna get me again," he said. He struggled to sit up.

Annette put her face against his chest and held him down. "No, he ain't," she whispered. "You're safe. He's dead."

"Dead? Did Dad kill him?"

"No," she said, kissing his chest. "Heart attack." She put a finger to his lips and lifted her head to look at him. "Don't think about it now," she said. "Just rest and be quiet. We'll be at the hospital soon and then everything'll be fine. Understand?"

He looked into her eyes. He didn't, but she seemed so relaxed, so in control, that he nodded.

"I love you," she said, and she kissed him again.

"Me too," he said, and he smiled and watched her.

"I'll call your mother and tell her that you're all right. And when you get out of the hospital, you can come and live with us for a while. Or have a room at my sister's. We'll get everything straightened out." Being with him again was making her think that things were possible.

He was so tired, but he was afraid to close his eyes because he did not want to wake up back in that bed. If this was a dream, he wanted to go on dreaming it. Annette was beside him. He had been lost and his father had been there. He had a terrible adventure, but it was all over.

"Dad saved me," he said.

When the policeman dropped Margaret off in front of her house, Minnie was standing on the front porch, waiting.

"Lila LeBlanc just called to tell me," she said. "I've got some water on for tea. Go get out of those wet things and put on your housecoat and it'll be ready."

She held the door open and Margaret came in.

"You poor thing. But what did I tell you? I've always said that there was something wrong with Sandy Whyte. You could tell just by looking at his hands. They're pudgy. Never trust a man with pudgy hands." Then Minnie gave out a little screech. "What in the name of God have you got on your feet? You look like some old hippy!"

Margaret sighed as she kicked the flip-flops off and walked barefoot towards the stairs. Maybe nothing much would change, but from now on she would be different.

CADENCE

TWENTY-SIX

"There they are!" Raymond shouted. "Pull over!"

Hal looked, but he could see nothing: a little inlet with a reddish bluff jutting out into the bay, a barren stretch of beach, muddy water that looked to be as thick as milk. They were in Danny's car with Gloria. The whole thing was her idea, and the others in the family hadn't wanted to come. "Waste of friggin' time" was Junior's version — he'd been trying to call Ginette all day, but there was no answer yet. Tomorrow morning he was going to drive to Halifax to talk to her. He was at home watching TV with Mama and Pop. Before they left, Mama had told Raymond and Hal that there would always be a room for them at the house. Pop said nothing, just nodded and turned away when Hal thanked them. They all knew that nothing would come of her offer, but she had made it.

All through supper Gloria and Raymond had been constantly looking at their watches, and telling Hal and Danny to hurry up. "The man at the tourist bureau said high tide was the only time to see them," Gloria said.

"And it'll be high in an hour," Raymond added.

The sun had started to go down, and they were on a dirt road past the mouth of the Petitcodiac River, driving alongside the narrow bay that opened into the Bay of Fundy. The tide was in and the water was so muddy that it was pink.

They were looking for sandpipers.

"Stop the car!" Raymond shouted again, and Danny pulled over.

"What do you see?" Hal asked.

"Right there," Raymond said, getting out and quickly walking down the road. "Are you blind?"

Hal followed along the roadside; he couldn't see anything. Gloria got out of the car. Danny rolled his window down and watched her as she stood squinting at the water. "What do you see?"

She shook her head. "Nothing."

Hal followed Raymond through the long grass beside the shoulder towards the edge of a little cliff that looked down at the rough beach covered with grey and brown pebbles. The air was salty and cool off the Fundy. He wished he'd brought a sweater. "Where?" he asked. There wasn't a bird in the sky, and nothing on the beach but sand and a huge stretch of smooth, little rocks.

"There," pointed Raymond. "Look. You dare to doubt me again?"

When Danny and Junior had come home last night, Raymond had been asleep on the veranda while Hal and Gloria sat watching the rain with Mama. Danny had bounded out of the car and run up the front steps. "The poor little bugger was right!" he shouted.

Hal was looking all around them, mystified. It was not until they were standing at the edge of the cliff that he realized the pebbles on the beach below them were not pebbles at all, but birds — hundreds of thousands of birds, all standing patiently and facing south. "Holy God," he said. The flock stretched along the shore for more than a hundred feet between the water's edge and the base of the cliff.

"Look," Raymond said, pointing. Out over the water, a large shadow was moving swiftly and flying low. It was heading north, then it darted quickly to the right and flew towards the shore: hundreds more birds, and they were coming to join the others. At the last moment, just as they reached the shore, the flock swerved abruptly to the south and skimmed down to settle on the beach. There was a flash of silver as the underside of their wings caught the setting sunlight, and then they dissolved in with the brown regularity of the rest. Raymond grabbed Hal's hand and squeezed it. Behind them Gloria called out, "I see them! I see them! Danny, get out here!"

He got out of the car and stood next to her. What was there to see? There was nothing down there. He looked at his brother and Hal, looked at the way they could stand so close to each other. Last night he had put his arm around Raymond, and the moment he felt those frail shoulder bones he had longed to hold him closer. When he looked over at his mother, she had turned away. Mama had given up on trying to hug her children long ago: they groaned in annoyance or twisted away from her. *Aw, Mama, knock it off.*

Out over the water, another small group of birds was flying towards shore. Gloria turned to him. "Look there," she said. "See those birds flying in?"

"Where?"

"Right there. Coming right towards us."

"Oh." Danny nodded. "That's it? I've seen more robins than that in the backyar——"

At that moment the new arrivals tacked suddenly in a burst of gleaming wings and settled onto the beach.

"Holy frig," he said softly, because the beach was suddenly covered with birds.

Gloria laughed at the look of dumb amazement on his face and gave him a little poke. "Mr. Smarty Pants."

"How many are there, do you figure?"

"Man at the tourist bureau said they expect a few hundred thousand in the next couple of days. They eat here for a week, double their body weight, and then fly to South America without stopping!" She looked down at the beach. *South America. All that way!* She thought about how long it had taken her and Mama to fly to Jamaica, hours and hours, all day long. "Just think," she said. "If they fly over the hotel where Mama and I stayed in Montego Bay they'd just be halfway there." The world outside of Membartouche suddenly seemed close and nearby.

As the sun sank lower, the breeze began picking up; below them millions of feathers ruffled slightly. There were tiny movements: a bird from the far end of the beach might skim above the others to the head of the flock and settle in there.

When Raymond had told him that there could be this many birds, Hal had imagined them swarming, teeming over the beach, running back and forth and scooting through the air. The intense determination in their stillness and quiet filled him with anticipation, as if he were about to arrive somewhere mysterious.

"They're all one thing," he said. "That's what's so strange. As if they all had the same purpose, and don't even need to think independently."

Raymond nodded. "It's chilly, I'm getting cold."

"Here," and Hal put his arm around him. "Me too."

"There's more coming in!" Danny called, and all of them turned to see another group shoot down from over the cape and alight with the others.

Hal held Raymond closer. "Who ever dreamed that a bunch of birds could make me feel so happy?"

"This is the place," Raymond said quietly, "isn't it?"

"What place?"

"For our ashes, dummy. It's ours. I mean, we found it together. We'll get Gloria to mix us up and scatter us down there at low tide."

"And maybe the birds will gobble us up and we'll end up in the rain forest."

"Bra-zeel," Raymond chirped. "Yi-yi-yi."

"Thank you, Carmen Miranda."

Raymond began to sing:

"*Braa-zeel,*
Where hearts were entertaining June,
We stood beneath an amber moon———"

"Humph. I can top that."

"Oh, yeah?"

"Oh yeah. *Oh, Rio, Rio by the Sea-o,*
Flying down to Rio and we've got to make time."

"Dammit," Raymond snorted, "you always win. You'll probably win the damn Widows' Tournament too."

At the same moment, they both turned their heads north and looked up the beach to the cape; then, with perfect synchronicity, their faces turned slowly southward, scanning the rich, brown carpet of sandpipers, and following the edge of the shore all the way down to as far as they could see. Both of them were thinking of their ashes, minuscule bits of Raymond and Hal, clinging to the birds' little claws; nestling into the feathers of their breasts, their wings; swimming in their little bellies.

Hal squeezed Raymond tighter and for a wonderful minute he believed in the possibility that all of their remaining time together could be shared as completely as this. No night sweats, no recriminations, no pain, no terror, no sobbing.

"Raymond, if you're winning the tournament, I want the last words I hear to be 'See you in Rio.'"

Raymond nodded. "Rio by the sea-o."

Just then Gloria clapped her hands and gave out a little shout because suddenly, and for no apparent reason, the entire flock rose as one, as if the whole beach were shifting and rising into the air.

Danny smiled as Gloria grabbed his arm and they drew each other close.

The flock lifted up and slid out over the pink water, and the air was filled with the sound of hundreds of thousands of tiny wings. It turned as one towards the open bay and split into four parts — each one darting free and swooping like a mysterious, rippling cloud. The inside of their wings caught the light of the sinking sun and shimmered like thousands of pieces of silver cascading above the darkening water.

ACKNOWLEDGEMENTS

Work on the first draft was made possible by a grant from
Canada Council Explorations for which I am deeply grateful.

I would like to thank the MacDowell Colony for the
generosity of a fellowship in 1995 and for the kindness of the
MacDowell staff. Thank you as well to the Philip Morris
Company for funding the fellowship.

I would like to express my gratitude to the Writer-in-
Residence Program of the Libraries and Archives Branch,
Government of Yukon, for four very productive and happy
months. Many thanks to everyone at the Whitehorse Public
Library — most especially to Julie Ourom, Mairi MacRae and
Janet Lee — for their generosity and support during my
residency there.

For taking the time to read the first draft, and for giving
me valuable and encouraging comments, I thank Rebecca

Brown, Polly Frost, Pauline Kael, Colleen Murphy, and Ray Sawhill.

For financial help and/or for providing wonderful places for me to live and write, my thanks to: Gary Akenhead, André Alexis, David Arnold, Ena Borde, Candace Burley, Betty Lou Daye, Rita Howell, Melanie Huston, Louise Joseph, Zoe Klein, Ellen Smith Leavitt, Elizabeth Leslie, Janet MacLean, and Dayne Ogilvie.

Thanks to the staff of Knopf Canada, especially to Diane Martin for her warmth and her wise editorial support.

Much love to my great friend Ken Garnhum for listening to rough versions of many of these pages.

And to Doug Guildford, for phoning me, thank you.